VICARIOUS

VICARIOUS

PAULA STOKES

**TOR®
TEEN**

A Tom Doherty Associates Book
New York

VICARIOUS

Copyright © 2016 by Paula Stokes

A Tor Teen Book
Published by Tom Doherty Associates, LLC
175 Fifth Avenue
New York, NY 10010

www.tor-forge.com

Tor® is a registered trademark of Tom Doherty Associates, LLC.

The Library of Congress Cataloging-in-Publication
Data is available upon request.

ISBN 978-0-7653-8094-4 (hardcover)
ISBN 978-1-4668-7620-0 (e-book)

Our books may be purchased in bulk for promotional, educational, or business
use. Please contact your local bookseller or the Macmillan Corporate and
Premium Sales Department at 1-800-221-7945, extension 5442, or
by e-mail at MacmillanSpecialMarkets@macmillan.com.

First Edition: August 2016

Printed in the United States of America

0 9 8 7 6 5 4 3 2 1

To Marcy,
for reminding me I could write any book I wanted to,
and for never giving up on Winter's story

VICARIOUS

REBIRTH

I can't seem to wipe away the blood. I rub my hands against my nightgown, but traces of the red remain, staining the lines of my palms and the crescents beneath my fingernails. I wipe harder, gathering and bunching the soft cotton inside my fists. The fabric has been slit up the center and I worry that I've been cut, that maybe the blood is my own. I try to ask what's happening, but there's a mask over my mouth and nose. Suddenly it hits me—I'm in an ambulance.

I don't remember how I got here.

The day returns in disordered fragments. A taxi ride that was short and frantic. A series of plane rides that stretched into forever. Before that, what? The apartment in Los Angeles? No, something else. Something with blood? I struggle to reassemble the memory, but the pieces won't fit.

My heart pounds like the hoofbeats of a frightened animal. I inhale sharply but can't get any air, like maybe the mask on my face is stealing oxygen instead of providing it. The ceiling above my head blurs. Everything starts to go gray.

But then my older sister, Rose, leans over the gurney. "I'm here, Winter," she says. "You're going to be all right." She reaches down to pet my straight black hair.

The ambulance comes back into focus. The next few moments are a whir of strong hands and sharp needle sticks. There is murmuring and beeping. The paramedics converse in meaningless letters and numbers. No one tells me what's happening.

Rose chides the men for scaring me. Despite the cramped quarters, they navigate around her with ease, never once telling her to move out of their way.

The hospital is a haze of white walls and overhead lights. The bed beneath me changes from hard to soft as the paramedics unload me from the stretcher. Rose's boyfriend, Ki Hyun, appears from somewhere. Not Ki Hyun. Gideon. He changed his name. We all did.

Rose is still by my side. She keeps telling me everything is going to be fine. "We're safe now," she says. "We're never going back there."

A pair of nurses peer down at me. A gloved hand runs across my bare thigh, lingering on a constellation of circular scars. The nurses swivel their heads simultaneously, their accusing stares falling like guillotine blades onto Gideon. I am sure that smoke lingers on his clothing, as always.

I try to tell them the scars aren't from him, that he'd never hurt me, that he was the one who saved me. He and Rose. But the words that dribble from my mouth are nonsense. The nurses act like they don't even hear them. Swallowing hard, I try again, but my lips form a single word I'm not expecting. *"Eonni."* Korean for elder sister.

"I'm right here," Rose murmurs. She unfolds my fingers and presses her hand to mine, lining up the cross-shaped scars on our palms. "Fingers to fingers and thumb to thumb. A pair of sisters like matching gloves."

The nurses part to allow a white-coated doctor into the mix. More meaningless letters and numbers are exchanged. All I can make out is his name, Dr. Bernard, and the word *psychiatrist*. I might not understand the alphabet speak, but I've studied English since I was a child. I know what a psychiatrist is. It means I'm crazy.

My arm tingles as a nurse injects me with something. My eyelids grow heavier. I struggle to listen to the soft words being exchanged by the doctor and Gideon.

"PTSD . . . inpatient care . . . possibly unstable . . ."

"I can take care . . . my responsibility."

"With all due respect . . . condition might deteriorate . . . outcome dependent upon . . ."

"I want to take her home."

"A couple of nights . . . observation."

"Don't. Want. Stay. Here," I say. Each word is a tiny battle.

"I won't let them keep you," Rose says. "Hospitals are for the dying, and we are only just beginning to live."

Thank you. I think the words, but when I try to speak, what comes out is, "Blood. Blood on my hands."

"Shh." She squeezes my fingers. "It was just a dream. There's no blood. You're safe." But then she lets go and I am adrift in a sea of white.

I struggle to lift myself, to balance my body on my elbows, but my head lolls back on my neck and my muscles all give in at once. I collapse back onto the bed, but not before I see Rose and Gideon standing silently against the wall of the room. Curling onto my side, I watch them talk to each other using only their eyes. Then Gideon turns toward the door and Rose follows. The hallway swallows them up.

"Eonni," I say again. Some part of my brain knows that Rose has only stepped away to speak to Gideon in private or perhaps to grab a cup of coffee, but I need her. A single tear makes its way over the crest of my cheek, following the contours of my face until it falls to the coarse hospital sheets below me.

"What is it, Winter?" a nurse asks. She bends low, frowning in concentration as she takes in my breathing, my temperature, that single rogue tear.

"I need my sister," I whisper.

The nurse pats my hand. "She isn't here right now, but don't worry. We're going to take care of you."

We're going to take care of you. That's what the women at the orphanage said when my mother left us there. That's what the people who brought us to America said before they handed us over to Kyung. That's what Kyung's men said before they started selling us by the hour.

I don't need these doctors and nurses with their weird alphabet speak and their judging eyes. Gideon will take care of Rose and Rose will take care of me. That was the plan from the beginning.

CHAPTER 1

THREE YEARS LATER

Rose is crowding me out as usual, the reflection of her slender elbow obscuring part of my face in the mirror. Her scattered powders and potions cover the marble vanity of the bathroom we share. They're made of all things bold and glittery, just like she is. In contrast, my neat little cluster of toothbrush, hairbrush, and eyeliner feels like an unruly child put in the corner.

"Move over," I say.

She's busy curling her eyelashes. I watch as she clamps a little torture device over one eye. People say we look alike, but what they mean is that we look alike except she's more striking. She has the same basic bone structure and pale skin, but bigger eyes, fuller lips, longer hair, and now, apparently, curlier eyelashes.

"You move over. I have plans tonight." Rose tosses the eyelash curler into the sink and blinks sweetly at my reflection before rummaging through the mess on the vanity to find a tube of mascara.

"Me too." I finger-comb my shoulder-length black hair, and then grab my eyeliner. A soft brush of black pencil across my lower lash line is usually all the makeup I wear.

"With Jesse Ramirez?" Rose wrinkles her nose at my pencil. "I could help you with your makeup."

"Maybe." I ignore her offer to slather me up with products.

Jesse's not my boyfriend, and even if he were, I wouldn't waste time trying to impress him by masquerading as someone else.

"Winter," Rose starts, her voice getting that whole mothering tone like she's forty instead of twenty. "You know Jesse loves you."

"No he doesn't. We just work together, all right?" I've caught Jesse staring more than once, but I'm fairly certain his feelings are more practical in nature. He wants what all guys want. Too bad for him.

Rose blots her eyelashes on the back of her hand and applies a coat of shiny red lipstick. She looks like something out of a black-and-white movie. I've never seen a dress with so much fringe before.

"You should just give him some. See what it's like to be with someone who actually cares about you."

I flinch slightly as I tug at her scooped neckline, pulling up the fabric to cover her cleavage. "Maybe you should try *not* giving some to everyone you meet."

"Funny." Rolling her impeccably made-up eyes, Rose twists her curtain of black hair up under a white-blond wig. "I'm going to Inferno. Come by later if you want."

Inferno is the club in the building next door. I've been there only a couple of times since I turned eighteen three months ago. "Are you . . . working?" I ask.

She smiles coyly. "Maybe."

"Then I'll just see you tomorrow."

Lately, Rose's idea of work has gotten increasingly provocative: modeling, club dancing, switch parties. Inferno holds a switch party every Saturday night. It's basically a make-out version of speed dating, where they turn out all the lights and everyone pairs up, hooks up, and then switches partners. As you can imagine, finding enough men isn't a problem, but the club usually ends up having to pay the women. Rose swears she doesn't let things go too far with anyone, that it's all about teasing and control, but sometimes I wonder. It's her body and she can do what she wants with it, but the thought of some dirty stranger's hands on my sister makes my insides wither.

I love Rose, but sometimes I don't understand her.

"When's your next therapist appointment?" she asks suddenly, as if the look on my face might indicate an impending breakdown.

"Why are you asking me that? You know I quit seeing her."

Rose arches a dark eyebrow. "I'm surprised you're getting away with that."

She means Gideon. He and Rose ended their relationship shortly after we left Los Angeles. Despite the breakup, they've remained friends and the three of us still live together in Gideon's penthouse. Which means now he's sort of our landlord, older brother, and boss rolled into one. It's complicated.

"He's so busy working that he probably doesn't realize I've stopped going," I say. This is a half-truth. My therapist's office seems to be a few weeks behind on billing, so that's why Gideon doesn't know I've been skipping sessions. "I'll make an appointment if I need to."

Rose acts like I might kill myself at any moment, but that's just her being dramatic. Maybe I was depressed in Los Angeles, but I got better once we escaped. My therapist here diagnosed me with PTSD, but even at its worst, it was never anything that serious. I just sometimes got my dreams confused with reality, or saw things a little differently than they actually were.

Now, other than the occasional nightmare or bout of anxiety, I'm fine. I don't need to waste time in Dr. Abrams's soothing blue-green office talking about how it felt to be repeatedly violated. Sometimes it's best to just move on.

"All right." Rose raises her hands in mock surrender. "You seem fine to me."

Rose lived the same life I did, but she doesn't have PTSD. No bad dreams, no missing memories. Sometimes I'm jealous that she seems to deal with everything better than I do. But then I'll catch her with this hollow look in her eyes and think maybe she just disguises everything for my benefit.

Maybe she's broken on the inside too.

She leans in to give me an air kiss on each cheek, and her jasmine perfume makes me sneeze. A row of shiny bracelets jangle against each other as she pulls a chunk of my hair forward from behind my left ear. It falls in front of my eye, kind of seductive-like. Satisfied, she smiles.

"I'm just going to put it in a ponytail." I lift my arm so she can see the plain black elastic band looped around my wrist.

She sighs deeply. "You're hopeless." She reaches out to hug me, and her warmth makes my rigid muscles start to loosen.

And then go tight again.

Sometimes when we touch, I flash back to the two of us huddled together in a tiny room in L.A. after one of our "dates." I'm sobbing. She's consoling. I'm hoping for death and she's demanding I stay alive.

She usually gets what she wants.

Rose spins around once to check her reflection in the full-length mirror mounted on the outside of the bathroom door. Fringe flares out from her slender body.

"Be safe," I say.

"But not too safe." Flashing me a grin, she sashays out into the living room.

Still trapped between here and thoughts of L.A., I grab the bar of soap and turn the faucet on all hot. Clouds of steam blanket the mirror as the scalding water turns my hands pink. I close my eyes and count to ten. My flesh protests, but I lather for another ten seconds and then rinse. The pain washes away the memories.

Someone raps sharply on the front door of the penthouse. It's probably Jesse, and I'm not ready. "Can you answer the door?" I ask.

No response. More rapping. I turn the faucet off and dry

my hands on an embroidered hand towel. "Eonni? Did you hear me?" I head for the living room.

Our cat, Miso, sits just inside the front door, his black-and-white tail twitching with anticipation. Otherwise, the penthouse is empty except for a whiff of jasmine perfume. Rose must have left when I was washing my hands.

"I'll be right there," I call. I head into my bedroom and grab my lightweight Kevlar body armor from a hanger in my closet. I slide it over my head and pull the Velcro straps tight. Then I open the top drawer of the nightstand and pull out a stun gun and a pair of throwing knives.

I'm in a slightly different line of work from my sister.

CHAPTER 2

There's a black hoodie folded neatly on my dresser. Tugging it over my head, I slide the stun gun into the middle pocket. I grab a few other things I'll need for tonight and then head for the hallway, slipping my feet into a pair of boots just inside the front door. Miso is still sitting like a sentry, ready to welcome or pounce as needed. I peek through the peephole and see Jesse standing in the corridor. Like me, he's wearing all black. His brown hair is mostly hidden beneath a black knit cap.

I open the door. "Hi."

Jesse steps into the penthouse. "Moo!" he exclaims with a smile, scooping the black-and-white cat into his arms.

"Why do you insist on calling him that?" I ask. Miso squirms a little but then stretches his neck up so he can lick Jesse's cheek.

"Because he's cow colored, and he seems to like it."

I lean in and scratch Miso between his ears. He purrs, but his attention is solely focused on Jesse.

My lips twitch as I remember the day I found the cat prowling back and forth in front of the fireplace. I half thought he was some unfortunate test subject that had escaped from Gideon's study, which also functions as a lab. But Rose told me later she found him in the alley, starving and scared.

"Look at you," I say, patting Miso's little round belly. "Hard to believe you were ever homeless."

Miso gives me a baleful look and then licks Jesse's face again.

"That cat likes everyone else better than me," I mutter. I bend down to strap a knife to each ankle and tie my boots.

Jesse drops Miso to the ground and the cat wanders off toward the kitchen in search of food. "I like you," he says. "Even better than Moo, but don't tell him I said that."

I like Jesse too—at least I think I do. In a normal life, we might be going out for pizza instead of sneaking across town to commit a crime together. Sadly, broken people do not live normal lives.

Jesse fiddles with his hearing aid and it makes a sharp whistling sound. My eyes flick to his disfigured ear, to the jagged scar running from his left temple to his jawline. He's never told me about his injury and I've never asked. I heard Gideon telling someone once that it happened in the army.

"I almost never see you with your hair down." Jesse reaches out to pet my dark hair, his knuckles accidentally grazing my skin.

I slide away from his touch. In one smooth motion, I take the elastic band from my wrist and pull my hair through it. I double the band and tug until I have a short but secure ponytail. Jesse's lips curl upward and something stirs inside me. I find it disconcerting, the juxtaposition of his war wounds with a smile that projects so much warmth.

I am not warm. That is one of the reasons I chose the name Winter.

"Just a minute." Dropping to the floor, I quickly do twenty push-ups and then spring back to my feet. Exercise helps turn off all the extraneous thoughts in my brain.

Jesse lifts his legs behind him, one at a time, in a halfhearted stretch of his quadriceps. "You ready for this?"

"Yes." I peek out into the hallway to make sure it's empty. Gideon, Rose, and I are the only people who live on this floor, but college students occasionally come up here to try to get on the roof through the utility room window.

We walk down the carpeted hallway, past the elevator to the stairwell. The penthouse takes up the entire top floor of a fifteen-story building, but I always use the steps. I have a bit of an elevator phobia. They feel like tiny moving cages to me.

"Do anything fun lately?" Jesse asks as we start to descend the stairs.

I shrug. "Nothing special." The last few days are a blur of sameness. Wake up. Work out with Gideon. Eat. Study. Lift weights. Study some more. Gideon has been homeschooling me with online lessons since shortly after we moved here. I was agoraphobic at first, and both he and Dr. Abrams decided that placing me in public school would be detrimental to my adjustment process. Sometimes I think regular school would be fun, but I still get nervous in crowds. Navigating the packed hallways and common areas would be a struggle.

A heavy metal door opens out into the lobby of our building. Persian rugs lie over smooth marble tiles, and crystal chandeliers hang from the painted ceiling. A long wooden bar runs the length of the room, empty except for a pair of businessmen sipping from wineglasses. At the far side of the lobby, a half set of stairs leads to Escape, Gideon's gaming club. Escape boasts three big-screen virtual reality gaming setups, computers for online play, and private rooms for other activities.

Jesse and I head for the exit. We pass two more men in suits at the revolving door that leads out onto the street. At first glance they look like lawyers or bankers, but they're too young and their necks are too broad. Their haircuts aren't quite slick enough. Athletes.

One of them makes eye contact and nods. He's got the look of a farm boy—muscular build, tanned skin, clear blue eyes. Wholesome. I don't really follow sports, but I recognize him from clips on the news. His name is Andy something and he almost led the state university to the college football national championship, but then he fell apart in the fourth quarter and we lost. Tough break.

I nod back. I like people who aren't perfect.

"Hey," he says, his voice husky and low. His eyes cling to my form a second too long, as if we know each other, but I'd remember if I'd met him before.

A third man behind him nudges both of the players forward. He stares at me with dark, unfriendly eyes as the three of them pass by. He's also lined with muscle but too old to be an athlete. Probably a coach trying to keep his players from doing something stupid and making the late-night news.

"Friends of yours?" Jesse asks as we step out of the revolving door.

"Not my type." I exhale a foggy breath and pull on a pair of gloves.

We live in an area of St. Louis called the Lofts, bordered by downtown on one side and poorer neighborhoods on the others. It used to be nothing but abandoned warehouses, but a wealthy developer bought them, razed them, and erected several blocks' worth of high-rise apartments. Many of the basements and ground floors feature clubs, bars, or restaurants, and the whole area functions as both home and a playground to the city's richest residents.

Jesse and I head west, the shadows absorbing our black-clad forms. Shards of snow and ice crunch beneath the soles of our boots. In front of the next building, tight clusters of club rats huddle together in the cold, thin filaments of smoke emanating from the orange glow of their cigarettes. They're waiting to get into Inferno. It's where Rose said she was going.

A guy in a down-filled NFL parka and a knitted ski cap moves from circle to circle, hoping to be called upon to peddle his wares. When it comes to drugs, pretty much everything is available if the price is right.

The dealer catches me looking and takes it as an invitation. "What you need, baby?"

I avert my eyes but he shuffles over and walks beside Jesse and me. The sweet scent of marijuana clings to his oversize coat. "I got stuff to make the pain go away, stuff to make you forget."

"I'm fine," I say tersely.

"Sounds like you need something to relax." He yanks open the side of his coat and digs down in a pocket, producing a clear vial of fluid. "This shit'll take you to heaven and back."

"Back off." Jesse slides between us. "She doesn't need anything from you."

The dealer looks ready to start something, but then Jesse lifts his sweatshirt high enough to expose the grip of his gun. The guy turns away, muttering under his breath. A trio of college kids on the other side of the street call out to him. He shimmies his way between two parked cars and then saunters the rest of the way across the road, his high-tops disappearing in the fog of a steaming manhole cover.

We pass a group of girls in glitter makeup and sky-high leather boots, shivering in their short dresses. The damp glow of the streetlight illuminates wide eyes and skin that is soft and perfect. They're not old enough to get into the club, but they're going to try anyway. They look good; the bouncer will probably let them in. A prickle of envy moves through me as I watch three of the girls link arms and huddle together for warmth, giggling and smiling at each other. I haven't had friends like that since the orphanage.

The Lofts end abruptly at a vacant lot that sits in front of an old train yard. Two girls, one with a shorn scalp and the other with a matted braid, are spooning under a knitted afghan where the lot meets the sidewalk. Braid Girl opens her eyes just briefly as our shadows pass in front of her. They've got a coffee can full of change and a sign made from a cardboard box that reads: *Ran away from abusive home. Please help.*

"Wait," I say to Jesse. I reach into the front pocket of my jeans and slide out a twenty-dollar bill. I always carry a little cash on jobs, just in case. As I bend down to place the money in the coffee can, I notice that people have put trash in it while the girls were sleeping. I fish out a crumpled-up napkin and a candy wrapper and tuck the twenty deep inside.

Jesse's teeth almost glow in the dark as he smiles at me. He should be urging me along so we can complete our mission, but that's not his style. I don't think I've ever seen him impatient or angry. "You're such a saint," he says.

"Hardly." He doesn't know my past, that I came from a place even worse than these girls.

We turn south and hurry along the wide sidewalk, blending in with the darkness like a pair of whispers. I slow a little as we pass a block of department-store window displays. They're still decorated for Christmas even though it's mid-January. Icicles hang like knives from the eaves.

Next, the baseball stadium rises up before us, the redbrick corners cutting into the sky. Fluorescent emergency lighting glows from behind the locked metal gates. Something cold slaps against my cheek. I look up as I swat it away. A handful of rogue snowflakes swirl in the streetlight's beam, remnants of last night's storm blown loose.

A strip of reflective buildings hovers a few blocks away, the nearest one topped with a ten-foot-tall iridescent ghost. It's the local offices for a software company called Phantasm.

Jesse and I are going to break in.

CHAPTER 3

"Shit. It's freezing out." Jesse hurries along the sidewalk.

I match my pace to his. "Explain to me why you couldn't drive again?"

"Because Gideon didn't want me to drive. Plus my car would probably break down at the worst moment."

I can't argue. For one, I don't even have a car. Gideon says it's dangerous for me to drive because of the sedatives I sometimes take. Second, Gideon Seung is the smartest person I know. He left Korea to attend graduate school here in the United States, completing a neurobiology doctorate in just four years. In L.A., he worked as a research consultant. After we arrived in St. Louis, he cashed in his investments to buy our building and open Escape.

Two years ago, he began selling a new kind of gaming technology out of the club. Ever since a business website did a feature on the tech a couple months ago, multiple software companies have been trying to buy it from him.

My lips flatten when I think about how angry Gideon became when he saw the article. Somehow the reporter had gotten a picture of him and posted it along with the story. Gideon is very private. We all are. He says we must never tell anyone who we really are or where we came from. It's a little paranoid, if you ask me. Kyung Cho, the man Rose and I worked for in Los Angeles, was probably angry when Gideon took us away, but he wouldn't spend his time or money looking for us. He probably just sent his people out to find some replacements.

I shudder. The idea that gaining my freedom might have doomed another girl to my former life makes me ill. I push the thought into a dark corner of my mind and do my best to lock it away. I'll need all of my focus to be successful tonight.

Jesse and I pause a block from the Phantasm building. I look up at the giant logo, take a breath, and center myself. "Escape route?"

"I've got it figured out." He touches my back lightly. "Just follow my lead, okay?"

Jesse and Gideon always do whatever it takes to assure that our work goes smoothly. I'm just stalling. Tonight is different from the jobs I've done before. We're not just committing some victimless crime—we're taking something from someone else.

It's a tangible threshold, a decision that might lead to harder ones. Gideon said I didn't have to do it if I didn't want to.

I want to.

I would do almost anything for him.

A figure in black exits the building and heads down the sidewalk away from us, a pair of handcuffs glinting under the streetlight.

"Security guards?" I ask.

"Two," Jesse says. "We'll need to evade them."

We cross the street in front of the Phantasm building and settle into the plastic shelter of a bus stop, just as the security guard turns around. Another burst of snow swirls down in front of us, the silvery droplets melting into the dark pavement. Jesse leans close and pretends to show me something on his phone. The guard's eyes flick toward us momentarily but then away. We're just two kids waiting for a late bus. I'm hoping one won't show up for at least a few minutes or it'll blow our cover.

The guard heads around to the back of the building and Jesse whips out a pair of mini binoculars. The lobby is empty except for a second security guard sitting at an information station in the center of the room. He's talking on the phone and flipping through a magazine. I can barely make out some sort of military tattoo on the back of his left hand. Jesse and I watch him for several minutes. He looks up only once.

Jesse reaches into his pocket and produces a key. Gideon bought our way into the building, but once we get inside we have to avoid the guards and gain access to the Phantasm offices on our own. Blood pulses through my veins, fear and excitement competing for my attention.

The guard finally drops the magazine and makes a big show of standing and stretching. He ambles toward the front of the building and checks each door to be sure it's locked before disappearing back into the depths of the lobby. Jesse peeks through the binoculars, expelling a series of slow, frosty breaths.

He turns to me and raises an eyebrow. We've worked together for the past few months—long enough that we can generally read each other's expressions. I nod sharply, my fingers curling into my pockets to feel for my headset and face mask, the pressure of my stun gun weighing comfortably against my abdomen.

Only the pale streetlight above our heads and a smattering of office lights in the nearby buildings dare to penetrate the icy dark. I slip on my headset as we both stand.

"You'd better make sure that thing is on tight," Jesse says. "Just in case."

I secure the headset tightly and then pull my mask on to obscure my face.

Jesse converts his hat to a face mask and slips it over his own headset. He grabs my hand as we dart across the street. Quickly, we use the key to enter the lobby. I hold the door behind me, slowly letting it fall closed so as not to make a sound. We skirt the periphery of the big open room to avoid the security camera that pans slowly back and forth. Pausing in an alcove outside the restrooms, we catch our breath and scan the area for the security guard. We're alone.

Jesse flicks his head in the direction of a conglomeration of steel cylinders and girders that's meant to be modern art. One at a time, we cross the lobby and duck low behind the sculpture. From here we can see the information station, the front doors, the escalators, and the hallway we know leads to a suite of Phantasm offices.

The company owns the first three floors of the building. We're looking for their server, which according to Gideon is in an office at the back of the second floor. Jesse and I creep onto the escalator and duck low, pressing our bodies tight against the metal so the guard won't see us heading up if he's coming down the other side.

My heart begins to race. I have no idea where the guard is. What if he sneaks up on us? I start to wonder why Gideon couldn't have paid a hacker to steal the information he needs from the safety of some darkened basement in another state.

We make it to the second floor unseen. The door to the suite has a numeric lock. Jesse sprays it with a luminescent powder. All of the numbers have been pressed at one point or another, but there are four that have been pressed a lot recently. 1-4-5-6. It takes him only a couple of tries to crack the code, and the door swings open.

Emergency lighting illuminates the office. A large wooden desk sits across from a waiting area built around an L-shaped fish tank. A framed picture hangs on the wall behind the aquarium. A bunch of men lined up in rows. Some sort of employee gathering.

"Come on." Crouching low, Jesse creeps farther into the suite. We pass the sprawling reception area and a set of cubicles that makes up the bulk of the department. The fiberglass walls are covered with memos and notices, the worktables laden with piles of papers and framed photographs of loved ones. My eyes are drawn to a purse dangling from the back of one of the chairs. Designer. Leather. Probably full of cash and credit cards.

We're not here for cash or credit cards.

The stillness of the room ripples and I lunge for my left boot, a silver blade appearing in my hand. Dropping to a crouch, I rear back my arm, ready to throw. But it's just a heater that has clanked to life in a corner, the leaves of a potted plant fluttering in the artificial breeze. Exhaling hard, I swear under my breath. Beneath my mask, my skin is slick with sweat. Why couldn't Gideon have asked me to skydive blindfolded or walk across hot coals or something?

Jesse leads me into a room at the back of the suite. As my eyes adjust to the gloom, I see a pair of desks and a dark wall of electronic equipment stacked six feet high. Wires dangle from some of the stacks. I pause in front of a computer mounted on a pedestal. Gideon provided me with a flash drive he said would automatically run a program to circumvent the server's password protection and download the information he needed. I plug the drive into a USB port and hope for the best. The screen lights up, and a progress bar begins to fill as something called HWARANG.EXE launches itself.

Jesse is standing in the doorway keeping watch. "What's it doing?" he whispers.

"Accessing the root directories."

"Tell it to hurry up." He glances down the hallway again.

The program takes about thirty seconds to install and then the screen goes dark except for a command prompt. Lines of text begin to scroll upward as files are copied onto the drive. For about fifteen seconds everything seems to be working smoothly. Then the computer beeps twice and the screen freezes.

"Something happened," I hiss. "I'm not sure if it's still copying."

Jesse crosses the room in a few quick strides. He peers at the screen, but although both of us have a working knowledge of computers, neither one of us knows enough to troubleshoot the problem. Just when I think we're going to have to abort, the text begins to scroll upward again. "Won't these files be encrypted?" Jesse asks. He watches the screen with me.

"Probably. But that won't stop Gideon for long," I murmur. "If he can't crack them, he'll just find someone else who can."

As Jesse turns to head back to his post, a bank of lights blazes to life above our heads. I spin around. The security guard from the desk downstairs is standing in the doorway. He's just a vague, blurry form, because my brain is focused on the gun in his hand.

CHAPTER 4

"**Against** the wall," the guard says. "Both of you. Hands up."

"Dude." Jesse gestures toward the tattoo on the guy's hand and lifts his sleeve to display a similar marking. "Seven hundred and sixteenth battalion. This isn't what it looks like." It's the old "Don't shoot me because we're the same" routine.

The guard isn't interested in brotherhood. "It looks like breaking and entering." His eyes flick to the computer screen for a fraction of a second. "And then some." He gestures with his gun. "Over there. Now."

We shuffle over to the wall he's pointing at, our hands half-raised as we move. With his gun still pointed at us, the guard slowly backs up toward the computer. His right index finger is still on the trigger as his left hand reaches out for the flash drive.

Jesse and I exchange another glance that conveys paragraphs of information. He shakes his head—an almost imperceptible movement—and I know what it means: *Don't do anything rash*. But I'm closer to the security guard. I have a better chance to take him out.

As soon as the guard's fingers touch the drive, Jesse and I both drop low out of the gun's aim. I lunge forward, my arms encircling the guard's legs, my head slamming against his thigh. He crashes into the computer and we both end up on the floor. There is a deafening crack as the gun goes off. Jesse dives on top of the guard, pinning his hand against the floor. I grab the gun and leap back to my feet.

I have never touched a gun before. My fingers tread lightly, like it's a viper that might turn on me. Adrenaline surges through me like venom.

Jesse wrestles with the guard. They trade punches. I pull the flash drive from the computer and tuck it deep into my pocket. Turning, I aim the gun at the guard just as Jesse lands a skull-rattling hit to his jaw.

My finger dances on the trigger. My blood, my breath, everything about me burns with life. My hands tremble. I could end this guard with his own weapon. It would be easy, too easy. *Do it,* a little voice whispers from the darkest parts of my brain.

He starts to shake. "No. Please," he says. "I have a wife, kids."

With the gun still aimed, I reach into the pocket of my hoodie with my right hand and pull out my stun gun. I'm not here to kill anybody. Jesse and I just need to get out of the building without getting any holes punched in us. Electricity crackles as I shock the guard. Once. Twice. Three times, just to be safe. He convulses and then goes limp. He's still curled in the fetal position when Jesse and I hit the doorway.

"Give it to me." Jesse points at the gun still in my hand.

I hand it over. We run full speed down the escalator, both of us vaulting over the bottom few steps. We head for the front of the building, the soles of our boots pounding like drums on the lobby's tile floor. I pull in front of Jesse as we reach the exit. My body feels lighter. Frost spews from my parted lips as the glass doors swing shut behind us. Too late, I see the gleam of white where the sidewalk meets the street. It's a flashlight—the other security guard.

He sees us and gives chase, screaming things that the night air distorts into meaningless syllables. Jesse and I turn and sprint past two blocks of office buildings. We cross into a small city park, veering off the paved walkway, trying to lose the guard in the trees. I hear the sound of snow crunching behind me. Swearing. Fabric rustling against branches. I push myself to go faster, weaving in and out of the foliage. Jesse and I run six-minute miles. This guy will never keep up with us.

The cold air stings my lungs as we fly past a playground and a set of cement restrooms. Sirens cut sharp lines of sound across the night. I can't tell if they're heading toward or away from us.

We exit the other side of the park, still running full-speed. We cut across the parking lot of a Mexican restaurant and then Jesse swerves left into an alley. Finally, we're heading back toward the Lofts. We hurdle trash bags and dodge rusted bicycles half-covered in snow. Behind us, the guard is swearing and grunting as he stumbles along. His voice fades as we pull away.

But the alley ends and there's more trouble out on the main street. A kaleidoscope of blue and red. Cops. Real ones. That was fast. I slow long enough to give Jesse a questioning look. Gideon has been known to buy off the police.

Jesse shakes his head. "We can't let them catch us."

I bite down on my lower lip. I've never had a job go quite this wrong. Gideon is normally so meticulous about planning for every contingency. My breath catches in my throat. Darkness plays at the corners of my vision like I'm in danger of losing consciousness. *Focus, Winter.*

The cops are coming at us from both directions. We change course again, flinging ourselves around a corner and onto another trash-covered street. The cold metal of the Arch peeks through gaps in the skyline. Jesse stumbles, just slightly, and I pull in front of him.

"The river," he mutters.

Wisps of fog dance around us. I veer toward the waterfront. The cops are boxing us in, but there's nowhere else we can go. The street ends and we're on top of the levee, at least fifty feet up. Below, unforgiving cobblestones. Beyond them, the Mississippi River, a thick ribbon of black current.

Jesse points at an unused railroad bridge, just a little off to the north. I glance over my shoulder. The cops are still coming. Their guns are out. Aimed. We head for the bridge. A chorus of warnings comes from behind, telling us to stop, telling us they'll shoot. A bullet zings past, but Jesse and I press onward.

The bridge is falling apart, the wood rotting, the girders caked with rust. Boards groan under my feet as I pick my way forward. In front of me, Jesse steps carefully from one metal tie to the next. I try to copy him, praying the planks won't give out. I look back. Two cops are waiting at the entrance. *They won't come out here,* I think, turning back around. *They're scared.* And then I see the haze in front of us light up. Blue and red circles flit like ghosts in the fog.

They're not scared. They have us surrounded.

Jesse reaches under his mask and slips his hearing aid from his ear. "Give me the drive."

I fish the flash drive out of my pocket, trying to ignore the cops crouched in my peripheral vision. Jesse slips the electronics into a waterproof pouch and secures the pouch in a zippered pocket. He reaches out for my hand as we step to the edge of the bridge. I look down at the swirling water and go dizzy. My heart thrashes around in my chest, a nightmare monster trying to escape from its closet.

"Is it too far?" I know the water in the middle of the Mississippi is plenty deep, but jumping from too high means broken bones, or worse.

"Not if we climb down the girders." Jesse steps smoothly over the bridge's railing and begins to descend the side of the truss, the metallic latticework almost invisible against the black of the river.

I follow him, clinging to the support beams as I gradually lower myself closer to the water. The frosty metal is slick beneath the fingers of my leather gloves. From this height I can see the white froth of the current. My eyes flick to the riverbank and then back to Jesse as I try to calculate where we'll be able to climb ashore.

"Stay vertical," he reminds me. "Hands against your body."

"Right," I say tersely. We've done some cliff diving in the past, but nothing that quite compares to this.

I guess I must still look scared, because Jesse reaches out and squeezes my arm. "Do you trust me?" he asks.

I nod. There's no other choice.

One at a time, we leap from the bridge.

CHAPTER 5

I slam into the frigid water and sink deep. Holding my breath, I fight my way back to the surface. Tucking my knees to my chest, I assume the fetal position to maximize my core temperature as the river carries me downstream. I paddle across the current toward the nearest bank, gradually steering myself to the water's edge. When I drag myself up on the frozen mud, I leap to my feet, ready to start running again. But Jesse is jogging toward me from where he crawled out of the river slightly upstream. He raises his hand in a high five.

"Are you serious?" My teeth start to chatter as I look back at the bridge. The flashing lights have disappeared. "That was *all* part of the setup? You could have told me." I use the fabric of my sleeve to wipe the fetid water from my eyes and then take a couple of deep breaths. I hug my arms to my chest to quell my shivering.

"If I did, your recording wouldn't have turned out as good. Gideon wanted to capture the adrenaline of the chase."

My recording. Right. My face mask was yanked up and over my head when I hit the river, but my recorder headset is still secured in place. Reaching up, I pull the five-pronged device from my head without even turning it off, twitching as a mild shock races through my body.

It's the latest version of Gideon's tech—a headset that records the sensory neurologic impulses of its wearer. Four of the device's prongs record neural impulses from different parts of the brain and the fifth sits at the base of the neck and records from the spinal cord. Gideon doesn't just give you the first-person visual of what it's like to run from the cops. He gives you what the runner is actually feeling, one firing synapse at a time.

He sells the recordings at Escape so people can live vicariously through us. For as little as twenty dollars, you can soar through the sky as a hang glider or drive 220 miles an hour in an official Indy 500 race car. You can dance with celebrities at the hottest clubs or hook up with a girl who would never give you the time of day. And now you'll be able to jump off a bridge into the Mississippi River. It's about being someone else, someone who does things you would never do. It's the ultimate in escapism.

"What about *your* recording?" I ask wryly. Just once I'd like to be the one with all of the information.

"Mine are never as good as yours, because of my sight," Jesse says. "And someone needs to know everything for when there *is* a real misstep, like with that security guard." He slips his hearing aid in and then jogs a few yards back toward where he crawled ashore. His voice grows muffled as he disappears into a thick patch of foliage. "That guy scared the crap out of me." Jesse reappears with a black garbage bag, knotted at the top.

"Oh, so he *wasn't* in on it?"

"Even Gideon can't buy everyone." Jesse says. "I can't believe you went for him like that. You could've gotten shot."

I shrug it off. I guess I was too adrenalized to feel scared. "So what? I'm wearing Kevlar." I unzip my hoodie as if to prove it. Immediately, I'm seized by another attack of shivering.

"Not on your face. Gid is going to have a meltdown when he sees that." Jesse pushes his wet hair back from his forehead and slowly works a knot out of the top of the bag.

"Maybe he'll be impressed for once." I tug the body armor over my head and toss it in the direction of Jesse's bag before slipping back into my waterlogged hoodie. "You know how he's always saying the only way to get stronger is to challenge yourself."

I've been recording Gideon's Vicarious Sensory Experiences, or ViSEs, for over a year and each job seems to get a little riskier. I started out doing basic adventure stuff, but after I gained some experience, I found myself BASE jumping from national monuments and running from cops. And tonight I got shot at for the first time.

But it's just the nature of the business. Once our customers have rock climbed and hang glided, most of them are ready to move on to something bigger and better. ViSEs are legal (even if what we have to do to get them isn't), but other than that, we're not much different from the drug dealers who roam the Lofts. If we want to maximize profits, we have to provide what people want.

Tonight's mission had two purposes. The police chase and bridge jump were for the visers. The information downloaded was for Gideon. Phantasm is one of the companies that's been pressuring Gideon to sell his tech. They want to produce mass quantities of playback headsets, widespread distribution of ViSEs online, streaming from multiple platforms. It's much more than Gideon could accomplish with his current staff, but he's not even considering it without a behind-the-scenes look at Phantasm's finances.

That's what he *says*, anyway. Personally, I think he's digging for company dirt to force them to back off. He's a control freak and the ViSE tech is his baby. I don't see him selling.

A gust of wind wraps its fingers around my middle, and my teeth start chattering again. Jesse pulls a thin gray blanket out of the bag and holds it out in my direction. I cocoon myself, willing the itchy fabric to suck the icy cold water out of my clothes.

"How much did you have to pay the cops?" I look up at the bridge again.

"Not much. You just have to know the right guys to approach." Jesse grins. "Some of them were so eager to shoot live fire that they probably would have paid *me*. We just have to make sure their license plates aren't readable on the finished recordings."

Easy enough to do with a bit of editing. I try not to stare as Jesse tugs his waterlogged sweatshirt over his head. He's built like a puma, thick and muscular, the outline of his abs just barely visible in the dim light. He slips on a dry T-shirt and a quilted parka and then starts to unbutton his pants.

I turn toward the river to give him privacy. There's something hypnotic about flowing water—the more I look at it, the more it calls to me. I inch closer to the edge of the bank. I imagine diving back in and surrendering to the current. Being swept downstream and swallowed whole.

I shake my head as if trying to dislodge the morbid thought. Once upon a time there was a girl named Ha Neul who wanted to die, but I am not that girl anymore.

Jesse taps me on the shoulder. "I've got stuff for you too. I don't want you to freeze to death on the walk home." He hands me a bundle of gray fleece. Dry clothes would feel good, but I can't bring myself to strip down here, in the middle of nowhere, especially not in front of him.

I toss my blanket back into the bag and shove the bundle of clothing under my arm. "Let's just get out of here. We can edit these and amplify the neural sensations tomorrow."

Jesse was right when he said keeping the plan a secret from me would result in a better recording. There's a natural adrenaline rush involved in running from the cops and jumping off a bridge, but it's a lot more intense if the recorder is actually afraid. The more Jesse and I train for a ViSE, the less scared we are when we record it, especially if we know it's all a setup. That's where Gideon's neural editor comes in. Natural sensations are the best, but when that isn't feasible we can modify what the viser feels, to a degree. We can't change things, like add a bridge jump where one didn't happen, but we can block certain impulses to obscure license plates, or amplify them to increase sensations like fear or pleasure.

To us, reality is just raw footage: Unclear. Desultory. Too shocking or not quite shocking enough. It's ironic that making something more real involves making it less real, but Gideon always says people don't want real. They want the *idea* of real, which involves production.

Jesse and I make our way up the bank of the river and onto the waterfront's cobblestoned streets. I try to ignore the fabric sticking to my legs and the water dripping from the cuffs of my pants as we head back to the Lofts.

"You can't go into the building looking like a drowned rat," he reminds me when we get close.

"I'm aware." I glance around for a private spot to change. The scarlet neon of an all-night Gas 'n' Go bleeds onto the sidewalk in front of us. Perfect. "Wait here." I duck into the restroom and slip on Jesse's gray fleece hoodie and black tear-away warm-up pants, balling my wet clothes under my arm. I roll the waistband twice so his pants don't hang down over my shoes and then stop to check my reflection in the mirror. My hair is slicked to the sides of my face like a pair of half-drawn curtains and most of my eyeliner has washed off, but at least I don't look like I've been swimming in the river.

When we arrive home, the line to get into Inferno has dwindled down to just a few high school kids still hovering in the cold. I wonder if Rose is in there, recording tonight's switch party for Gideon to sell. If she is, I'd rather not witness it.

Jesse and I cut through the lobby and duck into the stairwell. He walks me all the way to the penthouse.

"I'll get your clothes back to you soon," I say. He lives below me, on the seventh floor, which is actually the sixth floor since Gideon had the floors renumbered to skip from three to five when he bought the building. The number four is bad luck in Korean culture.

"Keep them if you want. They don't fit anymore." Jesse pats himself on the stomach.

I roll my eyes. Jesse complains that he's gained weight since he left the military, but 99 percent of it is probably muscle. I suspect he's fishing for a compliment, but I'm not in the mood to be manipulated. "You're not fat." I bite back a smile. "You're just fluffy."

He gasps in mock outrage. "You did not just call me *fluffy*. For that you owe me some of that tea you're always drinking."

I punch in the six-digit code and press my thumb to the sensor that unlocks the penthouse door. "I guess I could, as long as you're quiet so we don't wake Gideon." I slip out of my boots and step into the entry hall.

Jesse's body relaxes as he follows me inside and reaches down to unlace and remove his own boots. Just watching him, so comfortable in my personal space, makes me go tense. I hear my sister telling me to just "give him some" as she so delicately put it. Rose wouldn't have teased a guy and called him fluffy. She would have run her hands up his chest and around his neck and told him his body was perfect. My face reddens. Sometimes I wonder what would happen if I were completely uninhibited like she is.

When Jesse flops down at our kitchen table and looks up at me, this quickly becomes one of those times. His pupils dilate, circles of black swallowing up the hazel of his eyes. Points of wet brown hair cling to the skin of his forehead. He smiles his incongruous perfect smile.

I turn away and put on a kettle of water to heat. Then I quickly gather tea leaves, valerian root, passionflower, and a bit of ginger. I like creating my own flavors with fresh herbs and spices. My fingers fly with the paring knife, peeling and then dicing the ginger into smaller and smaller pieces to avoid looking at Jesse. I lean over the simmering water so he'll think the color in my cheeks is from the steam.

"You did amazing tonight." His voice is low.

I dump everything into the water and turn around, abandoning the tea to the stove. "You think?"

"Yeah. I panicked for a second when the gun went off. But you didn't. I swear you've got the reflexes of a cat."

I look over at the teakettle. It won't be done for a while. Jesse shucks off his quilted coat. All he has underneath is a white T-shirt stretched tight across his chest. He might as well be sitting here half-naked.

He catches me staring and his face lights up. I can read all sorts of things in his grin. What he wants, what he thinks I want. I wish I could throw myself into the kettle and drown, or maybe evaporate into steam. "Rose has faster reflexes than I do." I don't even know if this is true. It's just the first thing that comes to mind, and I want to distract him from whatever he's thinking.

"What's her deal, anyway? Does she actually like all that dancing and stuff?"

Maybe. "I don't know. So what if she does?" I ask, a note of defensiveness creeping into my voice. "Are you telling me you never recorded anything provocative?" I know Gideon has multiple sexual ViSEs for sale. I'm sure all of his male recorders have donned headsets and wigs and taken one for the team, so to speak.

Jesse's smile fades. "That was a long time ago, and I was desp—"

I cut him off. "So then why do you get to judge her?"

"Whoa." He holds his hands up in surrender. "Not judging anyone. I just know how much you worry about her."

"I do." I've never told him this. I didn't realize it was so obvious.

"I mean, why let guys paw all over her when she can do cool stuff like us?"

I asked Dr. Abrams about this once. She said sometimes victims of abuse seek out more abuse because it's the only thing they know. Rose says that's bullshit. She says it's about taking back the control that was stolen from us.

"Where we came from," I tell Jesse, "a girl needs an arsenal to feel safe. Beauty, her body—these are her weapons."

"Where did you guys come from?"

Hell. I don't answer.

Jesse leans forward. He reaches across the table and takes my hand before I can pull it away. "Okay, then. So what are *your* weapons?" His thumb massages the middle of my palm. I stare down at the military insignia tattooed on his forearm and the ring of random letters around his wrist. I've never paid much attention to Jesse's tattoos, but suddenly little details about him are starting to stand out. I hear my sister's voice in my head again. *You know Jesse loves you.*

Sweat beads up on my forehead. I yank my hand free, slide a knife out of the sheath still strapped to my left ankle, and set it on the table with a soft clunk. "Weapons are my weapons."

"Nice." Jesse takes the knife and turns it over in his hand. "Does Gideon know you have this?"

"Yes," I say. "He doesn't approve, but he knows he can't keep me from buying things that I want." I slide the other knife from its sheath and twirl the hilt between my palms.

Jesse lifts the knife he's holding to his shoulder and fakes like he's going to throw it at the wall behind me. "Where'd you get them?"

"The Internet." It's also where I learned to throw them. I watched a few videos and then hung a wooden target on the wall in my bedroom. Miso watched me practice from the hallway, his amber eyes curious but unafraid, his tail twitching at each dull thunk.

I look around for the cat but he's nowhere in sight. Probably curled up amongst the clutter in Rose's room. I set my knife on the table.

Jesse sets the other one next to it. "I have a great idea. Do you want to trade?"

"Trade what? Weapons?" Jesse carries a gun. I would love to trade with him.

"Recordings." He pulls his collapsed headset from a pocket and snaps a memory card out of a slot on the back.

"You know I don't vise."

I've told Jesse this, but I've never told him why. He doesn't know about my PTSD, my hallucinations, my time in the hospital. The reality-challenged are not meant to live vicariously.

"Never?" Jesse asks. "Not even your own recordings?"

"I did it a few times to help Gideon test the beta tech, but it's been years."

"It's not like you're tripping off it or anything," Jesse says. "It'd be like reviewing your performance. Aren't you even a *little* curious?"

I am, but it's difficult not to form an intimate connection with the recorder since you're experiencing the world from inside someone else's brain. I'm not good with intimate connections, especially not with Jesse. "I prefer the real world." The excuse sounds hollow even to me. "Also, I'm really sensitive to overlay."

Overlay happens when the viser isn't able to turn off his or her own thoughts and sensations, so external stimuli bleed through. The best visers are good at meditating, blocking out the whole world except for the ViSE. Otherwise you end up experiencing the recorder's sensations on top of your own, which can result in headaches, nausea, and disorientation.

"Maybe you just need to learn how to relax." Jesse goes to the kitchen wall and flicks off the light. The flame of the gas burner casts flickering shadows around the room.

"I don't think that'll help," I say. "My thoughts are a little harder to shut off."

He gives up. "Then just let me see yours." He holds out his hand.

I hesitate, but then fish my headset out of my pocket and extract the memory card. I pass it over to Jesse. In the dim light, his features are amorphous, his damaged ear, his scar, the slight bend in his nose fading into the gray. I wonder if mine are too—if my high cheekbones and sharp chin are softened. Gideon always says I wear a perpetually angry look, that my face repels people. Jesse is leaning toward me, though, anything but repelled.

"Fine," I say suddenly. "Let me have it." I've never vised from a guy's point of view. It could be interesting. Besides, the tea still has a few minutes to go.

Jesse slides his recording across the table. I catch a hint of sweat mixed with evergreen deodorant, the sweetness of the brewing tea threading throughout it. Just these simple scents might cause enough overlay to bring on a headache. I try to push them out of my head as I take the tiny card from him and slip it into my headset. *I smell nothing. I see nothing. I hear nothing. I feel nothing.*

The headset unfolds into what is basically a lightweight metal spider. I slide it onto the back of my head and position the prongs over the neural access points.

"Ready?" Jesse asks. "We go together."

I close my eyes and press PLAY.

Apparently, we're *not* going together. I should be standing just outside the Phantasm building, but instead:

I look into my own face as I open the door to the penthouse.

For some reason, Jesse started recording long before we reached Phantasm and I put on my mask. "What is this?" I ask.

"Don't worry. I'll cut you out of the finished product."

"But why would you start recording so early?" My head begins to throb at the temples from only just a few seconds of balancing the dual realities.

"Shh," he says. "This is just getting good."

I sigh, but try to focus on Jesse's recording. His eye was

permanently damaged at the same time as his ear, and therefore the left side of my visual field is framed by a faint blurry streak. It's almost unnoticeable unless you know to look for it. I skip forward.

We're heading down the stairwell. I see the fingers of my right hand brushing against the metal railing.

Even with the lights off, I'm not embracing the ViSE. Instead I experience it from a distance, like I'm watching the events play out on TV. As I reach up to fast-forward the recording again, I realize I look different to Jesse than I do when I look in the mirror. My skin is smoother, my eyes wider. It's almost like his brain is editing me.

Other people look different too. The girls trying to get into the club look softer, like lambs. The homeless girls seem so weak. It makes me curious about his past. What sort of history makes you view everyone as prey?

I skip forward to the actual break-in and then try to empty my mind and become Jesse.

We enter the Phantasm building. A sense of calm comes over me as we duck low behind the sculpture and then cross the lobby to the escalators. We head upstairs. I spray the keypad, crack the code, and head to the back of the office. My heart slows even more as we creep through the Phantasm suite.

Everything plays out pretty much like I expect until the guy busts in with the gun.

We're positioned against the wall. We exchange looks. I freeze up completely for a second as I see myself drop low and lunge for the guard.

My lips quirk into a smile as I admire my takedown move. Then I remember how Jesse's brain edited me earlier and wonder if I was actually half as agile as I looked.

My heart threatens to burst straight through my rib cage. I gasp for breath before leaping on top of the guard. I pin the hand with the gun to the floor. I see myself grab it. Then the guard is pleading and he's getting shocked and then we're on the run. Sharp spikes of air thrust in and out of my chest as I watch myself almost run directly into the second security guard.

I lose the momentum of the ViSE again as Jesse and I head for the river. I start to smell the ginger of the tea and feel the kitchen table hard beneath my forearms. Searing pain races through my temples and my stomach lurches. I try to empty my brain, but I keep flashing back to the freezing up, to the fear Jesse felt when I was in danger. I've never known him to be afraid.

With his military background and ViSE experience, he should be battle ready, always in control. That intense fear response *means* something.

Something I'd rather not think about.

CHAPTER 6

The teakettle whistles. I pull the headset off and fling it down on the table, flinching from the mild shock. Opening my eyes, I blink hard, clutching one hand to my churning stomach.

Jesse hears my chair scrape against the floor and opens his eyes. "Hey, you quit in the middle."

"I saw enough." My lips are tight. I jump up and go to the stove, nearly scorching my hand on the burner as I reach for the kettle. I crank the stove off, counting the beats of my heart as they pound in my temples. "The way you see me is weird."

Jesse removes his headset, folds it, and slips it into his pocket. "How so?"

"It's just different." I think of my wide, dark eyes looking at him from the doorway of the penthouse, my agile form attacking the guard in the server room. "I look so graceful to you. More like my sister than me."

He studies me carefully. "Maybe I'm not the one with the skewed perception."

"What is that supposed to mean?" I remove two mugs from the nearest cupboard, pouring each one of them exactly three-quarters full of tea.

"I don't understand why you're always putting yourself down. Comparing yourself unfavorably to Rose."

"I grew up in her shadow," I say simply. "Everyone finds her beautiful."

"Yeah, she's hot, and so are you. But the world is full of hot chicks. Not every girl can disarm a security guard and jump off a bridge."

I smile in spite of myself. It's true. Rose isn't one for adventure sports or martial arts. I used to question why Gideon didn't train her alongside me. He said she was old enough to make her own decisions, and she had no interest in fighting, at least not with her fists.

I suddenly feel lost in her absence, a satellite with nothing to orbit. Hopefully she'll be home soon.

I plunk both mugs down on the table. "Help yourself."

Jesse reaches past both mugs for my hand, but I pull it away. I try to step back, but the kitchen feels as if it's shrunk. I smell evergreen again. Jesse is everywhere.

"I don't feel like tea anymore." I turn and busy myself at the counter.

"What's wrong, Winter? What did I do?"

"You showed me that on purpose," I say, without turning around. "You knew I would figure out what it meant."

"What *what* meant?" He sounds honestly confused, and for a moment I hope I have it all wrong, that he's just another guy looking to score, like I told Rose earlier.

I spin and face him. "The way you felt when the gun went off."

"I was scared. I care about you," he says, like I'm the world's biggest idiot for not knowing this. He shakes his head. "Only you would find that to be a problem."

He's so . . . earnest. So willing. Maybe that's part of why I hold back. Good things have never come easily to me. If I can have him without a fight, there must be something wrong. "Jesse, our job is hard enough without . . . other things getting in the way."

"Other things?" He closes the gap between us in a couple of quick strides. "I know you care about me too."

"I do, but . . ." My voice fades away as Jesse pins me against the counter, trapping me between his arms. I see beard stubble and a nose broken one too many times. The hazel in his eyes blurs into different hues. He's too close. My brain sends all sorts of signals to the rest of me: *punch, kick, scream, run away.*

My muscles disobey. I am paralyzed.

"It's okay to care." He cups the side of my face in one hand.

I let myself get pulled further into his gaze. The colors twist and turn around me. An ocean of browns and golds. I wish I could regress to a point where this closeness would be exciting instead of terrifying. I'm not even sure how far back I'd have to go.

Too far.

"It's also okay to tell me to back off," he says.

Back off. The words get lost on the way to my lips. Jesse's face is still out of focus. I am still swimming behind his eyes.

He touches his cheek to mine and everything is amplified. His beard prickles my skin. My breath goes still. I clutch at the handle of a drawer behind me to keep from sliding right down onto the floor. Softly, Jesse's mouth brushes against my jaw, a single point of heat on my shivering skin. He holds my chin steady so I'm forced to look at him.

For a second, I am absolutely terrified that he's going to kiss me and I have no idea how I'll respond. Will I kiss back? Run away? Start to cry? I'm just a puppet waiting to see which string my handler will pull.

But then Jesse leans away and I regain some tiny degree of control. With one hand, he traces the curve of my eyebrow, my cheek, my throat. A strange collection of noises escapes from my mouth. I ball the fabric of his shirt in my free hand as my eyelids flutter shut. He presses his lips to my jawbone again, but this time he leaves them there.

"Jesse," I whisper. "Gideon might wake up."

"So come downstairs with me," he murmurs, his breath hot in my ear.

A wanting burns inside of me, hungry and raw, and with it the tinge of dread that always comes at the thought of getting too close. Reluctantly, I open my eyes. "I can't." The words fall from my lips in pieces. I tuck my head low so my hair obscures part of my face.

"I know." He nods. "I'm sorry."

He returns to his seat and my face flushes red. I can still feel his hands on me. His lips. A tremor races the length of my spine.

"The excitement of the night, you know?" he says. "I didn't mean to get carried away."

"It's fine." I return to my pseudo-work at the counter so I don't have to face him, swiping at the clean sink with a dish towel and then carefully folding and refolding it until the corners match up exactly. I peek into the nearest cupboard and find a container of mild sedatives. Popping off the cap, I shake out two of the pills and dry swallow them. "Headache," I explain as I close the cupboard. "From the overlay."

"Those can be brutal," Jesse says. "I can stay with you for a while until you're feeling better."

I shake my head. "I should probably try to study a little bit before I go to sleep."

"With a headache?"

"It's not that bad," I say. "Sometimes focusing on academics relaxes me."

"So what you're saying is that studying is so boring it puts you to sleep?" Jesse grins. "I still can't believe you go to high school on the Internet."

"It's just easier for me. Rose went to regular school for a year. She never talked about it much, though. I figured maybe she didn't want me to feel bad because I couldn't go too."

"Trust me," Jesse says. "You're not missing anything."

"Being around a lot of people makes me nervous anyway," I say. "I learn better in a controlled environment." I shift my weight from one foot to the other. "I should get to work. But thanks for everything tonight."

Jesse knows a dismissal when he hears one. He takes his untouched tea to the sink and dumps it. Greenish-brown liquid spirals down the drain. He washes his mug and then rinses it thoroughly. "I know it would make both our lives easier," he says. "But I'm not giving up on you, Winter. On us."

I take a tentative sip of my tea. "There is no us," I say, hating the cruel way it sounds. If I wanted any guy, I would want him. But right now, I can't be the girl he needs.

Jesse doesn't even flinch at my harsh words. He sets his mug in the drain pan to dry and then turns to face me. "Just because you say something, doesn't make it true."

I narrow my eyes. "Oh, really?"

He shakes his head. "Forget it. I don't want to fight with you." He slips back into his quilted jacket. "Drink your tea. Get your work done. I'll come get you tomorrow so we can edit the recordings before we go to Krav Maga." Jesse tugs his boots back on and slips out into the hallway.

I exhale deeply as the door closes behind him, both relieved and a little sad that he's gone.

Krav Maga class is how Jesse and I officially met. I had seen him around Escape once or twice, but we never really talked until we paired off for sparring. Jesse was the first guy who offered to go up against me, quick to point out that what I lacked in brute strength I made up for in speed and agility.

He scared me at first, with his tattoos and his mangled ear, and this air of intensity that made me want to look away when he came close. He didn't hold back when he was fighting me either. Jesse said I challenged him in ways guys didn't, that working with me would make him better. From that day forward, we were sparring buddies, showing up for the same Sunday afternoon class each week.

A couple months later, when Gideon wanted to pair Jesse

and me up for a martial arts ViSE, I found myself excited about the prospect of partnering with him. I knew he would push me to be my best. Gradually we became friends and he traded in his intense stares for smiles. Now I've grown to feel safe with him by my side. I should feel less safe after a glimpse into the predatory way he looks at the world, but I don't.

I know Jesse would never hurt me.

But why? Why does he see me as something other than a collection of vulnerabilities to exploit? I fetch my tablet from my bedroom and work through some physics homework to avoid thinking about it. I sip my tea repeatedly as I wrestle with the equations, downing almost the whole mug without realizing it. The warm liquid reminds me of Jesse's lips on my skin. My brain clings to the moment when I thought he was going to kiss me, replaying it, extrapolating out what might have happened if I had let it.

What might have happened if I were normal.

Abandoning my tablet, I head for the bathroom. I yank off the clothes Jesse loaned me and turn the bathtub faucet on extra hot. When the tub is full, I slide into it and duck completely under the surface, letting the scalding water cleanse away my shame and confusion.

CHAPTER 7

I dream of a small room and a man with one eye. Blood seeps like scarlet tears from his empty socket. I turn to run away from him and the room becomes a hallway that becomes a stairway that becomes a roof. The wind tugs at my body; the sky tries to wrap me in stars. Below me, a gazebo glows with red light. A line of black cars crawls like cockroaches through the streets.

An air conditioner exhaust fan chitters angrily near the roof's edge, one of its blades bent just enough to scrape against the side of the casing. For a second I let the wind push me close enough to the fan's razor-sharp blades that a lock of my hair gets snipped and sent out into the night. As it twists and flutters toward the gazebo, I think about just letting go, letting the breeze carry my body into the whirling blades, the wind scattering pieces of me throughout the city. Blood and flesh seeping into the cracked pavement. Flowers blooming wherever I land.

"Winter." Rose's voice comes from everywhere at once. I whirl around, but I don't see her. The one-eyed man stands in the doorway that leads back to the building. He watches me without speaking, his face stained with blood.

"Eonni? Where are you?" I ask.

She doesn't answer.

I turn back to the air conditioner. The blades spin. I step closer, hypnotized by the crackling noise.

Behind me, the one-eyed man laughs.

"Winter. No." My sister appears at the edge of the roof. She reaches out for me.

But it's too late. It's time to fall to pieces.

I wake with my hands tightened into fists, my heart large inside my throat. I'm curled up on the floor of my room, my neck bent at a strange angle. My muscles ache and my head feels like it's full of wet cotton.

At first I think I've sleepwalked. I used to do that right after we moved to St. Louis, especially when my dreams were particularly lucid. But then last night comes back to me. Trading ViSEs. The way Jesse's touch made me feel. Trying to drown my shame and confusion with a bath. I vaguely remember returning to my room after the bathwater went cold.

I don't remember going to sleep on the floor, but I do that sometimes when I'm anxious. Dr. Abrams calls this behavior "regression," because Rose and I used to sleep on a mat together when we were little.

There's a sharp knock on my door. "Winter. Are you all right?" It's Gideon.

I glance at my phone and swear under my breath. I'm already late for my workout. "Coming, *oppa*," I say. Oppa means older brother in Korean, but it's used outside of blood relations too. Although Gideon prefers that we speak English at all times, that desire does not extend to me disrespectfully addressing him by his first name. "Give me five minutes." Hurriedly I change into my *dobok*, my Taekwondo sparring outfit, and pull my hair back into a ponytail.

Gideon waits for me in the hallway already wearing his dobok and headgear. His dark eyes look me up and down in an almost clinical fashion.

"Sorry. I forgot to set my alarm."

Wordlessly, he turns and strides down the hallway, pausing outside of my sister's bedroom. "Have you talked to Rose today?"

Something in the tone of his voice makes my chest go tight. "No. Why?"

"I have something to ask her." He pauses. "It's nothing urgent."

The door to her room is cracked open. I knock. "Eonni," I say. No answer. I knock again and then push the door inward. Miso is sitting on the dresser, pawing gently at a bright red wig. I scoop him up in one arm and set the hairpiece on an empty stand between a wavy black wig and a silky blue one. Rose's bed is full of stuff—high-heeled boots, two dresses, three fashion magazines. There's no way she made this mess today. I would have heard her moving around.

"It looks like she didn't come home last night. Did you send her to Inferno?" I ask.

"She wasn't doing anything for me," Gideon says.

My chest tightens further. "She told me she was working."

"Rose has been doing a bit of . . . freelancing. You didn't know?"

"No." My teeth grate hard into my bottom lip. I knew Rose and I had secrets, but I didn't know we kept any from each other.

"I'm sure she's just crashed out at a friend's place," Gideon says kindly. "It wouldn't be the first time."

He's right. My sister is no stranger to staying out all night. Still, something feels off.

Gideon's phone buzzes in his pocket. He taps out a quick text and then says, "Come. It's getting late and I still have to pack for my business trip. Our workout will help clear your mind."

I follow him through the penthouse. A few sunbeams scatter their way through the miniblinds, just enough light to illuminate the Kandinsky print hanging above the fireplace and the private elevator that opens directly into the back corner of the living room.

"Where are you going again?" I ask.

"Chicago. Just for a couple of days." Gideon slides open the balcony door.

I step outside, the chilly morning air turning to ice in my lungs. A short flight of stairs leads up to the roof. It's empty up here except for an air-con unit and a ten-foot square drawn in chalk. My protective headgear sits in the southeast corner as always.

As I hurry over to it, something slams into me from behind. The blow strikes at the level of my kidneys and I fall to my hands and knees on the unforgiving cement. Instinctively, I curl over onto my back, my right forearm hooked in front of my face to protect my head.

Gideon stands over me, his mouth twisted into a mix of amusement and displeasure. "You're unfocused."

Frowning, I leap to my feet. "I wasn't ready." Blood blooms in the layers of torn skin on my palms. My knees sting from the hard landing.

"You must always be ready." Gideon reaches out, bracing my jaw with his thumb and forefinger for a moment as he studies me. To an outsider his actions might appear intimate, but his hands and eyes aren't cherishing me; they're searching for injury. Weakness. Apparently satisfied, he steps back and gestures at the headgear.

Being careful not to turn my back on him, I dress for battle. We bow to each other and then retreat to opposite corners. For the next hour we fight hand-to-hand, no breaks. Gideon and I are about the same height, but he's stronger and faster than I am and it is all I can do to stay on my feet. We do not use a mat because he says in life there are no mats, and I must learn to fall in a way that protects my bones and organs. It's all about the transfer of energy from the part that hits the ground first to the rest of the body. The whole self—physical and mental—must absorb its share of the blows.

There are more blows today than usual. I am slow, sluggish. I rest on my heels instead of springing forth from the balls of my feet. My chin hugs my chest instead of leading. Repeatedly, Gideon attacks and I struggle to dodge and block, ending up on my hands, my flank, my back.

"Did you stay up late after you finished your recording?" Curiosity glimmers in his eyes.

"Yes. Studying." The words come out sharper than intended. I lunge forward, my left arm lashing out in a ridge-hand strike, my right arm protecting my body.

My head snaps on my neck as Gideon lands a fist to my chin. I stumble backward, only barely regaining my balance before stepping outside of the chalk square. There are no chalk squares in life either, but there are enclosed areas and that is what the perimeter is supposed to represent.

Gideon's jaw tightens as he returns to his side of the square. "I thought perhaps you went out with Jesse afterward."

"He wishes." I drop back into horse stance.

"Is that so?" Gideon attacks again, but this time I am ready. I block him both high and low and sweep my left foot in a hook kick. He stumbles but doesn't fall. I follow up with a second attack, a knife hand and a crescent kick that sends Gideon outside of the chalk line. He recovers just before he falls, dipping into a bow. "Good," he says. And then, "It appears speaking of Jesse inspires strong feelings."

I attack again—a fist to the chin, a side arm to the gut. "Is there something specific on your mind?"

Gideon blocks both punches. "I just don't want you to get hurt."

I pause a split second to ponder the irony of that and end up on the ground.

When the hour is up, it is Gideon lying on his back half

outside the chalk square and I'm standing over him. A smile plays at his lips as he allows me to help him back to his feet. We bow to each other, remove our headgear, and then descend the stairs back to the penthouse.

Gideon gestures toward a Tupperware container on the kitchen counter. Inside are two rolls of *gimbap*, vegetables and fish cake wrapped in rice and seaweed.

"You made breakfast already?" I ask, surprised. I usually end up rolling gimbap or preparing some other small meal for us.

"I woke up early," Gideon says. "Unlike you." He smiles to show me he's teasing. "So I assume last night went all right?"

"Things went mostly as planned." There's no point in telling him about the gun going off. He'll see it soon enough and I'd prefer to delay any forthcoming lecture as long as possible. I wash and dry my hands and take the gimbap to the dining room table. I slip one of the quarter-sized pieces into my mouth as I take my usual seat. "Jesse has the flash drive with the downloaded information. Sorry—I forgot to get it from him."

"Hmm. There's something different about the way you're saying his name." Gideon's dark eyes cut into me like scalpels. I can almost feel him folding back layers, exposing secrets. Could he possibly know about what happened with Jesse in the kitchen? No—if he'd awakened, I would have heard him skulking around.

I swallow hard. "You're imagining things."

"Good." His smile is sharp and fleeting. "You have a long time for boys and dating. Better you finish your studies and learn to protect yourself first." He settles into the chair across from me and helps himself to a piece of gimbap. "How are your new courses going?"

"Fine. I think I'll enjoy Physics and World Literature. Calculus might not be quite as interesting, but I see no reason why I won't be able to get an A in every class as long as I work hard."

"Excellent. You make me proud."

I lower my eyes. Gideon is thirty years old, only twelve years my senior, but the closest thing I have ever had to a father. My real father left before I was born, or at least I assume he did.

I remember only my mother and Rose. One day when I was two or three, my mother woke us early and bundled us into our best clothes. She carried a basket with both hands, water and food for the journey. Rose walked beside her, her right hand wrapped tightly around my left one. We walked for hours and then took a train to the city. The ride stretched into eternity. The car was crowded with passengers—old leathery men with gnarled fingers and yellowing nails, school kids in their navy uniforms, mothers holding white-wrapped screaming babies. I was tired and hungry, but each time I reached for the basket of food, my mother slapped my hand away.

The mountains became rolling plains dotted with trees. Then Seoul rose up without warning, clusters of shacks bleeding into skyscrapers of metal and glass. Shortly after we disembarked, my mother stopped in front of a building and told us to wait on the steps for her. She disappeared into the lobby and never came back out. The building turned out to be the Singing Crane Orphanage. Staff members found us later and brought us inside.

When I was younger, I used to fantasize about why she left us there. I let myself believe she was a spy or a secret princess, that she abandoned us for our own protection and would come back for us once it was safe.

But now I know the reality is probably much simpler. She was too poor, too alone. She couldn't take care of us anymore.

I eat another piece of gimbap.

Gideon goes to brew some tea, but then his phone rings. His jaw tenses as he listens to someone on the other end. "She's with me," he says. "We'll be right there."

"What is it?" I can tell by the sound of his voice that something bad has happened. I grip the corner of the table to steady myself.

"That was Sebastian. We need to go down to Escape."

Sebastian "Baz" Faber is Gideon's head of security. When he's not at Gideon's side, he works out of an office in the club. "Why? What happened?"

Gideon's hands tremble a little as he slips his phone into his pocket. "There's been a break-in."

Baz peers out through the clear glass of Escape's front door. He's former military like Jesse, but he looks more like a stockbroker in his immaculately pressed dark suit. His bronze skin has paled slightly to match his slicked-back blond hair.

A wiry, dark-skinned man wearing thick glasses hurries over to us—Adebayo, the club manager. "Thank goodness you have arrived," he says in his clipped Nigerian accent.

"What happened?" Gideon pulls a lighter and a tin of clove cigarettes from his pocket.

Adebayo wrings his hands, sweat beginning to bead on his high forehead. "I cannot believe it. Our security is more than adequate. The odds are astronomical. If you calculate all the permutations of the recent burglaries in the area . . ." He trails off when he sees that all of us are staring at him. He used to be a statistics professor at a local university until he lost his tenure for taking bets on a school athletic event. Even though that was years ago, he still thinks obsessively of things in terms of their odds.

Baz gestures toward the back of the club with one of his meaty arms. "You guys need to see this."

We follow him across the main floor, past a row of vintage arcade games and the card tables where the college kids role-play. A narrow corridor at the back of the club leads to the ViSE rooms, where customers can enjoy their favorite recordings in complete darkness and silence.

And then there's the back office, which has been trashed.

I step into the room and survey the carnage. The file cabinet lies on its side, sheaves of paper splayed out across the floor. The desk drawers have been ripped from the desk and emptied across the long counter that runs along the back of the room. The cabinet where we keep the ViSEs, headsets, and neural editor has been stripped of its contents, one wooden door hanging askew on its hinges.

Jesse appears in the doorway, the flash drive from last night in his hand. "Hey," he says. His jaw drops. "What the hell?"

"Break-in," Gideon says. He steps forward and takes the flash drive from Jesse's outstretched hand.

"They took everything," I say.

"Everything but the cash." Baz gestures at the safe in the corner of the room. It appears to be undisturbed. "But it gets worse." He holds up a small envelope with two words written on the outside: *Who's next?* "No fingerprints on it. Or on this." He folds open the flap and a silver necklace falls out—a rose pendant. My sister's rose pendant.

But there's something else in the envelope too. A small blue memory card. A ViSE.

"I truly hope it is a forgery." Adebayo pushes his glasses up on his nose.

"What is it?" Gideon asks. He exhales a long stream of sweet smoke.

Baz hands the memory card to Gideon. "It's Rose," he says grimly.

CHAPTER 8

I grab for the card, but Baz pulls his arm away. "Gid needs to play it first."

"Why? She's *my* sister." The destruction swirls in my peripheral vision, the mess of papers, the cabinet door hanging open.

Gideon exhales another ribbon of smoke. He looks back and forth from Adebayo to Baz. "I assume someone has a headset available?"

Adebayo pulls a collapsed headset from his back pocket and hands it to Gideon, who unfolds it and inserts the memory card. Adjusting the headset to fit, he settles into the desk chair and lets his eyes fall closed. After only a few seconds, he plucks the cigarette from his mouth and grinds it out on the wooden desk.

"Terrible," Adebayo says. "How could something like this happen?" He laces and unlaces his fingers as he looks at me. "Such a beautiful young girl, your sister."

"What *is* it?" I whisper, not wanting to cause overlay for Gideon. "Is she all right?" I look from Jesse to Baz to Adebayo to Gideon, my panic growing as I consider each worried expression.

Gideon raises one index finger to his lips and I fall silent. All I can do is watch him vise . . . and wait. At one point his face contorts; at another he furrows his brow. But he doesn't speak. The red numbers of the desk clock creep upward. One minute. Two minutes. Five minutes. Five lifetimes.

Suddenly Gideon opens his eyes and blinks rapidly, as if he's not quite sure what happened. Then he removes the recording from the headset and stares at it for a moment, his jaw tightening in concentration. "Who has a tablet?" he asks. "I need to verify something." I reach out for the ViSE, but he shakes his head. "You don't want to play this, Winter."

"Yes I do," I say, even though when Gideon and I disagree, he always ends up being right. He doesn't answer. Instead he takes the tablet computer Baz hands him and inserts the memory card into a micro slot on the side. The room goes quiet as we all stare at him.

"What are you doing?" I ask.

Gideon taps at the screen and watches a stream of ones and zeros scroll past. "Hoping this isn't real." He taps again and the numbers convert to letters. It's all meaningless to me. I try to glean information from his expression, but his face remains neutral as he works.

"Oppa!" I say a bit forcefully. "What is it? What is on that recording?"

He swipes at the screen and the tablet goes dark. "I need to speak to Winter for a moment."

Baz, Adebayo, and Jesse head for the door.

"Jesse. Stay," Gideon says. Jesse turns and leans against the wall, his hands jammed in the center pocket of his hoodie. He looks like he'd rather be anywhere but here. Gideon gestures at the chair next to him. "Winter. Sit, please."

I want to refuse. There is too much energy coursing through me to be still. But something in the sound of his voice makes me obey. I lower myself into the chair next to his. "Just tell me," I say, trying to sound brave.

Gideon's face is ashen. "I'm sorry. Your sister is dead."

"What?" I shriek. "No. I saw her yesterday. She can't be. I don't believe you."

Gideon removes the memory card from the tablet. "I can tell by the neural sequences on this recording," he says softly. His eyes are wet.

I've never seen Gideon cry.

Never.

"She can't be dead. I would know." I hold out my palm. "Give me that. I need to see what you're talking about. I would feel something if she were gone, right? I would *feel* something."

Gideon blots his eyes on the sleeve of his dobok. He breathes in and out slowly, his gaze locked onto mine like we are the only two people in the world. "Are you certain you want to play this? It's the kind of thing you might not be able to unre-member."

No, I'm not certain. I am highly uncertain. In fact, I know I don't want to play it. I just want to rewind back to yesterday when Rose was leaving the apartment, tell her not to go or go along with her.

"I have to," I whisper. I have to because I know my sister isn't dead. If I play this recording, I can fix things. I can point out how it's all a mistake. A misunderstanding. Some sort of horrible lie.

"All right." Gideon slips the memory card back into the headset and hands it to me. He turns to Jesse. "Do not leave her side. I'm going to find Sebastian so we can review the security videos. I'll be back." He strides from the room.

I slip the headset on and adjust the prongs to fit, painfully aware of Jesse staring at me. "I'm going to a ViSE room," I mutter. "I can't concentrate here."

"I'm coming with you," Jesse says.

"Fine." There's no point in trying to object. Gideon told him to watch me and Jesse is as loyal as I am. Gideon probably saved him too, pulled him out of some miserable post-military existence and gave him a chance to feel human again.

I retrace my steps down the corridor and enter one of the

small, dark rooms. I slide into what looks like a dentist's chair and recline the head until I'm comfortable. Jesse pulls the door shut behind him, plunging us into total darkness. It's like someone lowered the lid of a coffin—complete sensory deprivation.

I hit the PLAY button on the headset.

I'm sitting in a hard-backed desk chair in what looks like a hotel room. Textured white walls. Heavy gray curtains. A crack in the plaster runs from the floor to the ceiling. A queen-size bed takes up half the room.

A shudder moves through me, independent of the ViSE. I have known many rooms like this.

"I'm here, Winter," Jesse says. I don't answer. Pain plays at the edges of my consciousness. I have to focus on the recorded world, not my own.

There's a girl tucked partially beneath the navy and gold coverlet, a girl with a shiny blond wig that sits crooked on her head. She's wearing a red dress adorned with sequins and lace.

I will it not to be Rose. Her dress had fringe. This can't be her.

I rise from the chair and move closer to the girl.

It's unmistakably Rose. Either I'm remembering her dress wrong or she must have changed clothes at some point.

A masked figure stands over her motionless body. He strokes her forehead with one gloved hand, pushing tendrils of her blond wig back from her face.

As I steel myself for what I might see next, I try to decipher information about the body I'm inhabiting. I'm fairly certain the recorder is a man. My face feels hot and tight like he's wearing a mask. The glimpses I've caught of his clothing are unhelpful. Black pants. Black gloves. He could be anyone. My stomach churns as I balance the dual realities.

The masked figure ties a tourniquet around Rose's right arm and probes for a vein. Producing a small vial from his pocket, he draws clear fluid into a syringe. With his thumb and forefinger, he flicks the body of the syringe to get rid of the bubbles. He slips the vial back into his pocket as I walk toward him. He jerks his head from Rose to me. I reach my hand up toward the back of my skull and suddenly a weak electric current moves through me. Everything goes black.

My eyes flick open. I bite my lip, trying to figure out what it all means, why anyone would inject my sister with drugs against her will. But then the ViSE buzzes back to life. I quickly shut my eyes again.

I'm submerged inside a kaleidoscope of colors. Two black forms move slowly around the periphery, like a pair of storm clouds interrupting an otherwise brilliant autumn day. I am bliss. I am flying. My whole body tingles. I am pure matter, splitting into individual atoms. I am atoms becoming protons and electrons. I am everywhere and nowhere.

It takes a second to understand what happened. The recorder has transferred the headset to my sister and the drugs coursing through my veins are causing euphoria. I'm inside of Rose now.

"What's happening?" I ask, my voice catching on the second word. I try to lift my head, my hands. I can't move. And then I feel myself floating up and away from my body.

Jesse rests a warm hand on my shoulder. I resist the urge to open my eyes, to cling to him. This isn't real.

But it feels real.

My vision sharpens, but now I'm looking down on the scene. The storm clouds become people. One large, one smaller. Both wearing masks. The smaller one holds something sharp and shiny in his hand. He bends low. A rush of warmth pulses up my arm. The kaleidoscope blurs into a rainbow and the smell of something sweet tickles my nose. A clove cigarette.

It could be part of the ViSE, or it could be . . . I open one eye. Yes, Gideon has slipped into the room. The end of his cigarette glows bright orange. He's holding a glass of water in one hand. Frowning, I try to concentrate.

The figure releases the tourniquet with a sharp snap and takes my hand. I can barely make out the cross-shaped scar carved into my palm. I try to speak but can't. A soft sigh escapes my lips.

"What do you want me to do with her?" the larger man asks.

It's definitely a man's voice, but it's low and stretched out. I don't know if it's how the guy sounds or if it's the drugs coursing through Rose's veins that are distorting things. My insides twist themselves into knots as I try to untangle what's real from what only feels real.

The smaller man doesn't answer. He turns his head toward the back wall and his partner nods. "The river. Perfect. If anyone finds her body, they'll just think she's a junkie who fell in."

The smaller man leans over me. He reaches out and touches my face with one hand as he peers into my eyes. Colors fade to gray. Suddenly the room goes black and then light. Bright white. Rushing, electric white. I gasp as I feel the cells in my body begin to hum. I am becoming part of the whiteness. The end of the tunnel reaches out for me and I plunge into its dark and icy embrace.

Jesse shakes me hard and I open my eyes, the outline of his broad shoulders slowly filtering into view. "Are you all right? You were thrashing around."

I don't answer. I keep feeling that tunnel, the rush of light and then darkness.

Panic crushes down on my chest. Rose can't be dead—she can't. I don't even know who I would be without her. Half a person. Empty. I breathe in slowly through my nose like Dr. Abrams taught me to do when I get anxious. I count to four, hold my breath, exhale for four, repeat. Then I yank my cell phone out of my pocket and call my sister. It goes straight to voice mail, like her battery is dead.

Or like her phone is at the bottom of the river.

Jesse stands at my side, his hazel eyes glinting in the dim light. I can tell he wants to know what it is, what I saw, but he's not going to ask me to describe my sister's murder.

"It's my fault," I say finally. My voice splits apart on the last word. I rip the headset from my skull and fling it across the room. "Someone killed her, and it's my fault."

"It's not your fault," Gideon says.

I rotate my body and drop my feet to the floor, but as I go to stand, my legs give out. I crumple, my knees hitting the soft, noise-dampening tiles of the ViSE room floor. I suck in a sharp breath, but nothing makes it to my lungs. There's no air here. Or maybe I've forgotten how to breathe.

"Get her," Gideon orders.

Jesse lifts me back to my feet just before I lose consciousness. He drapes me back onto the reclining chair. His hands feel soft, too soft; they don't even feel real.

Nothing feels real.

"This is a dream," I say. "This is a dream. This is a dream. Thisisadream." Maybe if I keep saying it, I can make it come true.

"I wish it were," Gideon says.

"It is—look." I reach across my body and pinch myself. The pain forces my eyes open. I'm in a ViSE room, with Jesse and Gideon. They're just vague blurry forms, their outlines illuminated by the cherry on Gideon's cigarette. I try again, biting down on the web of flesh between my thumb and forefinger. *Wake up, Winter!*

Gideon gently removes my hand from my mouth and wraps my fingers around the glass of water. He produces a pill bottle from his pocket and shakes out a small white circle.

I take the sedative from his fingers and wash it down with a couple gulps of water. I press the glass back into his hands. I'm not certain I have the strength to hold it.

"Should we call someone?" Jesse asks.

"Not yet," Gideon says. "Give us a few minutes, will you?"

Jesse squeezes my shoulder gently. He turns and leaves, pausing to retrieve the headset from the floor on his way out of the room. He's going to play it. He's going to play it and watch my sister die.

My hands have curled themselves into fists, my fingernails cutting crescent moon gashes into my palms. I am still trying to wake up from this nightmare.

"It's not your fault," Gideon repeats.

I look accusingly at him. "It *is* my fault, and *yours*. I should have been with her, but you—how could you let this happen? You let her freelance and it wasn't safe and now she's dead." The words spray out of my mouth like bullets.

"We don't know if this is related to her freelancing." Gideon lowers his head. "But you're right. I should have taken better care of her. I should've protected her. I failed you both." His voice cracks and he turns away from me. He walks to the far corner of the room. And then I hear the sobs, deep and racking.

I was expecting him to deflect responsibility, to tell me it wasn't my fault or his, to pin the blame completely on a pair of nameless assailants, or perhaps to say my sister's wild temperament is what killed her. This outpouring of pain and guilt surprises me.

Gideon sets the glass of water on the floor and sits next to me on the ViSE chair, his head buried in his hands. "Oh, Ha Neul. I keep thinking about what I could've done differently."

He hasn't called me by my real name in years, but we live artificial lives and spend our days creating artificial scenarios. I understand why he needs for something in this moment to feel real.

"Oppa," I say softly. I rest my hand on his shoulder and feel him go tense.

He turns to me, his face still damp with tears. Even in the darkness I can see a thousand emotions breaking loose, pouring forth. "I don't want to let her go."

"I don't either." I pull him toward me, loop my arms around the small of his back, press my cheek to his chin. "Could you be wrong?" I ask. "Is there any way . . ."

He pulls back, shakes his head. "I've studied the neural

sequences for death in a variety of species. The science is definitive." He blots at his face with the sleeve of his dobok again.

The ViSE recordings show neural patterns for pain and fear and so forth. It only makes sense they would show death too. Still, I'm not ready to accept it. "But Rose isn't one of your mice. She's my sister. Shouldn't I know?" I ask. "Shouldn't I feel different?"

"Everyone wants to believe that," Gideon says. "That our connections to the people we love are like psychic ropes that cannot be severed without both parties becoming aware."

"But it's not true?"

"Our bonds are real in our hearts, but not in our minds, not the way we like to think."

"I still can't believe it," I say. "What are we going to do?"

"We'll get through this together," Gideon murmurs. "We need each other now, more than ever."

We sit there in the dark, wordless for a while, only our ragged breaths disturbing the silence. Memories of my sister overwhelm me—I see her impish grin as she leans over me at the orphanage, tugging on my hair until I wake up. I remember us climbing up to the roof as kids, sitting cross-legged next to the herbs and vegetables our caretakers were growing while we read the English books Rose had "borrowed" from her class at school. And then there was L.A.—all of our hope for a better life so quickly crushed, but Rose never let despair overtake her. She was there after every single night to hold me until the pain went away. And later, when I got numb to it all, she still made a point of holding me, of promising me that one day things would be different.

And now they are, but it all seems meaningless if she's really gone.

I try to imagine going home without her. Falling asleep, waking up, eating, breathing—how am I supposed to do these things without my sister?

Another wave of pain washes over me. I rest my head on Gideon's shoulder as the tears start to fall.

He takes my right hand in both of his. "I know," he whispers. "I know."

We've never really been close like this before. In L.A. I thought of him as a stranger, someone to respect from a distance. He was my sister's friend, not mine. And then once we came here he told me to think of him as an older brother, which I do, but physical affection isn't something that comes naturally to either of us.

Right now I feel as if his hands are holding me together. I wonder if that's how it was for my sister when the two of them first met.

"She knew you were different," I say. "She told me about you. How you wouldn't even touch her, how all you wanted to do was talk about Korea, where had she grown up, did she miss it, what memories did she have that she refused to let fade."

"I was very homesick at that time," Gideon says. "But it was still wrong of me to buy her attention like that. Don't make excuses for me. I am not different. I am not better than the other men."

"Yes you are," I say defiantly. "Each time she met with you, she'd come back with a light inside of her. She didn't talk about it because she didn't want to make the others jealous, but I could see it, the hope. And then sometimes she'd tell me stories when I couldn't sleep. I'd drift off to the sound of her voice, thinking about how the three of us would go far away and be a family someday."

Gideon turns to face me. "She spoke of you often, her little sister with the big, big heart. So strong, yet vulnerable. She worried you would break and that she'd never be able to put you back together."

It's strange to hear myself described as someone with a big heart. I've blocked out a lot of the memories of L.A., but perhaps in some ways the girl I used to be was better than the girl I am now. Now I feel so cold, almost incapable of loving anything.

"As much as being trapped where you were pained her, it hurt her worse to see you in the same situation," Gideon continues. "She would have died a thousand times over to free you from that hell."

"And you would've died to free her."

"Not just her. Both of you," Gideon insists. "You are my family, Ha Neul. I made a promise to your sister that I would do everything in my power to watch out for you, to take care of you and keep you safe. That is a promise I intend to keep for the rest of my life, if you let me."

CHAPTER 9

I have no idea how long we sit there in the dark, in the quiet nothingness where my sister still lives through our spoken stories. But when we finally return to the back room, Baz, Adebayo, and Jesse are all huddled in a circle. They fall silent when they see us.

Adebayo begins picking up the papers scattered across the floor, stacking them neatly on the corner of the desk. "Do you wish for me to telephone the police?" he asks Gideon. "The percentage of violent crimes solved is substantially higher when the authorities are involved in the first twenty-four hours."

Gideon leans against the doorframe, his thumb striking the silver wheel of his lighter repeatedly. He locks eyes with me and I know what he's thinking—involving the police could be dangerous for us. I'm illegal. Rose and I came here in a fake adoption. Gideon was a legal resident, but when we changed our names, we all got forged documents. There's no guarantee we wouldn't be arrested or deported if we were investigated and our papers didn't pass scrutiny.

But this is my sister, the girl he risked his life for, the girl who would have died a thousand times over to free me. I don't know why Rose and Gideon broke up, but I do know that he still loves her. I can hear it in his voice every time he says her name. Maybe there's some chance we're wrong, that the ViSE is fake, but it's so good Gideon can't tell the difference. If so, then we need all the help we can get.

"What do you think?" I ask.

Gideon sighs. "Look at it from a cop's point of view. The only clue we have is a ViSE, which isn't admissible evidence. Do you really think the police will put their best people on this case?"

No one speaks. Jesse might know cops who are willing to help out with recordings, but we've all had bad experiences with law enforcement. In L.A., Rose once tried to tell a cop we were being trafficked. He took her statement on the street and promised to investigate. Then he made a deal with Kyung's men—free girls in exchange for his silence. My sister got beaten. She told me it was random, that a client became violent with her, but I knew the truth. She was punished for what she did.

Still, one bad cop doesn't mean they're all corrupt. And we do have other clues. "But we have the note," I say. "And evidence of a break-in."

"But no fingerprints," Gideon reminds me. "And publicizing the break-in will scare the building residents." He turns to Adebayo. "I think it best to handle this discreetly for the time being. Tell the staff we'll be closed today but opening up tomorrow. I've got backups of all our recordings, but I'll need to make copies and get new playback headsets made, so we won't be able to offer ViSEs for at least a couple of weeks. Come up with a reason. Maybe that we're upgrading the technology or something similar. I don't want anyone to know we've been compromised."

"Understood. I'll make the necessary arrangements." Adebayo adjusts his glasses again and casts a quick glance at each of us before scurrying out of the room.

"You know, there's more than one reason not to involve the cops," Baz says. "The legal system is inefficient, inept. Criminals go free . . ." He trails off meaningfully.

"We are not killers," Gideon says.

"In my experience everyone is a killer." Baz's gray eyes go cold. He leans back against the wall. "Or a victim. Some people just need a little coaxing to choose a side."

The implication of his words hangs silent in the air. Rose and I used to speak of killing Kyung and his men, slashing them to ribbons, stealing back our papers, and then running away into the night. But those were just the desperate fairy tales of powerless girls. Neither of us really *wanted* to hurt anyone. I'm quite sure Gideon never did either.

But maybe things are different now.

"I'm just saying, sometimes the only way to end something completely is to end it completely." Baz shrugs. He might as well be talking about sports scores or a movie he saw.

"But what if somehow we're wrong? What if she's not dead?" I ask. I know that I am grasping, but the best things in life happen because people choose to believe the impossible. Dead men come home from the war. Corpses wake up in the morgue. There has to be a chance, some infinitely tiny chance Rose is still alive. And if there is . . .

"Winter," Gideon says. "You can't make things true just by wishing. You saw her die. You felt it inside of you, did you not?"

I did. I didn't just watch *my sister* die, I lived it—the pinch of the tourniquet, the sting of the needle, the rush of the drugs. It was as if it happened to my own flesh. My stomach lurches as I think of her lying in that bed, of the drugs coursing through her veins, diluting her thoughts, stopping her heart. It felt so real then, so why does it feel so impossible now? *Rose is dead.* Those three words don't even make sense together. I bury my face in my hands.

"Are you okay?" Gideon asks. "I can call Dr. Abrams or take you to the hospital if you think—"

"No." The last thing I want is for Gideon to find out today that I've been skipping appointments. "And no hospital."

Hospitals are for the dying, and we are only just beginning to live.
"But I think we should go to the police. I won't accept that Rose is really gone unless I see her body. Or at least until we find her killers and they tell us why they did it. Oppa, I need to know."

"She's gone." Gideon's voice has taken on an unfamiliar edge.

Baz clears his throat. "I know a detective on the force, if you really want to involve the cops. Someone we can trust. And I can call up a couple of independent investigators as well."

"All right." Gideon nods. "We'll find out who did this and make sure that they pay. I promise you, Winter."

"I want to help too," I blurt out.

Gideon, Jesse, and Baz all turn to me, a firing squad of concerned looks. Then their eyes flick back and forth as they exchange glances with one another.

Rage brews in my gut. "I know what you're all thinking. Poor Winter. She's not strong enough to handle this."

Are they right?

"Maybe I'm not," I say, answering both them and the voice in my head. "But I need to be productive, to focus on something. Or else I'll focus on the fact that she's not here."

"Winter," Gideon says. "You should concentrate on your studies." He gestures at the crude note written on the envelope. "It's not safe. They could come after you next."

"I don't care," I say. "I can't study right now." What I don't say is that it doesn't matter if they come after me, because if Rose is dead, I'm basically dead too. She looked out for me. She listened. She kept me sane. Without Rose, all I have is Gideon, but I can't talk to him the way I talked to my sister. Without Rose, I'll go back to being that girl I was when we first arrived, thrashing at invisible monsters and screaming about blood that doesn't exist.

I can feel the pull of that girl already, the darkness spreading inside me like I've swallowed a bottle of ink. Part of me wants to walk out of here, go back to the penthouse, crawl into my sister's bed, and go to sleep there—for good. But then the men who hurt her might go unpunished. I force myself to refocus. "It looked like a hotel room. Jesse and I could scout around the city and figure out where she was. Maybe someone saw her or there's security camera footage of her killers."

"Better yet, we can start by looking at online ads for the hotels along the river," Jesse offers. "See if anything matches up to the room in the ViSE. We can do that without even leaving the building."

"I guess that would be all right," Gideon says to Jesse. "But if you find anything, you're to report to us, not go investigate on your own."

Baz turns back to me. "Is there anything else I should know? Did Rose mention being afraid of anyone?"

"She wasn't afraid of anything," I say.

"Do you know where she went last night?"

"She said she was going to Inferno." I drop my eyes to the floor. "She told me I should meet her over there."

"But you didn't?" Gideon asks.

My face flushes as I think about Jesse and me sitting at the table, trading ViSEs while my sister was being killed. I think of his hands on my face, his lips on my skin, the warring feelings inside me.

I am the worst sister in the world.

Jesse jumps in. "We were both kind of tired after our big run from the cops. Clubbing wasn't exactly our top priority."

"We'll check out Inferno," Gideon promises. "In the meantime, Winter, I don't want you alone until we find who did this. I think you should come with me to Chicago tonight."

"No," I say. If I go with Gideon on his business trip, I won't be able to do any investigating. He'll have me tripling up on my study modules just to keep me busy while he spends all day in boring meetings. "I'll be fine. I'm eighteen. I can stay by myself."

"I know you can," he says. "But humor me. I won't be able to concentrate if I have to worry about your safety."

"Please don't make me go," I beg. "Someone needs to be here to take care of Miso."

Gideon sighs. "All right, but I don't want you to be alone. Perhaps Sebastian can—"

"I can stay with her," Jesse blurts out.

Gideon narrows his eyes at Jesse. I start to protest but then fall silent. I don't want Jesse *or* Sebastian looking over my shoulder, but maybe I can use Jesse's feelings for me to my advantage.

"Fine," Gideon says. "Jesse will stay with you. And I'm calling the other recorders. No one goes anywhere alone for the time being."

"How did they break in?" I ask. "What about the cameras and the alarm system?"

"Someone shot the back camera with a paintball around three a.m. and the door to the alley was jimmied open," Baz says. "I'm still trying to figure out how they circumvented the building's security system. Clearly whoever it was knew what they were doing."

Last night's close encounter with the Phantasm security guard flashes to life. That happened just after midnight. "Could this be retaliation for Phantasm?"

"Unlikely," Gideon says. "Even if you two were somehow identified immediately, how could anyone from Phantasm have figured everything out, found Rose, and taken her so quickly? Not to mention, all you did was borrow a little data. This would be an excessive response."

"What exactly did we borrow?" I rub my temples with my fingertips.

Gideon snaps open his lighter again. "Obviously I haven't gone through it yet, but mainly some accounting files. I already told you, I want to see how Phantasm's financials hold up before I even think about their offer." His voice is perfectly level, but I'm still struggling with the idea he would ever willingly sell the ViSE tech.

"How did you know where the server was located?" I ask.

"I have someone on the inside."

I turn to look at Jesse. He holds his hands up in a "it wasn't me" kind of way.

"You really think it's a coincidence that we stole information last night and then this happened a few hours later?" I ask.

"I don't know. I'm not sure what to think." Gideon pulls out another cigarette and tucks it between his lips. "I received a call here at the club a couple of days ago—a man saying he had been recorded without his permission, threatening to do whatever it took to make sure the ViSE never made it to the street."

"What? I can't believe you—"

He waves me quiet. "No one had turned in any ViSEs featuring other people recently, so I figured he was just some paranoid crackpot. If you're all following my safety protocols and keeping your headsets covered, no one should know they're being recorded, right?"

"I guess, but can we find out who it was by checking your call log?" I shift my weight from one foot to the other.

"I'll have Sebastian look into it."

"Are you sure that's everything that's happened?" I ask.

Gideon runs a hand through his black hair. It falls in soft peaks, still slightly damp with sweat from our workout. "I knew Rose was getting reckless, but I was doing my best to watch out for her. I swear I had no idea she was in real danger." He removes the ViSE from the headset and slips it into his pocket. Then he lifts Rose's pendant in his hand, holding it up so it reflects the light.

I'm sure her room upstairs is full of more jewelry like it,

but suddenly I feel like Gideon is clutching the last tangible piece of my sister. "Can I have that?" I ask.

"Of course." He drops the necklace into my palm.

I look down at the sinuous twists of silver, at the intricately formed pendant with its individual petals. Beneath Rose's necklace is the cross-shaped scar in my palm. I trace the intersecting lines with my index finger. The past rushes back to me.

Rose and I gave ourselves the scars on the same day, our first day working for Kyung. Back then we were still Min Ji and Ha Neul. The other girls told us the first time would be the worst. They said each "date" would get a little easier and then eventually we'd get numb to it, learn to switch off until our client was finished.

I can't recall the first man, only certain moments. I spent most of the time focusing on the television. It was one of those summer blockbuster action movies. Fires, explosions, people dying—all of it preferable to what was happening in the real world.

Afterward, one of Kyung's men escorted me back to the building where I shared a room with Rose and two other girls. He didn't say a single word to me. I might as well have been an animal or a product. I went to lie down on the mattress where I slept at night, watching the red numbers on our digital clock crawl upward. Tears came like a storm. As each number changed, I wondered why I was the only one back so soon. Had I done something wrong? Surely, the other girls were out eating and dancing. They were being showered with gifts. They would come back laughing and giggling and make fun of me when they found out how my date had gone.

Shame and fear took turns assaulting me. I had performed poorly and Kyung would punish me. Maybe he would even send me away from my sister. Where was she? I needed her desperately. I crawled from my mattress to hers, pretending I could feel her next to me. That's when I found the knife tucked inside her pillowcase. Small, the kind you might use to peel fruit. When I pressed the blade into my skin, the pain comforted me. I felt human again. I looked down at my bleeding palm and cut myself again the other way—a perfect cross. Blood seeped out of both wounds, not a lot, but enough to make me light-headed. I collapsed to my sister's bed and drifted into dreams.

Eventually, she stumbled in the door, her hair mussed, her makeup smudged. When I saw the dried tears on her cheeks, I sat up suddenly, my bleeding hand forgotten. "Did he hurt you?"

She came to me and kissed me on the forehead. "I'm all right," she said. "I'm just sad."

"I'm sad too. I don't want to do it again."

"I don't want you to do it again," she said. "I'm working on a plan, all right? For now just try to look plain. Maybe no one will choose you."

As she looked down at me, her brow furrowed, and I realized I had left spots of blood on her sheets. I hid my hand behind my back but I was too slow. She wrenched my arm forward, grabbed my wrist, and pried my fingers open.

"Ha Neul, what have you done?" My sister examined the pinkish fluid still oozing from my hand. "Kyung will be angry if he finds out. He'll think you tried to hurt yourself on purpose."

"I'm sorry, Eonni," I said. "I couldn't help it."

"Hurting yourself won't fix things. Pain is not the answer." She bit her lip in concentration. "Here, I'll do it too. We can tell people we were being silly, being blood sisters." She took the knife in her hand and carved the same cross into the flesh of her left palm. Then she tucked the knife away at the bottom of her trunk, beneath her clothing and books.

Lifting up her hand, she said, "Promise me you will never cut yourself again."

"I promise." My eyes held fast to the blood oozing from her palm.

She twined her fingers through mine, and my whole body tingled as our blood touched. "Fingers to fingers and thumb to thumb," she said. "A pair of sisters like matching gloves."

Gideon flicks his lighter, the sharp sound of the metal striker pulling me back to the present. I never cut myself after that day, but I did other things when no one was looking. I stare at the flame dancing behind his curved palm, and then at the glowing ember that flares up on the end of his cigarette as he inhales. I don't remember the first time I plucked a still-burning cigarette from an ashtray and pressed it against the skin of my thigh. I haven't done it in years, haven't wanted to, haven't needed to. But now I open myself up to the circle of fire, imagining the searing heat and the eventual numbness of charred flesh. Suddenly I'm dying for a pain I can actually control, a pain that would bring peace instead of crushing me to ashes.

CHAPTER 10

Gideon takes the stairs back to the penthouse with me. I am still fantasizing about his glowing cigarette, about adding to the cluster of scars on my thigh. Just once, to clear my head.

No. Rose's voice is a whisper inside me. *Pain is not the answer.*

Pain is all that I know in this moment.

He unlocks the door and we both step into the entry hall and slip out of our shoes. Miso curls around my ankles. I scoop him up and hold him to my chest, his head wedged under my chin.

"I wish I could cancel this trip," Gideon says. "I hate leaving you alone."

"Apparently I won't be alone," I say, heading into the living room with Miso. I roll my eyes. "I'll be with Jesse."

"He cares for you," Gideon says. "I trust him."

I trust him too. But part of me can't stop replaying the events of last night, wondering whether my sister might still be alive if I had done anything differently. I sit cross-legged on the white rug in front of the fireplace and release a squirming Miso from my arms. He bats playfully at a tuft of white fur, attacking the rug like it's another animal.

Gideon frowns. "That cat is a menace."

"Oh, be nice," I say. "He doesn't mean to muss your precious home furnishings."

Gideon sits down next to me. We both lean back against the sofa. Miso's eyes widen at the sight of a second human on the floor for him to play with. He pounces on Gideon's foot, his teeth biting down on the fabric of his sock.

"Ouch." Gideon shoos the cat away. He rests his hand on mine. "Are you certain you'll be all right without me?"

Lying to Gideon is not something that comes easily, but I've mastered the art of vague, evasive statements. "I have your number, remember? I can call if I need something."

"And you won't do anything rash?"

"You can trust me, oppa." Two true and one mostly true statement. Not bad.

About an hour later, there is a knock at the door. I go to it expecting Jesse, but it turns out to be the cop that Baz mentioned. He introduces himself as Detective Ehlers and flashes a badge. I fetch Gideon from the study.

Gideon lets Ehlers play the ViSE and then gives him a picture of Rose. I tell him about some of her favorite clubs and then watch as he skulks around in her bedroom, his gloved hands gently going through her things. He takes several photographs and then promises to have a tech run her phone records.

"I'll try to get back to you with more information in a couple of days," he says.

A couple of days feels like forever. Gideon was right about the police. Even Baz's friend isn't going to prioritize finding out what happened to my sister.

Ehlers gives Gideon his business card and tells him to call if he thinks of anything else. After he leaves, Gideon turns to me. "You should eat something."

I start to tell him I'm not hungry, but then I realize that Gideon's headset with the recording of the overdose is resting on the kitchen counter. I want that ViSE in case I need to review it.

"I just need something to drink." I go to the cupboard and remove a glass. I turn on the sink and let the water run until it becomes cold.

"I assume you're not going to Krav Maga?"

"Is it all right if I don't?" I fill the glass three-quarters full and then turn off the faucet.

Gideon nods. "You should rest. I'm going to go pack. My plane leaves at three p.m. Jesse will be here in a couple of hours."

As soon as Gideon disappears into his bedroom, I snatch the headset from the counter and remove the recording. I hurry down the hallway, duck into my room, and shut the door behind me. I set the untouched glass of water on my dresser, my eyes lingering for a few moments on my small collection of snow globes. Most of them are from cities where Jesse and I have recorded ViSEs or Gideon has traveled for work. I guess they're an odd thing for someone like me to collect, but I like the idea of perfect moments captured in glass.

As opposed to the worst moment ever, captured on a ViSE.

I can't bring myself to play the recording again. Why would anyone hurt my sister? Were they interrogating her? Is that why she was being drugged? Or was it simply a clean and convenient way to end someone's life?

Pulling the cover from my bed, I lie down on the floor. *Regression,* a voice whispers. I don't care. Today of all days I am allowed to seek comfort in the past. I think of Rose and me as children, snuggled side by side on a bamboo mat, the heated floor beneath our bodies keeping us warm during the long chilly nights of winter. I think of us at the orphanage, on separate cots pushed close enough together so that we could reach out for each other in the night. And then later, in the hospital, Rose curled up against me. Two sisters, one bed.

I wrap my arms around my comforter and pretend she's here with me. Finally, my thoughts start to slow and my mind goes quiet. I'm not sure how much time passes before there is a sharp knock on my bedroom door.

Reluctantly, I untangle myself from the folds of the blanket and rise to my feet. I cross the room and open the door.

Gideon stands in the hallway. He looks as if he's aged five years since this morning. "My cab is here," he says. "I'll see you the day after next."

I walk with him to the door of the penthouse and embrace him lightly as we exchange good-byes. Jesse is in the living room watching television. I must have slept through his arrival. His eyes lock onto mine. I try not to think about last night. Being here with Jesse might be scarier than being all alone.

"So are you going to help me look for that hotel room?" I ask.

Jesse studies me for a moment before responding. "Gideon said a detective was looking into that."

"Yes. A detective who said he'd try to get back with us in a couple of days. I want to do something *now*." I shift my weight from one foot to the other.

Jesse sighs. "I knew coming here was a bad idea."

"What?" I ask. "Gideon said we could try to find the hotel."

"He also said if we found anything we should tell him or Baz and not go check it out by ourselves." Jesse arches an eyebrow. "That okay with you?"

I perch on the arm of the sofa. "What if Gideon is wrong? What if she was just knocked out? She could be lying half-unconscious or injured somewhere. We should look for her just in case." I'm not sure if I still believe in this possibility or if I'm just trying to convince Jesse to help me. I'm not sure what I believe in right now.

"Winter." Jesse presses the remote and the TV goes dark. "Gideon's not wrong. He's never wrong."

"Everyone is wrong sometimes." I cross my arms. "And even if he's not, we should find her, Jesse. She deserves a proper funeral."

"True," he says. "So you're saying you just want to check out the hotel if we can find it?"

"I figure we can start by trying to talk to the desk clerk from last night. Oh, and I want to go to Inferno and ask if anyone saw anything."

Jesse rakes both hands through his thick brown hair. "Shit. You are impossible. I never should have volunteered for this. Gid almost fired me last month, you know? I'm trying to stay out of trouble."

"What did you do?" I ask. Gideon has never fired anyone to my knowledge. He's too paranoid about his personal information getting leaked.

"Something stupid," Jesse says darkly.

"Well, I won't let him fire you—I promise." I pause. "You know I wouldn't willfully go against Gideon's wishes, but I'll go crazy if I do nothing. You saw me earlier, in the ViSE room. That's what happens when I stop moving and start thinking. The blackness swallows me up."

Jesse shakes his head as he exhales deeply. "I hated seeing you like that. Okay. Inferno doesn't open for hours. Grab your tablet. Let's look for the hotel room."

I get my computer from my bedroom, taking a few minutes to change out of my dobok at the same time. When I return to the living room, Jesse has already found a list of local hotels along the Mississippi River with the GPS function on his phone. We search each website, but it's tedious work, especially since some of them provide photos of only their most elegant suites.

I flinch each time a room with a crisply made bed pops up on the screen. It's like a door that's been locked inside of me is slowly creeping open, spilling out a past I don't want to acknowledge, let alone relive.

"What about this one?" Jesse asks.

Biting back a wave of revulsion, I force myself to concentrate on the computer screen. The web page is for the Riverlights Hotel and Casino. There's a picture of their deluxe single. Plaster walls. Gray curtains. A navy bedspread.

"It looks like the place," I say. "Will you go there with me?"

Jesse reaches out for my hand. My fingers fall easily between his. He squeezes gently. "Are you sure you're up for this?"

I nod. "I have to know for certain."

Jesse parks in the hotel's garage, so we have to cut through the casino to get to the Riverlights lobby. Solitary elderly people are lined up at the slot machines, their jaws going slack as they press buttons repeatedly. Ignoring them, I scan the small clusters of men hunched over the craps and blackjack tables. I don't know if I'll be able to identify either the recorder or the man who shot Rose full of drugs with almost nothing to go on, but both Jesse and I are wearing headsets under our winter hats so we can record everything we see. I search the whole room, looking for anyone who might be the same size and shape. Anyone who might look or feel familiar.

Jesse strides up to the hotel's front desk, where a red-haired clerk is flipping through a celebrity gossip magazine. Her long manicured nails curl under at the ends like talons.

"Excuse me, miss," Jesse says. "Did you work last night?"

Her eyes narrow. "Maybe. Why?"

He flashes her his perfect smile. "Do you remember seeing a blond woman in a red dress in here?"

The woman snorts as she flips another page in her magazine. "That's half of our weekend clientele," she says. "You got a picture?"

He turns to me. I fumble in my pocket for my phone. Flipping to the photo gallery, I am not surprised to find I have only one recent picture of Rose. She's been known to sneak through people's phones and delete any images of her she feels are even the slightest bit unflattering. The one she's left me is dreamy-looking and slightly out of focus.

The clerk raises an eyebrow, unimpressed. "Sorry. Don't recognize her," she says.

"She's Korean," I say. "Really pretty."

"She might've been with two guys," Jesse adds.

The clerk smirks but then shrugs helplessly. "It doesn't ring a bell."

Discouraged, I turn away from the front desk and walk to the large picture window that looks out onto the river. The twisting water beckons to me, its curves flashing deadly white. Jesse follows me and puts a hand on my arm.

I shake off his touch. My heart pounds inside my chest, light and fast, a rabbit being chased by a cat. "I need to find her, Jesse. Even if she's in the water."

He sighs. "Come on." He tows me past the desk clerk who is busy texting on her phone. He bypasses the elevators and ducks into the stairwell. Our feet echo on the cold metal as we ascend to the second floor.

"What are we doing?" I ask.

"Making sure this is the right hotel. We can't check the whole Mississippi."

He's right. We might not even have picked the correct river. There are other ones within driving distance of the city.

The second-floor hallways are both empty. Undaunted, Jesse proceeds to the third floor. Empty. Then the fourth floor. A pair of doors are propped open halfway down the hall, a housekeeping cart parked just outside. Jesse takes my hand like we're a couple returning from a leisurely lunch. As we stroll past the rooms where the maids are working, he looks into one and I scan the other. It's more obvious in person than online. It's the same gray curtains, the same navy-and-gold coverlets.

We're in the right place.

"Now what?" I ask.

"Now we can check the water."

My chest tightens as we descend back to the main level. We cross the gaming floor and head out into the cold. A Metro-Link train hisses by on an elevated track, slowing near the far end of the parking lot to let off a group of casino patrons and hotel employees. I watch the stream of people disembark and head down the stairs, searching for any sliver of familiarity.

"Winter. Let's go." Jesse rests a hand on my lower back and I turn away. A smooth concrete path littered with dead leaves and patches of ice leads toward the river. It's just over the hill. What if the whole area is cordoned off with yellow police tape? What if I see Rose there, bobbing in the black water?

"Are you going to be okay?" Jesse's voice is full of concern.

Are you going to be okay if we find her body? That's what he means. I don't answer.

Jesse slips his hand in mine as we traverse the path, guiding me around the slick spots. *I have to know.* I repeat those four words over and over in my head like a mantra. We turn onto the street that runs along the riverbank. The frozen cobblestones glint like jewels in the sun. I don't see any police tape or dead bodies. So far, so good.

It's not until we make our way down to the shoreline that I recognize the futility of our task. The river is wide, the current strong. The water is full of mud, driftwood, and litter. We're going to be searching for Rose in a giant churning garbage dump. Even if she's right in front of us, we might not find her.

Jesse senses my hopelessness. "Come on," he says. "I know where we can get a boat. Maybe things will look different on the river."

On the river, things look even worse.

Starting just north of the Riverlights Hotel and Casino, we cruise along the western bank in a motorboat Jesse borrowed from a guy who owns one of the riverfront restaurants.

"It's too big to search everywhere," Jesse says. "I'm going to stay near the shorelines."

"Good idea," I say. "She could have crawled up onto the bank somewhere."

He licks his lips like he wants to say something, but finally he just nods.

"Do you see anything?" I ask. The riverbanks are a rainbow of grays and tans, the water greens and blacks. Complete contrast to Rose and her red dress.

"Nothing," Jesse says grimly. We hug the bank until we're about a mile south of Riverlights, our eyes skimming the vegetation. The high grass is full of debris—beer bottles, dirty diapers, old truck tires—but there's nothing that could be Rose. Jesse pilots the boat across the river. Water slams into clusters of rocks and driftwood in the middle, its fierce current occasionally sending a shard of broken wood tumbling downstream.

The icy wind burns my skin and thrashes my hair against my face. I pull my hat down low over my ears. Jesse turns north and steers along the opposite bank. We're fighting the current now, so it's slow going. My eyes begin to water from the cold. Suddenly he yanks the wheel hard to the right so the hull is pressed up against the reeds and stops the motor.

"What is it?" I ask. "What do you see?" I peer into the high grass but see nothing except clods of mud and a half-buried rubber tire. Wait, no. As the wind folds the vegetation away from me, I see a flash of red.

CHAPTER 11

"Eonni!" I am over the side of the boat before Jesse even brings it to a complete stop, sloshing through the knee-deep water.

"Winter, wait." Behind me, Jesse swears loudly.

I ignore him. I ignore the wind biting at my exposed skin and the soft mud squeezing at my ankles. Pushing my way through the high grass, I make my way toward the red.

Desperate.

Hopeful.

She could be alive.

There has to be a chance.

But as I draw close, I see it's not my sister.

It's just a scrap of cloth tangled in the reeds.

Jesse comes up behind me. He's wearing gray hip waders that keep him dry. "Jesus Christ. You could've at least waited for me to anchor the boat." He makes his way through the high grass and reaches out with one gloved hand to grab the scarlet fabric.

"Let me see."

He tucks the red cloth into his pocket. "Once we're out of the water."

I try to protest, but my teeth start chattering and I can't get the words out. I turn and retrace my steps through the mud. Jesse helps me over the side of the boat. My whole body is shivering now, my pants soaked almost up to my knees.

"Now let me see," I demand.

He pulls the ball of crumpled fabric from his pocket. He holds it up and a couple of sequins flutter to the floor of the boat like glittering drops of blood. Both of us stare at the red cloth without speaking. Then finally Jesse says, "It looks like part of her dress, right?"

"That could be from anyone," I say. "It could have been there for weeks."

"Fabric left in water would break down quickly. This can't have been in the river for more than a few days." Jesse's voice is deadly serious.

I hug my arms around myself for warmth. Inside of me, something snaps, subtle, pinching, like a guitar string. The scrap of red *does* look like a piece of her dress.

Jesse takes me home and follows me up the stairs to the penthouse. When I open the door and slide out of my shoes, he starts to do the same.

"You don't have to babysit me," I say. "I'll be fine."

"Nice try, but I promised Gideon I'd stay with you," he says. "You need to get out of those wet clothes before hypothermia sets in. I could try my hand at making some tea if you want to take a bath or something."

"All right." I am too hollowed out to argue.

I show Jesse where I keep the loose tea and fresh herbs. Then I head for the bathroom. My knees buckle when I see all of Rose's beauty products scattered across the vanity. Slumping to the tile floor, I pull my thighs up against my ribs, but tears elude me. When I played the ViSE, I felt like she was gone. Then, afterward, I let hope creep into my heart. But finding the fabric from her dress makes me realize I'm being stupid. Not stupid, crazy. I don't want to let her go. It makes me think of something Dr. Abrams said once, about how the mind creates delusions because people simply cannot live with reality. And so we block out what we don't want to remember and we change what we refuse to accept. That's what I'm doing—making loopholes, finding irrational reasons to believe Rose is still alive. *I've studied the neural sequences for death. . . . The science is definitive.* I'm rejecting reality for my own version of events.

Delusional. The word stings, even inside my own head.

My wet jeans are sticking to my legs. I should be freezing, but I just feel numb. I curl my arms around my knees and dig my nails into my palms, embracing the pain. Jesse knocks on the door a few minutes later, probably wondering why there's no water running. I don't answer. He knocks again and then opens the door a tiny crack.

I am coiled into a ball. Lifting my head, I see him looking in at me. I drop my face back to my knees.

He slips inside the little room and sits down next to me. "Do you want to talk about it?"

I shake my head violently.

We sit side by side for a few minutes, listening to each other breathe. Then Jesse says, "I've lost people close to me. I saw their bodies." He looks over at me. "It doesn't help. I don't want you to have to go through that."

I blink rapidly. "I just can't believe she's gone."

"I know. It feels the same way even if you're there. Even if you watch them die." He leans back against the wall. "Everything sort of speeds up and slows down simultaneously. It's like people are dying, but the pain, the blood—it doesn't feel real."

"Jesse," I whisper. I never thought about who else might have been injured alongside him in the army. I never thought about the people he might have lost.

"Sorry," he says. "I shouldn't make today about me."

"I don't mind." I reach up and run my fingertips along his scar. "Tell me. It might help."

Except for his accident, Jesse's history is a blank to me. You can't grill someone about his past without offering up some information about your own. I've never wanted him to know I used to be a sex worker, at first because I was embarrassed, and then later because I didn't want it to wreck the apparent crush he has on me. As much as I try to deny his feelings, part of me thrives on them. I'm broken and he still likes me. I don't want to give that up.

He leans back against the bathroom wall and looks up at the ceiling. "I went into the army as soon as I turned eighteen. There was a critical need for MPs—military police—so they offered me a signing bonus. My parents told me not to go. My mom worried I'd get hurt. My dad is just not a huge fan of the American government."

I have never heard Jesse talk about his parents before. For some reason I imagined he was an orphan like me. "Where are your parents?"

"They're in Albuquerque," he says. "Anyway, I was nineteen by the time I deployed. My job was basic—be part of a routine checkpoint on a road that led to a makeshift US camp in Afghanistan. Easy breezy," he continues bitterly. "Locals come. We stop them. We check their cars for weapons or explosives. We let them go." He rubs at his disfigured ear. "There were five of us working that day. We had just finished our shift and were heading back to camp. I was driving. It was dark. We were all tired. I remember my staff sergeant was telling a joke, something about a one-legged man in a bar. I should have been paying better attention. Maybe then I would've seen something." He says all of this in an emotionless, clinical manner, like he's practiced it before. I can almost see him sitting at a table with a couple of superior officers, going through the story one piece at a time while someone takes notes and fills out paperwork.

"Jesse," I say again.

"They told me later it was the back passenger-side tire that triggered the IED. That's probably why I lived. I just remember all this heat, my body flying through the air. All I could smell was smoke and blood, burning flesh. I saw my friends, some dead, some screaming. Then I passed out. I woke up in the hospital." He stares straight ahead at the cabinet underneath the sink. "Everyone else died, Winter, even though it was my fault. And to this day, I still sometimes have to remind myself they're gone. Sometimes I feel more dead than they do."

I turn and brush my mouth against his jawbone. The gesture surprises both of us. He stiffens a little; then he reaches out and pats my hand. I want to tell him what happened wasn't his fault, but I know those words won't help. It's the same way he doesn't tell me everything is going to be all right. We didn't grow up in that world, the world where reassurances change things.

"I'm sorry," I say finally.

"Yeah," he says. "Me too. But enough about me. You need to get out of those wet clothes before you get sick." He rises to his feet, starts the tap, and tests the water against the back of his hand. He turns back to face me. "Do you need help with . . . anything else?" It's an innocent question, but I am embarrassed at the thought of him undressing me like a child.

"I'll manage," I say. "But could you get rid of that stuff?" I point at the counter, at Rose's collection of powders and potions.

"Sure." Scooping the bottles, compacts, and tiny vials into his arms, he unceremoniously dumps them into the cabinet under the sink where they're at least out of sight if not out of mind. "I'll be right outside."

I shuck off my zip-up hoodie and still-damp jeans and then sink into the hot water, embracing the heat as it wraps around me. Jesse has managed to get the temperature just right, almost hot enough to scald my skin, but not quite. I slouch down so only my face is above the surface.

My sister is dead. I shouldn't think about it, but even without her beauty products hoarding the counter, this room is full of Rose: the smudge of her trademark crimson lipstick where she blotted her mouth on our hand towel, the lingering hint of her jasmine perfume, her fingerprints on the mirror above the sink. It's just like Jesse said. She is the one who lives here. I am the ghost.

I close my eyes and try to concentrate on the way the warm water unlocks the knots in my muscles, but all I can think of is how Rose used to run herself a bath when I was blow drying my hair or brushing my teeth. She would toss dried lavender under the spigot and it would perfume the whole room.

A random memory flits in and settles in my mind. I was maybe seven or eight. It was Christmas at the orphanage in Seoul and one of the staff members had bought little gifts for each of us. I received my very first snow globe. It was made of cheap plastic, with a cluster of pine trees and a deer inside of it. I had never seen a real deer before and it felt like the most magical thing ever, like a unicorn. Rose told me that one day we would find the place where snow fell on deer. We could live there if we wanted, like queens of the forest.

That night, one of the older girls tried to steal the globe from next to my cot. Rose caught her and made her give it back. The next day, that girl fell down the stairs and broke her arm. She came back from the hospital a couple of days later and never bothered me again. I always wondered if Rose had pushed her.

I don't know what happened to that snow globe. It's just one more thing that was lost or stolen from me in Los Angeles.

The water begins to cool and I know I'll have to get out soon, but I don't want to. I want to stay here, submerged. Am I really supposed to keep on living like nothing has changed?

Everything has changed.

"You need anything?" Jesse calls through the closed bathroom door.

"I'm fine. I'm getting out now." I pull the bathtub stopper out of the drain with my toes. The water makes a long slurping sound as it starts to disappear. I step carefully out onto the bare tile, wrapping a thick, fluffy towel around my entire body.

Of course I didn't remember to bring dry clothes in with me. I peek out of the bathroom door and don't see Jesse. I can hear the television in the living room. Quickly I scoot from the bathroom into my room and shut the door. I pull a pair of dark jeans and a gray long-sleeved T-shirt from my closet and dress quickly. The warm fabric feels comforting against my skin.

My phone rings. It's Gideon.

"Winter," he says. "Are you all right?" That seems to be the question of the day.

"Fine."

"Is Jesse with you?"

"Yes."

"Good. My plane just landed. I was just checking in."

"Have you talked to Sebastian or Detective Ehlers? Is there any news?"

"The phone record was a dead end. Sebastian said the call was made to me from a disposable phone that's now inactive. But whoever killed her knew their way around Escape," he says. "The back office is the only room that was searched."

I flinch at the cold and clinical way Gideon says "killed her." Obviously he's not holding out hope. It makes sense, though. Gideon has always been a man of science, and if his data says the ViSE is real, then he'd have no reason to think otherwise.

"If it was the man on the phone, he's probably someone who has vised with us," Gideon continues. "Either he was looking for a particular recording or he was after revenge."

"Revenge for what?"

"I don't know. If Rose was recording people without their permission, maybe she saw something she wasn't supposed to see, even if it didn't make it onto a ViSE."

"But why would anyone record themselves committing murder?"

"Clearly they know the cops won't take ViSEs seriously, but we will."

"Is there any way to generate a list of all the customers who played Rose's ViSEs lately? Maybe this guy went through the stock before attacking her."

"We don't keep records of who buys what," Gideon says. "For privacy reasons."

"Right," I say. "Well, if you find something out, anything at all, you'll tell me, won't you?"

"Of course I will. Sebastian has promised to keep me updated." Gideon says good-bye and then disconnects the call.

I slide my phone into my pocket, finger-comb my hair, and then go out into the living room where Jesse is splayed out on the sofa. He's on the phone, but whoever is on the other end is doing all the talking. Football highlights are playing on TV. Two mugs of tea sit on the coffee table.

"Gideon?" I mouth.

Jesse nods. He gestures toward the mug nearest to me.

I lift it to my lips and sip it cautiously. I taste hints of lemon, ginger, and honey in the soothing liquid. "You did well."

Jesse says, "I understand. I will. Good-bye," and then hangs up the phone.

I perch on the arm of the sofa. "He didn't believe me when I said I was fine?"

"He didn't believe you when you said I was here. He figured you sent me home."

"So untrusting." I take another drink of my tea.

"Well, you did *try* to send me home," Jesse points out. He reaches for the TV remote. As he skims through the channels, a news show catches his eye. He pauses long enough to let the anchor talk about a "series of dangerous crimes."

"Are you looking for my sister on the news?" My voice wavers slightly. I don't know what'll happen if they find her body, if I see it being pulled out of the river. I'm not sure if I want Jesse around at that point.

"I was looking for *us* on the news. Remember?"

Oh. Right. The Phantasm robbery feels like it happened a million years ago. It turns out the anchor was referring to a pair of carjackings in the Green District—the wealthiest part of town.

The TV cuts to a commercial and Jesse punches the remote again. A familiar face flashes onto the screen. It's the football player I saw in the lobby last night—Andy Lynch. Two sportscasters are discussing how he just declared himself NFL draft-eligible for the following season. The picture they post of him is boyishly handsome, his sandy-blond hair flopping forward into his face.

Jesse changes channels again and we watch a few minutes of another news show. There's a clip about a shooting in the Bricks, a rough area of town, followed by clips about a broken water main and a school district where two kids were diagnosed with meningitis. Nothing about our break-in.

"Do you think that's weird?" I ask. "We didn't make the news, but a broken water main did?"

Jesse sets the remote on the coffee table. "Maybe Phantasm handled it privately with their security company. Or maybe they tracked what we downloaded and it's no big deal, so they don't really care."

He's probably right. Classified corporate secrets would most likely be harder to access, but it still feels odd to me that no one reported such a high-profile crime.

It makes me think about what Baz said downstairs, how not involving the police in Rose's murder would mean we could take matters into our own hands, if we so desired. Maybe Phantasm has plans to come after us.

Maybe they already did.

CHAPTER 12

"YOU really don't think they're involved somehow?" I ask.

"Phantasm?" Jesse scratches his chin. "They'd have no reason to hurt Rose, would they?"

"I guess not." I rub my temples. "I can't even think straight right now."

Jesse punches the mute button on the remote and turns to face me. "Sit down," he says. "You should rest. Most people in your situation wouldn't be able to think at all."

My situation. My sister, gone forever. None of it feels real. I sit down and stare off into space while Jesse flips aimlessly through the TV channels. I know he said that seeing her body wouldn't help, but maybe he's wrong.

I head into my room and check the local news and police websites to see if anyone has mentioned finding a body in the river. Nothing. I check the most recent news stories in other cities along the Mississippi too, just in case. The fact that no one has reported anything here or in Festus or Ste. Genevieve gives me a surge of hope.

And then a surge of shame. I'm doing it again, making up my own reality.

Delusional.

You have to let go, Winter.

Easier said than done.

I grab my tablet and try to distract myself by working on

some physics homework, but the words and numbers blur together and I can't remember any of the equations. I look up my reading assignment for literature class, but it's even worse. I'm supposed to be starting *Antigone,* a Greek play about a girl who is punished for wanting to give her brother a proper burial. I can't read that now. I might not be able to read that ever.

I power down the tablet and lay my head on my desk. The walls of my room start whispering *Rose, Rose, Rose.* Maybe Gideon and Jesse are right. Maybe it's better if I'm not alone.

I return to the living room, but she's still everywhere—her sparkly shoes just inside the door, one of her sweaters tossed across the back of the sofa. I head into the kitchen to make some more tea and notice her essential oils all lined up in a row inside of a cabinet. I go to shut the door but then pause. She used to tell me that sniffing the lavender would calm me down. I uncap the little bottle and inhale deeply.

"Hey." Jesse's voice comes from right behind me.

I whirl around and nearly crash into him. The glass bottle slips from my fingers and shatters on the floor. I swear under my breath and reach for the paper towels.

He goes for the broom in the corner. "Let me get it so you don't cut yourself."

Normally I would argue, but today I just sink into a chair. "I can't breathe. I can't stop thinking about her. I almost wish we'd gone to Krav Maga. At least that might have distracted me for a couple of hours."

"We can spar on the roof if you want," Jesse says.

I shake my head. I'm not sure it's a good idea for me to be on the roof right now. "I'm going to go down to the gym," I say.

Jesse nods. "Sounds like a plan."

I duck back into my room and change into some workout clothes. When I head for the front door of the penthouse, Jesse makes like he's going to follow me. I lift a hand to his chest. "I know you think you're taking care of me. But I need to breathe, all right? There are plenty of people at the gym. Nothing bad is going to happen to me there."

"Okay. I'll be here. Call me if you need me." Jesse bends down to kiss me on the forehead.

Surprisingly, I don't flinch from the gesture. It feels comforting, almost familiar. Funny how someone's lips can feel so different from one day to the next. "Go home, Jesse. You don't need to sit here and wait for me. I'll call you when I get back."

"Promise?"

"Promise."

The gym on the second floor is the only thing in the building Gideon doesn't own. He rents the space to one of those big corporate chains. Today it's fairly busy, all of the New Year's resolution people sweating it out on the exercise bikes and treadmills. I head into the side room where the dumbbells and free weights are kept. I'm the only girl in here, but the guys don't seem fazed by my presence.

Midway through my second set of hammer curls, someone taps me on the shoulder. I'm so surprised that I nearly drop a fifteen-pound dumbbell on my foot. Whirling around, I intend to give the guy a piece of my mind when I see it's Mr. Football, Andy Lynch, the same guy I just saw on the news.

"So are you just never going to speak to me again?" His voice is a mix of confusion and pain.

"What?" I set the weight back on the rack and debate trying to repeat the exercise with the twenties.

Andy doesn't answer. He just cocks his head to the side and then looks sheepish. "Sorry. I thought you were someone else."

"You might mean my sister," I say slowly.

"Rose?"

My jaw drops slightly. Rose doesn't tell most of the guys she meets out at the clubs her real name. She gives them the name she uses when recording her ViSEs—Lily. "Yes. Do you know her well?"

"Not too well. We went out a few times. I thought we were hitting it off," Andy says. "But we had a disagreement and now she won't talk to me."

My jaw drops even farther. Rose was *dating* the local football star and never bothered to mention it? Could this have anything to do with her freelancing? Is Andy one of the guys she was recording without permission? I look him up and down—he's got nice hair and muscles, the kind of guy most women would find attractive. But he's so wholesome that I'm not convinced ViSE sex with him would be a huge seller.

And Gideon wouldn't sell anything explicit without Andy's permission anyway. Because ViSEs are actual sensory memories, people who appear in them can't sue for infringement, but Gideon still errs on the side of caution. Famous people are capable of making a lot of noise, and he doesn't need money bad enough to sacrifice his privacy.

Maybe Rose planned to record Andy and convert the footage to images she could sell to a tabloid or something.

"What?" Andy asks. "Why are you staring at me?"

"No reason," I say. "But aren't you going into the NFL this year? Better get used to girls staring at you."

He chuckles. "I doubt I'll ever get used to it. So did she say anything to you about me?"

He thinks Rose is blowing him off. If only it were something like that. I blink back tears. *Focus, Winter.* Maybe he knows something helpful. "A little bit," I lie. "What did you two fight about?"

"Her . . . line of work."

She wouldn't have told him she was a recorder. He probably means the switch parties. I can see how that might be problematic for a guy. "When's the last time you talked to her?" I ask.

"A few days ago? Why?"

"I haven't seen her today and she's not answering her phone." I try to make it sound like it's nothing serious. I'm not going to tell a total stranger that she's dead. For all I know he had something to do with it. I'm not ruling out anyone until I have more information. Also, saying it makes it true.

I'm not ready for it to be true.

Andy pulls his phone out and dials. After a few seconds he hangs up. "Straight to voice mail. Looks like we're both getting blown off," he says. "I knew it was too good to last."

"Look," I say. "Don't take it personally. Rose has issues. More than the average girl."

"More than you?" Andy touches one of the fresh bruises on the inside of my arm.

"That's not what you think. I do a lot of sparring and martial arts. I'm always covered in bruises." I pull my arm away. "Where's the last place you saw Rose?"

"My house. She came to a party. We got into an argument. She left and quit answering my calls."

"I see." I can't think of anything else to ask that won't seem strange, so I grab the weights again and start working on another set. My muscle fibers twitch and shake as my arms protest the workload.

Andy grabs a twenty-pound weight and rests one knee on a nearby bench. He holds his arm at a right angle and kicks the weight back to work his triceps. But he doesn't seem like he's ready to quit talking. "Does she have a boyfriend?" he blurts out. "Was she just messing with me?" Despite the hulking muscles and the T-shirt with the sleeves cut off, he looks so sweet, more like a wolf puppy than an actual wolf.

I decide to throw him a bone. "I never heard her say anything about a boyfriend."

A tall, stringy-haired kid wanders up to Andy before he can reply. I watch curiously as the kid pulls out a copy of *Sports Weekly*. Andy is on the cover with a couple of other NFL draft hopefuls. "Hey, man. Do you mind?" the kid asks.

"No problem." Andy sets his weight down on the bench to sign the magazine. The kid takes off and Andy catches me staring. He rolls his eyes like "What can I do?" and then goes back to his curls.

"If I see her, I'll let her know you're looking for her," I say.

I leave Andy in the free weight area and head out to the main room to hit the treadmill. Thirty minutes later, I'm drenched in sweat, my heart is racing, and it's the first time I've felt calm all day. I unroll a mat and do a quick stretch of all the major muscle groups. Andy puts his weights down and strides over to me when he sees me heading for the door.

"I'm leaving too. Can I walk with you?" he says hopefully.

"Why?"

"I don't know. We could talk more?"

I start to refuse the offer, but then I remember I know things he doesn't. Maybe he thinks I lied to him and Rose is tucked safely inside the penthouse, avoiding him. Or maybe he believed me, but his brain has gotten to that itchy desperate place that reaches out for any tiny bit of hope. There's no way I can put him out of his misery without telling him the truth—a truth that will only hurt him worse. "You know what? Sure. Let's go."

He heads for the elevator as I head for the stairs. "We live on the top floor, but I always walk up," I say. "I don't like elevators."

"Okay." He changes direction and follows me into the stairwell without questioning it.

"So is that why you're working out here?" I ask. "Hoping to run into my sister?"

"Lame, huh?"

"You're not lame. He seems like a decent guy. I hope Rose wasn't just playing him to get something scandalous on a ViSE.

He keeps pace with me on the stairs. "Why are you wearing her necklace?"

"What?" I almost forgot I had the pendant on underneath

my workout T-shirt. It must have bounced out from my collar as I was running up the steps. "Oh. We share jewelry sometimes."

A couple minutes later, we're standing in front of the penthouse door.

"Penthouse, huh?" Andy says. "Nice."

"We live with our . . . brother," I say. I've never had to explain my relationship with Gideon to a stranger before and I don't feel like getting into the details. I punch in the entry code, press my thumb to the sensor, and open the door to a dark and empty apartment. "Sorry. She's not here."

"It's cool. I just thought maybe . . ." Andy cranes his neck to get a look inside.

"Do you want to come in?" I pause in the doorway. "Our brother is out of town. We can talk more if you want."

Andy jams both hands in his pockets. His shoulders slump forward. "That's all right."

"How long have you known my sister?"

"Not that long. I met her about a month ago." The way he looks when he says it makes it seem like longer. He shifts his weight from one foot to the other, his blond hair falling over one eye. He looks exactly like the photo of him they showed on the news. "Can I give you my number?" he asks. "Even if she doesn't want to call me, I'd love to hear from someone that she's okay."

A lump forms in my throat. I'd love to hear that too. "Sure." I type his number into my phone. "If she shows up, I'll tell her to call you." I wish she *would* show up, that I would open my eyes and find out the whole day has been a dream. Even a hallucination. I'd go back to the therapist—to the hospital, even—if it meant I could have my sister back.

I shut the door, my muscles trembling in protest under the smallest force. I'm going to be sore tomorrow. Stripping off my sweaty clothes, I hop back into the shower. I find myself replaying my conversation with Andy, feeling a twinge of jealousy that my sister could make a big football star fall for her in just a couple of dates. Then I feel guilty for feeling jealous of Rose, so I try to concentrate on finding her killers. Surely there are clues I'm missing. Like Andy. Why wouldn't she have told me about him? What else might she have conveniently forgotten to mention?

I shut off the water and blot myself dry. I change back into my jeans and long-sleeved shirt and wrap a towel around my wet hair. I can't stop thinking about my sister, about the fact that she was keeping secrets from me. I have to know what they were.

Tears rise up from nowhere as I hit the doorway to her room. Everything is so Rose—from the scent of her perfume in the air to the mess of clothes and magazines on her bed to the décor itself: red comforter, red curtains, black lacquer. How could she have left me? How could someone have stolen her away? I hear Baz and Gideon arguing in my head. *We are not killers. Everyone is a killer . . . or a victim.* I will not be a victim. I will not let whoever killed Rose get away with it. Fighting to stay in control of my emotions, I paw through the stuff splayed across her bedspread and then drop to my knees to peer under the bed. There's nothing but a few mismatched shoes and a small stuffed bear with the words "You're unbearably cute" emblazoned across its chest.

I go to her dresser and start yanking open the drawers. I try to see down to the bottom of each without disturbing any more of her things than I have to. As my fingers touch the cool jade of a carved bracelet, my eyes sting and my vision goes blurry. I wipe away a rogue tear.

I have no idea what I'm looking for, what sort of evidence I might find that my sister had a whole other life I don't know about. There are no drugs, no hidden cell phones. There's no locked diary of secrets. All that stares back up at me are Rose's pajamas and a couple of knotted necklaces.

And then I see a sliver of something shiny and red protruding from beneath a folded pair of pajama pants. It's a music box shaped like a heart. Why would she hide that in a drawer? With shaking fingers, I undo the gold clasp and fold back the lid. A delicate porcelain ballerina spins to the tinny music of Beethoven's "Für Elise." The base of the box is full of tiny blue memory cards. I pull in a sharp breath. These are Rose's ViSEs. I always keep the original copies of mine, but I never knew she did too.

Why search the present for clues about what happened, when I can search the past? Better yet, if someone went after Rose for a recording she made, I might be holding it in my hands.

CHAPTER 13

I take the music box back to my room. There are nineteen memory cards scattered across the velvet. Overlay or not, I'm going to play them all.

I snap the first card into the slot on my headset and slip it over my ears. Closing my eyes, I recline back on my bed and press PLAY.

I'm in a dressing room of some sort. Black-and-white floor, black lacquer furniture. The air smells like a mix of perfume and styling products. Around me, women are tugging on dresses and adjusting necklines. Several of them are wearing diamond tiaras.

"Chop-chop." A man with short black hair wearing a shiny gray suit and a metallic gold tie claps his hands together. "We need you dressed before next year."

It's the New Year's Eve fashion show, I realize. Each year, one of the city's philanthropists holds a fashion show with some of his designer friends. The whole event is for charity, so no one is paid, but still, getting to walk in the show is a huge honor. I vaguely remember Rose telling me about it afterward, going on and on about the pretty dresses she got to wear.

My hands reach out and stroke the fabric of a gown hanging on a hook. It's off-white, a mix of silk and lace, the neckline and hemline adorned with pearls. I slip the dress over my head and the man in the gray suit zips me up.

A stylist pulls me over to a chair and a team starts working on my hair and makeup simultaneously.

I let out a sharp giggle. "Sorry," I say. "I didn't realize this would be so much fun. I feel like a movie star."

"You look like one too," the woman applying my makeup says. "I wish I had your legs."

If the stylists know I'm wearing a wig, they don't say anything. I fast-forward through the next few minutes of prep time. Rose must have recorded all of this just in case anything interesting happened backstage. The real ViSE will be the actual fashion show, the feel of strutting down a runway with all of the city's elite watching.

I'm standing in line between a tall black girl in a flowing turquoise gown and a shorter girl with strawberry-blond hair who keeps tugging at the hemline of her silver cocktail dress. A row of painted feathers adorn the bottom of it and each time she adjusts herself another feather falls to the ground. I reach out to touch her arm. "You look great," I say.

She smiles. "You too. I'm so afraid I'm going to fall in these stilts and flash my thong underwear to the entire city."

I look down at her shoes—silver ankle boots with heels long and sharp enough to be knives. "You won't fall," I tell her. "And if you do, you just own it—get back up, keep going. Everyone loves that."

"You're right," she murmurs.

We move forward as the girl in front of me heads out onto the runway. Music pounds from the ballroom, the bass coursing through my blood and vibrating the stage beneath my feet. A man cues me and I step out from behind the curtain. I glance down at my own tall heels but then I am going, walking confidently down the runway, the soft fabric of my dress swishing against my legs with each step.

The ballroom is decorated in white, gold, and silver. Every pair of eyes turns toward me as I strut past. Women in brightly colored dresses ooh and aah. Men in tuxedoes clap politely. Flashes go off from both sides of me. My lips twitch as I fight the urge to smile. I pause at the end of the runway and strike two poses. More cameras go off. As I turn, I see Gideon sitting a few rows back. He raises a champagne glass toward me, a grin plastered on his face.

I wink at the girl in the cocktail dress as we pass, and then head back to the curtain as the audience continues to clap. Backstage I am whisked toward a garment rack, where two girls hurriedly help me change into the next dress.

I walk in four different gowns before the ViSE ends and I open my eyes. I feel slightly queasy from playing such a long recording, but I also feel something else—exhilarated. It's almost like I actually just participated in a high-profile fashion show in front of half the city. I shake my head at the thought. I went to sleep early on New Year's Eve. That is one night where people who don't like crowds are better off staying inside.

I rub my stomach gently as I go through the ViSE again in my head. I didn't recognize anyone besides Gideon, but that doesn't mean Rose didn't know any of the other models or people in the audience. I might need to play each recording multiple times to really glean clues from them, but given my sensitivity to overlay, it could take me days to get through them even once.

Sighing, I set the first memory card to the side and select another.

I'm standing in the middle of a long line outside of a dance club called Zoo.

Zoo is the area's newest club. You generally have to be with somebody rich or famous to get inside. Unlike most of the basement clubs, Zoo boasts its own building, a converted warehouse located right at the edge of the Lofts. Rose never mentioned going there, but it's the kind of place even some-one as gorgeous as she might have struggled to get into, unless Gideon pulled some strings. It's a great venue to record at, because anyone who likes dancing or partying would proba-bly kill for a chance to spend the evening there.

I *don't* like dancing or partying. I'm dreading this recording.

Reluctantly, I force myself to focus.

Security guards dressed in black suits prowl the perimeter of the building. They pause frequently, muttering into their headsets. A tight cluster of girls in front of me are speculating about what sort of sexual favors they'd have to offer the bouncer to go to the front of the line. I sigh as I reach down to dislodge a dead leaf that's caught on the heel of my shoe. The girls flip curious but unwelcoming glances over their shoulders before judging me unworthy of their attention. Two of them start speaking in fake British accents and pretending to be European pop stars. Another girl suggests they should all make out.

"That might work," I say. "If you're willing to repeat the show once you get inside."

"Obviously you don't know or you'd be inside, wouldn't you?" The girl's British accent is horrible.

"Care to bet me who can get inside first?" I ask.

"Twenty bucks," the apparent ringleader says. She's got ketchup-red hair and lipstick to match. Her pale skin is practically turning gray in the cool night air.

"Don't waste my time," I say.

The girl paws through her wallet and pulls out a wad of cash. "Fifty," she suggests.

"Deal." I yank the neckline of my dress down just slightly and saunter up to the bouncer. He raises an eyebrow. I whisper something in his ear and then slip some money from my purse into the bouncer's palm.

I can't make out what Rose says to the bouncer or see how much money she gives him, but it feels like more than fifty dollars. It would be completely like my sister to take a loss to put some mean girl in her place.

The bouncer nods at me and moves the velvet rope so I can enter the club. I stride back to my place in line just long enough to pluck the crumpled bills from Ketchup Hair's hand. The girls stare at me, their brittle features a mix of surprise and loathing.

Inside, the club pounds with a bizarre mix of angry-sounding classical music and death metal. Smoke machines fill the floor with glaciers of fog, and glitter confetti swirls through the air like fake snow. Throngs of people are writhing to the endless beat, bodies brushing up against me as I move toward the center of the room.

I pause the recording for a second and open my eyes. My heart is thudding rapidly. I'm not sure if it's from the sensory overload of the smoke and lights and music, or if it's just the feel of being surrounded—and touched—by strangers. "Not real," I remind myself. I let my eyes fall shut and continue.

There are four metal cages balanced on platforms draped in white sheets. Inside three of the cages, scantily clad girls are dancing. In the fourth one, two guys are fighting. One hits the other in the mouth and spots of blood spatter across the white sheet. The small crowd of people around the cage cheers.

Turning from the violence, I make my way through the crowd. A girl dressed in a sheer green dress and thigh-high boots approaches me. She's got stick-straight white hair that hangs to her waist.

"Dance with me," she says.

I reach out to stroke her hair and she smiles. Our bodies twist and sway to the pounding drumbeats. A couple of guys in the crowd break away from their partners and circle around us—one dark skinned with dark hair, the other pale and blond. The lights flash and move overhead, blinding me for a few seconds. The music pulses through my blood.

The dark-skinned guy pulls me into his arms. "What's your name?" he asks.

I recognize him—Lamar Silver. He's a local rapper who's supposed to have his own reality TV show this summer. He's also known for starting up an animal rights charity and working with inner-city youth. All that and handsome too—the kind of guy who reduces most girls to stammering and blushing. I'm amazed at how cool and collected my sister is feeling.

"Lily," I say.

"Lily," he repeats. "That's pretty."

My lips curl upward in response. He drags his fingertips up the side of my rib cage and then leans in like he's going to kiss me. I press one finger to his lips and then pull away. He laughs.

Suddenly a hand clamps down on my wrist. A girl spins me around and pulls me toward the center of the dance floor. "I've been watching you for like ten minutes," she says.

She's wearing a brown-and-black wig that makes me think of burnt toast, but I recognize her. It's Natalie, another of Gideon's recorders. I've spoken to her only a couple of times in passing.

"Do you actually know Lamar Silver?" she asks.

"I know of him."

"And you passed up a chance to kiss him?"

"I think he was just flirting." I flip a glance over my shoulder. Lamar is now dancing with the white-haired girl, his hands crawling their way up her naked back.

I pause the recording again to study Lamar. The way he went from my sister to the other girl in five seconds convinces me he doesn't have any serious interest in Rose. To him, she's just a girl out dancing at a club.

"I saw some hockey players up at the bar," Natalie says. "And Stellan Hillberg, the fashion designer. This place is unbelievable."

"How did you get in?" I ask.

"The same way as you, I imagine—Gideon."

I shake my head. "I was going to surprise him with this recording. Do you know how many people would love to see the inside of this place? I can't believe we both had the same idea."

"Don't have a meltdown. I'm sure we can have completely different experiences." Natalie cocks her head toward one of the cages. "I might see if I can find a hot guy or two to battle with me later." She winks.

I can see my sister editing this clip, cutting out the exchange so Natalie appears to be just a strange girl who wants to dance with her.

Natalie twists seductively around me. Her hands stroke the sides of my face. She pulls me in close, pretends like she's going to kiss me. "I see this guy who's totally staring at you."

"You act like that's not an everyday occurrence," I say.

"No, but there's something creepy about this one."

"What?" I can barely hear over the loud music.

She gestures toward the back of the room. The people are packed in tight. My eyes linger on a man in a long gray leather coat. His features are completely obscured by the pulsing lights and the black fedora he wears pulled low. I laugh a fluttery little laugh before turning my attention back to Natalie. "He's a little overdressed, isn't he?" I say.

I struggle to get a better look at the guy, but Rose turns away from him too soon. Without thinking, I open my eyes as I fight the ViSE, and the landscape of Zoo overlays itself on my bedroom. The effect is immediately disorienting. My stomach churns. Quickly I let my eyes fall shut again.

It's impossible to move independent of the ViSE. I know this, but I'm dying to turn back and study the crowd, to see who Rose and Natalie are talking about. But I stay trapped in her body and let the recording play out until the end, my eyes doing their absolute best to scan the blurry figures for anyone who might be familiar. The dancing continues for a few more songs, but I don't see anyone I recognize, and as far as I can tell, neither does my sister. She works the crowd, dancing with several attractive guys but never letting them get too close.

I stop the recording and open my eyes. The real world rushes back all at once—the stark black and white of my room in direct contrast to the pulsing lights and garishly bright dresses at Zoo.

Removing the headset, I massage my temples for a few moments. I breathe in and out slowly until my nausea subsides. Then I find a blank notebook and a permanent marker in one of my drawers and open it to the first page. I write #1 and next to it the words *NYE fashion show*. I label the memory card with a 1. Next line: #2: *Zoo dancing*. I label that card with a 2.

I grab my phone and scroll through the list of contacts to find Natalie. She's only in my phone because Gideon made all of his recorders exchange numbers, but judging from the way she and Rose joked on the ViSE, my sister knew her better than I do. I leave a voice mail message asking her to call me back. Reluctantly, I slip the headset back over my ears.

I'm about to start the next ViSE when my phone rings. I pick it up expecting Natalie, but it turns out to be Jesse.

"How are you doing?" His words are slow and precise. Hostage negotiator voice.

"I'm all right."

"Are you still at the gym?"

"No, sorry. I was just getting ready to call you."

"You stayed at the gym for three hours?"

"I've been home for a little while," I hedge. "You want to help me with something else?"

A pause. A long breath. "With what?"

I fidget with one of the prongs on my headset. "I need to get into Zoo."

"I thought you were going to Inferno."

Damn it. I forgot all about that when I found Rose's ViSEs. "I can get into Inferno on my own, but I know my sister also did some work at Zoo lately. Natalie told me there was a creepy guy there who seemed like he was watching Rose." I push away a prickle of guilt. Technically not a lie. Natalie did tell me, on the ViSE. And I'm sure she'll tell me again once she calls back.

Jesse whistles long and low. "Until something even flashier opens up, Zoo is kind of off-limits to commoners like you and me, even on a Sunday night. You'd have to be a rock star or a professional athlete to—"

Perfect. I cut him off. "Never mind. You just gave me a great idea."

"I did?"

"I ran into Andy Lynch in the gym. I bet I can get him to take me."

Jesse makes a choking sound. "After that fumble on the four-yard line, he might not be cool enough to get in either."

"Be nice. So he got nervous and screwed up. He was on the news. He's on the cover of *Sports Weekly*. That's cool enough for Zoo."

"I didn't know you read *Sports Weekly*," Jesse says dryly.

"I don't. Some guy came up to Andy when we were working out and—"

"So now you're gym buddies with Andy Lynch? I thought you liked working out alone."

"Seriously? Now is not the time to get jealous," I say. "Besides, he's in love with Rose, all right? Apparently they were dating. He was working out downstairs hoping to catch a glimpse of her on his way in or out."

"I'm not jealous," Jesse says. "But think about it. Rose gets killed, possibly because of a ViSE, and now Andy Lynch is suddenly your best pal? Maybe he had something to do with it."

"Andy?" I scoff. "Doubtful. He seems more like a puppy than a murderer."

"If you say so." Jesse still sounds a bit miffed. "But Gideon is going to want me to go with you."

The phone beeps. I look down at the display. Natalie. "I have another call I have to take," I say. "I'll call you back." I switch over.

"Hey, Winter," Natalie says. Her voice has that "heaping with sympathy" sound to it and right away I can tell someone has told her about Rose.

"Hi. I guess you heard about my sister. I've been playing some of her ViSEs and I saw one with you two at Zoo."

"Yeah?"

"You and Rose were dancing. You said some guy had been staring at her."

"I did?" Natalie doesn't say anything for a few seconds. "Sorry, I've run into her more than once at Zoo, and I get pretty trashed when I go clubbing."

"It was a night Lamar Silver was there. The guy you were talking about was wearing a long gray leather coat."

"Oh, right, the guy in the hat and coat. Who keeps their coat on at a dance club? Yeah, I saw him checking out your sister several times that night."

"Did you recognize him?"

"No," she says. "But Rose didn't seem worried about him."

"Did you see him there more than once?" I ask.

Natalie exhales deeply. "Maybe? I'm not sure. Sorry."

"Do you know if my sister was dating Andy Lynch?" I ask suddenly.

Natalie coughs. "The quarterback?"

"Yes."

"If she was, she never mentioned him." Natalie pauses. "I always got the feeling Rose wasn't looking for a relationship."

"Could the guy at Zoo have been Andy Lynch?"

"Hmm. I don't think so, but I can't say for sure."

"That's all right," I say. "Did she ever seem worried to you? Afraid?"

"I only knew her from the clubs, but Rose never seemed afraid of anything or anyone," Natalie says. "At least as far as I could tell."

CHAPTER 14

As soon as I hang up with Natalie, I call Andy.

He picks up immediately. I can hear the clanging of weight stacks in the background. "I went back to the gym," he says.

And I thought *I* was obsessed with exercise. "Don't you have stuff to do besides work out?"

"Officially I don't go back to school for another week. Assuming I go back at all." He clears his throat. "Exercise helps keep my mind off stuff, you know?"

"I do," I say. "I'm calling to ask you for a favor. I still haven't heard from my sister and I'm starting to worry. She actually didn't come home last night. I didn't want to tell you that earlier, because I figured you'd assume, well, that she was with another guy. But I don't think that's what it is." Without mentioning ViSEs or Rose's job as a recorder, I try to explain why I want to go to Zoo. "I know Rose has gone there multiple times recently and I talked to one of her friends who said a guy there seemed to be following her around."

"But if you really think something might've happened to her, shouldn't you get the police involved?" Andy asks.

"I did," I say. "We talked to a detective, but Rose has stayed out all night before and he didn't seem all that concerned. I'm going a little crazy just sitting around, though. I'd feel better if I were out looking for her." I'm amazed by how easily the half-truths flow from my tongue. After talking to Andy in the gym, my gut doesn't really think he had anything to do with what happened to Rose, but I still can't bring myself to tell him the whole story.

"Okay. I can get you into Zoo," Andy says, his relaxed voice going taut with worry. "It still packs up every night, though. It'll be easier to get in if we go earlier."

"Maybe ten?" I suggest.

"Sounds good. I can pick you up."

"All right."

I hang up and check the time. I've got about two hours to go through more of Rose's ViSEs. The next one is a recording of Rose bungee jumping from a bridge downtown during last year's Fourth of July celebration. It's a ViSE that Gideon probably would've assigned to me if crowds didn't make me so uncomfortable. No one stands out on the recording except for Rose, Gideon, and a man from the ropes company.

Next.

I'm sitting in the audience of an auditorium. Around me, a few people are raising their hands in the air, but most are slinking down in their seats, feigning interest in their phones. My hand is waving wildly. The guy on stage points at me and suddenly I'm being escorted from my seat by a couple of stagehands.

"Are you afraid of knives?" the man asks. He's a full head taller than me with hair as black as raven feathers and eyes to match. He's wearing all black except for a satin cape adorned with silvery stars and moons.

It's the circus, I realize. I can't remember how long ago the circus was in town.

I shake my head as I stare at the trio of shiny blades in the man's hand. "I'm not afraid of anything."

A murmur runs through the crowd. The man sets the knives on a nearby stool and wraps his lean fingers around mine. He kisses the back of my hand.

"Good. You have nothing to worry about. I almost never miss."

Another murmur from the crowd, this one tinged with laughter.

The knife thrower's assistant leads me to a wooden wheel at the far end of the stage. She looks critically at my outfit and declares in a thick accent that I will be fine. I step onto wooden pegs for my feet and she secures my wrists and ankles with leather straps.

She produces a black silk handkerchief from some invisible pocket in her sequined costume. "Do you wish for a blindfold?" she asks.

I shake my head. My heart pounds as the assistant walks toward the far side of the stage. Music plays from the speakers as the knife thrower shows his three knives to a man in the front row to prove they are real. Then the knife thrower casually juggles them as he steps up to a line directly across from me.

Our eyes meet. He sets two of the knives on the stool and lifts the third one high in the air. Fear races through my veins as the overhead lights glint off the blade. The thrower kisses the tip of the blade and then rears back his arm. A sharp thunk sounds from the area of my left ear. He lifts the second knife with an exaggerated flourish. My whole body tenses. He throws again. This one thunks to the right of my head. The third knife lands between my legs.

I pause the recording for a second, holding one hand to my chest in a feeble attempt to slow my racing heart. I can't believe my sister recorded this ViSE without a blindfold. It wouldn't have been nearly as exciting without the sense of sight, but still. I got so enthralled by it I forgot I was supposed to be looking for clues.

I start the recording again, trying my best to study the faces of the performers and audience members, looking for anyone who seems familiar or out of place.

The thrower's assistant fetches the knives from the wooden circle. She returns to his side and pulls out her blindfold again.

"Now do you want a blindfold?" the man asks.

I shake my head as the assistant blindfolds him. The audience gasps. My body goes tense with fear.

Thunk. Thunk. Thunk. This time the knives land on either side of my chest and above my head. The assistant retrieves them again and returns them to the still-blindfolded knife thrower.

"And now, for the pièce de résistance," the knife thrower starts.

A stagehand comes up and double-checks the leather straps holding me to the wheel. Then he straps the assistant to a second set of buckles so her body is perpendicular to mine.

"I will take a blindfold," she says. *"I am not as brave as our audience volunteer."*

There is a rustling noise as the crowd whispers again. The assistant's body is pressed against mine, pinning me tightly against the wooden wheel. And then the stagehand gives a lever on the side of the wheel a sharp yank. I close my eyes for a second as I start to move. But then I open them. The room is spinning. The crowd is gasping. Thunk. Thunk. Thunk. The knives hit in rapid succession. The audience cheers. I expel a sharp breath. My muscles go weak with relief. The stagehand helps both of us off the wheel. I smooth the wrinkles from my form-fitting dress and lift a hand to my head to make sure my wig is still tightly pinned in place. The crowd rises to its feet as the assistant and I sashay into the spotlight. The knife thrower meets us center stage.

Movement at the side of the auditorium catches my eye. It's just a silhouette, thanks to the harsh stage lights, but I see a guy in a long coat and a hat turn and head up the far aisle. My temples begin to pound, the pain radiating to my forehead.

Nausea begins to well in my gut. My phone rings. I ignore it. I need to see who is in the coat.

I try to focus on the shadowy figure but it's impossible because Rose isn't interested in him. She's linking arms with the knife thrower and his assistant, taking multiple bows while the audience cheers.

My phone rings again. I pause the ViSE and open my eyes slowly. The pounding at my temples is crescendoing now. My stomach is roiling violently.

"Hello?" I say, my voice wavering slightly.

It's Jesse. "Hey. Just wanted to let you know I'm coming back up. Are you going to Zoo?"

"Can you hold on for a minute?" I ask. Dropping the phone

before he has a chance to respond, I rush to the bathroom, fall to my knees, and vomit into the toilet. My nausea quickly subsides, but my headache still lingers. I rinse my mouth out with warm water, and then make my way back to my bedroom.

Collapsing on my bed, I grab my phone again. "All right, I'm back."

"Everything okay?"

"Yes. And yes, I'm going to Zoo. Andy is picking me up around ten."

"I want to come with you," Jesse says.

"I can handle Andy Lynch," I say sharply. "You don't need to worry."

"Please, Winter?"

I expected Jesse to threaten to call Gideon if I didn't let him have his way. This one-word plea takes me by surprise. Affection stirs in my chest, an unfamiliar feeling. I soften. "Fine, you can come, but I don't know if Andy's going to be able to get you in or not."

"It's not really my scene, anyway. If he can't, I'll just prowl around outside waiting for you, but at least I'll be nearby if you need me."

"All right. Dress as nice as possible just in case. Zoo is pretty strict with the dress code."

"Got it," Jesse says. "I don't have much in the way of clubbing clothes. I might have to go buy something. Should I bring my headset?"

"No. You don't need to. I can wear one of Rose's wigs."

"Okay. See you later. Call me in the meantime if you need anything."

"I will." I hang up the phone and finish the circus recording, but the guy in the coat and hat is gone. I remove my headset and label the memory card with a 3. I tuck the notebook and Rose's music box into the locked cabinet where I keep my recorder headset and copies of my own ViSEs. Tomorrow I'll play the rest of her recordings. I wish I could do them all now, but the overlay is hitting me too hard. If I push it, the pain and nausea will dilute my focus and I could miss something important.

Besides, it's time to find an outfit to wear to Zoo. Like Jesse, I don't own any clothes fancy enough to get me into the city's most popular club, so I venture back into my sister's room and head for her closet.

I skim past the first three garments—including the dress with the fringe I thought she was wearing last night. Squeezing my eyes shut, I try to envision her outside the bathroom again, spinning in front of the full-length mirror. I lift the scarlet fabric to my face for a closer look. I know it was this dress. Why would she have come home and changed?

Sighing, I flip past the last couple dresses until my hand stops at a short, silky number at the very back of the closet that's more free flowing than form fitting. Like most of Rose's dresses, it's red. I hold it up against me in the mirror. I look like a totally different person, but not one that scares me. I remove my long-sleeved T-shirt and pull the dress over my head.

I flinch at my exposed collarbones, but at least my bra isn't showing. Undoing the zipper of my jeans, I slide them down, immediately feeling the softness of silk against my skin. Stepping out of the bunched-up denim, I give the bottom of the dress a hard tug. The flowing fabric falls to the middle of my thighs and that's as low as it's going to go. Hesitantly, I peek into the mirror again. I know I look fine, but my breath sticks in my throat. Sweat glistens on my upper lip. There's no way I can leave the house dressed like this.

I duck back into Rose's closet to look for other options and notice a pair of black leggings balled up on the floor. My breathing returns to normal as I slide them on. Better. I start looking for a pair of shoes to match.

In addition to the pair of strappy heels she has tucked inside the front door, she's got five other pairs of shoes tossed haphazardly on the floor of her closet, three of which are so tall and sparkly that they look like part of a circus performer's uniform. I find some black suede boots with a medium heel and decent ankle support. Shaking out my hair, I let it fall forward so the edges skim my shoulders and then apply my standard eyeliner. I'm ready.

Except I forgot about my headset.

I pull my hair into a low ponytail and then grab my headset from my room and slide it on. Heading back into Rose's room, I don the wavy black wig and adjust it so it hides the metal prongs. Soft tendrils curl around my face. I peek at myself in the mirror—not too bad—and then check the clock. It's only nine thirty. There's plenty of time to walk over to Inferno and find out if anyone there saw Rose last night.

Inferno is only a parking lot away, but my skin is red and raw from the frigid wind by the time I slip into the building. The lobby is decorated all in red and black—art deco, minimalist, as simple as Gideon's building is opulent. Stairs at the back of the lobby lead down into the club. There's no line yet since it's still early. There's not even a bouncer.

I've been to Inferno a couple of times, but only when I was looking for my sister. I glance around, my eyes lingering on the tongues of fire painted on the walls. Clubs are apparently wasted on me. I don't understand why anyone would pay to hang out here. A few couples cluster together at the bar, sipping drink specials and tapping their feet to the techno rhythm. I take a seat next to them and wait for the bartender to approach me.

She sidles over with a bright red beverage napkin. "Can I see some ID?"

"I'm just looking for someone," I say. "My sister. A blond Korean in a red dress. I'm trying to find out if she came in here last night."

"Doesn't sound familiar," the bartender says. "Sure you don't want a drink? Maybe a soda or something?"

I slap a twenty-dollar bill down on the bar. "Does that help your memory at all?"

She eyes the money greedily. "You got a picture?"

I show her the cell phone picture as the music bleeds from one song into the next. A girl starts dancing all alone in the center of the room.

The bartender nods. "Yeah. I've seen her in here before. She's a switch-party girl, right?"

"Yes. Did you see her last night?"

"Oh, I didn't work last night." She smirks as she pockets the twenty.

Bitch. "Is anyone here who *did* work last night?" I ask through clenched teeth.

"You want Julian," she says. "Let me get him for you." She disappears into the back.

A few minutes later, a skinny guy with inky black hair and a tattoo of a pentagram on his temple slinks out of the kitchen. "You looking for Julian?" he asks.

"Yes. I'm also looking for my sister." I slap a second twenty-dollar bill down on the bar and show him the picture of Rose on my phone.

"Oh, Lily," he says. "Yeah, she comes in here some." He glances left and right, wringing his hands like he's either nervous or strung out on something.

It makes sense that Rose went by her alias at Inferno since she sometimes recorded ViSEs here. "Did you see her last night?"

Julian shakes his head rapidly, his pupils dilating. "I think she said something about stopping by, but she didn't make it, unless I missed her."

I slip my phone back in my pocket. "She's a hard person to miss."

"She's not in trouble, is she? Lily has always been cool to me." He grins—a mouth full of yellowing teeth. "She's a solid tipper."

I write my phone number on the red napkin left by the other bartender. "Call me if you think of anything else."

I head out into the cold and back across the parking lot. I barely make it back to the penthouse before someone is knocking. It's Andy. When I open the door, he stares at me a little longer than I would like.

I hug my arms across my chest. "I don't look good enough to get in, do I?" Maybe the leggings are too casual. Or maybe I need more makeup.

"No, you look great," he says. "It's just weird to see someone else wearing her clothes."

"Do you care if my friend comes with us?" I grab Rose's coat from the hall closet. "I told him you might be able to get him in. It's either that or he's going to call every five minutes to check up on me."

Andy shrugs. "The more the merrier."

Jesse shows up less than a minute later. To my surprise, he's wearing a pair of dark suit pants and a dress shirt made of some kind of shiny turquoise material. His hair is combed forward, the left side carefully arranged to hide most of his disfigured ear. I've never seen him look so polished—almost like a different person.

"You look beautiful," he tells me.

This time I resist the urge to cross my arms. "You look nice too." I smile tightly.

"Yeah, you both look great." Andy shakes his bangs back from his face. "We should have no problem getting in. I showed up for Zoo's grand opening back in November. They love me over there." He looks back and forth from Jesse to me. "So what are we looking for again?"

"According to my sister's friend, a guy in a long gray leather coat and a black fedora, who may or may not have been following Rose," I say, realizing exactly how absurd it sounds. "Or anything weird."

"I'm sure there will be no shortage of weird," Jesse says.

CHAPTER 15

He's right. It turns out tonight is a special "Blackout at the Zoo" theme night. There are the same cages of dancing and fighting, only now the entire club is dark, lit only by rotating black lights in the ceiling and sparse emergency lighting around the perimeter.

"We're never going to find anyone in this," Jesse says. "The dude could be up on a pedestal in one of the cages and we wouldn't be able to see him."

I'm about to agree when someone shouts, "Lynch!" A guy the size and shape of a refrigerator taps Andy on the shoulder. I'm guessing he's one of Andy's teammates. "I need to talk to you about something." The guy gestures toward the back of the club.

"Be right back." Andy lets the guy tow him toward the VIP room.

Jesse and I lean against the wall, watching the dancers sway under the undulating purple lights.

"It's kind of pretty." The first thought that jumps into my head.

Jesse brushes the sides of Rose's wig back from my face. "You're kind of pretty." His lips hover close to my earlobe so I can hear him over the music.

"Not compared to these girls." Everywhere I look, lithe supermodel types parade around in obscenely short dresses and tall high heels. So much skin. It makes me wish I could have worn some leggings on my arms too.

"Whatever," he replies. "You don't need glittery false eyelashes and caked-on makeup to be hot." He glances around at the crowd. "Some of these chicks probably spent hours disguising themselves before they left the house. What's the point? The guy you're with has to be okay with the real you."

A current of pain jolts through me. Jesse wouldn't like the real me, the girl who spent years being violated and victimized. "You combed your hair to cover your ear," I point out.

"Yeah, but that's just part of the disguise." Jesse looks down at his shiny shirt. "This isn't who I am. I bought it for tonight. My ear, my scar—they're part of me. I don't *need* to hide them from anyone."

I wish I felt like he did, like I didn't need to hide my scars. Like people wouldn't judge or pity me if they knew my history. I wish I were as strong as Jesse. Almost without thinking, I touch my right hand to where I know the angry pink line lingers, just beneath the forward sweep of his brown hair.

He blinks rapidly and then reaches his hand up and twines his fingers through mine. Leaning in close to me, he says, "Are you okay being here?"

The scent of either cologne or aftershave tickles my nose. I take my hand back and step slightly away. "Why wouldn't I be?"

"You said crowds made you nervous. Doesn't get much more crowded than this."

He's right. Maybe I'm finally getting over my fear of other people. Or maybe I just feel more comfortable here because I've already experienced this place in a ViSE. "It's not too bad," I tell him.

Jesse nods. "Do you want to dance?"

I imagine his hands on me, his eyes skimming their way down the lines of my body as we move to the music. I shake my head. "We need to stay focused on why we're here."

"Okay." Jesse scans the room again. "Hey. Is that Isaiah?" He points across the club at a tall African-American kid who is slipping gracefully through the crowd of dancers.

"Looks like it," I say. Isaiah is Gideon's newest recorder. He's sporting a head full of braids—a wig—which means he's recording. We watch as he escorts a petite girl with long dark hair toward one of the bathrooms.

"What do you think that's about?" Jesse asks.

"Drugs or sex, I'm sure," I say. "Nothing else happens in bathrooms at a club, right?"

Gideon won't sell ViSEs of torture or sexual assault, but almost everything else is fair game. If you're willing to do it, chances are someone out there is willing to buy it. Some people feel like ViSEs encourage risky behavior, but Gideon's philosophy is the opposite—if we can provide people the experience in a safe environment, they'll be less likely to go out and do it on their own. I remember arguing with him about the sexual ViSEs once, telling him no one's first time should be someone else's experience.

"No one's first time should be with a girl who isn't willing," he responded quietly.

I never brought it up again.

"I wonder if Isaiah got the message about not working alone," Jesse says.

"Let's find out." I cut across the crowded dance floor toward the women's restroom, with Jesse right behind me.

A guy who is dressed in a maroon shirt and black pants—a bartender, maybe—holds up his hand. "Bathroom is occupied right now."

"We know." Jesse gives him a gentle shove out of the way and we stride right past.

I lift a hand to my mouth when I see what's going on. I was wrong about the drugs or sex part. Isaiah and the girl are fighting. She's only half his size but she's throwing punches like a heavyweight. Her fist connects with his stomach and he doubles over. She lands a right hook to his jaw and he stumbles backward against the sinks, his lower lip wet with blood.

Jesse and I spring into action. I step between the girl and Isaiah and Jesse grabs her. He pins her back against the wall.

The girl blinks rapidly, like she's not sure where we came from. "Is this part of it?" She looks over at Isaiah.

"Part of what?" Jesse asks. "What's going on?"

"Jesus, Ramirez." Isaiah wipes the blood from his mouth with one hand. "Talk about sneaking up on a brother." He turns to the girl. "Sorry, babe. We're going to have to do it over."

"You were recording?" I say in disbelief. "You think there's a big demand for the experience of getting beat up by a girl?"

Isaiah chuckles. "*She's* recording. Not me."

Jesse steps back and the girl removes a black wig to reveal a headful of coppery twists partially mashed by a recorder headset. "I'm Helene," she says. "Isaiah's girlfriend."

"I still don't understand," I say. "Does our boss know you're letting other people record?"

"He won't care once he checks out this footage," Isaiah says smugly.

Jesse smirks. "Because you think people will pay big bucks for the honor of kicking your ass?"

Isaiah ignores Jesse. "Winter, haven't you ever wanted to slap the shit out of some guy who won't take a hint? Maybe he asks you to dance or he asks you for your number and you're polite at first but he won't let it go, even follows you into the bathroom like a creeper." Isaiah gestures around the cramped room with a flourish. "I present the Bathroom Beatdown."

"Pretty sure if Winter wanted to slap the shit out of some guy she'd just go ahead and do it," Jesse says.

I bite back a smile. He's probably right. "I guess I can see the appeal of this, but please be careful."

"Yeah, about that." Isaiah looks over at Helene. "Give me a second, babe." He pulls Jesse and me to the other side of the room. Dropping his voice he says, "Gideon told me about your sis. I only met her once but she seemed cool. I'm sorry for your loss. It probably seems disrespectful as hell that I'm out recording, but I still got to eat. Knowing Gideon, he'll be back up and running in a week, and I need to have something new to offer him."

"How did you even get in here?" Jesse asks.

Isaiah grins. "I got my ways."

"Have you seen a guy in a gray leather coat?" I ask. "Maybe wearing a fedora too?"

"I don't think so, but I haven't spent much time checking out the guys tonight." He gestures at Helene. "You see anyone wearing a gray coat up in here tonight? With a hat maybe?"

She shakes her head. "Nothing like that. I've seen a few girls who probably ought to *put on* a coat." She clucks her tongue. "Transparent is not a dress color."

"Cool. Thanks anyway," Jesse says.

"Be safe," I add, as we head for the restroom door. The guy in the maroon shirt is gone. Maybe he didn't want to hang around to be yelled at by Helene and Isaiah for letting us get past him.

Back out in the club, Jesse and I muscle our way up to the bar and ask the two bartenders currently making drinks if they've served anyone in a gray leather coat tonight or anytime recently. Both of them just shrug.

"How can people be so oblivious?" I mutter as we turn away.

"Speaking of oblivious." Jesse gestures across the dance floor. "Superchoke is heading in this direction. I'm not sure how much of what's going on you want him to know."

I turn around. Andy is working his way through the crowd toward us. A pair of girls stops him on the way over. He shakes each of their hands.

"The less he knows, the better," I say. "I told him I was worried about Rose because she didn't come home last night, but nothing else."

Jesse nods. "That's what I thought. I'm going to get into one of the cages—get an aerial view of the whole place. If there's a guy in a gray leather coat here, I'll find him."

"Don't get your ass kicked," I say just as Andy reaches my side.

"Who said anything about fighting?" Jesse winks.

To my surprise, he sidles up to a cage full of dancing girls who happily welcome him inside. I shake my head as the girls twist and writhe around him. I never would have figured Jesse for a dancer, but he moves like he's completely comfortable. One of the girls plants a kiss on his jawbone. I force myself to look away.

"So is he your boyfriend?" Andy asks.

"No. We work together, but we're just friends."

"Are you guys recorders like Rose?"

I clench my jaw to keep my mouth from falling open in surprise. I'm shocked at how much Rose confided in Andy. It's great that she trusted him, but no one is supposed to know we're recorders and I'm not about to violate the rules Gideon put in place to keep us safe.

I give Andy my best blank look. "What's a recorder?"

He chuckles. "Oh, so that's how it is? Very hush-hush? Okay. I'll play along."

Before I can respond he slides his arms around my waist and sweeps me out onto the dance floor. "A recorder is some-one who makes ViSEs. Do you know what those are?"

"Everyone knows what ViSEs are," I say. "Everyone around here, at least." People come from neighboring states to try them. Gideon even has some rich customers who fly in from the West Coast to vise.

"Do you ever do it?"

I feel the pressure of the metal headset beneath my wig. "I don't think I would like it." I try to slide away from Andy. "I don't really like to dance either."

"So fake it. You're not going to see much with your back

pressed into a corner." He raises my hands in the air and swings them from left to right. "Your sister is all kinds of dancer."

"That doesn't surprise me." Reluctantly I move my feet in time to the music, swaying my hips as I systematically scan the room looking for the guy in gray. Each song bleeds seamlessly into the next. I try to keep enough of a space cushion around me so I'm not brushing up against other people.

Andy snickers at my awkward dancing. "Do you want a drink?" he offers.

"I don't drink." Another activity best avoided by the reality challenged.

"Maybe you should." He winks at me. "It takes the edge off."

"Maybe I like the edge."

"Ouch," he says. "Feisty."

"You went back in the VIP room with your football friend, right?" I ask. "You didn't see anyone in a coat and hat?"

"I haven't seen anyone in a coat anywhere tonight. People either left them in cars or checked them."

I sigh. "You're right. This is hopeless."

Across the room, Jesse climbs out of the cage to the chagrin of the female dancers. One whispers in his ear as he turns to shut the door behind him. A spike of jealousy moves through me like a faulty electric current. But I'm being stupid. I can't be the girl he wants. He deserves someone who can.

He holds my gaze through the dark as he makes his way around the gyrating dancers. I can't even see his eyes, but I can feel them on me. Like my own personal eclipse, the room falls away until there is nothing but grayness and Jesse's dark form superimposed upon it. He looks taller. Half his face is bathed in shadow. He looks like someone has gouged out one of his eyes. My heart thrums in my chest. Then Jesse steps out of the circling black lights and his form is the same as always. Two eyes. Just a trick of light.

"Any luck?" I ask.

"Nada," he says. "You want to do more asking around?"

I shake my head. "Let's just get out of here."

The three of us begin making our way to the front door of the club. I grab Rose's coat from the coat check and fling it around my shoulders. As we step out into the cold, Jesse says, "So where to? Do you know of anywhere else Rose spent a lot of time recording?"

Andy turns toward me, his lips twisting up into a smile as he watches me squirm at being so blatantly caught in a lie. My face flushes red in the frosty air. A few flakes of snow swirl around us.

"What?" Jesse looks from me to Andy. "Oh, man. Didn't you say they dated or something? I thought he knew that much at least."

"I did." Andy fishes his keys out of his pocket. "But someone here has trust issues."

Jesse whistles long and low. "Dude. You have no idea."

Ignoring Jesse, I give Andy a defiant look. "Fine. So I know Rose is a recorder. Her boss doesn't like for people to talk about it."

The snow starts coming down harder. It looks like we're due for another blizzard.

"Let's go," I say, frustrated at wasting so much time on a dead end.

We head across the parking lot. "Well, she has to be somewhere," Andy says hopefully. "Maybe the cops will come up with something." He presses a button on his keychain and the doors to his Range Rover unlock with a shrill electronic chirp. Another button and the engine roars to life.

We're only a few yards from the Range Rover when my eyes are drawn to a car in the next row. Black. Midsize. Completely nondescript. There's a man sitting in the driver's seat.

A man wearing a coat and a fedora.

CHAPTER 16

"Guys," I start. "Don't look, but there's a guy wearing a hat and a coat in a black car one row over, and I think he's watching us."

Jesse keeps his eyes trained on me, but Andy starts to turn his head.

The sedan's engine suddenly springs to life. The driver backs up quickly, shifts into drive, and squeals his tires as he heads for the exit.

"Shit," Andy says. "Sorry."

I am already running toward the Range Rover. "Let's go after him."

We peel out of the parking lot in pursuit of the black car. Andy drives like a race car driver and we quickly gain on the sedan, pulling ever closer as it heads for the riverfront. Snow-flakes slap the windshield and immediately get shunted to either side by the wiper blades. Andy accelerates until the Rover is vibrating, the seams rattling so hard I start to worry they might come apart. The arrow on the speedometer jumps and twitches as it climbs higher and higher.

"What are we going to do when we catch up to him?" he asks.

"Cut him off," I say. "Force him to pull over."

"And then what?"

"Leave that to us." Jesse produces a black pistol from beneath his seat.

Andy catches a glimpse of the gun in his peripheral vision and his sun-kissed skin goes pale. He lifts his foot from the accelerator. "Holy shit. Is that thing real?"

"Real enough," Jesse says.

"Don't slow down," I bark.

Andy speeds up again, cutting across an empty parking lot. For a moment the Rover tilts up on two wheels as he jumps a curve and ends up back on the road. We're closing on the sedan when a train whistle sounds in the distance—long and shrill. Red lights flash in front of us. There's a set of tracks just ahead. The sedan speeds up. The black-and-white gate begins to lower. The flickering lights of a passenger train appear in the distance, moving deceptively quickly.

We should stop. We need to stop. But instead I hear myself saying: "Hurry. Gun it!"

The sedan slips under the gate at the last second. It rockets over the tracks, practically going airborne from the shock of hitting the metal at high speed. Andy swears loudly but bears down on the accelerator.

I try to calculate the distance to the other side of the tracks with respect to how fast the Rover and the train are traveling.

We're one hundred yards away.

The train whistle bleats.

Fifty yards.

We might make it.

Twenty yards.

The train roars. All I see is the white of its headlights.

Or we might die.

Metal screams on metal. Sparks shoot from the train's wheels as the engineer sees us coming and tries to slow down. It's too late. He'll never stop in time.

CHAPTER 17

Andy swears again, slamming on the brakes and screeching to a halt just in front of the gate. I jolt forward, the shoulder belt keeping me from hitting the windshield. I feel Jesse slam into the back of my seat. The train bleats angrily as it rushes past, its fluorescent headlights reflecting a ribbon of silver metal into the night.

"Damn it," I say.

"Sorry. No point in getting us killed." Andy glances over his shoulder at Jesse as he holsters the gun. "You good back there?"

"Fine," Jesse says. "Thanks for stopping. Winter might have a death wish, but I don't." He leans forward. "I don't suppose you got close enough to see the license plate?"

"I doubt it." I yank off my wig and press the STOP button on my headset.

Andy glances over at the pile of black waves splayed across my lap. "So you were actually recording the whole time?"

"Don't worry. I promise not to sell the footage of you," I tell him. I rewind and play the recording from the time we left Zoo onward. Unfortunately, I can't read the license plate's numbers.

By the time the train has passed in front of us and the black-and-white gate rises, the sedan is long gone.

"What now?" Andy asks.

"Home, I guess." As I lean back in the passenger seat, I try to figure out what came over me there for a second. Am I really so intent on avenging Rose that I would kill myself and two friends in the process? And if so, what does that make me? Determined? Obsessed? I bury my face in my hands.

"Are you okay?" Jesse reaches one hand forward to squeeze my shoulder. I nod violently without making eye contact. If I look at him, I know what I'll see. Sympathy. Empathy. Jesse knows what it's like to lose people. Jesse knows his way around this hell.

A fissure opens in my chest, rage and sorrow threatening to spill out and overwhelm me. I take in a deep breath and hold it until the crack stops widening. I can't lose control. Not here, with Andy. Not anywhere. Rose would tell me to stay strong—to fight it.

I lock the pain away and force myself to focus. Who is the man in the coat and fedora? Why was he following Rose? The answers swirl around but ultimately elude me, melting into the night like the snowflakes battering the car windows.

Back home, Andy drops Jesse and me off in front of the building. "Let me know if there's anything I can do," he says. "And call me and fill me in on what the cops say."

"I will," I say.

It's after one in the morning when Jesse and I head inside. Both Escape and the lobby bar are closed. The quiet mixed with the ornate surroundings is almost like being in a museum. Jesse and I head for the stairwell. As the door falls shut behind us, he squares his shoulders and lowers his voice in an imitation of Andy. "So yeah, let me know if there's anything I can do."

I snicker as we start climbing the stairs. "You don't have to be such an ass."

"I don't trust him. I saw you guys dancing together. He didn't exactly look like he was missing Rose too much."

"Don't be an idiot." Jesse's jealousy is sweet but I could never replace Rose in anyone's mind.

"We are who we are, you know?" he says with a grin. He stops on the seventh floor. "I'm going to shower and change really quick and then I'll be up."

"You don't have to stay with me if you don't want to."

Jesse touches the knuckles of his left hand to my cheek. "I want to."

I blink hard. "All right. See you soon."

He disappears into the hallway and I head toward the top floor, my progress slightly hindered by Rose's boots. *We are who we are.* I know Jesse was just kidding around, that he didn't mean the words seriously, but still, they fester inside of me. Rose always said we could be who we choose to be. That just because I was weak didn't mean I couldn't become strong. What's the point of living if people can't change?

I pause on the tenth floor to catch my breath. I hear a second set of footsteps, but I can't tell if they're coming from above or below me. I peer upward but I can't see anything in the dim stairwell lighting. I look down. "Jesse," I call. "Is that you?"

No response.

Shrugging, I continue toward the penthouse, but I'm unable to fight off the feeling that I'm not alone. I wish I had brought my throwing knives with me, but weapons aren't allowed inside Zoo. I pause midstep between the twelfth and thirteenth floor, listening closely for the sound of anyone else.

Nothing.

I exhale deeply and shake out my arms. I'm probably still caught up in the adrenaline of the night—the club, the car chase, the train that could've killed us. "Don't lose your mind, Winter," I mutter.

I push open the door to the top floor. The hallway is empty as usual. I punch in the key code for the penthouse and place my thumb on the sensor. The alarm system beeps and unlocks the door.

That's when I feel the barrel of a gun against my temple.

CHAPTER 18

For a second, I think about making a move, but that's a lot easier when I'm recording a ViSE and have had at least some time to prepare for things like this. "What do you want?" I ask calmly.

"Inside. Now," a man growls.

I don't recognize his voice, but I suspect he's distorting it on purpose. I let him push me inside the darkened penthouse. I start calculating how long it'll be before Jesse arrives.

Too long.

My chest goes tight as my brain starts to play through all the possible scenarios. Is this the guy who killed my sister? Is he planning on sending Gideon a recording of me too? My ViSE headset weighs heavy in the pocket of Rose's coat. I wish I hadn't quit recording back in the Range Rover.

"What do you want?" I repeat.

"I need all your ViSE stuff," he says. "I don't want to hurt you."

I nod slightly. I don't want to make any sudden movements in case he's got his finger on the trigger. I'm not giving him the recordings, but I need to get him to drop the gun somehow. Hand-to-hand I at least have a fighting chance. "It's in my room," I say slowly, a plan starting to formulate. "It's down the hall."

He jams the gun against the back of my head. "Let's go."

I head for my room. My throwing knives are on top of my dresser, but can I reach one without tipping off my assailant?

I hope so.

I have never stabbed anyone.

That's about to change.

I pause outside my bedroom, my breath whispering harshly in my ears. Resting my hand on the knob, I focus on the angle the door will swing in, on the precise location of my knives. I envision the exact movement I'll have to make to grab a knife, the whirling around, the strike of my arm, blade moving through the air to connect with the intruder's neck. No. I need to aim low—a nonlethal target. A muscle or tendon, just enough to incapacitate. I need to know exactly what happened to my sister.

I turn the knob and push the door inward. "It's right here on the dresser," I say. Without warning I drop low out of the gun's aim and lunge for the nearest knife. I make contact with the handle and spin around. The intruder is too close for me to throw. I flail in the darkness, praying the blade hits its mark before I get shot.

But Rose's coat limits my mobility and I end up missing him completely.

Shit. Plan B. I lunge for his gun, my free hand forcing the barrel up and away from me.

He lashes out with one of his feet, landing a solid hit to my left knee. A grunt of pain escapes my lips. My legs fold underneath me and I crumple to the floor in a heap. I try to roll out of the way but the guy steps on my hand, digging in the heel of his boot until I release my grip on the knife. He kicks it behind me and points his gun at my chest. My breath catches in my throat as I wait for him to shoot me point-blank.

But he doesn't.

His menacing silhouette towers over me. He's wearing all black and a face mask, just like the men in the ViSE. It could be the bigger man from the recording, but I can't tell for certain.

My kneecap feels like it's splintering into pieces. My eyes are trained on the gun, but I force myself to slowly widen my visual field, taking in more of my bedroom, looking for the best way to escape. I'm not giving up. I'm not giving him what he wants.

As if the assailant can read my thoughts, he backhands me across the face with his gun. My neck snaps painfully; my ribs hit the edge of my bed.

He bends low to me and suddenly it is the weight of his body and not his weapon that terrifies me. He wraps one hand around my neck and begins to squeeze. "Where is it?" he asks.

I feel the cold steel of metal against my temple again. I gag. He squeezes harder. The delicate structures of my throat begin to collapse under his force.

"I lied," I choke out. "I don't have anything here." Blackness is threading through my vision and I don't know if it's from lack of oxygen or fear or both. I try not to exhale, conserving the air in my lungs while I probe the carpet behind me with one hand, searching for my knife.

"Then where is it kept?" he asks.

"What are you actually looking for?" I rasp, hoping he'll give me more information. I let my body slump toward the floor. If I fake being weak and scared, maybe he'll relax his hold. Not that I have to fake the fear part. Terror is racing through my veins, my heartbeat galloping after it like a runaway horse.

"You know what I'm looking for." He hits me with the gun again, so hard that I taste blood.

I shake my head, do my best to look frightened. "Please don't hurt me," I whimper. Limply, I use one hand to try to break the hold he has around my neck. It's what he expects me to do. My other hand lies uselessly behind me.

Or so he thinks.

My fingers crawl slowly over the carpet in search of my knife. The darkness is expanding in my brain. My lungs are on fire. Rose and I might meet again soon.

"Why did you hurt my sister?" I ask. "What did you do to her?"

"I don't know shit about that little whore."

"She's not a—" His grip is too tight. I can't form the words. The air feels heavy around me, like water pressing down on my skull. The room begins to fade away.

I channel my rage to keep from passing out. How dare this man judge my sister. He doesn't know her. He doesn't know what we've been through, what we've survived.

The room is halfway gone.

Three-quarters gone.

My fingers locate the knife's hilt and something inside of me snaps. Gasping for breath, I swing the knife toward the intruder, no longer caring if I wound him or kill him outright.

But I'm too late.

Before the blade can find its target, the room dissolves completely. Darkness wraps around me and my body goes limp.

CHAPTER 19

The pounding wakes me. Faster. Harder. Relentless. It's like someone is building a house inside my brain. Groaning, I lift my fingertips to my temples.

My hands are wet.

Why are my hands wet?

Blinking slowly, I open my eyes. Blood. There's blood on my hands. Nausea overwhelms me. Trembling, I wipe my fingers violently on the fabric of Rose's coat.

The intruder! I leap to my feet, or at least try to. Too late I remember the kick to my knee. All I can do is wobble before crashing back to the ground. More pounding. I realize it's coming from the vicinity of the living room.

"Winter! Are you in there?" Jesse's voice, frantic but muffled. "Are you okay?"

I manage to turn over onto my hands and knees. Oh no. There's blood on the carpet. There's blood on Rose's dress. I peek down the front of it. My skin is intact. Hesitantly, I raise a hand and check for scalp wounds. Nothing.

It's not my blood.

What have I done?

Still more pounding. "Let me in," Jesse hollers.

"I'm coming." The words fall from my lips, weak and breathy, my throat sore inside and out.

Half walking, half crawling, I fight my way to the living room and open the door.

Jesse storms into the penthouse, his hair sticking up, his eyes wild. "Are you all right? It looks like there's blood in the hallway." His hands go immediately to my face. I wince as he finds a tender area. And then he sees my hands, my fingers still wet with someone else's blood. He pales. "Winter. What the hell happened?"

"It's not mine," I whisper. "Someone broke in. He jumped me right outside the door."

Jesse pulls a gun from the small of his back and shields me with his body. "Stay behind me," he orders. He quickly goes through the penthouse, checking each room for the intruder. When he gets to Rose's room, we both hear a scratching sound from the closet. Jesse lifts one finger to his lips. Brandishing his weapon, he yanks open the closet door. A ball of black and white fur tumbles out.

"Miso!" I say. "How did you get stuck in there?" The cat gives me a reproachful look before trotting off toward the living room. Jesse and I follow him. The whole apartment is silent now. I open the front door and peek out into the hallway. There are a few elongated drops of something red on the carpet, like someone was running away. "I think he's gone."

"I'm going to check the utility room and the roof, just in case," Jesse says.

I limp behind him as he uses the light on his phone to make sure no one is hiding in the little room that houses a smattering of cleaning supplies and various apartment fixtures. There are footsteps in the dust on the floor, but there's no way to know who they're from.

Jesse cuts between a chipped porcelain bathtub and an old washing machine and opens the window on the far wall. "I'll be right back."

"Be careful," I say.

He crawls out onto the roof and comes back a few minutes later. "No sign of anyone. No blood that I could see." We turn back toward the penthouse together.

Jesse bends down to consider the splotches of red on the carpet. "Gid is going to kill me. We should call the cops. If you hurt the guy badly, he might not have gotten far."

Did I stab him? I wanted to stab him, that's for certain, but I thought I passed out before I got a chance. "We should call Gideon first," I say. "He's working directly with a detective on the police force that he trusts." I punch in the security code and press my thumb to the sensor.

Jesse doesn't say anything until we're back inside the penthouse and the door is locked behind us. Then he pulls out his phone. "Fine. We'll call Gideon."

"I'm going to change clothes." I limp toward my room.

"Give me a minute and I'll help you. You look like you can barely walk." Jesse has his phone to his ear, waiting for Gideon to answer. After a few seconds, he frowns and slips it back into his pocket.

"At least someone is getting good sleep," I mumble. "We can try him again in the morning."

"I'll text him later." Jesse reaches out for me. "But are you sure you don't want to call 911? The guy might still be nearby. Or he might have gone to an ER for treatment of a stab wound."

I think again of the street cop Rose approached in L.A., of the way he pretended to be on our side and then used the information against us. "Detective Ehlers can access those records tomorrow."

"Okay," Jesse says. "But I'm not leaving you again. Come on. Let's get you cleaned up and then you can tell me exactly what happened." He supports me under the arm and I'm relieved to find I can bear weight on my left side now.

I lead him into my bedroom where he flips on the light. Miso is curled up at the foot of my bed, sleeping peacefully as if nothing happened. If only that were true. There are streaks of blood in the center of my beige carpet. As I pull open my dresser drawer to get new clothes, I catch a glimpse of my reflection in the mirror. A triangular bruise is spreading across the left side of my face and there's a small cut above my eyebrow.

Jesse lifts my throwing knife from the carpet. The black blade is soiled with blood. "Where did you stab him?"

"I don't know," I say. Immediately I wish I could take back the words. I can't tell Jesse I don't remember stabbing the guy. Who stabs someone and forgets? This is another reason I don't want to talk to the police tonight. My story sounds crazy.

"What did you say?" Jesse fiddles with his hearing aid. It whistles sharply and then goes silent.

"Um, I'm not sure. He was strangling me and I couldn't really see. I just flailed out with my arm and hoped for the best."

"And then what?"

"He ran off," I say. "And then I guess I passed out."

Jesse bends down and touches the blood on the carpet with one finger. It comes back smudged with maroon. "It's not a lot of blood," he says. "Are you sure it's not yours?"

"You think I imagined all this?" I ask. "And that I cut myself and went outside and bled in the hallway?" *Promise me you will never cut yourself again.* I would never break a promise to my sister.

He shakes his head quickly. "Of course not. But Gideon told me you sleepwalk sometimes and I know how dreams can seem a little too real." He touches the cut above my eyebrow, his fingers making their way through my dark hair, looking for other injuries. I spy the grip of the intruder's gun under the edge of my bed. I reach down and grab it, keeping the barrel pointed at the floor. "This real?"

Jesse's eyes widen. "Where did you get that?"

"The guy left it behind."

"Let me see it."

I give Jesse the gun. Holding it in the fabric of his T-shirt, he flips it around so he can look at the handle. "The serial number's been filed off."

"What does that mean?"

"It means we can't trace the owner. Was he wearing gloves?"

"I think so."

"So the only fingerprints on this gun are yours." Jesse wipes it clean on his shirt. "Did he say anything to you? Did you get a good look at him? Would you recognize his voice?" His jaw goes tense as he waits for my reply to his barrage of questions.

"He said he wanted all of the ViSE stuff. He had a mask on. I don't know if I would recognize his voice. It didn't sound familiar to me."

Jesse frowns. He slips the gun into the pocket of his sweatpants.

"Can I keep that?" I ask.

"The gun? Gideon is not going to—"

I massage my knee with one hand. "Why does he even have to know? I'm eighteen, Jesse."

"Which is not old enough to legally own a gun."

"So? You were shooting at people before you were legally old enough to own a gun."

"It's different in the military. It's regulated."

"But what if the guy comes back? I could use it to protect myself."

"You shouldn't have to protect yourself," Jesse says. "Let's get that blood off you and then I'll stay up and keep watch so you can get some sleep."

The blood—right. It's drying on my skin, becoming a part of me. With the clean clothes still clutched in my hands, I limp toward the bathroom.

Jesse waits in the hallway while I trade the bloody dress and Rose's leggings for a pair of sweatpants and a T-shirt. Then I hold the blade of my knife under the gushing tap until the water runs clear. Finally, I splash water on my face and scrub my hands until I manage to get all of the blood out of the tiny grooves of my fingertips.

Jesse knocks on the door. "Everything okay in there?"

"Almost finished." I dry my fingers on the hand towel and then grab my knife and head into the living room. Jesse trails behind me. Flopping down on the sofa, he grabs the remote and flips on the TV.

I place my clean knife on the coffee table and lower myself to the cushion. I try to extend my left leg, wincing in pain as my knee struggles to lock in place. "He kicked me in the knee," I grumble.

Jesse kneels in front of me and takes my leg in his hands, bracing his fingertips on either side of my knee joint. Behind him, the Discovery Channel is playing a show all about the primates of Madagascar. "Extend," he says.

I raise my leg as high as I can.

"Good. Back down." I lower my foot to the floor, comforted by the pressure of Jesse's hands. He gently manipulates my knee in different directions, taking note of when I wince. "I don't think anything is torn or broken," he says. "But I can take you to the ER if you want."

I shake my head. "I don't like doctors. They'll take one look at my bruises and think I'm an abuse victim. They'll end up calling the cops or social services."

"So big deal. Just explain to the cops and social workers that you're a martial arts badass and you always look like this," Jesse strokes my bruised cheek.

"I'd rather not," I say. "Gideon was right. No cops, except for Detective Ehlers."

"Are you secretly on the FBI's Most Wanted List or something?"

"I'm an illegal alien," I admit, staring straight ahead at the TV. "If anyone goes snooping through my papers, I could get deported and Gideon might get in trouble too."

"Oh shit, Winter. I didn't know that." Jesse rubs at his chin. "Not that it would help right this minute, but have you thought about applying for a legit visa?"

"It's complicated," I say, staring straight ahead at the TV. "Winter Kim isn't even my real name." It's probably not that complicated, but I haven't thought about it, because doing it would mean going back to being the girl I used to be, at least temporarily.

I watch as a lemur jumps from tree to tree. So free. So weightless.

I don't want to go back to being that girl, not even for a minute.

I need for her to stay dead.

CHAPTER 20

Jesse props my injured leg up on the coffee table. He goes to the kitchen and returns a couple of minutes later with a Ziploc bag full of ice. He rests the ice pack on my knee and then sits next to me. Cocking his head to the side, he gives me a long look.

Too long.

"What?" I say sharply.

"I was just wondering what your real name is."

"Ha Neul," I say. "Ha Neul Song. Or how we say in Korea—Song Ha Neul."

"Song Ha Neul," Jesse repeats. My name rolls off his tongue like something pleasing that he's tasting for the first time. "That's perfect."

"Why?"

"Because it sounds both pretty and badass."

I look down at my knee and fidget with the ice pack so he won't see my blush. "I can't believe we're sitting here talking about my name when I just stabbed someone."

"Would you rather talk about that?"

I shrug. "It's strange to think about. This is the first time I've really hurt someone. All that training with Gideon, but I've never done worse than use the stun gun."

"Which hurts," Jesse points out. "And you've knocked me around in Krav Maga pretty good."

"It's not the same as cutting a person."

"What did it feel like to stab the guy?" he asks.

I feel sick just thinking about it, and then more sick because I don't remember doing it. What if this isn't the first time? What other horrible things might I have pushed into the holes of my eroding memory?

Jesse winces at the stricken look on my face. "Sorry. Inappropriate question."

I elbow him in the ribs. "Morbid, anyway."

"Yeah. I guess." His turn to stare straight at the TV. Something called an aye-aye looks out from a dark tree with a pair of glowing eyes. It looks more like a cartoon character than a real animal.

"Did you ever hurt anybody in the army?" I ask.

"I never got a chance." He looks down at his wrist, at the ring of letters inked there.

I think back to our conversation in the bathroom and realize his tattoo is a list of initials, memorials to fallen comrades. "Jesse . . ." Our eyes meet, and a channel of pain opens wide. For a moment, I want to spill everything out right there onto the living room sofa. Every hurt. Every horrible memory. I want him to know he's not alone.

"I wanted to go back, you know? But they medically discharged me because they said I couldn't serve in combat zones anymore," Jesse says. "I hear fine with the hearing aid, but I'm not fit for missions because it could malfunction. The same goes for my cornea transplant. I have to be extra careful not to injure my eye, and there's always a chance I'll reject the graft and lose part of my sight."

"Do you really miss it that much?"

"Yeah. I mean, most days were pretty boring, but the work felt meaningful. I wish I had made at least one arrest or intercepted some explosives or something. Maybe then it would be easier to face my parents. They think I'm just some dumb kid who was brainwashed by the promise of machine guns and adventures."

"What does it feel like?" I ask. "Shooting a gun." Gideon started training me in martial arts when I was sixteen. I have studied Aikido, Taekwondo, Kendo, and Krav Maga. I've learned to fight with a staff and a bamboo sword, but Gideon has never been allowed anywhere near a gun. And for me, forbidden is usually synonymous with desired.

"It's a powerful feeling, knowing you can incapacitate someone with the pull of a trigger. The actual gun going off is a mix of jarring and exhilarating," Jesse says. "I can make a ViSE for you next time I go to the range if you want to know what it feels like for me."

"You'd do that for me?"

"Sure." Tugging his sleeve down over his hand, Jesse picks up the intruder's gun and looks thoughtfully at it. Then he sets it on the floor and pulls his own gun from beneath his shirt. It's black, blunt nosed, a lot like the Phantasm security guard's weapon. Jesse flips a lever on it and ejects the magazine. Popping out one of the small, shiny bullets, he says, "They don't look like much, but they can do a lot of damage."

I twirl the bullet around in my fingers, thinking about what it would feel like tearing through flesh at high velocity.

"People say it feels like getting hit by a sledgehammer," he says.

I take the clip from Jesse's hand and fumble the bullet back into it. I gesture at the gun he's still holding. "Show me how it works."

"Winter," he warns.

"I'm not going to go buy one on the street," I say. "I'm just curious. I mean, this is twice now in two days someone's pointed a gun at me. It makes sense for me to know how to use one. Knowledge is power, right?"

Jesse frowns but hands the gun to me, being sure to keep

the barrel pointed away from us. He shows me how to hold it, how to flip the safety on and off, how to extract the clip. I practice a few times until the gun feels less scary. I imagine myself at a gun range, like on TV, like when the detective's girlfriend hits the center circle with every shot and then smiles mysteriously before crediting her skill to video games. Gideon would never let me have a gun, but somehow just holding one makes it seem like less of a big deal.

I return the gun to Jesse and he slips it back into his waistband. For a while neither of us says anything. A sweet kind of drowsiness settles over me as I rest my head against Jesse's shoulder. I could fall asleep like this.

But then he nudges me. "So, I showed you mine. You going to show me yours?"

"My what?" At first I think he's talking about my weapon. There's not a lot of demonstration involved with a knife.

"Your tragic history, Ms. Kim. Or should I say Ms. Song?"

Talk about ruining the moment. I scoot away from him on the sofa, pulling my legs up between us as a barrier, wincing as I flex my injured knee. "What makes you think I have a—"

Jesse rolls his eyes. "Because Gideon collects shattered youth, right? It's a solid hiring strategy."

"Not just youth," I murmur. Adebayo is close to fifty and Baz is probably at least a few years older than Gideon.

"I'm sure the desperate and downtrodden make faithful employees," Jesse continues. "What was it with you? Drugs? Gambling? Prostitution?" At my look he continues. "Oh, come on. Don't get offended. The way you act around men sometimes—"

"How exactly do I act around men?" My hands curl into fists.

Jesse glances down at my white knuckles. "Like you want to beat the shit out of them, even the ones who care about you . . . like me. Like you find us all repulsive."

"I don't find you *that* repulsive." I try to joke my way out of the question, but all Jesse does is tilt his head to the side and let out an exasperated sigh. I pick up my throwing knife and consider its blade. "You don't know anything about me."

"Which is why I'm asking," he says. "I *want* to know more. The past is the past. Why does it have to be a secret?"

I twirl the hilt of the knife between my palms. "It's a hard thing for a girl to talk about. Maybe I don't want you to think less of me."

Jesse reaches for the knife in my hands. He sets it on the table and then twines his fingers in mine. "You don't have to tell me anything if you don't want, but nothing you say would make me think less of you. I don't give a shit about the person you used to be, except she can't have been all that bad or I probably wouldn't like you so much now."

"What if you're wrong?"

"I'm not," Jesse says. "Besides, look at me. I went into the army thinking I was going to kill me some bad guys, be a big shot, prove to everyone I was someone who mattered. And I came home a year later, used up, spent, with the initials of four guys who died because of me inked onto my arm. The government doesn't even think I'm good enough to be cannon fodder. Who am I to judge?"

Used up. Spent. Words I know well.

Maybe it's because he already seems to know half the story anyway, or maybe after the day I've had, I just don't have the energy to build any more walls. Whatever it is, it gets me talking. "Rose and I grew up in an orphanage in Seoul. When I was twelve and she was fourteen, we learned we were going to be adopted by Americans." I pause. "Adoption doesn't happen much in Korea. Bloodlines are too important and no one wants to raise someone else's child. Even being adopted by foreigners seemed odd for girls our age. Usually people want tiny babies. But the staff told us we were going to a Korean-American family who had lost their teenage daughters in a car accident. Rose had forced me to study English from the time

I learned to read, insisting that we'd have more opportunities as bilinguals. I remember thinking how that moment proved her right. We were so excited about coming to the States. Only when we got here, the adoption turned out to be fake. Our adoptive parents immediately turned us over to a businessman named Kyung."

"Kyung." Jesse stretches the word out to two syllables—key young. "He dealt in girls?"

"Among other things. I think we were just a hobby for him, a way to keep his clients and staff happy," I say bitterly. "We should have tried to run away. We talked about it a couple of times. But there were two other girls. They told us stories about how runaways ended up in gangs—branded, beaten, addicted to drugs. They made it sound like working for Kyung wasn't that terrible compared to the alternatives. And with no money and no papers, in a strange place, I guess we let ourselves believe it." I stare down at my lap. "And then with each passing day, running away just felt like more of a dream, not something that could actually happen. Eventually Gideon came along and fell in love with my sister. He got us out. He saved us."

Jesse reaches out and turns my head so I'm forced to meet his gaze. I never knew eyes could hold so much pity.

"Don't look at me like that," I snap. "I'm fine. Rose and I got through it together. She took the brunt of it. Men always seemed to prefer her."

"So that's why you're afraid to be touched, and she seemed to crave it? Just different ways to deal with the same shit?"

"I'm not *afraid* to be touched. I just don't like it. And Rose, I think for her it's about taking back control." I swallow hard. "Or it was, anyway."

Jesse nods. "Well, that's a horrible story and I wish it hadn't happened to you, but I'm glad you told me. It explains why you're kind of—" He pauses, searching for the right word.

"Cold?" I suggest.

"Guarded," he says softly.

The primate special ends and a show about snipers replaces it. As the men don complex disguises laced with actual vegetation, I jump at the chance to change the subject. "They always say combat changes people, makes things less black and white. Did it change you?"

"Nothing has ever been black and white to me," Jesse says. "I'm more of an 'ends justify the means' kind of guy."

"So right and wrong are fluid? Dependent upon the outcome?"

"Basically."

"So you would do something terrible to get something you really wanted?"

Jesse's jaw goes tight. "I have done terrible things."

"Like what?"

He doesn't answer for a few seconds. Then he shakes his head. "Forget it. Too much depressing conversation for one night." He pats his leg. "You should get some sleep. I make an excellent pillow."

I'm curious, but I don't want to force him to talk. I know what that feels like. Frowning at his muscular thigh, I ask, "But aren't you tired too?"

"We'll do it like I did in the desert. Take turns. I get first watch. I'll wake you in a couple of hours."

"All right." My whole body feels heavy as I arrange myself on the sofa. I opt for a throw pillow instead of Jesse's leg, but he scoots close enough to me that when I twist onto my side, his arm rests gently on my shoulder, an overlapping triangle of heat connecting us. For at least ten minutes, my brain does nothing except concentrate on the warmth, extending it outward, toying with the idea of what it would feel like to fall asleep in Jesse's arms.

And then, just as I decide I might like that someday, I think back to our conversation.

I wonder what kinds of terrible things Jesse has done.

CHAPTER 21

Sleep drags me once again into a tangle of dreams. Hallways stretch out interminably long and mazelike. Rows of closed doors mock me, whispering *choose choose choose*, as if all but one lead straight into hell. My footsteps echo in my brain. My breath spikes in and out of my chest. I am not alone in the maze of hallways. I am running from someone.

Or something.

Winter. Rose's voice in my head.

"Eonni," I whisper. "I need you."

I'm here.

There is grunting and snarling from around the next corner. A creature that is half man and half beast appears in the corridor. It wears the head of the one-eyed man. I stop. Turn, double back. Just when I feel like I am safe, the creature appears in front of me, only now it wears Gideon's head. I retreat again, and it wears Jesse's head. Andy's head.

My head.

There is no escape. I am a human sacrifice in the Minotaur's lair. The doors fall away, all except two.

Choose.

"But how do I know which one?" Both doors look exactly the same.

Fingers to fingers and thumb to thumb.

"I don't understand."

There's no time to figure out what Rose means. I plunge through the nearest door. There is nothing but black space on the other side. I fall faster and faster. Air whistles by, soft, then sharper. From somewhere, the one-eyed man laughs.

And then I hear something else—Jesse's voice calling my name.

I open my eyes and see the purple-gray of morning filtering through the blinds. I'm in Rose's room—the floor hard beneath me.

I sit up sharply, the folds of her comforter falling away. She is everywhere, too close. Her rose pendant hangs heavy around my neck; her clothes and magazines are still piled at the end of her bed.

"Hey." Jesse is peering at me through the partially open door. "Why are you sleeping on the floor?"

I ignore his question. I don't feel like explaining the customs of my childhood or my apparent psychological regression to him. "Why would you put me in here?"

He yawns. "I didn't. I dozed off and just woke up. I was looking for you."

A sharp pain shoots through my chest. "I came in here by myself? Sleepwalking?"

"I guess." He shrugs. "Maybe I was suffocating you on the couch and you came in here because of the blood in your room."

"Maybe." It's been a while since I've sleepwalked. I thought it was something else I had outgrown. I thought I was normal. Healed.

Now I'm starting to wonder.

I should probably make an appointment with Dr. Abrams. It was silly of me to stop going to therapy, but it had started to feel redundant—the same questions, the same answers. I felt stable. I was acing my classes, doing well at my job, and even starting to make friends . . . if Jesse counts as a friend. I figured I'd go back when I ran out of sedatives or if I felt like I *needed* to go.

Maybe I need to go.

The panic must be written all over my face, because Jesse slides through the open doorway and sits down on the floor next to me. He touches the back of his hand to my face like he's checking for a fever. "You're probably still shaken up from last night."

With one finger, I reach up and trace the dark circles under his eyes. "You said you'd wake me to take a turn keeping watch," I say accusingly. "So you could sleep too."

"I lied."

I massage the side of my cheek that's been pressed into the pillow. My eyes feel like they're full of sand. I hear a sharp, snarling sound as I rub them—it's coming from the TV in the living room.

I arch an eyebrow. "You watched that channel all night?"

"I watched your apartment all night," Jesse says. "I got a hold of Gideon a couple hours ago. Needless to say, he's freaking out. You're supposed to call him as soon as you wake up."

I groan. "I think I'm going to pretend I slept for another hour or two."

Jesse swallows back a yawn. "Better yet, let's not pretend. I could use more sleep. I feel kind of delirious."

I flinch at the word. It's too close to *delusional*. "Go ahead. I don't think anyone is going to try to break in now that it's daylight."

"Cool. Just give me about an hour to recharge my batteries."

"Of course." I wish I could recharge *my* batteries in an hour.

Jesse returns to the living room and stretches out on the sofa. I head to the bathroom, splash some water on my face, tame down my hair, and go to the kitchen to brew myself a cup of tea. I dice some ginger and lemongrass and add it to loose green leaves. Before the water even begins to boil, I can hear

Jesse's even snoring. I glance over and smile to myself. There's something innocent and peaceful about a person lost in sleep, even someone with a dark history and an unconventional sense of morality.

Maybe Jesse doesn't know himself as well as he thinks. If he didn't care about right and wrong, he'd be getting rich by stealing or selling drugs instead of working as a recorder for Gideon. War does things to people, just as my old life did things to me, but that doesn't mean you can't overcome them. *We are who we are.* I prefer to think as Rose did. *We choose who we become.*

When the tea is ready, I pour myself a mug and stand in the doorway to the living room, watching Jesse's chest rise and fall. Then I slip into my bedroom and grab the comforter from my bed, carefully skirting the bloodstain on the carpet on my way in and out.

Jesse stirs as I drape the blanket over him, but he doesn't open his eyes. Rolling onto his side, he exhales deeply and tunnels into the folds of fabric. He twitches, his lips forming silent words. I wonder if he's dreaming, if he's haunted by his own one-eyed man.

I return to the kitchen and grab my tablet. I check again for any news of a body in the river and then work through a few homework problems for my calculus class. As I finish my tea, the sun rises full and hot. The morning brings a Zen-like sense of security. Like I said, no one will try to break into the penthouse in broad daylight. And if they do, Jesse and I will take care of them.

Ducking back into my room, I grab my notebook and the music box full of Rose's ViSEs from my locked cabinet. I add the ViSE from the Phantasm break-in and the overdose recording in with the others, just so none of them get misplaced. Then I sit cross-legged on my floor, a safe distance from the spots of blood, my back up against the wall. I place two of my throwing knives within easy reach.

Grabbing my headset, I prepare to insert the next ViSE. Last night's memory card from Zoo is still in there. Maybe I should play that recording again, just to make sure nothing jumps out at me now that I've slept.

I slip on the headset and press PLAY. I fast-forward through our arrival to the club, pausing long enough to hear Jesse tell me I'm pretty. Everything plays out just as I remember until he exits the cage.

He makes his way around the gyrating dancers. The lights overhead change their pattern and the room grows darker. Half of Jesse's face is bathed in blackness. My heart thrums in my chest. Then Jesse steps out of the circling black lights.

I remember how distorted Jesse's form had looked last night. Now it's easy to understand why he looked like the one-eyed man for a moment. It was just because the club had changed the lighting.

I play the ViSE to the point where we're leaving the club, focusing on the car in the parking lot and on the street, but the license plate is just a blur. I give up and trade the memory card for another one of Rose's recordings.

I'm sitting at a blackjack table in Riverlights Hotel and Casino, sliding forward a stack of chips. The music playing over the loudspeaker is being drowned out by the beeping and chiming of a bank of nearby slot machines. The dealer flashes me a sharp smile and then deals me a pair of face cards—I win. Adrenaline surges through me as the dealer doubles my chips. I bet big again. I win a few more hands and a crowd starts to form behind the table. The guy sitting next to me gives me an appraising look. "What's your secret?"

I grin. "I guess I'm just getting lucky tonight."

The guy's gaze drifts below my neckline. "What about me? Do you think I have a shot at getting lucky tonight?"

"Probably not." I use my index fingers to pull my lips down into a sad face.

"Didn't think so." He gets up and leaves.

Another guy sits down—Andy Lynch. "What about me?" he asks. He gives me a boyish smile.

"Maybe." I run my fingertips up his arm. "Give your luck a try."

Andy starts betting and wins a couple hands. He increases his wagers to equal mine, but I'm having better luck. He stays on an eighteen. Dealer has nineteen. I have twenty-one. He hits on a sixteen and busts. Dealer busts. Blackjack for me again.

Gideon must have paid off the pit boss so Rose could amass a string of impressive wins. Even she wouldn't try to record in a casino without permission, especially considering she must have used fake ID to get in.

"How about you just give me your phone number?" Andy says, slurring his words slightly. "You can be my proxy. I'll wire you over a few grand next time you're coming here."

I lick my lips. "What fun would that be? Maybe I like to watch you suffer." I gather all of my chips into an impressive pile, scoop them into my purse, and then get up from the table.

"At least tell me your name," Andy calls after me. "I'll save up my suffering for you."

"Figure it out," I say.

I try to dissect the tone of Rose's voice. Is she bored? Flirting? Seriously interested? Normally I can read my sister, but not this time.

I sidle across the room to the roulette wheel and put a thousand dollars' worth of chips on red-7. People murmur—a mix of concern and admiration. The wheel spins. The ball bounces. Around me, everyone leans in eagerly to watch. The ball stops on red-7. I just won thirty-five thousand dollars.

The ViSE ends. It had to be a setup. Rose would have told me if she won thirty-five thousand dollars at roulette. I would have noticed her coming home with two hundred new pairs of shoes. Maybe Gideon is doing gambling ViSEs as a sort of advertisement for the casino. Maybe they think that once you've tasted the thrill of victory, you'll be likely to come back for more.

The next two recordings are Rose singing at an open-mic night and Rose in the front row of a pop concert. Interesting, but nothing suspicious. No man in gray leather.

I update my list. So far it reads:

#1: NYE fashion show—Gideon
#2: Zoo dancing—Natalie, man in gray coat
#3: Bungee jump—Gideon
#4: Knife thrower—Man in gray coat
#5: Blackjack—Andy Lynch
#6: Open mic
#7: Front row concert

Seven ViSEs down, another twelve to go. I creep over to my doorway and peek out at the sofa. Jesse is still curled on his side, my comforter pulled halfway over his head. I take a few big breaths, shake out my arms and legs, and grab the next ViSE from the music box.

I'm standing on the porch of a three-story house with a gabled roof. I knock. The front door opens. Andy Lynch steps out onto the porch, his eyes locked onto mine. "I'm glad you came," he says.

I open my eyes for a second and debate stopping the recording. It's a little creepy eavesdropping on Rose and Andy now that I know they were dating, but Jesse's right—I shouldn't trust Andy just because he seems like a nice guy. He might know more about what happened to Rose than he's letting on. Pressure starts to build at my temples and I quickly close my eyes again.

"Nice place," I say.

"My parents' house," he says. "They're in Hawaii for a couple of weeks."

Andy is wearing an NFL jersey with a long-sleeved shirt underneath. He looks down at the porch and then back up at me, a small smile playing at his lips. I can smell the alcohol on him from a foot away.

Watching Andy highlights how limited ViSEs actually are. The recordings share only sensory impulses, not actual thoughts. This might seem like a drawback, but considering that my usual thought process during a ViSE is anything from *Did I forget to feed Miso?* to *I sure hope this recording turns out well*, it's obvious having access to a recorder's actual thoughts would be problematic.

If Rose was afraid of Andy, I might feel her muscles tense or her pulse accelerate. If she was really into him, I might feel butterflies in her stomach or arousal. But all I'm feeling is the nausea beginning to creep up on me since I'm not concentrating.

Pausing the ViSE, I take another quick look around to make sure the penthouse is secure and Jesse is still asleep. Then I return to my room, lie back on my bed, and try my best to relax every single muscle in my body. My fingers, my face, even the muscles of my eyes. The more I empty myself, the more Rose will seep in.

Andy turns back toward the door. A dog barks. He swears under his breath. "Someone let Touchdown out of the basement. Let's go around the side."

I follow him across the snowy yard. Music and laughter float over a wooden privacy fence. We pass through the gate into a backyard full of athletic college guys and pretty girls. They're split roughly into three groups—crowded into the hot tub, tossing a football back and forth along the back fence, and clustered around a giant fire pit in the center of the yard.

Andy finds a spot for both of us near the fire but then promptly gets called away by a couple of his friends. I watch the tongues of flame dance in the air as I wait for him to return. Tapping one foot, I dodge the wayward sparks that rocket out from the blackening wood. Across the dimly lit yard, Andy is gesturing with his whole body as he converses with his friends.

Sighing, I relocate myself to the deck, where there are eight people crammed into the hot tub.

"Come on in," a guy yells. "Always room for one more." I give Andy one last look and then unbutton my coat and drape it over the deck's railing. Hurriedly, I slip out of my heels, shimmy my dress up over my head, and slide into the hot tub in my bra and underwear. I shudder as my cold skin hits the bubbling water.

The guy who coaxed me in scoots close, his breath reeking of beer and tortilla chips. I slide just far enough away from him so that our hips aren't touching.

Andy catches my eye from across the yard. He heads toward the deck but then stops just short of the wooden steps to talk to a muscular older man who looks out of place.

It's the guy I saw him with in the lobby—the one I figured was a coach. This is probably the party Andy mentioned that Rose went to a few days ago. I can tell it's recent from the snow on the ground.

My lips turn downward and I let the guy next to me press his leg against my own. I look up at the stars and can just barely see the outline of wispy clouds, gray against the black sky. Someone passes me a bottle of whiskey and I take a long swig, and then another. The liquor burns my throat, but it warms the skin of my face and neck.

The mix of smoke and alcohol makes the backyard hazy, but I see movement in the yard next door. The silhouette of a man.

It could be just the neighbor making sure they're not burning down the neighborhood, but he's roughly the same size as the guy from the circus ViSE, and it looks like he's wearing a fedora. I try to follow his movement, but Rose has other ideas.

Andy gestures toward me. I stand up in the hot tub and immediately start to shiver. Andy breaks away from the guy on the steps and wraps me in a towel as I slide gracefully over the hot tub's side. I slip back into my heels and grab my coat and dress from the railing. Together Andy and I head in the back door.

"Come on." He nuzzles the place where my neck meets my shoulder. Chills race down my spine as he tugs me up the stairs to the third floor.

His room looks like the typical frat boy hangout, complete with inflatable Bud Light furniture and empty pizza boxes stacked in one corner. He wraps his arms around me and pulls me close. I smell hard liquor on his breath.

With almost no warning I get to find out Andy is a really good kisser. I've never played a kissing ViSE before and not being able to pull away is weird. I feel a little dirty doing this, but it's all in the name of finding my sister's killers. And it's not real. The visual of Andy fades away as Rose shuts her eyes, amplifying all of the other sensations.

The feel of his arms around my back. My racing heart. The sensation of floating as he lifts me off the ground and lays me gently on his bed. I kick off my shoes. His lips find mine again. Sweet yet urgent. His hands slip beneath my towel.

Trembling, I reach up to fast-forward again. But then:

His phone rings. I open my eyes.

A sigh. He rolls over and checks the display. "I have to take this."

"But all you've done so far tonight is ignore me," I protest. I gather the towel around me.

"I'm sorry, Rose. Just give me five minutes." He pulls away and leaves me on the bed. I crawl beneath the covers, my heart still pounding with desire. The clock ticks upward. One minute. Two minutes. Five. Ten. Andy paces in the hallway, speaking in tones too soft for me to hear.

I feel lines forming on my forehead. Sitting up, I reach down and pluck my dress from the floor. I tug it over my head. Grabbing my coat and my shoes, I head for the doorway.

"Wait." Andy follows me downstairs, but he's still got the phone to his ear. "Don't leave."

"I'm done being ignored," I snap. I am out the front door. The freezing cold energizes me. I am walking at a fast clip toward the front of the neighborhood. And then I see a shadow of someone crossing behind me. I stop. Turn. My eyes study the manicured lawns.

"Rose, please," Andy hollers. He hurries toward me.

I force myself to concentrate on the periphery of my vision. The moonlight illuminates the silhouette of a man hiding in the bushes. He's got his head ducked low, but then he turns at the sound of Andy yelling, and I catch a glimpse of his face.

It's Baz, Gideon's head of security.

CHAPTER 22

"What are you doing?" Jesse taps me on the shoulder.

I open my eyes. Immediately my bedroom overlays on Andy Lynch's neighborhood, and a burst of nausea assaults me. I pause the recording and curl onto my side, slowly breathing in and out through my nose until the urge to vomit dissipates.

"I thought you never vised," Jesse says.

After our talk last night, I can't bring myself to lie to him. "I'm playing my sister's recordings."

He kneels down and brushes my hair back from my face. "Are you going to throw up?" He reaches out and grabs a small trash can from the corner of my room.

I shake my head slowly. "I just need a minute."

"Where did you get Rose's ViSEs?" he asks.

"I found the originals in her room." I sit up slowly and show Jesse the heart-shaped music box.

He paws through the memory cards. "How many are there? Is this all of them?"

"There's nineteen, but that doesn't seem like very many. Maybe she only recently started saving them."

"How many have you played?" Jesse's fingers skim across the memory cards again.

"Eight. It's slow going for me." I show him my notebook. "Even when I try my best, the overlay still makes me sick."

"You should give them to Gid. Let him and Baz go through them for clues."

"I will," I say. "After I finish playing them. No one knew Rose better than me. I might be able to pick out things no one else can."

Jesse nods to himself as he consults my list. "Can I help? I could play some of them for you. Maybe the ones that would make you . . . uncomfortable?"

"Sure." I have no desire to experience my sister grinding up against drunk frat boys on the dance floor or making out with total strangers at switch parties. "Look at this," I say, removing my headset and handing it to Jesse. He loosens it slightly and then slips it over his ears. "Just start from where I paused it. You see the guy in the bushes?"

Jesse leans back against the wall, closes his eyes, and plays a few seconds of the ViSE. "It looks like Baz."

"It does. I think he's the guy in the hat and coat I've seen on three of Rose's ViSEs now. Pretty sure that was him at Zoo last night too."

Jesse pauses the recording and opens his eyes. "You know we could've gotten killed, right? You scared me a little."

"I scared myself a little. I'm not sure what came over me."

Jesse closes his eyes and fidgets with the headset again, his mouth scrunching up in a frown. "But why would Baz run from us? Why would he be following us in the first place?"

"No idea." I hop to my feet and start pacing back and forth across my room. "What reason would he have to hurt Rose? They barely even knew each other."

"Should I play this from the beginning?"

I flush. "Not unless you want to hook up with Andy Lynch."

Jesse snickers. "Maybe before he went all choke in the national championship." He gives the headset back to me and I add the ViSE to my list. *Backyard party—Andy Lynch—last week?* Jesse arches an eyebrow at me as I label the memory card with a number 8. "Did *you* play the whole thing?" he asks.

"How far do things go with Superchoke? I bet someone would pay for that action."

"Quit being an ass." I ignore the questions as I snap the lid to the music box closed and lock it in my cabinet. "Forget Andy. Do you think Baz could really be involved with what happened to Rose? I need to go talk to him."

"We should wait and talk to Gideon first."

I glance at the time on my phone. "Gideon is probably in a meeting."

"Yeah, but Baz might be dangerous, Winter. You heard the way he talked about not involving the cops. I wouldn't mess with him."

"Gideon trusts Baz and I trust Gideon. There has to be an explanation. I'm going to go talk to him, with or without you."

"Okay. Give me five minutes and I'll be ready." Jesse ducks into the bathroom, emerging a few minutes later smelling suspiciously like my deodorant. He looks thoughtful as he rubs the beginnings of a beard. "I'll come back and help you with the rest of the ViSEs later, if you want. That way we can play them all and the overlay won't get you as much."

"All right." Jesse knows I have them now, so there's no point in refusing his help. Plus, there's no guarantee I'll find the answers I want, but there's a high probability I'll end up seeing things I don't want to see. I don't want my last thoughts of my sister to be of some guy disrespecting her.

"What are you going to say to Baz?" Jesse asks.

"Oh, probably something like 'Why the hell were you following my sister?' "

"I'm sure that'll go over well."

It actually goes over better than Jesse imagined. Baz is sitting at an out-of-use gaming table when we arrive at Escape. His head is bent over a screen.

Adebayo is behind the bar with a clipboard, doing what appears to be inventory. The main room of the club is empty except for a smattering of die-hard gamers. Up on the platforms, a group of kids are playing Rock Wars, two of them fighting over who gets to be the drummer. A couple of tables over from Baz, a group of Korean college kids in headset microphones are hunched over their laptops, playing some kind of role-playing game.

I slide into the chair next to Baz. I'm not going to tell him I saw him in one of Rose's ViSEs. He's one more person who will try to confiscate them. I peek over his shoulder. He seems to be reviewing security footage on his tablet.

Jesse stands behind my chair, his fingers curling around the edges of it protectively.

Baz hits a button and his tablet goes blank. He looks up, the dark circles under his eyes more pronounced than usual. "Was there something you needed, Winter?"

"I know you were following Rose," I blurt out. "Why?"

"Following Rose? Why would you think that?"

"Someone told me," I say.

Baz slips the tablet into a black leather sheath. "Fine. It's no big secret." He lowers his voice slightly. "Gideon asked me to keep an eye on her."

"Why?" I ask again.

Behind me, Jesse says nothing, but his hands move from my chair to my shoulders. I'm not sure if the motion is meant to be comforting or restraining.

"Because he was worried about her," Baz says. "Why do you think? She was a hot single girl running around the Lofts by herself. Not to mention she'd been acting reckless."

My sister was always kind of strong willed, but I never viewed her as reckless. Probably because I never saw anyone willing to stand in the way of her doing whatever she wanted. "How long were you following her? Did you ever see her with a boyfriend?"

Baz folds his hands carefully and rests them on the table. "A few weeks. As I'm sure you know, I saw her with different men."

A few weeks? Gideon said he got a threatening phone call a couple of *days* ago. "Why so long?"

"I don't know. I don't get paid to ask questions." He stares at me. "You're not supposed to be asking questions either, are you?"

I ignore his warning. "Was there one guy who stood out more than the others? A guy she actually seemed to like, who she wasn't just recording?"

Baz shrugs. "Not that I could tell, but I generally only followed her to the clubs and casinos."

"What about in the Green, at Andy Lynch's house?" I say sweetly.

Baz doesn't answer at first. We all know I've caught him in a lie. His eyes flick rapidly around the club. "Gideon wanted to be sure she wasn't involved in anything dangerous," he admits, squaring his shoulders. "Andy and his teammates have a reputation for gambling, for extending their credit a little too deeply with the Riverlights pit bosses. Gid didn't want Rose caught up in that."

"Have you been following *me* too?"

Baz looks up at Jesse, who is still hovering behind me. "You already seem to have a shadow."

Jesse lifts his hands from my shoulders as I swivel around on my chair to glare at him. "I have not been following you for Gideon," he says. "Thanks, dude," he tells Baz. "I have to work with her."

I turn back around. "Did you follow Rose two nights ago?"

Baz shakes his head. "I can't watch her twenty-four seven."

"Why were you at Zoo last night?" I ask. "Why did you run from us?"

"Wow. You know everything, don't you?" Baz's lips slant upward, just slightly. "Gideon wanted to know if you were putting yourself in danger, looking for Rose's killers. I told him how you appeared to be behaving, staying with Jesse. I

— 175 —

left out the part about how you almost got crushed by a train. I figure he has enough to worry about right now."

Before I can ask anything else, my phone rings. Gideon.

Baz glances over at the display and smirks. "I'll let him answer any other questions you might have. I'll be in the back office if you need me." He rises from his chair and strolls across the gaming floor.

Jesse wanders toward the bar area to give me some privacy. I answer the phone. "How are your meetings going?" I ask.

"Fine. Jesse told me what happened. Are you all right?"

"Yes." I'm suddenly glad Gideon is out of town and not here to see the bruises that have sprung up around my neck from nearly being strangled. "You told me you didn't think Rose was in any danger; so then why were you having her followed for weeks?"

"Why are you questioning my judgment?" Gideon continues without waiting for a response. "So Jesse didn't see the guy who jumped you? It was just you and the intruder?"

I pause. Around me, the video games chatter and sing. The table of college boys are still focused completely on their laptops. Adebayo is chatting with a female gaming attendant. No one is paying me any attention.

"I didn't make this up, all right?" I say softly. "Jesse might not have seen the intruder, but he saw the gun the guy left behind."

Jesse is sitting at the next table now, which is unfortunately only a few feet away. He's pretending to be doing something on his phone, but I know he can still hear me. He *thinks* he doesn't care about my past, but would knowing about the PTSD—the hospital, the *crazy*—change how he feels?

"What can you tell me about the guy?"

"I don't know. He had a mask on. He said he wanted all the ViSE equipment. I told him I didn't have any."

"What happened to him?"

"He ran away after I stabbed him."

"Hang on. I have another call," Gideon says.

I turn to Jesse. He's still fiddling with his own phone.

He glances up at me. "Your turn to get a lecture?"

"Basically."

"He lectures because he cares, you know?" Jesse gives me a half smile.

"I know. I just wish he—"

Gideon comes back on the line. "Is Jesse there with you?"

"Yes. We're at Escape, actually. Everyone is here."

"Take the phone to a ViSE room and put me on speaker so I can talk to you both at once."

I wave an arm to get Jesse's attention and gesture for him to follow me. We cross the main gaming floor and duck into one of the ViSE rooms. I flip on the light and close the door behind us. Moving to the center of the room, I set the phone on the ViSE chair and activate the speaker.

"Go ahead," I say.

"I'm sending you both to Miami Beach tomorrow to record a shark-diving ViSE," Gideon says.

"Cool," Jesse replies.

I give him a dirty look and turn back to the phone. "Are you sure that's a good idea? I want to be here until we . . ." I trail off. If I say something like "know for sure," I'm going to get another lecture. "In case there's anything I can do," I finish.

"I understand your hesitation, Winter." Gideon's voice softens. "But there's nothing you can do to help. Detective Ehlers has people investigating. Sebastian is doing additional work on his end. We might as well continue building our ViSE inventory while I work on a new editor and more playback headsets. You've always wanted to dive with sharks, haven't you?"

I am both terrified of and fascinated by sharks. "Yes, but not now," I say. "Oppa, I can't just go to work like everything is fine. Let me stay here. You can use me as bait. Maybe the guy will try again."

"We are not using you as bait," Gideon says firmly.

"Fine. But you don't need to send me away. I don't even know how to scuba dive."

"The dive operators will teach you."

"I don't care. I don't want to go." My voice hitches. I know I'm whining, but I almost never ask Gideon for anything. He can't make me go out of town now. I'm not going to forget what happened just because I'm in a different place. It won't help. "Plus, who will take care of Miso? You're always work-ing. You'll probably forget to feed him."

"Natalie can take the cat for a few days. This is for your own safety. You're a decent fighter, Winter, but if someone wants to grab you, there are plenty of people who can make it happen."

"That's not true. You've made me strong. I can defend myself."

"You're strong, but you've become a bit rash." Gideon pauses. "I reviewed the footage from Saturday night. You should've let Jesse handle the security guard. You got shot at. You could have died."

"I'll be more careful," I say, suddenly glad Baz didn't tell Gideon about the close call with the train. "If you let me keep the gun the intruder left behind, I could—"

"No," Gideon says. "No guns. The most dangerous weapon you have is your brain. Give someone a gun and they tend to quit using it."

"So then why do Jesse and Baz have guns?" I protest. "Come on. If you let me keep it Jesse will show me how to use it safely."

Gideon sighs. "Jesse. Take the phone off speaker for a mo-ment, please."

Reluctantly Jesse picks up the phone. He nods. His eyes darken. "I don't think now is the time to—fine. I understand."

Jesse sets the phone back on the ViSE chair. "Do it." Gide-on's voice is tinny through the phone speaker.

Jesse removes a gun from the small of his back and slides

out the clip. He hands the weapon to me with the barrel pointed down.

My pulse accelerates. The weight of the gun in my hands feels powerful. It feels right. "I can't believe it," I start. "He's actually going to let you—"

Before I can even think, Jesse drops low. His elbow connects with my gut. I stumble backward toward the ViSE chair. Jesse slams my hand against the chair. The gun falls to the ground.

We both dive for it, but he's quicker than I am and has obviously done this before. He scoops up the gun with one hand and then lunges at me.

"Sorry, Winter." Jesse's muscular arm snakes around my throat. My neck ends up wedged between his forearm and biceps, the chain of Rose's necklace cutting into my skin. My throat burns as I gasp for air. And then I feel the cold steel of a gun barrel jabbing into my ribs. "It's done," Jesse says.

A long beat of silences passes. Then Gideon clears his throat. "Now do you understand why I don't want you to have a gun?"

"Tell him you understand," Jesse whispers in my ear.

"No." The same sick desperation from last night engulfs me. I need to win this, just like I needed to beat the train.

Hurt him, a little voice in my head says.

CHAPTER 23

I don't want to hurt him. Jesse is not the enemy. I refuse to let my sister's death turn me into someone who is violent and unhinged.

But I still want to win.

"Winter?" Gideon says.

I make a wheezing sound and Jesse loosens his hold a tiny bit. He's not going to hurt me. He's just trying to prove a point.

A point for Gideon.

I stop struggling and lower my eyes to the ground. "Fine. I understand."

The instant Jesse starts to let me go, I strike backward with my fingertips, aiming for his eyes like I learned in Krav Maga. He grunts in surprise and releases me completely. I duck low and rear back with my elbow, landing a direct hit to his groin. As I spin around, he doubles over.

"Shit." Red faced and gasping, Jesse sinks to his knees.

I wrench the gun out of his hand. "Guess who has the gun now," I tell Gideon.

"She fights dirty," Jesse says.

"You probably went easy on her," Gideon replies. "She is well aware that not all men will be so kind."

I lower my body onto the ViSE chair next to the phone, rubbing my neck with one hand. "Are we talking about Kyung? Was it one of his men? Is that why we're bringing up the past?"

"What did I tell you about using that name?" Gideon says coolly.

"I told Jesse," I say. "He knows about Los Angeles." I expect to get a lecture about how we're not supposed to talk about our past, how privacy is paramount, but Gideon just brushes it off.

"Fine. I do not know if Kyung or his men were involved in this," he says. "All I know is that I'm not there to watch you, so you're going to Miami where you'll be safe. It's not up for negotiation."

"Not up for negotiation?" I'm tired of being told what to do. If it isn't Gideon or Rose, then it's Jesse. I've been legally an adult for three months but no one seems to think I'm capable of making my own decisions about anything. "You're not my father and I'm not a child," I blurt out. "I don't have to obey you." Out of the corner of my eye, I see Jesse's eyes widen.

"I may not be your father, but I am still your boss. Which means you *do* have to obey me when it comes to work-related things. I already made the reservations and emailed them to both of you."

"You can't—"

"I can and I will. I promised your sister I would never let anything happen to you. I will honor her wish, even if it means that you hate me. Do you understand?"

I sigh deeply. I can tell he's not going to back down. "Fine. You win. I'll go to Florida."

"Your plane leaves at seven a.m. tomorrow," Gideon continues. "Take care of each other. I'll see you both when you get back." He pauses. "You can take me off speaker now."

I turn the speaker off and hold the phone to my ear. "You're off."

"Thank you," Gideon says.

"For what?"

"For leaving."

"Not like you gave me a choice," I mumble. But then after a few seconds I tack on a grudging "You're welcome." I might not agree with everything Gideon does, but he is still my elder and the closest thing I have to family. I know that he means well.

I duck out of the ViSE room and head for Escape's exit. Jesse is right on my heels.

He follows me through the main lobby and into the stairwell. I do my best to ignore him, but when he continues past the seventh floor, I stop on the landing and turn to face him. "How could you do that?" I ask. "I might have to go to Florida with you, but I don't forgive you for that little stunt."

"Sorry. It was kind of a dick move."

"Especially going for the throat the day after some guy almost strangles me," I remind him. I turn back to the stairs.

"Again, I apologize," he says. "I lose sight of that kind of stuff when I'm fighting. I just wanted it to be over quickly." He coughs. "But you took kind of a cheap shot yourself."

As we head for the top floor, I think for a second about the little voice in my head that wanted me to do more than just elbow Jesse in the groin. I know what it's like to have tunnel vision in a fight. "I guess I did. Sorry," I mutter. "But sometimes I swear it's like he has you brainwashed." I wriggle out of my boots in the hallway outside the penthouse.

"You don't get it," Jesse says. "He has all of us brainwashed, except for you. You're his family. You'll never get fired. I need this job, Winter. Gideon basically owns me. It kills me to say that, but recording pays a lot more than anything else I can do. And Gid's not normally a bad boss. I'm sorry he made me jump you like that."

"So then how about you make it up to me?" The words fly out of my mouth, almost flirty sounding, before I can even think about what I'm saying.

Jesse touches me on the arm. "How would I do that?"

His touch combined with the cadence of his question sends a tremor through me and I quickly avert my eyes. "I have an idea."

Jesse follows me into the penthouse. As I close the door behind us and lock it, I try my best pleading look. "Can you find some other girl and go? Tell Gideon I'm with you?"

"He already got us plane tickets. We can't send someone else in our places because our IDs won't match and there's not enough time to get fakes made," Jesse says. "And you know Gid. He'll check up on us when we're expected to arrive, or maybe even before then. He'll pay someone to hack the passenger manifest to make sure we boarded the plane if he suspects we're playing him."

"Damn it. You're right." Gideon doesn't leave anything to chance. He trusts no one.

Jesse flops down on the sofa. "What if we do the ViSE as quickly as we can and change our tickets so we can come home early? Gid won't check every flight to make sure we're *not* on it. We'll just have to avoid him for a couple of days once we get back. You can crash with me if you want."

I slouch back against the wall separating the living room from the kitchen. Normally I would love to go to Florida. But not now. Not when I feel like each passing second means Rose's killers are slipping farther away.

"There's no other way," Jesse says. "If we try to get out of the job, we'll spend all our time avoiding Gideon and not learn anything. Besides, we can play the rest of Rose's recordings on the plane or while we're stuck in Miami and maybe find some fresh clues to follow once we get back here."

"Good idea," I admit. "At least it's using our time wisely."

"So what now?" Jesse asks. "More ViSEs?"

"Plenty of time for that. Let's try to do something we can't do in Florida."

"Like what?"

"Like check out Phantasm." I think about how Andy

mistook me for my sister at the gym. "Maybe Rose got grabbed on accident. Maybe they wanted me. What if the guy I stabbed wasn't looking for a recording my sister made? What if he was looking for ours?"

CHAPTER 24

"You want to skulk around Phantasm in the middle of the day?" Jesse asks. "How are we going to get in?"

"I'm still working on that part."

He rubs at his scar. "Actually, I have an idea. Have you been to Miguelito's?"

"The Mexican restaurant? I've never eaten there, but I seem to remember running past it the other night. It's not too far from Phantasm, right?"

"About a half mile."

"And this gets us into the building how?" I ask.

"Trust me." Jesse picks up his phone and starts dialing.

We pull into the parking lot of Miguelito's twenty minutes later. In the daylight, the squared-off brick building looks more like a bomb shelter than a restaurant.

"We're going to make a special delivery to Phantasm," Jesse explains. "No one can resist free food, right?"

I wrinkle up my nose. "You think an international software company is going to welcome us in if we show up bearing burritos?"

"Oh, yes." Jesse puts the car in park and turns off the ignition. "These aren't just any burritos."

I slide out of the car and slam the door shut behind me. "It's worth a try, I guess."

Two guys in baggy chef pants and black T-shirts are sitting on milk crates, smoking cigarettes, outside the loading dock door. Jesse bumps fists with one of them as we pass by. The back room is full of trash cans and empty boxes. The scent of old grease and chili peppers makes my eyes water. A set of silver shelves in the back hallway sags under the weight of cartons of paper products. Turning the corner, we pass the cooks' line, where two guys and a girl are working to rap music blaring from a flour-caked transistor radio.

Jesse ducks into a little room that seems to be doubling as a manager's office and a pantry. A dark-haired guy with the beginnings of a beard is hunched over a computer screen. He drums his fingernails on the desk as he scrolls through what looks like price lists.

"Miguel." Jesse says it with a Spanish accent, which for some reason makes me smile. I stand back, browsing the large cans of pinto beans and boxes of brown sugar like I'm at the grocery store.

"Jesse. My man. It's been too long." Miguel turns away from the computer, stands, and claps Jesse on the back. "What brings you here?"

"Well, it sure isn't the cooking," Jesse jokes.

Miguel's eyes widen. "Shh. You crazy? My mama will hear you and come with her shotgun."

"We need to make a delivery," Jesse says. "Only it's a place that hasn't technically ordered anything. Do you still have the fishbowl full of business cards?"

"Yeah. We got it." Miguel stands and peeks his head out into the hallway. He flags down a passing waitress and has her fetch the fishbowl from the dining room. She returns a couple minutes later and hands the bowl to Miguel.

"Can we borrow the catering truck too? We need to look legit."

"As long as you bring it back in one piece," Miguel says.

I take the bowl from Miguel and dump all of the business

cards out onto his desk. I start going through them individually, crossing my fingers for the Phantasm logo.

A plump woman with a long black braid pokes her head inside the office door, her chocolate eyes melting at the sight of Jesse. *"Mijo,"* she says. "I thought I heard your voice." She pinches one cheek like she's known him since he was a baby and then wraps him in an embrace. "You should call your father. He asks about you every week, and every week I have to tell him I haven't seen you."

"Sorry," Jesse mumbles. "I'll call him soon."

"They worry about you. Your poor mama." Releasing him, the woman turns to me, her eyes hardening with judgment. "And who is this?"

"Tía María, this is my friend Winter," Jesse says.

I'm halfway through the cards, still looking for a Phantasm one. "Pleased to meet you," I say.

"You too." She smiles again, lines forming at the outside corners of her eyes. She touches Jesse on the back of the neck and leans in close, murmuring something in Spanish I'm fairly certain is about me. He answers her in Spanish and they both smile.

"I worked here for a few months," Jesse tells me, "when I first got out of the army. Maria is my aunt and Miguel is my cousin."

"And you are a brave soldier and a good man," Maria says. "Never forget that." She floats out of the office and I finish going through the business cards. I get lucky with one of the very last ones: Darren Ritter. Technical support specialist. Phantasm.

We order Mr. Ritter a nice variety of burritos and other food at a discount rate.

"What did your aunt say about me?" I ask while we wait for the food.

Jesse laughs under his breath. "She said, 'Pretty, but too skinny.'" He winks. "I agree with the first part."

My face gets hot, as much from the touch as the compliment. "Thanks. I've never heard you speak Spanish before."

"I've never heard you speak Korean," Jesse says.

I speak to him in Korean, the corners of my lips tugging upward in a smile.

"Whoa." He blinks rapidly. "What did you say?"

"I said that you're pretty but too skinny." I pat him on the stomach. His abdominal muscles tighten under my touch. I snicker. "Did you really just suck it in? You are the vainest guy I know."

"I'm not vain," Jesse insists. "But I was kind of a big kid and there's a lot of heart disease in my family. I'm just a little paranoid of waking up a hundred pounds overweight someday."

"I promise I'll let you know before you're a hundred pounds overweight," I tell him. "If you're nice, I'll even introduce you to some healthy Korean food."

"Sweet. Are you offering to cook for me?"

"No. But I'll take you out to a really good restaurant and let you buy me dinner." I grin.

"Deal." Jesse gives my ponytail a gentle tug. "She also asked about the bruises on your throat. Does it hurt?"

"Not really, but I guess it looks horrible, doesn't it?" I adjust the collar of my shirt to cover up more of my neck.

"I just wish I had been there," Jesse says. His expression is so earnest and sad, like he failed me by going home for a half an hour to shower and change clothes.

"You can't protect me from everything," I say.

Once the food is ready, Miguel helps up pack up the catering truck. Jesse and I arrive at Phantasm just in time for lunch, our headsets concealed beneath matching Miguelito's caps. I start recording as we approach the doors. There is one security guard patrolling the cavernous lobby and two more behind the counter.

"Delivery for the tech support department," Jesse says.

One of the security guards directs us to the suite on the second floor. We step onto the escalator, each carrying a stack of three disposable catering pans in insulated bags. A trickle of employees heading down the opposite escalator turns around to look at us. I can hardly blame them. I haven't eaten all day and my mouth is watering from the scents of salsa and seasoned meat.

Normally I would look away—the less eye contact you make with other people, the more invisible you are. With invisibility comes safety. Today I make a point to focus on each person I see, capturing their faces on my recording.

The main door to the suite is standing open and the secretary has her eyes trained on her computer screen. We glide in with our pans, and at first I think we might be able to just walk right past her.

But then she looks up. It's Natalie. She's wearing a wig, but it's definitely her. Recognition flashes in her eyes too, but she doesn't say anything. I follow her gaze and see a video camera mounted in the far corner of the reception area. It's trained directly on her desk.

"Free corporate lunch." Jesse balances the pans on one arm while he pretends to look at a voucher. "For Darren Ritter."

Natalie plays along. If I had known she worked here, we wouldn't have had to go through the fishbowl of business cards. She must be how Gideon got the key to the Phantasm building. She clicks at her computer. "He's actually working remotely today," she says. "But I'm sure the rest of the staff will appreciate the food. I'll show you back to the break room."

She starts down the main corridor, but then the phone rings. "One second." Sighing, she hurries back to the desk. Snatching the phone from its receiver she says, "IT and development. How may I direct your call?" She starts talking to someone in a different department.

"We'll find it," Jesse says. He strolls back, past the rows of cubicles, right toward the server room. He ducks through the door.

A couple of guys in khaki pants and T-shirts are at the stacks of equipment. They look up in confusion. "What are you doing back here?" one of them asks.

Jesse gestures at the pans. "Sorry. Thought this was the lunch room."

"Nope. Go back to the end of the cubicles and it's the first door on the left."

"It's the door marked *Staff Lounge,*" the other guy adds, shaking his head.

"Subtle," I say as we head back down the row of cubicles.

Jesse shrugs. "You never know what you might find out when you burst in on people unexpectedly."

We find the staff lounge and take our sweet time setting up the containers of food on one of the round lunch tables, rolling back the foil, arranging the sauces in front of each tray. Slowly, curious employees trickle back.

"What's this?" A middle-aged woman in a gray pantsuit looks over the pans with an expression of disdain.

"Free lunch from Miguelito's. Somebody won it for putting their card in the fishbowl," I tell her.

A man wearing a checked shirt with a striped tie wanders back, followed by a girl with thick glasses who seems to be his assistant. She starts rummaging around in a cabinet and returns with a stack of Styrofoam plates.

"The secretary almost turned us away," Jesse says. "It's like she's an extra security guard or something. You guys working on some top-secret stuff?"

No one answers. No one's expression even wavers. If they heard about the break-in, they're not talking. I loiter behind the pans, labeling each of them on a napkin.

Jesse tries again to engage the employees in conversation. "Any of you know Darren Ritter? He won this lunch, but I guess he's out of the office today. Too bad."

"Darren. Right," the woman in the pantsuit says. "He works from home sometimes."

Slowly the word spreads around the office and more employees arrive. Everyone grabs plates and starts loading up on chips and burritos. We loiter around for a few more minutes, pretending to answer questions about the food so we can eavesdrop on conversations and record more employee faces, but there's only so much to explain about the food we provided. I start wondering why we went through the trouble to get into the Phantasm suite for ten minutes. Did I really think someone was going to talk about the recent security breach in front of a couple of restaurant workers? Shaking my head in disgust, I gather up the cloth catering bags and tuck them under my arm. Jesse and I both head back to the lobby. I pause for a minute to watch the fish swimming lazily in their aquarium, twenty or so Asian men staring down at me from the framed photo on the wall.

Natalie stands up when she sees us. "Let me walk you out." We walk down the corridor. There's another photo of corporate executives right inside the door to the suite. More disapproving dark eyes.

"What are you doing here?" Natalie hisses.

"What are *you* doing here?" I ask.

"I'm temping. Gideon told me to get a job here. He needed a key to the building and the door codes for a ViSE."

And here I thought Jesse had cracked the code to the suite on his own. I guess that was another part of our recording that was pure theater.

"Is that all?" Jesse asks. "Because if so, you can probably quit."

"I'm also supposed to be gathering intel," she murmurs, glancing around furtively. "Eavesdropping on executive gossip. Recording as much as possible. Phantasm is pushing to buy Gideon's tech. Gideon wants to know what they plan to do with it."

I nod. "We did the ViSE. He had us grab some financial

information from the server. I wonder why he didn't just have you do the whole thing."

"Those programmer guys sometimes work until eight p.m. and I'm not a break-in-after-hours kind of girl. Besides, computer stuff is not my area of expertise. I can barely work my phone." Natalie shudders. "I can't believe that was you two. The execs have been questioning people about it all morning."

"You can't tell Gideon you saw us here, all right? I'm trying to figure out exactly what happened to my sister and I thought maybe it had to do with the break-in." I look desperately at her.

"I won't say anything, but you owe me one." Natalie grins. "Nah. It's not like delivering free Mexican food is a crime anyway." Her face goes serious. "I'm so sorry about Rose."

The phone rings again. Our heads swivel toward the secretary's desk in unison.

"I have to go." Natalie turns away.

I reach out and grab her arm. "Wait. Have you found out anything?" When she looks confused, I add, "Executive gossip? Intel?"

"Not really. I've only been here two weeks." Her eyes flick to the framed photo. "I've only seen one of those guys."

This picture is more casual than the one behind the fish tank. It looks like it was snapped at a corporate picnic. Several older men are posing behind a blue-and-white banner with Hangul—Korean letters—on it. *Usu Annual Festival,* it reads. I scan the rows of stern-faced men, each trying to look more serious than the next for the camera.

That's when I see him. He's in the back corner, almost completely obscured by a man in the second row. I suck in a sharp breath. Slowly, I lean in closer to the photograph, expecting it to change, expecting to realize my eyes were playing tricks on me. But the man in question doesn't morph into someone else. And though I can't see his whole face, I recognize him. I know I do.

It's the one-eyed man from my dreams.

CHAPTER 25

"What did you see?" Jesse asks as soon as we're back out in the hallway.

"I'm not sure." I step gingerly onto the escalator, one arm holding on to the railing while my other hand calls up the photo gallery on my phone. I stopped long enough to take a picture so I could study the man without having to vise. I enlarge the image I snapped. It's definitely him. He's got his body turned slightly away from the camera so only half of his face is showing, but I would know him anywhere.

I just never expected him to be real.

The giant lobby seems to stretch out into infinity. I don't want to say anything until we're back outside, or better yet in the catering truck where no one else will hear. I feel Jesse's eyes on me every step until we push through the glass doors and escape out into the frigid air.

Where I immediately start to doubt myself again.

I check my phone. The picture hasn't changed. "I know one of the guys in that photo."

"Know him?" Jesse unlocks the doors and hops into the driver's seat. "How?"

I slide in beside him and toss the cloth bags in the back. "I'm not sure. Korea, maybe. Or L.A. This is going to sound crazy, but I see him in my dreams sometimes."

"Like when you're sleeping?" Jesse backs the truck out of the parking space and heads for the street.

"Yes. I don't know what Gideon might have told you, but I don't have *daydreams*, all right?"

"I just meant—"

"I know what you meant." He meant hallucinations. "That time in my life is over. I'm not crazy anymore."

"Let's forget I said anything." Jesse buckles his seat belt and slips on a pair of sunglasses. "So you dream about some guy and he shows up on the wall of the company where we broke in. How exactly is that possible?"

"I don't know. Maybe he's one of the men I . . . knew in L.A. and I just blocked it out."

"Did you get his name?" Jesse turns the corner and heads toward Miguelito's.

"The picture wasn't labeled."

"Maybe Gideon would know," Jesse says.

"Except we promised him we wouldn't snoop around."

"So then . . ."

"We figure it out on our own. Once we get home, maybe we can plug the image into a search engine and come up with something."

"Okay," Jesse says. "It's worth a try."

I flash him a grateful look as he pulls into the restaurant parking lot. We drop off the keys and catering supplies with Miguel and then cross the parking lot to Jesse's car. We're only halfway there when Jesse takes off running.

"Son of a bitch." He skids to a stop next to his car and kicks at one of his hubcaps.

The driver's side window has been shattered and all four tires have been slashed.

"Damn it." He walks a slow loop around the car like he can't quite believe it. "Someone is on a mission to get all of us."

"This is kind of a rough neighborhood," I say. "Maybe it's

not related." I pull my hands into the cuffs of my shirt and hug my arms across my body to stay warm.

"Let me call a tow truck." Jesse steps away and dials his phone. I hear him explaining to the guy on the other end what happened, where we are, and that he'll be out of town so he'll need to leave the car at a tire shop for a few days. After he hangs up, he unlocks his door and fishes a pocketknife and a tin of mints out of the center console. Then he turns to me. "They're backed up. He said it's going to be a couple of hours. I'm just going to leave the keys with the hostess. We can take the train home."

"Sure." My eyes scan across the damage to Jesse's car, looking for anything that might be a clue. There's no way to know if it's related.

Jesse jogs inside the restaurant and returns a couple of minutes later. The two of us cross the Miguelito's parking lot and head for the nearest MetroLink station. It takes us about fifteen minutes to get there. The platform is crowded as usual, people waiting for multiple trains. Jesse and I stand behind the yellow line, both staring forward. Even underground, the cold air bites at my skin. I let my hair out of its ponytail, arranging the ends so they cover my ears.

"At least Florida will be warm," Jesse says.

"True." I exhale a frosty breath. "Was there anything stolen out of your car?"

"Not that I could tell."

"Are you going to report it to the police?"

"What's the point?" he says. "They don't give a shit about this kind of vandalism."

"Do you think it's the same people who got Rose and broke into the penthouse?"

"I don't know." Jesse pulls his knit cap down low over his ears. "I'm getting pissed off just thinking about it."

A couple of guys push past us in quilted NFL parkas. One

of them looks like the kid who tried to sell us drugs the other night, but it was dark then and I can't be certain.

Jesse's phone rings. He pulls it out of his pocket and glances at the display before answering. "Yeah?" he says. "I'm on my way home actually."

I wander a few feet away to give him privacy. I blow on my hands in an attempt to thaw my rapidly freezing fingers. As much as I don't want to leave town right now, it will feel nice to have the sun on my face, to swim in the Atlantic Ocean. Of course, then there is the small matter of sharks. I have never seen a shark, not even in a zoo or an aquarium, but I remember reading and rereading a book about them back at the orphanage. So beautiful. So deadly.

I hear the rumble that means a train is drawing near, but I'm not sure which way it's coming from. I glance over at Jesse. His back is to me and he's still on the phone, his other hand covering his ear to block out the noise. I lean over just far enough to look into the dark tunnel at the end of the platform. I can't see the train yet, but I see the reflection of headlights.

And then someone bumps me from behind. I feel hands on my back, pushing me forward. My ankle wrenches as I try to turn. Too late. I am falling. I claw out at the air, but there's nothing to grab. I land hard on the MetroLink tracks.

CHAPTER 26

Glancing up, I see a guy dressed in black pushing his way through the throng of people on the platform.

"Winter!" Jesse nearly drops his phone when he sees me on the tracks. "What are you doing?"

I point down the platform as I scramble to my feet. "That guy pushed me!" I look left and right, hoping to see the navy uniform of a transit officer, but it's like they say in the movies—there's never a cop when you need one.

The tracks are only about three feet below the platform, but just as I'm about to head for safety, I catch a glimpse of the train bearing down on me. I freeze up. The wind blows my hair back from my face. The train clatters on the tracks. I can see its rectangular headlights shining through the gloom. I can envision the red and blue stripes on the front of it. It's close. So close.

Winter, move, a little voice says. I know I need to move.

But it would be easy to stand here, to be done with everything.

To be with my sister again.

I'm so tired. It would be quick.

"Damn it, Winter!" The sound of Jesse's voice snaps me out of my trance.

He's moving toward me. People are gathering around,

panicked. They're pointing. They're talking on their cell phones. Some of them are even snapping pictures.

I dive shoulder-first for the safety of the platform, rolling once on the hard concrete as the train roars into the station. Jesse runs to my side and kneels next to me. All of the color has drained from his face.

"Jesus Christ," he says. "You just took ten years off my life."

Now that I'm safe, the crowd starts to disperse, a couple of kids clapping as if what happened was all a big performance. Jesse pulls me into a seated position as the train slows to a stop. I sit just beyond the yellow stripe, trembling as passengers begin to disembark.

"Are you okay?" he asks. He's still completely pale.

I nod. "Did you get a look at the guy who pushed me?"

"All I saw was you down there playing chicken with the train."

"I'm sorry," I tell him. "I zoned out for a second. I didn't mean to scare you."

"Well, you did." Jesse shakes his head. "I thought you were going to die."

People hurry past with big purses and shopping bags. A few of them flip us curious glances. Most people don't sit on the cold concrete in the middle of winter. I slowly rise to my feet as the train pulls out of the station. "I wonder how long before the next one arrives." I turn to consult a nearby schedule.

"I know it's cold, but how about we walk home instead?" Jesse suggests.

I shrug. "All right."

We head back up the steps. Jesse wraps his fingers around mine as we leave the MetroLink parking lot and turn toward the Lofts. I would normally object to this, but I suspect he's doing it so he doesn't have to worry about me wandering out in front of a bus or something. I'm not going to, but after the scare I just gave him, I suppose the least I can do is let him hold my hand. My phone buzzes with a text. My fingers are still shaking and it takes me a couple of tries to access the message with my free hand:

If you go public with that recording, next time the train won't miss.

I don't show Jesse the text until we're home, safely locked away in the penthouse.

"Did you respond?" he asks.

"I tried." I curl my arms around my body. I'm still a little shaky. "The number won't accept incoming texts."

"We need to show this to Baz and Gideon. They might be able to trace it."

"To a disposable phone," I say. "Or some anonymous texting app. Besides, Gideon is paranoid enough as it is. If I tell him someone pushed me onto the MetroLink tracks, he'll probably want to put me in the witness protection program." I flop down on the sofa. Miso wanders out of the kitchen. He jumps up and crawls into my lap.

Jesse sits next to me. "We both just want you to be safe." He reaches out and strokes Miso's head. "What's up, Moo?" Miso purrs but for once doesn't abandon me for Jesse.

I lean back and let my body sink into the cushion. "Sometimes I wonder if this whole thing is just a huge mistake. Some crazy guy thinks someone caught him doing something wrong on a ViSE, but maybe we didn't. Or maybe we did and edited it out without even knowing. I never pay attention to the people in the background. Do you?"

"Not really." Jesse gives me a long look. "So do you want to talk about what happened back there?"

I don't, but I need to give him some kind of explanation or he'll probably call Gideon. I pet Miso's soft fur. "Like I said, I didn't mean to scare you. I guess it was one of those deer-in-headlights moments."

Jesse reaches out to pet Miso. The cat's toes flex, his tiny claws catching in the fabric of my shirt. "I don't believe that, Winter. I've worked with you long enough to know you're not a deer-in-headlights kind of girl."

"You're right," I admit. "It was more like . . . have you ever peeked over the edge of a cliff and thought about jumping? Not that you want to jump, but just like what would happen if you did?"

Jesse exhales a big breath of air. "Well I'm all about cliff diving, but not if it's going to end in a horrible death."

"I didn't want to die," I say. "I swear. I'm just tired. I feel so powerless. Do you ever feel like that? Like you have only the smallest say in what actually happens to you?" I run my fingers through Miso's fur again, comforted by the soft vibration of his purring.

"Well, yeah. But you're talking to a guy who handed control of his life over to the military and then was disappointed when they gave it back." Jesse pauses. "So staring down a train made you feel in control?"

"Yes. Because in that moment I was in charge of my future."

"Or at least whether you were going to have one, I guess."

As if sensing that Jesse needs comfort, Miso stands, stretches, and crawls across me to the next cushion. Jesse scoops him up into his arms and touches the cat's forehead to his. "What do you think, Moo?" he asks. "Think we need to do a better job taking care of Winter?"

"I don't need either of you to take care of me," I say. But I give Jesse a half smile.

He sets Miso on the coffee table and then turns to me. "Question," he says. "Have you talked to your therapist since you found out Rose was dead? Even on the phone or something?"

I sigh. "I told you I wasn't trying to hurt myself. Someone pushed me. You saw the text."

"I believe you," he says. "Still. You've been through a lot lately."

I start to ask him how he even knows I have a therapist and then I remember Gideon mentioning her in the office at Escape after I watched the recording of Rose.

"I'll make an appointment when we get back from Florida, all right?"

"Thank you," Jesse says.

We stare awkwardly at each other for a few seconds and then he says, "Do you still want to look for the one-eyed man?"

"Right." I almost forgot about the weirdness at Phantasm. "I guess we could start with him and then finish up the ViSEs if there's time."

"Okay." Jesse gets my tablet from where I have it charging on the kitchen counter. He brings it to the coffee table and opens a search engine. We both lean in toward the screen, our shoulders brushing.

According to sources on the Internet, Phantasm has offices in eight American cities but the company was purchased last year by a Korean *jaebeol,* a powerful industrial corporation, called Usu. I remember seeing that name on the banner in the picture with the one-eyed man. A search for Usu returns over twenty thousand websites. I scan the main page for the corporation and find out that Usu owns over thirty companies in industries ranging from textiles to technology to pharmaceutical development.

"Great," Jesse mutters. "This won't take long at all."

We start by going through all of the executive and employee photos on the various Phantasm web pages, but we don't find anything. We split up the list of Usu affiliates—me on my tablet and Jesse on his phone—and click through as many photos as we can find. After about an hour of searching, we're both ready to admit that it's hopeless. Some of the smaller Usu companies don't have photos of their executives or staff and there's no guarantee the one-eyed man still works for Usu.

I upload his picture from my phone and try to search by image, but after another hour of clarifying and enlarging and scrolling through unrelated web pages, I'm forced to accept the fact that the Internet isn't going to give up his identity. I do a last-ditch search for "Korean men" plus "one eye" and get a gruesome return of about fifty people who have been shot, stabbed, or mauled, but none of them are a match for the man from Phantasm.

Jesse turns away from the screen, like maybe looking at mangled faces is hitting a little too close to home for him.

"Sorry. I didn't think." I power down my tablet.

"It's fine," he says. "What next?"

Glancing at the time, I frown. We lost a lot of time walking home. "I want to play more ViSEs, but I've got to take Miso down to Natalie's apartment and then start packing if we're going to Miami tomorrow morning."

Jesse and I have gone away together before, but Gideon always went with us. Thinking about a couple of nights alone with Jesse in a hotel room makes me even more nervous than the idea of him sleeping out on the living room sofa. I can't hide from him in a tiny enclosed space. He'll see the real me. And maybe he won't like what he sees.

This thought should fill me with relief—maybe then he'll finally give up on us—but instead it makes me want to abort the whole plan. *You have become one of those girls who wants him to want you, even though you don't want him.* No, that isn't true. Part of me does want him. I feel it every time we're in the same room, but I don't think it's enough to make things work.

"It'll only take me ten minutes to throw some stuff in a bag. Let me help you go through some of Rose's ViSEs while you deal with the cat and pack," Jesse says. "Overlay doesn't bother me at all."

"All right." I retrieve my notebook and the music box from my room and set them on the coffee table. Part of me feels weird sharing my sister's personal experiences with Jesse, but strangers have played these recordings. There's nothing personal about them to her. Not to mention, there are still eleven more ViSEs to go and I could use some help if I'm going to make it through all of them without throwing up again. "Anything without a number hasn't been played."

Jesse pulls his headset out of his pocket. He selects one of the memory cards and inserts it with a click. He slips the headset over his head, adjusting it so it fits snugly. Then his eyes fall closed.

"Be sure to let me know what kind of ViSE it is and who's in it," I say. "I don't want to miss anything."

"Trust me," Jesse says. "You don't want any of this action. It's a switch party at Inferno." He makes a face without opening his eyes. "I'm kissing a frat boy. Who wears a backward hat to a club? How does a guy like that even get in?"

"Money, probably." After noting the ViSE in my notebook, I leave Jesse to his switch party and focus on gathering together the things I'll need for our trip. By the time he finishes the ViSE, I'm almost done packing. "Did you see Baz?" I ask. "Or anything weird?"

He shudders. "Plenty of weird stuff, but I didn't see anyone I know." He hands the card to me so I can number it and then selects another one. "Nice," he says, closing his eyes again. "Salsa dancing with a bunch of creepy dudes."

I crack a smile. I'm really glad Jesse is with me.

CHAPTER 27

I **have** to wake up at five a.m. the next morning to go to the airport. For once, I don't oversleep.

Jesse is sitting on the sofa waiting for me. "I called us a cab already," he says. "You need help?" He looks expectantly at my duffel bag and backpack.

All of my luggage together probably weighs only thirty pounds. I roll my eyes. "I think I can manage. Thanks." I draw the living room curtains across the rectangle of dark sky beyond the glass. Only Gideon would think a seven a.m. plane ride was a good idea.

"Ready?" Jesse holds the door open.

I step out into the dimly lit hallway. As we head to the stairwell, the morning feels heavy around me, like it's holding secrets.

Our footsteps echo on the concrete stairs. Jesse reaches the bottom first. He opens the door to the lobby with a faint squeak and I slide through behind him.

Jesse takes a seat at the long bar, one foot tapping idly against the base of his stool. I stride to the front door and peer out into the purple-black morning. The city is a wasteland of frozen streets, of silver and gray corners backlit by the waning moon. There are no people. No cars. The air is sharp and cold. Steam filters up from a nearby manhole cover.

Just as I'm about to turn back to the warm lobby, a cab pulls up to the front of the building, its headlights cutting white streaks through the gloom.

Jesse materializes at my side, his duffel bag hooked over his shoulder. He gestures to the taxi driver and approaches the vehicle. I follow him, but inside I hesitate. It still feels like a bad idea to be leaving town while Rose's killers are out there somewhere.

Both Jesse and I sleep through the first leg of our trip. We make it to Philadelphia without incident, but our plane to Miami ends up delayed for over three hours thanks to an equipment malfunction and wing deicing. Jesse dozes on and off in the airport while I take turns fidgeting in my chair and pacing back and forth. There are too many people here. Too many strangers. Most of them are staring into their phones or tablets with glazed-over eyes, but occasionally I feel someone looking at me. I wish I had something to do to pass the time. I don't feel comfortable vising out in the open like this, but I hate the thought of wasting time doing nothing.

I try to work on my homework again, but it all seems so pointless right now. I end up taking a sedative and then going through all of my text messages, looking for any hint Rose might have been in trouble. There's nothing—just a bunch of "I'm fine" or "I'll see you soon" messages. She never was much for answering her phone. I check the news websites for St. Louis, Festus, and Ste. Genevieve again, just to make sure no bodies were pulled out of the Mississippi.

Jesse wakes up about an hour before we take off. "You hungry?" he asks. "You didn't eat breakfast, did you?"

"I'm fine," I say, even though my stomach is growling.

He goes off in search of food and comes back several minutes later with coffee, tea for me, potato chips, a sandwich, and something called donut holes that I have managed to live six years in the United States and never try.

"So these are really the middle parts from donuts?" I ask.

Jesse balances his coffee between his legs while he wrestles with the seal on his bag of potato chips. "Um, I think places make them separately now."

"But why eat four or five of these instead of eating one whole donut?"

"Because they're good?" Jesse's bag opens with an explosive pop, sending sour cream and onion potato chips flying all over his lap and the floor. "Shit," he says.

My shoulders twitch as I try to swallow back a laugh, but when the two kids sitting across from us start pointing at him, I can't help it. My giggles turn into full-blown laughter as Jesse fishes a couple of soggy potato chips out of his coffee. The sensation almost feels foreign. I can't remember how long it's been since the last time I laughed this hard.

"I'm glad you're finding this amusing," Jesse says with a grin. He gestures at the tea and donut holes. "Better eat up before I destroy your food too."

The donut holes are surprisingly good. I take a second one and chew it slowly, thinking my way through each ViSE of Rose's that I've played, trying to remember if there was anything unusual going on in the background.

An announcement crackles through a speaker above our heads. Our flight is finally boarding. Jesse hops to his feet, stretching his legs.

We get in line behind a young couple decked out in matching resort T-shirts. I wish Jesse and I were going to Florida on vacation. I've never gone anywhere on vacation. The gate attendant scans our tickets without even glancing up at us. "Welcome aboard," she says robotically.

Amazingly, Jesse falls asleep *again* once we get settled into our seats. We haven't even lifted off and I can already hear him snoring. The flight attendant comes by to make sure our seat backs and tray tables are in the proper position and smiles down at him like he's a newborn baby. "He looks so peaceful," she coos. "You take good care of him, all right?"

All I can do is smile tightly. Clearly Jesse isn't my brother, so whenever we go places together people generally assume we're boyfriend and girlfriend. I try to envision that life: Jesse and I returning to college after our winter break instead of going to record a ViSE. Days filled with lectures and library dates instead of exercise and martial arts training. Nights spent cooking for each other and then curling up together on the sofa to watch movies. Gideon has told me more than once that I should talk to Dr. Abrams about the possibility of going to college, but I can't seem to reconcile such normalcy with the person I am.

I look over. Jesse's eyelashes are feathered shut, his face muscles relaxed. I don't think I've ever slept so soundly in my whole life. I creep just a little bit closer to him, resting the side of my forearm against his, as if mere proximity will make some of that peace rub off on me.

The plane pushes back from the gate. I pay careful attention to the safety demonstration even though I've flown several times before. Our takeoff is smooth and uneventful, and the pilot quickly climbs to our cruising altitude.

Jesse stirs slightly as the flight attendant comes by with her drink cart. I ask for ginger ale and accept the little plastic cup filled mostly with ice. I sip it absent-mindedly as I try to piece together the seemingly unrelated clues and events of the past few days. It just all feels so disconnected. Pulling a pen from my backpack, I make a list of possible suspects on the back of the beverage napkin.

—*Baz. He was following Rose.*
—*Andy. He was dating Rose.*
—*Kyung. Somehow found us?*

—Phantasm. Retaliation? One-eyed man?
—Paranoid customer? Thinks we caught him on a
recording?

I consider the list, hoping something will jump out at me, but nothing feels quite right. Baz seems too loyal to Gideon to be involved. After spending time with Andy in person and on Rose's recordings, it's hard to believe he would ever hurt her. I see no reason why Kyung or his people would want to kill Rose. The other two . . . I just don't know.

I crumple the napkin and tuck it into my pocket. Slouching down in my seat, I hide my headset under a knitted hat and work my way through three more recordings, numbers 11, 12, and 13. There's another clip of Rose and Andy gambling, one of Rose being picked out of the audience to be a magician's assistant, and finally another switch party. I debate saving it for Jesse but then decide to just go ahead and play it.

I'm leaning against the wall at Inferno, my eyes scanning the crowd. Suddenly the music cuts out, replaced by the recording of a gong. It rings eleven times.

A redheaded woman I recognize as a DJ for a local radio station steps up to the microphone. "You know what that means," she says. "Time to start switching. As always, the rules are simple. We'll turn the lights down and the music up. You find someone to get to know, and when the song ends you leave that person and find a new someone. Oh, and don't do anything I wouldn't do . . . so basically do anything you want." She laughs.

I cringe as the lights dim and a hard rock song starts playing.

I move toward a tall guy who is leaning against the wall. He hesitates a moment and then lets me pull him toward the center of the room. He wraps his arms around me and we start dancing. Even in the faint light, he can't bring himself to make eye contact.

"First switch party?" I ask.

The guy nods without speaking.

"Relax. Just have fun," I say.

"I'll try." He chuckles awkwardly, but some of the tension leaves his body.

I can't make out specific features, but I can see that he's Asian, with spiked-up hair and glasses. He reminds me of the way Gideon looked in Los Angeles. At least my sister picked a shy guy. Maybe this won't be as horrible as I think.

We dance close together until the song fades. I give him a gentle kiss on the cheek. He disappears back to the periphery and a strong hand clamps down on my wrist. The hand belongs to a broad, muscular guy with a shaved head.

"What's your name?" the guy asks.

"Lily," I say.

"That's almost as hot as you are." The guy brushes strands of hair back from my face and kisses me on the neck, his teeth nipping gently at my skin. A rush of heat moves through me.

I pause the recording for a second and look over at Jesse. His eyelashes flutter but he's still asleep.

"I'm Mark," the guy says.

I start to reply, but he crushes his lips against mine without warning. I try to step back, but his arms are tight around my waist. One hand drops to the curve of my hip as he thrusts his tongue into my mouth.

My stomach lurches and I have to hit PAUSE again. I flail for the airsickness bag in the seat pocket in front of me. My hands shake as I peel it open and hold it beneath my chin. Slowly, I breathe in through my nose and out through my mouth until the urge to vomit fades. I don't recognize the song that's playing in the ViSE, but I hope it's a short one.

I put my hand on Mark's chest and push him back a little. "Easy there," I say. I bite down gently on his lower lip. He groans. I run my fingernails over his shaved head. We kiss repeatedly as we dance close together.

"Do you want to go somewhere?" he asks.

I laugh lightly. "I'm fine where I am."

Luckily the song ends and Mark goes in search of his next victim. I play bits of the next two guys, neither of whom are familiar, fast-forwarding when things get uncomfortable. And then I end up in the arms of someone I recognize.

"Hey." Isaiah looks down at me, the braids of his wig falling forward to obscure his face. "You work for Gideon too, right?"

I rest my hands on his waist. "Who?" I ask innocently. "I'm sure I don't know what you mean."

"Riiight." He strokes the back of my neck, his fingers crawling up under my wig to graze the lowest prong of my headset. "I've seen you at Escape before. You stand out even in the dark."

"Do I?" I press my chin to Isaiah's chest and flutter my eyelashes as I look up at him.

"Yep." He laughs lightly. "You don't actually have to kiss me or anything. I just came by to say hi."

"So you're saying you don't want to kiss me?" I ask in a little-girl voice.

"Pretty sure no guy would ever say that." Isaiah brushes his lips against mine, softly, and then when I don't pull away, a little harder.

His kiss is warm without being threatening. I blink hard. Somehow I've gone from being nauseated to blushing in five minutes. I glance over at Jesse again. His mouth is open slightly. I can see the tiny grooves in his lips. I suddenly wish I had let him kiss me in the kitchen the other night. My head starts to pound from the dual realities. I let my eyes fall shut.

"You know who I saw here?" Isaiah says as we break apart.

"Who?"

"Baz."

"Gideon's Baz?"

"The one and only." Isaiah kisses me again. "He's a little old for this crowd, don't you think?"

I shrug. "I don't judge, as long as he stays away from me."

Isaiah laughs. "You doing anything fun for Thanksgiving?"

I toss my hair back from my face. "I don't know. I don't really like big meals and football games."

Isaiah laughs. "You should check out the parade. It's a good time."

"Maybe," I say coyly.

"I'll look for you." He spins me around once as the music fades and then disappears into the mass of bodies. I pull another guy into my arms.

I go through five more men before the clock strikes midnight at Inferno and the switch party is officially over. Unfortunately it's all downhill after Isaiah. The guys seem more drunk and more aggressive. Rose does a good job of controlling each encounter, but I still struggle to stay engaged and have to pause the recording repeatedly to let my nausea subside. At one point I see Baz leaning against the wall, but it doesn't look like he's hooking up with anyone.

By the end of the recording I'm clutching the airsickness bag again. I put my headset away and ask the flight attendant for more ginger ale. I manage to get a little sleep, waking up only once to move Jesse's head off my shoulder. He doesn't wake until the plane touches down, wheels bouncing roughly as they transfer from the air to the runway.

When the plane arrives at the gate, Jesse and I take the escalator down to the exit level, where we grab our checked bags and then wait for a taxi. It's only five o'clock in Miami, but I'm exhausted from the long day in the airport after waking up so early. I toy with my headset, extending and collapsing it repeatedly as we make our way to the head of the line.

"At least we get away from the cold for a few days," Jesse says.

"Two days," I say. "I'm back on a plane the day after tomorrow at the latest."

The South Florida traffic is brutal. It takes us half an hour to go a couple of miles. Our cabdriver drives with one hand on the steering wheel and the other hand flipping the pages of a foreign newspaper. At one point we veer into the adjacent lane and almost get hit by an SUV. Eventually, the traffic thins out, the driver abandons his paper, and my life seems slightly less at risk. I lean my head against the vinyl seat and let my eyes fall closed. When I wake up, this time it's my head on Jesse's shoulder.

"Your hair smells good, but your head weighs a ton," he informs me.

"Funny, on the plane I found yours to be rather weightless," I reply.

Jesse smiles. "I know you don't want to be here, but if you have to be, I'm glad I got to go with you."

"Me too," I say, relaxing as he gives my leg a gentle squeeze. "How's your knee?"

"All better." I rub a hand across the front of my neck. "My throat too."

After a handful of swear words in a language that sounds like Russian and one more close encounter with a car in the next lane, the cabdriver turns off the highway. The taxi slows to a stop at a large four-story hotel just a few blocks off the water.

Of course our room isn't ready, even though it's almost six p.m. Jesse and I leave our bags with the bellhop and eat dinner at the hotel restaurant, making small talk about tomorrow's shark dive over chicken enchiladas and a heaping basket of nacho chips.

"You're a horrible influence on my diet," I tell him. "I never eat unhealthy American food unless I'm with you."

Jesse inhales sharply, like he's offended. "This is *not* unhealthy American food. It's Mexican." He dips a chip into a steaming bowl of queso, frowning at the cheese's bright orange color. "Sort of."

I smile. "What was it like to grow up biracial?"

Jesse chews the nacho chip with a thoughtful look on his face. "It was cool," he says. "I'm an only child, which is unusual for a Mexican family, but we lived in a neighborhood with a lot of friends and relatives, so I never felt lonely. My parents made sure I learned to speak both English and Spanish as a kid, which really helped." He reaches for another chip. "I know it's something kids struggle with a lot, but I guess I was really lucky in that aspect. I almost feel like I had the best of both worlds." He winks. "Especially when it comes to food."

"It always comes back to food for you, doesn't it?"

Jesse swallows and then takes a drink of soda. "Basically," he says with grin.

Gideon calls while we're waiting for the check. "Sebastian found the guy who attacked you on the building security feeds," he says. "Not without his mask, though."

"So nothing helpful?"

"Not yet."

"Have you heard anything from Detective Ehlers?"

"He said there was nothing overtly suspicious on Rose's phone record. Mostly calls from you and me and a few from a guy she might have been dating. He's going to follow up. He's also confident he's located the hotel where she was killed, and he has people going through the list of registered guests, but that's a tedious process."

They're all things Jesse and I discovered on our own, but Gideon doesn't know that.

"Can I speak with Jesse for a moment?" Gideon asks.

I hold the phone out to Jesse, who quickly wipes his hands on his cloth napkin before accepting it. He says, "Yeah," and "I will," and "I promise," probably all of which are in response to Gideon telling him to watch out for me. Then he hangs up and sets the phone on the table. We pay the check and return to the front desk, where we find out our room is ready and the bellhop has already delivered our bags.

The hotel room is nice, with two queen-size beds, a big-screen TV, and a small kitchen. I claim the bed closest to the door. Grabbing a pair of sweatpants and a black T-shirt from my duffel, I duck into the bathroom and change into them.

After splashing water on my face and brushing my teeth, I head back into the main room, where Jesse is lying on his stomach in a pair of plaid pajama pants and no shirt. His back is layered with muscle, a faint tan line evident at his neck and shoulders.

He rolls over when he hears me coming. My eyes are drawn to his tattoos. In addition to the initials of his friends who died and the military insignia on his right arm, he's also got an elaborately decorated skull on his shoulder and an eagle with a Mexican flag wrapped around it on the left side of his chest.

"Sexy." He gestures at my outfit.

I snort. "You too. Don't cover up on my account. Get comfortable."

Jesse laces his fingers behind his head and smiles a slow grin. "I usually sleep naked." He arches his eyebrows suggestively.

There's no way a former army MP sleeps naked. He probably sleeps in full gear with a loaded machine gun snuggled in the crook of his arm. "Go ahead." I give him the eyebrows right back. Then I yank the bedspread from my bed and leave it balled up on the floor. "You know I saw this TV show not too long ago about how hotels never wash their comforters. The investigators found all kinds of horrible stuff on them—fleas, mites, blood . . ."

Jesse makes a face but doesn't budge. "Did they find snakes?" he asks. "Giant camel spiders? Otherwise I think I'll survive."

"I don't know what a giant camel spider is, but it sounds terrible." I shudder. "Aren't soldiers supposed to zip their tents closed or use mosquito netting or something to keep out the bugs?"

"Yeah. Unfortunately. It would have been nice to be able to sleep under the stars without worrying about the wildlife or other humans." He sounds wistful, like he's remembering an unspoiled wilderness instead of a war zone. "In the desert, there are more stars than you ever thought possible. Ten times as many as you can see here."

"I like listening to you talk about your experiences." I sit cross-legged in the center of my bed. "Even the sad ones. I hope someday I find something I love that much."

"If you do, I hope the world doesn't take it away from you." Jesse looks over at me from his bed. "It was the one time when I felt like I was doing what I was meant to do, like I had a real purpose, you know? I was part of a team trying to make the impossible possible for people who are oppressed."

"Being one of Gideon's recorders isn't purpose enough for you?" I say dryly. "We make the impossible possible for people who are lazy and afraid."

"I know, right?" Jesse says. "Sometimes I just want to say, 'If you really want to dive with sharks, why don't you just tell your fear to get lost and go do it?'"

I wonder if it's really that easy for him. "Is now a bad time to tell you I'm afraid of sharks? Normally I'd be already nervous about tomorrow, but I've been focusing so much on finding Rose's killers that I'm too exhausted to worry about anything else."

"Your fear is what's going to make this an epic ViSE." Jesse's voice is full of pride. "I love how you're the kind of girl who runs toward the thing that scares you, not away from it."

I can't bring myself to tell him he's only partially right about me, that what scares me the most is other people, and that I run away from almost all of them. That the only people I even talk to are the ones who haven't grown weary of chasing me. That's partially why I do all the adventure stuff, why no job is too dangerous for me. Because I'm compensating. Because if I do a bunch of incredibly daring things, then no one can call me a coward.

"What about my fear of elevators?" I ask.

"You're not *afraid* of them. You just don't like being enclosed," he says. "That's a survival instinct. A lot of military guys won't take elevators either, because being in one is an indefensible position. Plus," he adds, "no one would pay for an elevator ViSE, so who cares?"

He's got a point. And as usual, he knows exactly what to say to make me feel better. "Speaking of ViSEs, I went through another three on the plane. Lucky number thirteen is another switch party. Baz was there. So was Isaiah. He's only been working for Gideon for a couple of months, right? What do you know about him?"

"Isaiah is a good guy," Jesse says. "He was probably recording it too. There's no way he's involved in this."

"I wonder what Helene would think of him recording stuff like that." Isaiah seems like a nice guy and he treated Rose like a gentleman. I don't want to think of him as someone who cheats on his girlfriend.

"They can't have been together for too long," Jesse says. "Otherwise I would have heard him talk about her."

I remember Isaiah mentioning Thanksgiving in the recording. Jesse's probably right. He could've made it when he was still single. "Well, I hope the rest of the ViSEs aren't switch parties," I say. "I couldn't tell if the nausea was from the overlay or from making out with a bunch of strangers."

Jesse sits up. "Give the recordings to me. I slept so long on the plane that I hit my second wind. I can probably get them all done for you, right now."

"But it's getting late and we have to wake up at seven," I protest.

"It's like nine o'clock and I slept half the day. Just give them to me." Leaning over the edge of the bed, he pulls his headset out of his duffel bag. He unfolds the spiderlike skeleton and slips it on his head.

"If you're sure." I slide out of bed and give him the music box of ViSEs along with my notebook, averting my eyes from his bare chest. "Don't forget to write down who is in them and anything that seems odd. The recordings of the Phantasm break-in and Rose's overdose are in there too, if you want to play those once more in case we missed something." I still haven't been able to bring myself to experience my sister's death again.

"No problem," he says.

"All right. See you in the morning. If you don't get through them all, we'll finish them tomorrow." Sliding safely under my own covers, I give him a little wave and then click off the light over my bed.

"Good night, Winter." Jesse reaches up for his own light.

And then we're alone in the darkness.

CHAPTER 28

Panic claws at my chest as I open my eyes. The furniture is in the wrong spot; the walls have moved. Then I remember where I am. Miami. The hotel room. I sit up slightly. I'm in the bathtub. I know I fell asleep in bed this time—I remember Jesse saying good night to me from across the room. I must have sleepwalked. I tell myself it doesn't mean anything, that the symptoms were brought on by the stress of my sister's death. But fear thrums slow and steady beneath my skin.

I pause in the bathroom doorway to gather my bearings. Just enough moonlight trickles through the blinds to illuminate the outline of the room. My bed is empty, the sheet neatly folded back as if I rose in the middle of the night to go to the bathroom but never returned. Jesse is lying on his stomach, the sheets twisted around his naked back.

"Nice necklace."

I whirl around at the sound of the voice. Rose is perched on the dresser. Reaching up, she adjusts her blond wig. Her red dress is wrinkled, matted and torn in places, and she's barefoot. But otherwise she looks fine. My gaze goes immediately to the door that leads to the hallway. It's closed. Bolted.

I lift a hand to my neck—the rose pendant hangs in the hollow of my throat, even though I know I wasn't wearing it when I went to sleep. "You're not real," I whisper, glancing over at Jesse again. He mumbles something but doesn't wake.

"Of course I am," she says.

"No. You're not really here. You're dead."

"Do you want me to be dead?"

"What kind of question is that? You know I don't." Tentatively, I reach out for her with one hand. I half expect my fingers to pass right through her forearm, like she's a ghost. But she feels solid. Warm even. She rotates her arm and touches her hand to mine—the scars on our palms line up.

There is something very right about that.

"Gideon-oppa says I make my own reality sometimes to avoid the truth."

Rose flicks her wrist as if she's batting away my concerns. "You have more important things to worry about. You're in danger, little sister."

"Danger?"

Before she can respond, the door to the hallway creaks open and a dark figure bleeds into the room. Rose's eyes grow wide. "Run," she says. She throws herself at the menacing form. He grabs her by the hair. Lightning flashes from outside the window and I recognize the intruder. It's the one-eyed man from my dreams. He's holding a knife. With one violent thrust, Rose's body goes limp.

"No!" I scream. I lunge for him and then he turns toward me. I lash out with my fists and feet, but they glance harmlessly off his muscular frame. It's like punching stone.

He tosses me back onto the bed like I am made of feathers. His face leans low. I reach up and jab at his empty eye socket. My fingers penetrate the skin, slipping inside the gaping flesh. For one horrifying second I feel my body being pulled into his.

I yank my arm back. "Let me go!"

"Winter," he says calmly. He's pinning me against the bed now, his hands firmly cupping my shoulders, one knee bracing my legs.

I scream again but he doesn't relax his hold.

"Wake up, Winter."

Gasping, I open my eyes to see it's Jesse holding me, not the one-eyed man. When he releases me, I sit up so quickly I nearly tumble off the end of the bed. My throat feels like I swallowed a bucket of sand. I can manage only a single word: "Rose."

Jesse sits next to me on the mattress. He rubs my back as I slowly choke out what I saw. "It was just a dream," he murmurs.

I let my head dip low, my hair fall forward to hide my eyes. Then I turn and bury my face in his chest, his bare skin cool against the hot tears beginning to fall. "It felt so real, like I watched her die," I say. "And that man was there—the one from Phantasm."

"Shh." Jesse strokes my hair. "We'll find him, okay? I promise I'll help you figure everything out." Slowly, he lays me back down and arranges the covers around me. Then he rises to return to his own bed.

"Could you maybe . . ." I trail off, struggling to form the words. Eventually I just pat a spot on the mattress next to me. "Just for the rest of the night?" My voice hitches.

He nods soberly. "If you want." He slides under my covers.

I turn to face him. "Thank you," I whisper.

"Come here." He pulls me close, curling his arms around me. For a second I'm scared. The tight embrace reminds me of too many terrible memories from when I worked for Kyung. But Jesse's not touching me like the men used to. He's just holding me, stroking my hair. Over and over until I feel calm. By the time my breathing is back to normal, I have molded my body to his. Our heartbeats have fallen into an easy rhythm, their overlapping cadence comforting me.

My eyes are even with his collarbone. I watch it rise and fall with each breath he takes. I slow my breathing even further to match his, and finally I feel safe. It's like we're on a ship, a ship inside of a bottle, the rest of the world locked away outside the glass.

A soft aching spreads throughout me. I could lift my chin, so easily, and pull Jesse's head toward mine. *Kiss him.* I could touch my lips to his and just let go—let him have control. Maybe it's what I need. Maybe then I wouldn't feel alone anymore. Being with him like this feels so familiar, so right. A hard breath escapes my lips.

Jesse's chin tucks against his neck as he looks down at me. "You okay?"

I hide my face in his chest. "I think so."

"You want me to move?"

"No."

He lifts up on one arm, brushes my hair back from my face, and gives me a gentle kiss on the forehead. "Go to sleep, Winter. I'll keep the bad dreams away."

CHAPTER 29

Jesse's still sleeping when I wake a few hours later. Surprisingly, I feel rested. No more nightmares with him beside me. His arm is heavy across my middle. I slide out from his loose embrace and head for the bathroom.

The scalding water of the shower brings the real world into focus. All I can think about is Jesse. His naked chest. The twining scents of sweat and evergreen deodorant. The part of me that so easily replaced a nightmare about my sister with desire for something else.

I dry off and wriggle into my swimsuit, a one-piece navy racing suit I bought for a previous job. The bruises on my neck have gone from purple to an ugly greenish color. Maybe I can put on my wet suit without the dive operators noticing. In the meantime, I layer a hooded sweatshirt and a pair of warm-up pants on top of my suit. I know it's warm outside, but I've been on boats before and the wind can get chilly, especially after the dives when I'm wet. I peek at myself in the mirror and add my standard smudges of black eyeliner.

When I finish in the bathroom, Jesse is sitting at the foot of his bed, a small leather case of toiletries dangling from his right hand.

I can't quite meet his eyes. "The shower is all yours," I say.

When he's finished getting ready, we head downstairs and order a quick hotel breakfast of cereal and fruit. I cut my pineapple into smaller and smaller bites while Jesse eats and makes small talk. I'm still finding it hard to look at him.

Finally he touches my shoulder. "Did you sleep better—"

After you got in bed with me? "Yes," I say quickly.

"Glad I could help," he says. Then he continues, "I played all the remaining ViSEs after you crashed out—one cage dancing, one as an extra in a music video, one swimming with dolphins, the rest with Andy Lynch." He rolls his eyes. "I think that dude might have a drinking problem, but other than that, nothing really stood out to me." He crunches a big spoonful of cereal. "And nothing on the overdose or Phantasm one either. I mean, obviously they changed their door code, and that's the only private info we recorded. What if the ViSEs are a dead end? Maybe we should concentrate on identifying the man from your dreams. You could ask Gideon if he's someone from your past. Maybe if you know who he is, then he'll stop haunting you."

He's right. Gideon will be angry that we disobeyed him and went snooping around Phantasm, but if he can give me answers that help me sleep, it will be worth it. I never expected the one-eyed man to be real—I need to know who he is. "Good idea," I say. "Thanks for helping."

A Jeep Cherokee pulls up outside. A tall guy gets out and heads toward the front door of the hotel.

"I think that's our ride." Jesse pats his pocket and frowns. "I've got to run back to the room for a second. Tell them I'll be right there."

"All right." Blotting my mouth with a napkin, I grab my gear bag and intercept the tall guy in the hotel lobby. "I'm Winter," I say. "Jesse will be right down."

The guy reaches out to shake my hand, and I resist the urge to pull it away. His grip is tight but his smile is friendly. "I'm Eli," he says. "Sam is outside."

Sam and Eli are brothers whom Gideon has hired for other diving ViSEs. They have experience taking tourists out to watch dolphins and to cage dive with different species of sharks.

I loiter in the parking lot of the hotel until I can see Jesse making his way through the lobby. Then I step up into the vehicle and slide my way along the wide bench seat.

Jesse exits out into the sun with his folded recorder headset dangling from his hand. He slides into the back of the Jeep next to me.

I poke him in the ribs. "Kind of an important thing to forget."

He leans in close so only I can hear him. "I spent the night with this hot chick," he says. "Sorry if I'm a little distracted."

I blush. "As long as you focus when we start playing with sharks."

Jesse grins. "You really are scared, aren't you?"

"Maybe a little."

He slips his hand around mine and squeezes my fingers. "I won't let anything happen to you—I promise."

Eli looks back over his shoulder and smiles at us. "Ah. Young love."

I swallow back a lengthy explanation about how it isn't what it looks like, how Jesse and I are just friends. I don't even understand what's happening between us. I definitely don't know how to explain it to anyone else.

Jesse doesn't say anything either. He just squeezes my hand again and smiles to himself.

Sam navigates the traffic with surprising ease and in about ten minutes we pull up at the Miami Beach training facility. Eli spends a few minutes going over all of the safety contingencies related to both diving and sharks while Sam fetches gear for all four of us. He returns with a cart of air tanks, harnesses, wet suits, fins, and even neoprene booties that he says will keep our feet warm if we're in the water for an extended period. I feel a burst of relief when he hands Jesse and me each a titanium diver's knife, but then he makes a point of saying the knives are useless against the sharks. They're more for cutting ourselves free of netting or kelp if we get tangled.

Sam starts to explain the bigger pieces of scuba equipment and I ask if there's any way for me to get decent recordings without going through the whole multiday scuba training first. Sam and Eli offer to teach me to SNUBA, which is like a cross between snorkeling and scuba diving but takes only a couple of hours to learn.

Jesse already has his diving certification, so he observes as I go through all of the basic SNUBA training in a pool. The regulator is similar to a scuba-diving apparatus, but instead of breathing air from a tank on my back, I breathe it through a hose that links to a tank in a raft on the surface of the water. I can't go as deep as a diver, but I can go deep enough that Gideon will never know the difference.

After I'm finished, we gear up and board Sam and Eli's boat. Jesse stands next to me at the railing, the wind whipping our hair back from our faces. Above our heads, the sky is a mass of thick storm clouds, its deep gray color disturbed only by the flight of an occasional seagull.

"Sunny Florida," I grumble.

"At least it's not snowing." He rests a hand on my lower back.

We're heading for a spot only a few hundred yards offshore that Sam and Eli claim is a good place to find hammerhead sharks. The graceful creatures often travel in large groups that will look impressive on a ViSE but according to Eli are generally not dangerous.

Generally not? As I stand at the edge of the boat, I feel like I'm swallowing my own heart. The water is clear enough that I can see the sharks waiting for me. Lured by a mix of chum, the hammerheads have come right up to the side of the boat. They're only about six to eight feet long, but there's something so lethal about the sinuous way they cut through the water, their T-shaped heads tracking the movement around them.

Jesse falls gracefully backward off the edge of the boat in full scuba gear and then accepts a metallic prod from Eli. His main job is going to be to protect me, should I need it, but he's also recording a ViSE.

Not wanting to be outdone, I make a big show of sliding backward into the ocean and then doing a quick check of the SNUBA gear. I'm ready . . . except for the sharks.

Luckily, they've backed away from the boat because of the splashing we made entering the water. I sink slowly beneath the surface, focusing on the lightness of my body. At first it's just me, Jesse, and the clear turquoise ocean. Then a flash of silver—a bright school of fish. Curious. Hungry. Their mouths snap up bits of chum residue. I forget to breathe and the pressure builds up around my head. As I exhale slowly through my mouth, the hammerheads begin to return. One of them swims close enough to bump me, but he's not interested in trying to eat something that's almost as large as he is. Still, his sleek body hits me with a surprising amount of force.

Jesse pokes at the shark with his prod and it swims off. My fear starts to wane. The shark seemed more curious than menacing. I drift deeper in the water, exploring the far reaches of my breathing tether. Below me the ocean fades into blackness.

I explore the various angles the buoyancy of the water affords my body. I float, swim, sink, circle. The sharks grow used to my presence and accept me as part of the ocean. I chase after a bright red-and-blue fish and have a couple close encounters with an impressive tuna who comes to investigate us.

Off in the distance a dark shape rockets past like a torpedo—a bigger shark, a tiger or maybe a bull shark. Both species have been known to attack humans. My heart punches against my breastbone. Embracing my fear, for the sake of the ViSE, I stay submerged for another minute, scanning the water methodically for the bigger shark. Then I slowly float to the surface and signal that I'm ready to reboard the boat.

Jesse rises alongside me. He hauls himself up the boat's ladder and then helps me back onto the deck. Water streams from his wet hair. "What did you think?"

"It was amazing," I say. "Did you see the bigger shark go by?"

"What?" He points at his ear. He must have taken his hearing aid out to dive. "Sorry. I'm half-deaf today."

I decide there's no point in worrying him now that I'm safely back on board. "I said it was amazing!" A smile spreads across my face.

He wraps me in a wet hug, lifting me off the deck for a moment. "You did great. I knew you would rock."

I cling to him for a couple of extra seconds, thinking about how the worst is yet to come. Our next dive is farther offshore, where we're going to actually seek out bigger sharks. But Jesse's right. I can survive this. He brushes his lips against my forehead when I finally pull back, and I hang on to him long enough to go in for a kiss on the cheek. He's not expecting it so he turns at the last second and I end up getting a mouthful of beard stubble.

Looking down at me, he says, "Let's try that again." He turns his head so that his cheek is facing me, but when I lean in to kiss him, he turns back so our lips touch. Quick. Painless. So fast I might have imagined it. But then he presses me against the boat's railing. One hand cradles my face while the other caresses the back of my neck.

"Jess—" I start to say. But his lips swallow up my words, and this kiss is not quick. Jesse's mouth is warm, wanting. I wrap my arms around his neck and feel our bodies fold against each other as I lean into the embrace. His tongue tastes my bottom lip and my knees start to buckle. He reaches out to steady me.

And then a seagull caws, reminding us of where we are. Jesse releases his grip on me. He glances toward the boat's cabin, where Sam is studying the controls and Eli is looking off into the distance. "Sorry. I guess we shouldn't do this at work."

He looks anything but sorry.

I flash him a shaky smile and turn away into the wind. My insides are spinning and twisting like runaway carnival rides, but once again, guilt brings them to a screeching halt. I shouldn't be feeling this way when my sister is dead.

After we eat a light lunch, Sam and Eli take the boat farther out from the shore, trailing turtle decoys and looking for tiger sharks as they head toward the Gulf of Mexico. People have swum with tiger sharks outside of a cage, but neither Jesse nor I have any wish to die today, so we will be recording our ViSEs from behind bars.

There's a reef area a few miles offshore that draws lots of diverse wildlife. As we approach them, I see a fin slicing across the water's surface. Once again my heart lodges neatly in my throat. Unlike the smaller hammerheads, these sharks can weigh more than a car and have been known to attack everything in their paths.

Jesse wraps an arm around my shoulder as I stand at the boat's railing staring out at the ocean. "I'll be right there with you," he reminds me.

"I know. I'm fine."

Sam and Eli drop a cage and secure the SNUBA set-up to the top of it. Then Jesse and I enter the cage together. The water is cooler out here, the wind nipping at the exposed skin on my face as I sink beneath the surface. When I open my eyes, I see that a pair of tiger sharks have come to investigate the cage. Their monstrous bodies, the length of Cadillacs, cut through the water like huge circling torpedoes. I won't need to do any neural amplifying. The rows of serrated teeth, the dead black eyes—there is nothing scarier than a giant shark.

On cue, the larger of the two sharks rockets up toward the surface. Sand swirls in the turbulent water. When it clears, tendrils of red curl before me. Looking up I see the blood spreading out on the surface. Pieces of . . . something fall through the cage bars. A turtle maybe, or a big fish.

A third shark appears, a mako, smaller but no less deadly. A few brave fish venture close to nibble on the leftover scraps of food. The largest shark swims by, dragging a fin against the cage. The bars rattle sharply. The sharks disappear as quickly as they arrived, and for a few moments Jesse and I float in the water alone.

Or are we?

Shadows fade in and out in the distance. Slow. Fast. Waves? Sharks? I can't tell. I glance over at Jesse. He's spinning lazy circles in the water around me, seemingly unconcerned by the sharks' behavior.

We float upward, away from the bottom of the cage. The metal groans under the weight of the water. The smaller tiger shark is back. I can tell them all apart. The bigger tiger is a monster, fifteen feet long at least. It's the stuff of nightmares and horror movies. The other one is maybe ten feet and has a fin that flops to the side as it swims. And then there's the mako, its giant black eyes receding into its head as it slices through the water. Floppy Fin races directly at the cage but then swerves away from the collision at the last moment.

I feel like food. Like a mouse dropped into a snake's enclosure. My heart rattles in my chest. I'm fairly certain I'm sweating inside of my wet suit. Can the sharks sense my fear? I want to close my eyes, but I don't. That would cheat the visers out of one of my senses.

I kick my fins up and down to hover in the center of the cage, being careful to keep all of my extremities away from the bars. The tigers swim in patterns. They circle around. They circle below. I wonder if this is what it's like for their prey, if they toy with it for a while before striking the killing blow. Slowly I exhale and then take in another breath of air.

And then the cage ricochets against the side of the boat with a deafening clang and hard metal slams into me. One of the sharks must have rammed us.

The world goes dark for a second as I instinctively close my eyes. When I open them, Jesse signals me to surface. *About time.* I kick my feet and reach skyward, but I don't go anywhere. My diving boot is caught on the cage.

I tug hard. Still stuck. I imagine the shark returning for another hit.

Its teeth closing around my ankle.

Bones snapping like raw spaghetti.

Bending down, I fumble with one hand, trying to free the loop of neoprene that has snagged itself on the bar. The mako swims by, leaving behind a wake that pushes my body away from the side of the cage. I flail in the water, yanking with all of my strength. And then I see the monster tiger shark glide past, its mouth wide enough to swallow me whole, its jagged teeth eager to tear me to pieces.

It fades into the distance.

Reappears.

Circles out away from me.

Dives low.

It rushes the cage, all dead eyes and sharp teeth.

I open my mouth to scream as the shark slams into the bars.

And my foot.

But there's no piercing pain, no curls of blood in the water. Struggling to remain calm, I try once more to free myself, this time by removing my fin and the boot that is snagged. But the boot has no zipper and the stretchiness of the material makes it cling to my ankle. Pressure builds up in my face and head again.

Frantic, I wave my arms, hoping Sam or Eli can see me from above the water. Where is Jesse? Why did he surface without me? Why hasn't he seen that I'm trapped? A cluster of bubbles escape my lips. My head feels like someone is crushing it in a trash compactor. I can't remember what to do to make the pain go away. The water fades from blue to black as I start to pass out. The last thing I see is a blur of gray as big as a bus, a set of knifelike fins heading for the cage again.

CHAPTER 30

I wake up on the beach, lying on my side. The memory of the sharks rushes back, assaulting me like snapping teeth. Biting back a scream, I test my limbs, one at a time. Left hand. Right hand. Left foot. Right foot. Everything seems to be attached. I exhale, slow and shaky, as I look up at the sky.

The night sky.

I blink rapidly, but the stars are still there. How is that possible? We did the second dive right after lunch. I sit up, glancing around me for my phone. The beach is dotted with bursts of activity—a couple walking along the water, the flickering light of a bonfire just down the way. Above my head, palm trees sway in a gentle breeze, their thick waxy leaves blotting out part of the moon. A chill runs up my spine as I realize I'm wearing the warm-up pants and hooded sweatshirt I wore over my swimsuit, but I don't remember putting them back on.

"Winter?" Jesse is staring at me like he's not quite sure I'm real.

"What happened? What time is it?" I grab the gear bag between us and work the buckle with trembling fingers.

"The sharks decided to try to eat the cage," Jesse says. "Your boot was stuck. Don't you remember?"

"Yes. Sharks. Teeth. What happened after that?"

"You cut yourself loose and I fished you out of the water.

Sam and Eli were a little freaked out. They made me promise not to sue."

I remember the crushing feeling in my head as I struggled to escape. I got so scared I forgot to breathe. "I cut myself loose? But I passed out. Did I almost drown?" My voice is shrill with panic.

Jesse furrows his brow. "You never passed out, did you? I surfaced and expected you to follow. When you didn't, I thought you were being a hotshot and staying to get the perfect footage for the ViSE. A couple of minutes passed but I didn't see a lot of bubbles from your breathing. Then I noticed the line being jerked from below. I got worried, so I went down to get you and saw you trying to take off your boot."

My hands finally manage to loosen the plastic buckle on the gear bag and I begin to unroll the waterproof Velcro seal. A small group of boys pass by us, chattering and laughing. "But I *remember* passing out." I shudder.

"Maybe just for a few seconds," Jesse says. "But you were conscious when I pulled you out of the water. And also for the ride back to the pier. I thought maybe you were in shock, but then you seemed to snap out of it. When we docked, you said you wanted to rest on the beach. I was going to take you to the hospital if you didn't wake up soon."

Jesse's memory makes sense, but it's completely foreign to me. "Did I hit my head or something?" I do a cursory check of my skull, looking for sore spots. Sand rains down from my hair.

Jesse looks concerned. "Not that I know of. I suppose you could have hit it on the cage bars."

I finally fish my phone out of the bag and see it's almost seven o'clock. "I've been lying on this beach for four hours?"

"Yeah. Diving tends to take a lot out of someone. Especially your first trip . . ."

Another chill ripples through me and I'm not sure if it's

from the lost time or ocean breeze. "The last thing I remember is the biggest shark hitting the cage. Maybe if I play the ViSE I'll be able to put everything back together."

"You can try," Jesse says. "But you took your headset off once we got you out of the water."

"Let me see what's recorded."

"Are you sure you want to do that right now?" he asks. "Maybe we should get some food first. Go back to the hotel where we can relax."

"It won't take that long." I'm not going to be able to relax until I know what happened. I slip on my headset and play the ViSE from the beginning. At the part where I expect to lose consciousness, pressure builds up inside my head. And then:

Around me, the water is churning. A dark shape circles. My throat goes tight. Then suddenly, violently, the shark slams into the cage. I try to inhale, but I can't. It's like my lungs are closing up inside me. I tug at my boot again. It's stuck. Everything goes dark for a second. And then I reach down and manage to free my knife from where it's strapped to my leg. Quickly, I cut away the neoprene material and swim toward the surface.

Jesse appears in front of me. One arm encircles me from waist to shoulder in a rescue hold. Together we rise. Eli hauls me out of the ocean and I scramble over the edge of the boat and end up on the hard deck looking up at the sky. The brothers begin to argue. Jesse looks down at me, water dripping from the ends of his brown hair.

"Winter Kim, you have got to stop scaring the shit out of me," he says.

I cough but don't speak. With one hand I reach up to remove my headset.

The ViSE goes dark, a slight shock moving through me.

"I don't remember anything after my boot got stuck," I say.

"Haven't you repressed bad memories before?" Jesse asks gently. "I'm sure you were really scared. Maybe this is just one of those times."

"Maybe," I say. "I did that back in L.A. But I was hoping those times were over."

We take a taxi from the beach back to the hotel. I recline my seat and try to get comfortable as our driver dodges in and out of the South Florida traffic. Grabbing my phone, I get online and attempt to book us the next flight home. No seats are available tonight so I make us a reservation for tomorrow. By the time we make it back to the hotel, my head has cleared and I feel mostly recovered from my ordeal.

"What do you want to do for food?" Jesse asks.

We pass the check-in desk and turn the corner toward the stairwell. "I'm not sure my stomach is settled enough to eat anything," I say. "Maybe some room service later."

"That'll work."

Jesse glances back at me over his shoulder as we head for our room on the second floor. "We can watch bad TV together. Maybe *Jaws* is on."

"Not funny," I say, but I like the idea of relaxing for once.

But then he slides his key into the slot and pushes open our door, and the evening's plans rapidly change.

Someone has ransacked our hotel room.

"Son of a bitch," Jesse says.

The sheets from both beds are balled up on the floor and the mattresses hang askew from the box springs. Our duffel bags have been emptied onto the floor. Even the Bible has been pulled from the top drawer of the nightstand. I scan the wrinkled linens and the pile of clothes strewn around my bag. It doesn't take long to figure out what the thief was after.

Rose's music box lies open on the carpet. It's empty.

The ViSEs are missing.

CHAPTER 31

"Damn it." I retrieve the empty music box and set it on the nightstand. "I never should have let those out of my sight."

Jesse pounds one fist lightly against the wall of the hotel room. "I can't even believe this."

"What are we going to do? Clearly there's something crucial on one of those." Desperation creeps into my voice.

"I swear I didn't see anything important," he says. "But I guess I could've missed something in the background. Let's go ask the hotel clerk if they've got security cameras. Maybe we can figure out who did this."

We return to the front desk where the girl on duty has unfortunately just come on shift. She tells us that only the head of security can review the day's tapes and he won't be back until tomorrow morning.

"So then there's no one on duty now?" I ask. "No security all night?"

"We have a couple of guys working the parking lot and can page the supervisor if needed." She pauses. "Why? Did someone break into your room? I need to call the police if there's been a burglary."

"Forget it," I say. "We'll just come back tomorrow. We're leaving town in the morning, so there's no point in involving the police."

"Well, you should still make a report because—"

"I'll take care of it once we know if anything was stolen," Jesse tells her.

"Well, okay but . . ." Her voice trails off as she wilts under his penetrating gaze.

We head back to our room. I pause in the hallway, studying the lock for signs of forced entry. None. I check the window on the far wall. Double-paned glass, locked.

"I don't understand it," I say. "How'd they get in? How'd they even know we were *here*?"

Jesse flops down on his bed and covers his face with his hands. "What a total nightmare. Do you think Gideon figured out you had Rose's ViSEs and sent someone to steal them?"

"Did you *tell* him I had her ViSEs?"

Jesse removes his hands and looks over at me. "I wouldn't do that to you."

Almost without thinking, I start tidying my side of the room. "You wouldn't go behind my back about Rose's recordings, but you would jump me and try to strangle me just to help Gideon prove a point?" I hold a long-sleeved T-shirt against my chest and neatly fold it into a square.

"Well, I can assure you I won't be doing that ever again either. I'm still kind of sore in certain areas." Jesse grimaces. "But you know how hard it is to disobey Gideon. I never know for sure when he threatens to fire me if he's being serious."

"Right." I reach for another wrinkled shirt. I smooth it, begin to line up its seams. Normally it's hard for me to disobey him too, but lately it hasn't seemed quite as difficult. Losing my sister has changed me. I don't know if it's desperation, necessity, or both. All I know is that Rose used to be the strong one, but now I have to be strong too. Part of being strong means making my own decisions, even if I know Gideon wouldn't agree, even if I might choose wrong.

Jesse exhales deeply. "I'm sorry. I feel like this is my fault somehow."

"Why?" My fingers grab the next balled-up piece of fabric—the sweatpants I brought to sleep in.

"Because I'm the one who told you there was no other choice except to come here and do the ViSE."

"It's not your fault, Jesse. But if whoever took those recordings thinks I'm going to stop looking for them, they're crazy. All this does is reinforce that I'm getting closer."

"I hope you're right. Maybe we'll recognize someone on the security footage tomorrow. But right now I'm so hungry I can barely think straight—I'm going to order some food." He tosses me the room service menu. "What do you want?"

I shake my head. "All I want is to kick myself for being so stupid. I should have kept those ViSEs with me at all times."

"You had your mind on other things. You weren't stupid."

I did have my mind on other things—on Jesse. Which *is* stupid considering everything that's happened lately. But sometimes adversity brings people together. I'm not sure I would have survived today without him. Even having him here right now takes the edge off this latest disaster.

After I finish cleaning up my side of the room, I rinse myself off in the shower and change into clean clothes for sleeping. Jesse orders a burger and fries for himself and a plate of grapes and sushi for me, even though I insist I'm not hungry.

"You should eat something," he says. "Diving burns a lot of calories." He goes to the minibar and removes a tiny bottle of vodka from the fridge. "I need a drink. This day has been hell. First, I thought those sharks were going to bite us in half. Then we get robbed."

"I know. Can you believe Gideon sent me here for my own safety?" I snort. "Good thing almost dying on a regular basis pays well. Toss me one of those." I gesture at the vodka.

"I thought you didn't drink?"

"I'm making an exception for today."

"Okay." Jesse twists open a little glass bottle and hands it to me.

I hold the bottle up to my lips, the sharp smell of liquor stinging my nasal passages. I pause, feeling like I'm standing at a tangible threshold—one that maybe I shouldn't cross. Hesitantly, I take a half swallow. "Just because we lost the ViSEs doesn't mean we can't still hunt down Rose's killers," I say.

"What are you thinking?" Jesse asks.

I take a long drink, the bitter liquid numbing my throat. "The only suspects that make any sense are someone from Phantasm or one of the guys who knew her from a club—some deranged ViSE junkie who thinks she recorded him doing something he doesn't want anyone to know about."

"You definitely don't think Andy is capable of hurting her?" Jesse asks.

I shake my head. "From what I can tell, he was crazy about her. Plus he seems so harmless. I guess maybe if he was on drugs or out of his mind or something."

"From what I saw, he definitely drinks a lot," Jesse says.

I barely hear him. The bottle of vodka trembles in my fingers as I am suddenly consumed by a horrible possibility. *I'm* the one who is sometimes out of my mind. Today wasn't an isolated incident. I've blacked out before. Maybe I'm missing other gaps of time I don't remember losing. Maybe the reason I'm so consumed with the idea of finding out what happened to Rose is because some part of me already knows.

Maybe I hurt her, and I blocked it out.

There's a sharp knock at the door and Jesse rises to accept our trays of food. I gulp the rest of the vodka and grab another bottle of liquor—whiskey this time—from the minibar. I tilt my head back and finish it in a single shot, wincing as it burns a trail of fire down my throat. But at least I'm not shaking anymore.

Jesse signs the white charge slip and then sets my tray on my bed. "What is it?" He settles in across from me and grabs his bacon cheeseburger. "You look like you're going to throw up."

"What if I hurt Rose?" I blurt out. "What if I killed her?"

"What?" Jesse blinks rapidly. He sets the burger down unbitten. "Why would you say something like that?"

My body is warm and hazy from the alcohol, but my head feels clearer than it has in days. "It just kind of fits. If I could forget cutting myself free today, maybe there are other things I can't remember."

"Yeah, but—"

"This isn't the first time something like this has happened to me," I say miserably. "I blacked out during the break-in at the penthouse. I know I stabbed the guy, but I don't remember doing it." I look up at Jesse. "And there have been other instances of lost time in the past, especially back in L.A."

"That doesn't mean you hurt Rose."

"True, but no one besides me seems all that interested in finding her killers. Is it because you guys *know* what happened and are just trying to protect me? Tell me the truth, Jesse. Did I hurt my sister?"

CHAPTER 32

"No." Jesse shakes his head. "I know what happened today freaked you out, but come on. You loved Rose more than anything."

I flinch at the past tense of the word *love*. Every reminder that she's really gone cuts me a little deeper. "But one of the figures on the ViSE was smaller—about my size. And I overslept the next morning, almost like I'd been out extra late and didn't remember it. What if I did it and blocked out the memory?"

"Please don't think that." Jesse downs another miniature bottle of vodka and then comes to sit next to me on my bed. He takes my hands in his, slowly tracing the scar on my palm with one finger. "You would never hurt her, Winter."

Rose told me once that when we first came to St. Louis, the doctors wanted to keep me in the hospital because they thought I might hurt myself or someone else. Gideon wavered. Rose refused to let it happen. The two of them could take care of me better than some overworked nurses, she said. They fought about it and eventually Rose threatened to hurt herself if Gideon sent me away. That way we'd both be sent away and we'd still be together. She loved him, but she chose me. She said she always would. I don't even remember any of the fighting they supposedly did. More lost hours. Hours so far gone I didn't even realize I was missing them until this moment.

What if the doctors were right and Rose was wrong?

"Do you want me to call Gid?" Jesse's voice is full of concern.

"No." I set my tray of uneaten food on the nightstand and sink back to the mattress.

Jesse reclines next to me. "Come here." He pulls me close and kisses me on the forehead.

I nestle into the crook of his arm. "I feel lost. I don't even feel like myself without her."

"I know." He rubs my back gently. At first I tense beneath his soft touch, but then I relax. *You run toward your fears.* I focus on the sensation of his hands moving across the thin material of my T-shirt. *You would never hurt her.*

"You don't think I hurt her?" I ask.

"No." Slowly, his touch grows firmer.

He shifts his body until we're both on our sides, lying face-to-face. His eyes are closed, but the corners of his mouth twitch slightly. I'm close enough to see the tiny grooves in his lips. He runs one finger across the narrow strip of skin that exposes itself when my shirt rides up in the back.

I don't know if it's the alcohol or the adrenaline of the day or something else, but I'm not scared. I press my face into Jesse's chest, inching closer to give him better reach. I want to be normal. I want to be connected. I think of Rose telling me I need to experience what it's like to be with a guy who cares about me. Maybe she was right. Maybe if I just let whatever happens happen, it'll break the curse and I'll be able to feel things and trust people.

"Say it again," I whisper.

"You didn't hurt your sister." Jesse's fingers slide beneath the hem of my shirt. He's using both hands now. No one has ever given me a massage before, and it's as if he's kneading out eighteen years' worth of knots.

I exhale hard, my breath hot against his skin. I feel a tremor move through him. He presses his lips to my hairline—another chaste kiss, the kind Rose used to give me at bedtime at the orphanage. I angle my head upward and trace the contours of his chin and jaw with my mouth, the texture of his beard stubble fascinating me. My hands find their way beneath his T-shirt. I explore the muscles of his chest with my fingertips.

Groaning softly, he glances down at me. "You probably shouldn't do that."

"I want to," I say. Jesse shared his secrets with me and he didn't judge me for mine. And whether or not it's true, I could tell by the look on his face that he thinks it is absolutely impossible I had anything to do with what happened to my sister.

Rose was right. He really does care about me. I want to care about him back. I want to let my guard down, to be touched and not filled with dread. I want something decent to come from the horror of the past few days. It's not wrong to crave a bit of comfort after enduring so much pain. My sister would understand. She would want this for me. My lips make their way around to the other side of Jesse's face, trailing gentle kisses from his chin up to his disfigured ear.

His body goes tense. At first I think it's because he's not used to being touched there. But then he pulls away. "Winter, you're drunk."

"No, I'm not. I had two drinks. Just enough to relax for once."

"Okay. But you've gone through a lot lately. I know you're in a vulnerable pl—"

I place one finger on his lips. "Stop protecting me. It's sweet, but it's not what I need right now."

Jesse swallows hard. "What do you need right now?"

"I need to feel human." I pause. "Whole. Connected." I lean in to kiss him.

He moves away. "We should talk first."

"*Now* you want to talk?" I ask. "About what, exactly?"

"About you and me." Jesse sits up suddenly and reaches for a half-empty minibottle of liquor on the nightstand.

I slip it out of his fingers and set it next to my uneaten food. I'm afraid he's going to tell me about how much he cares or how he's liked me for months. I'm not in the same place as he is, not yet anyway. I don't want talk of serious feelings to ruin this moment. I don't want to change my mind. "Let's talk later." I pull him back down to the bed with me.

Jesse looks like he's going to protest, but I trace my lips across his earlobe, exhaling against the skin of his neck. His whole body convulses. His eyelids fall shut as our mouths tentatively brush against each other. And then there is only heat. Our lips connect. Break apart. Meet again. His tongue gently coaxes my mouth open. I embrace his warmth, pull him tight against me.

"You are incredible," he whispers between kisses. He rolls onto his back and positions me on top of him, my shirt still riding up, our warm skin pressed tight together. My whole body is liquid. No, my whole body is helium. I'm flowing, floating. For once the pain is fading. Jesse's hands are in my hair, on my back, on the curve of my hip. He slides my shirt up over my shoulders. I freeze up, suddenly aware of how exposed I'll be.

"The light," I say.

Jesse reaches over and flicks the switch. The room goes dark and I can breathe again.

"You okay?" he asks.

"Yes." I let him tug my shirt over my head. He drops it to the floor of the hotel room. I stare deep into his hazel eyes as I trace one finger along his scar.

"Nothing has to happen," he says. "I can just hold you."

Everything feels so right, as if my body has been waiting for this. "I want things to happen," I murmur. I tug at his shirt, pulling it over his broad shoulders and flinging it to the floor. I bend low, pressing my lips to his eagle tattoo on his chest. "I want you."

Now it's Jesse's turn to go tense. "Winter?" He runs one hand down the bruise on my face. "Are you sure?"

"I'm sure."

Jesse's whole face lights up and he shakes his head in disbelief. He pulls me down against him, tangling his hands in my hair again.

Tears well in my eyes, but for once they're the good kind. One falls, splashing down on his neck, finding its way into a crevice between two hard tendons.

He reaches up to trace the hollows of my eyes. "You're crying."

"I'm just happy. It'll be the first time since . . ." I trail off, not wanting to empower my sexual assaults by acknowledging them in this moment.

"It'll be the first time," Jesse says firmly.

Our mouths find each other in the dark. His kisses deepen and his hands caress me. I am a thousand swirling emotions, like no one has ever touched me before. He tugs gently at the drawstring of my sweatpants. My brain starts pushing panic buttons, but I silence them one after the next. This is Jesse. This isn't some slimy businessman, some stranger who paid to own me for a couple of hours. Jesse cares about me. I reach out for Rose's words.

Jesse loves you.

Jesse loves you.

Jesse loves you.

But then, without warning, Jesse pulls away from me.

"I can't do this," he says.

CHAPTER 33

I open my eyes. "What's wrong?"

"I just can't. I'm sorry."

"Too much liquor?" I ask.

He makes a mock offended face. "No. Trust me, I *can*. I just—it suddenly feels like a bad idea."

I inch away from him on the bed. "Oh. So you changed your mind." I can't keep the hurt from leaching into my voice.

Jesse buries his face in his hands for a few seconds and then raises himself up and swings his feet around so he's sitting on the edge of the bed. He rakes both hands through his hair. "It's not that I changed my mind. I'm not sure I've ever wanted anything more in my whole life."

I focus very hard on a spot on the ceiling. "So then what's the problem?"

"You," he pauses, struggling for the right phrasing, "got so tense."

"What?"

"It was like you went rigid, like you just wanted it to be over." He sighs. "I don't want it to be like that."

"Sorry," I say, which is probably the stupidest thing ever. Who apologizes for being afraid to have sex? I swear under my breath. I went so many years not wanting anyone to touch me, and now that my head is finally able to cope with being touched, my body is finding new and creative ways to push people away.

"Don't apologize," Jesse says. "I shouldn't have rushed you."

"You didn't rush me. I wanted to." Certain parts of me still want to.

He flicks the light back on. "I don't know what to do. I would hate it if we were together and you regretted it later." His eyes soften.

I curl the sheet tight around my body. This is about who I used to be. Jesse said he wouldn't judge me, and he's not, but he's always going to treat me like I'm fragile.

Like I'm damaged.

I think about how different it is from the way Andy treats me. To him, I'm normal. Just another girl.

Is it wrong that I am desperate to be normal?

"What?" Jesse asks.

"Sorry. I was thinking about Andy."

Jesse recoils like I slapped him. "Ouch. Cold, even for you."

"You know that's not what I mean. But I like how he acts around me. He treats me like I'm normal."

"And what do I treat you like?"

"A wounded animal," I say. "A victim." I know Jesse can't help it. He's protecting us both. I know he means well, but I refuse to be a victim anymore.

I stretch out in the bed, staring up at the textured ceiling of the hotel room. Jesse doesn't have anything to say about how he treats me. We both know why he does it. We both know he might always do it.

We both know it's never going to work for me.

Tears rise up like a flash flood. I don't want to lose Jesse completely, but I don't want to spend the rest of my life constantly being reminded of how broken I am, either.

He sits on the edge of the mattress and watches me cry, one

hand brushing my hair back from my face. Finally he says, "Tell me what I can do to make this better."

"You wish I'd never told you about my past, don't you?" I ask.

"No." He shakes his head violently. "As much as I hate the thought of what you went through, I want to know all of you, Winter. I just don't want to hurt you more."

"I'll be fine. I just need a few minutes to calm down." I wipe my eyes with the back of one hand. "I think I might get some air, walk down to the pool."

"You can have the room to yourself if you want," Jesse says softly. "I'm going to take a shower."

"All right." I stare at the ceiling again until Jesse disappears into the bathroom. When I hear the water start to run, I cry harder. I hate that I hurt him, but it needed to be said. I know he wants to be with me. It's better he know now why it might never happen.

I think about what it felt like to be so close to Jesse, to almost be loved. A wound opens inside me at the sheer loss of possibility. I fight back another wave of tears.

Slipping out from beneath the covers, I trade my sweatpants for a pair of jeans. This room is suffocating me. I put on my shirt, finger-comb my hair, and grab one of the keycards.

I unbolt the door and open it. A blast of chilly air wafts in from the hallway and my skin turns to gooseflesh. The hotel must keep their air con on about sixty degrees.

Letting the door fall shut, I turn back to survey the room. The only hoodie I brought is full of sand from the day's outing. I glance around at Jesse's side of the room. He's replaced all of his clothes back into his duffel bag, which is half tucked beneath his bed.

He won't care if I borrow a sweatshirt. He's always trying to get me to wear his clothes. I cross the room and start to unzip his bag, but then I notice one of his hoodies folded neatly behind it—all the way under his bed, almost completely out of sight.

Grabbing the sweatshirt, I tug it over my head, comforted by the faint scent of Jesse's deodorant that holds fast to it. As I'm heading back to the door, I slip my hands into the hoodie's middle pocket almost without thinking. My fingers graze hard plastic. A lot of hard plastic.

I pull out a handful of blue memory cards, my insides going even colder as I see my neatly labeled numbers on them.

CHAPTER 34

It takes me a moment to process what I'm seeing, but then dread washes over me. Does this mean . . . No, it can't. I swallow hard. But there's no other explanation. Jesse staged the hotel room burglary in order to steal the ViSEs. That's what he was doing when he left me in the lobby at breakfast and went back for his headset. It was all a lie. Which means there must be something horrible on one of these recordings—something that implicates him in Rose's death.

My throat feels thick. I struggle to breathe. Should I try to play them right now, before he gets out of the shower? If I do, he might catch me. I've been so sure Jesse would never hurt me, but someone who would craft such an elaborate lie could be capable of anything. I could go out for that walk like I planned, but I don't feel safe vising in a public place. I could wait until he's done showering and lock myself in the bathroom to play them. That's a smart idea. A rational idea.

I am not feeling rational.

I have to know what he's hiding from me.

Stripping off the hoodie, I take the ViSEs back to my bed. One at a time, I slip each of the cards I haven't played into my headset. It doesn't take me long to find it. A ViSE of Jesse and Rose.

Jesse is standing in the hallway outside the penthouse. "Your hair is wavy," he says.

I remember the wig I wore to Zoo. Rose must have been wearing it to record this.

"Do you like it?"

"Sure. But I like it regular too." He looks down at me. "Are you going to let me in?"

Without speaking, I open the door wide enough so that he can enter.

"So did you mean those things you said on the phone?" he asks, his voice low. "Or are you just messing with me?"

"Oh, you'll know when I'm messing with you." My lips curl into a grin.

Jesse cocks his head to the side. "I have to say I'm surprised. You've never acted like you were into me."

"Maybe it just took me a while to figure out what I wanted." I shut the door and lead Jesse into the living room.

"You sound funny," he says. "And you're acting weird. Have you been drinking?"

I let out a throaty, but girlish giggle. "I'm just happy to see you."

"Well, I've been drinking," Jesse admits. "I needed a little liquid courage."

"Why?" My smile widens.

"I don't know. I'm nervous." He clasps his fingers together in front of his body.

"You worry too much," I say, pressing him back against the living room wall.

A sharp pain spikes through my chest.

"Me? You worry—"

I silence him with a kiss. His eyes widen but then fall shut. And so do mine. He tastes like liquor and breath mints. He wraps his arms around me. Heat radiates through me as his mouth traces its way down my neck to my collarbone.

He groans softly. "I can't believe this is actually happening."

"I can." Opening my eyes, I break away and lead him to the sofa.

The pain extends down into my stomach and up into my throat. No wonder Jesse didn't want me to see this.

I can't play this.

I *have* to play this.

I can only bear to engage the recording in small snippets, opening my eyes wide every few seconds to block out some of the experience. The ViSE plays out like a movie montage, a series of separate scenes fused together by my beating heart.

Beat.

I pull him down onto the sofa with me.

Beat.

More kissing. "What are you doing?" he says. Instead of answering, I begin to unbutton my shirt.

Beat.

Jesse stares for a moment. Then he folds back the fabric, his mouth tracing the curve of my left breast. His hands are everywhere. Soft. Caressing. "You are so beautiful. So much more than I deserve."

Beat.

He shucks off his shirt and then pulls me in close, his strong grip locking our bodies together. He kisses me hard as his hands explore the flesh of my back.

My breath hitches; blood courses through my veins. I'm not sure how much more I can take. I pause the ViSE and open my eyes for a moment. The hotel room is quiet. Jeese is still in the bathroom. Bile burns in my throat. I squeeze my eyes shut again. I have to know exactly how far this goes. I have to know how deep the secrets run between Rose and me.

I lie back and pull him down on top of me. Our bodies twine together. I can feel how much he wants me. But still, his touch is so gentle. "Are you sure?" he murmurs. "I don't want to hurt you."

I rock against him and pleasure explodes in my brain. I exhale sharply. "I want you to hurt me."

"Winter?"

My eyes flick open. Jesse stands in the bathroom doorway wearing only a towel. His face is ghost pale. I yank the headset off without even pressing pause, flinching from the shock. My face goes red with shame and then anger at the thought I should feel ashamed. Clearly, Jesse is the one who should feel bad.

"Why didn't you tell me?" My voice wavers slightly.

"Tell you what?"

"I want you to hurt me," I spit out. "That does sound like something my sister would say."

Jesse tightens the towel around his waist and steps toward me. "It's not what you think."

I scoot backward. "Stay away from me." I dig in my duffel bag and come up gripping one of my throwing knives.

"Winter . . ." Jesse's voice falters.

I position both my bed and my blade between us. "If it's not what I think, what is it then?"

Jesse sighs. He slips on a pair of pajama pants and lets the towel fall to the floor. He approaches me again, both hands raised in surrender. "We both know you're not going to throw that at me."

"Don't be so sure." I gesture at the headset. "Did I know about this? And block it out? Was I mad at Rose?" Finally a guy seems to like me and she has to go and seduce him. Maybe I care about Jesse more than I realize.

Maybe some part of me hated my sister.

Maybe I killed her.

"It's complicated." Jesse sits on the edge of his bed, a storm of emotions flitting across his face.

"Oh, I bet it is." I toss the knife, headset, and ViSEs into my bag and yank my sandy sweatshirt over my head. I can't be here anymore. It's not even the fact that Jesse was with her. It's the way he held her, like she was made of porcelain. Like she was perfect. "If she was so much more than you deserve, what am I? Some cheap replacement?" I look away. "How long were you two—I mean, why keep it a secret? Everyone preferred her to me. I would have understood."

"I don't prefer her to you," Jesse says. "I never have. Just listen."

But I can't listen. I keep playing the ViSE in my head, feeling his soft touch, hearing him say things that a guy would never say to a girl unless she *mattered*.

"How come you're not more upset that she's gone?" My face is wet. I don't even remember starting to cry.

"I am upset, but only because of what it's doing to you." Jesse makes his way toward the foot of my bed, positioning himself between me and the door. "Winter, please. There has never been anything between me and your sister."

"How stupid do you think I am, Jesse?"

"Did you finish the recording?"

I shudder a little at the implications of that. "I saw enough."

"If you don't believe me, you need to play the end."

"No thanks." I push past him and head for the door.

He grabs me before I make it out into the hallway. Spinning me around, he forces me up against the wall of the hotel room. "Your sister didn't record that ViSE," he says. "It was—"

I cut him off, wrestling free of his grip. "*Seriously?* What is that? Some bullshit version of the 'it wasn't me' defense? I know my own home. So try again."

I expect him to deny it, but he doesn't say anything. He just waits.

Watches.

"Well?" I finally prompt. "You're expecting me to believe some other girl invited you into the penthouse and seduced you?"

"I can't believe there's no part of you that remembers. Not even after tonight. I thought maybe when I touched you—" His voice cracks. He buries his face in his hands. "Jesus Christ, what does that make me?"

And then it hits me, like the fifteen-foot tiger shark ramming into our cage. "*Me?* You're trying to say *I* recorded that?"

Jesse stares at the plush carpet. "I didn't know." His voice is hollow. "I didn't know you black out, that you forget things. Gideon told me afterward."

I laugh—a brittle metallic sound. "You're trying to say I invited you over, seduced you, and then forgot all about it? Wow, you must not have been very good."

Jesse deflates like I stabbed him. "I deserve that," he says. "Trust me, you can't hurt me worse than I've hurt myself over this. Imagine falling for a girl who spends months pushing you away only to one night seem crazy about you." He glances up at me. "And you know it's too good to be true, but you let yourself believe it anyway because you've wanted her for so long. And then the next day she doesn't remember any of it. And then you find out she's got PTSD, that she represses *bad* memories. And all you can think is that maybe you took advantage of a girl with . . . problems. That if she knew what had happened she'd hate you, and you wouldn't even blame her."

"Stop it." I squeeze my eyes shut for a moment and press my fingertips to my temples. "Just stop it. You're lying to me. Rose lied to me. Next thing I know, Gideon will be lying to me."

"Gideon." Jesse shudders. "I have never seen him so pissed in my entire life. He threatened to break every bone in my body. That's the only reason he told me about your condition. The only reason he didn't fire me—or murder me—was because I told him I was falling for you."

"No." I shake my head. "They trained you in the army, right? To trick people. To manipulate. You're really good at it. You staged a *burglary* to hide this from me." My whole body is shaking. Words are flying out of my mouth, sharp, uncontrolled, a spool of barbed wire unraveling. "That's insane. You're the crazy one, not me."

Jesse continues like I didn't even say anything. "Every time I see you, all I can think about is how it felt to be so close to you. How much it *meant* to me. And how to you it must've meant nothing. You apparently never wanted it to happen." He rests his forehead in his hands.

"Because it *didn't* happen!" If I did that, then God only knows what I've done and forgotten about. Jesse is manipulating me. He has to be. I remind myself of the way everyone looked in his Phantasm ViSE. Like prey.

I will not be prey.

"You're a liar." I sling my duffel bag over my shoulder and grab my backpack from the floor. "I might black out after a shark nearly eats me, but there's no way I would forget something like us . . . whatever. There's no way I would do it in the first place."

"Really? Because it seemed like you were going to do it about thirty minutes ago," Jesse says softly.

I think back to the two of us in bed together, to the way my body called out for his. He's right about that moment and I hate him for it. But he's not right about this ViSE. "What kind of person tries to use someone's psychological problems to manipulate her?" I snap. "But that's how you're wired, isn't it? Everyone is just a collection of vulnerabilities."

"Not everyone," Jesse says. "Not you. You really didn't feel anything . . . familiar about what happened?"

"Stop talking." I refuse to acknowledge the multiple times Jesse touched me and it felt comfortable, like it was meant to happen. *Or had happened before.* No. That just means he's good at . . . touching girls. I can't even look at him. "If that were me, the card would have ended up with my ViSEs, not Rose's. Nice try, though. You're very convincing."

"Winter. Don't leave. Just think about it for a couple minutes."

"Screw you, Jesse." I rip open the door to the room and flip one last glance at him over my shoulder. "Oh, wait. I guess I already did, right?"

I barely remember the stairs to the lobby, the cab ride to the airport, the ticket counter, the security checkpoint. I spend six hours at the gate waiting for a standby spot to open up, but it's mostly a blur. The only thing I remember is sitting with my back to the terminal, so I don't have to see the display of snow globes in the souvenir shop across the corridor. Normally I'd want to examine them all, to pick them up and shake them, to buy the one that called out to me the most. Unfortunately, this is one memory I don't want captured in glass. This is one trip I just want to forget.

CHAPTER 35

When I get off the plane in St. Louis, I follow the trail of people in front of me down one level to the baggage claim area. Snatching my duffel bag from the wide silver carousel, I head for the nearest bathroom. I duck inside a stall and pick through my folded clothes until I find my knives. I tuck one in the center pocket of my hoodie and the other into my left boot. At the sink, I splash a little water on my face and pull my hair back into a ponytail. Then I head for the taxi line.

The wind slices between the terminal and the parking garage, cutting through my clothing, chilling my blood. I raise my hood over my ears and pull my arms inside my sleeves, hugging myself to stay warm. Around me, sagging travelers tuck their chins low against the bitter cold.

"The Lofts," I say when I make it to the front of the line, waving off the cabbie's offer to put my bags in the trunk. But as he pulls away from the curb, I decide I don't want to go home. Gideon might be waiting for me. Who knows what Jesse told him? He'll yell at me for leaving Miami on my own when I could be in danger. He'll put me under house arrest in the penthouse and call it protection.

My chest aches. I've spent years learning to protect myself, trying to make myself invulnerable. And yet I let Jesse close enough to hurt me. He told me himself that he wasn't a very nice guy, that he did terrible things in the name of getting what he wanted. I guess I thought I was an exception to that.

Sighing, I sink back against the cracked vinyl seats. I've got twenty minutes to figure out where to go, but right now my brain is fixated on one thing, and I can't find the strength to lock away my feelings.

Ignoring the talk radio blaring from the speakers, I close my eyes and give myself over to the pain. I think about what it felt like to kiss Jesse, to be held by him. I let the tears fall. How could I have misjudged him so badly? Could he have faked the emotions in our Phantasm ViSE in order to fool me into believing that he cared? Could he have faked *everything* since the day we first worked together? I don't want to believe that.

The cab leaves the highway and turns left onto a two-lane road. Clusters of houses and shops are replaced by trees. We're skirting the perimeter of the Green. A row of gated streets hides an entire network of sprawling estates.

"Wait," I say. "Let me out here."

The driver looks at me like I'm crazy. In my jeans and hoodie I definitely don't look like Green material.

"My friend lives nearby," I explain.

When he pulls over, I grab my bags, slide out into the cold, and toss him a couple of folded bills. Now all I have to do is find Andy's house. As the cab pulls away from the curb, I kneel down and fish my phone out of my backpack.

Andy answers right away. "Winter. Any news about your sister?" His voice is heartbreakingly hopeful.

I need to put him out of his misery. Letting him have false hope is cruel. "Nothing new," I say. "But are you at home? Can I stop by for a few minutes?"

"Sure." A pause. "I live at 17 Winghaven. In the Green. You need directions?"

"No. I'm actually in the neighborhood. See you soon."

I sling my bags over my shoulder, tuck my hands inside the

cuffs of my hoodie, and jog to keep warm. My breath makes frosty clouds as I head toward Andy's place.

There's a rent-a-cop parked at the entrance to the neighborhood, but all I get is a raised eyebrow as I stroll by. Number 17 is the fifth house on the left—I recognize it from the backyard-party ViSE.

I knock tentatively on the front door, my knuckles going red in the frigid air. A dog barks. Andy answers, wearing a pair of tear-away pants and a T-shirt. His hair is sticking up in the back like maybe my phone call woke him, even though it's after lunchtime. He studies me for a few seconds before speaking, taking in my red eyes and my luggage. His forehead creases with worry.

"Are you okay?" he asks finally.

"Yes." I fidget with the strap of my duffel bag. "But we should talk."

He nods. "Come on in."

I slip inside and a wave of comfort surges through me. The living room ceiling is vaulted and there's a huge flat-screen TV in the corner, but that's where the grandeur ends. The black leather sofa is bleeding stuffing from one corner and the coffee table is covered with ashtrays and empty beer bottles. Football pads are piled in a recliner and cords from a gaming console snake across the hardwood floor. Something about the clutter makes me feel safe.

"Sorry," he says. "It's kind of a mess. My parents are out of town. I had some friends over last night."

A German shepherd lopes into the room.

"Touchdown," I say. I bend over to ruffle the dog's brown and black fur as I set my bags on the ground. He puts his paws on my chest and tries to lick my face. I turn so that he gets cheek instead of lips.

"That's right." Andy whistles sharply and Touchdown sits back on his haunches, his brown eyes looking somewhat chagrined. "How did you know his name?"

I probably heard Andy say it on a ViSE, but I can't exactly tell him that. "Rose must have mentioned him at some point."

"Figures. He always gets more love than me." Andy pats the dog on his head and then shoos him away. Touchdown sprawls out on his belly in front of the TV. Andy turns back to me. "I'd offer you food, but all we have is beer. I was getting ready to order a pizza. You game?"

"That would be great." I realize I haven't eaten anything since lunch yesterday.

My phone buzzes in my pocket—undoubtedly a text from Jesse. I don't answer. I don't even check. There are only a handful of people who have my number, none of whom I want to talk to right now. I move a rumpled football jersey aside and perch on the edge of the sofa.

Andy's eyes flick toward my vibrating pocket for a second, but he doesn't say anything. "What kind of pizza do you like?"

"Anything is fine."

He fishes his phone out from beneath a stack of sports magazines and orders a large pizza with extra pepperoni. Before he can put the phone down, it rings. He frowns at the screen. "I've got to take this. I'll be right back." He disappears into the kitchen.

I huddle on the sofa, my arms crossed over my chest. I tap one foot repeatedly as I try to figure out how to tell Andy that Rose is dead.

A few minutes later he returns with two bottles of beer in one hand and a two liter of soda in the other. "Pick your poison."

I point at one of the beers and Andy opens the bottle and hands it to me. So much for not drinking. Right now I would take anything to distract me from what happened in Miami. "You know you're contributing to the delinquency of a minor, right?" I lift the bottle to my lips and take a long swallow, embracing the sour flavor.

Andy winks. "You won't tell on me, will you? I've gotten

more than enough lectures from my agent lately." He sets the bottle of soda down on the coffee table and opens the other beer. He downs half of it in one gulp. "So you said you needed to talk to me. What's up?"

Rose is dead. My mouth refuses to form the words. I decide to start with the easier reason I came here. "You said your parents are out of town?"

Andy's eyes widen slightly. "Yeah. Why?"

"I need a place to stay for a day or two. I'm avoiding my brother."

"You can stay here if you want," Andy says. "But will your boyfriend have a problem with it?"

"I don't have a boyfriend." The words stab me in the chest like a handful of needles.

"Oh, right. He's just your coworker." Andy gestures around him with one hand. "Then welcome home."

My phone buzzes again. I peek at it but don't answer. It buzzes again. And again. Does Jesse really think I'll answer a call if I won't respond to a text? I silence it completely and tuck it into my pocket.

"Your *coworker*?" Andy raises an eyebrow.

"Yes." I take another drink of my beer.

"So you never filled me in on what the police had to say about Rose's disappearance," he says.

"Oh. I—" The bottle slips out of my hand and lands on its side on the coffee table. Beer spills out on the wood. Damn it. I don't see any napkins nearby, so I contain the spill with the sleeve of my hoodie. Andy heads for the kitchen again and returns with a roll of paper towels. I blot at the varnished wood.

"Forget the table." He leans forward. "Did someone threaten you? Did someone you know do something to her? Maybe your *coworker*?"

Oh, he did things to her, all right. I hide my trembling hands in my lap. "It's not like that. Jesse and Rose were . . . close."

"So then how come you never went to the police? I called

the station to ask if there had been any news and they had no record of a missing persons report ever being filed."

I furrow my brow. "No, that's not true. We filed a report with Detective Ehlers. My brother asked for him specifically because a friend said it was someone we could trust."

The doorbell rings and Touchdown starts barking. I flinch.

"Relax." Andy vaults up from the sofa again and heads for the door. "It's just the pizza guy."

Feeling silly, I turn to watch him flash a gold credit card at a kid in a red-and-blue uniform. Andy and the guy share a laugh about something and then he shuts the door. He returns to the sofa and drops the pizza box and a stack of napkins on the coffee table. "So you really talked to a detective?"

I nod. "There's something you should know, though. She's not missing." I fiddle with the ball of damp paper towels. "Rose is dead."

"What?" Andy's jaw drops. "How? When?"

"Someone killed her," I whisper. "They threw her body in the river, but they sent a ViSE of the whole thing to our boss." My eyes start to water. I bite my lower lip to keep it from trembling.

"Winter, I am so sorry. Oh my God." Andy leans in to give me a hug.

His touch makes me think of the recordings with him and my sister. Even though they were full of drinking and flirting, I could sense how much he cared about her in them and I can feel it now too. "I apologize for not telling you sooner," I say. "I'm still struggling to accept things myself."

"Maybe that's why the missing persons department didn't know anything about her. You probably talked to a homicide detective." Andy offers me a pizza napkin from the coffee table as a tissue. "Do the cops have any idea who did it?"

"Our boss thinks someone killed her over something she accidentally recorded on a ViSE, but no one seems to know anything for certain." I dab at my eyes with the napkin.

"I'm sorry. That's horrible." Andy looks down at his lap for a few seconds. Then he says, "Is there a funeral planned?"

I shake my head. "I'm not ready for that yet." I'll probably never be ready for that, not even if they find her body someday. "I'll let you know."

Touchdown wanders over and sniffs at the pizza box. Andy shoos the dog away. He and I stare at the pizza for a few seconds, but now that the truth is out in the open, neither one of us can bring ourselves to eat.

"I need to go to the gym," he says finally. He hops up from the sofa and paces back and forth. "Do you want to come?"

Normally I'd say yes, but I'm not sure how long it's been since I slept. I'm too physically and emotionally drained to exercise. "I don't think I'm up for it," I murmur.

He nods. "My brain is going a little crazy right now. I need to blow off some steam so I can think. Will you be okay here by yourself?"

"I'll be fine. I'm just going to rest." I tug my hooded sweatshirt over my head and kick off my shoes.

Andy's gaze falls on my neck, on the bruises that are finally starting to fade. "Did you get karate chopped in the throat or something?"

"Something like that," I say, not wanting to get into the details. He looks like maybe he's going to change his mind and stay with me, so I make a shooing motion with my hands. "Really. Go. I'm all right."

"Okay. I'll be back." Andy grabs his keys from the coffee table and hands me the TV remote. "Call me if you need anything."

A blast of cold air enters as he slips outside. I curl onto my side and pull my knees up to my chin for warmth. I flip through the cable channels one by one, half hypnotized by the blinking lights and moving forms on the screen. I don't really watch much TV these days.

I used to watch it in L.A. all the time. I would ask my

"dates" to put it on to relax me. Really all I wanted was something to focus on besides what was happening. I learned a lot of American slang and customs from all those hours of movies and primetime shows, but after we escaped to St. Louis, TV became just one more thing that reminded me of a past I needed to forget. Occasionally I'll watch a K-drama on my tablet when I'm feeling anxious. There's something comforting about hearing people speak Korean, even if I hardly ever speak it myself anymore.

I pause on a horror movie from a few years ago. A killer traps a girl in a cage and then sprays her with acid. Fabric smokes, skin sizzles, and giant bloody welts open up on the girl's torso. The violence should be disturbing, but I just feel numb. The next channel is showing a baby panda being resuscitated. Even the veterinarian starts to cry when the little black-and-white ball of fluff opens its eyes, but I can't feel anything. It's like I've run out of emotions.

I'm not sure how much time passes while I'm skimming through the channels. Eventually, I flick off the TV and glance around the living room—the comfortable furniture, the display case of trophies, the mess of football gear and fast-food remnants. *Normal,* I think. But this isn't my normal. I feel safe here, because I'm hiding—hiding from the fact that my sister is dead and I don't even know who killed her. Hiding from the guy who I thought cared about me but ended up hurting me, just like every other guy I've known.

Every guy except for Gideon. I grab for my phone and dial his number.

He picks up on the first ring. "Are you all right?" he asks.

"I'm fine. Have you heard anything more from Detective Ehlers?"

"No," Gideon says. "I'm sorry." And then, "Jesse told me what happened."

"Which part? The part where I almost drowned, the part where I had some sort of psychotic blackout, or the part where

I got to experience Jesse having sex with my sister?" I wait for the forthcoming lecture, expecting Gideon to chastise me for leaving Miami by myself.

"All of it," he says calmly. He sounds very Zen. There's no lecture, only steady, even breathing. "Where are you?"

"With a friend."

"You should go home," Gideon says. "Give Jesse a chance to explain."

"He slept with your ex-girlfriend and then tried to say it was me and that I just blacked it out. And you're going to take his side?"

"I would never take anyone else's side, but it's a little more complicated than that."

"Really? Because that's fairly complicated all on its own."

"We're worried about you," Gideon says.

"I'm fine," I say. But then, with no warning, I start to cry. Huge racking sobs. "I feel so alone. I can't believe she's gone."

"Tell me where you are. I'll send someone to come get you."

"If I go home, will you be there?" I ask.

"I'm still out of town. I had to make another trip, but I'll be back tomorrow. If you don't want Jesse around, I can have Sebastian—"

"No," I say. "I just need—I don't know. I can't deal with everything right now." My words come out in bits and pieces. "I'm all right where I am."

"You don't sound all right," Gideon says.

"I think I just need to sleep," I say. "I'll come home tomorrow. I promise."

"Okay." He pauses. "We can talk about planning a funeral service, if that would help you deal with things."

"No," I say, more sharply than intended. I lower my voice. "Not unless we find her body. We *need* to find her body." Even as I say it, I know it's futile. The Mississippi River empties into the Gulf of Mexico. We might never find her.

"You're right," Gideon says after a short pause. "I'll call Ehlers and see if there's anything more the police can do. Get some rest. Maybe tomorrow will be a better day."

"Maybe," I say, but I don't believe it.

I have a feeling tomorrow will bring nothing but pain.

CHAPTER 36

I sense the figure leaning over me even before I open my eyes. The instant my brain registers it isn't Andy, I slam the palm of my hand into the guy's nose. I roll from the sofa onto the coffee table and reach down for one of my knives.

And then I recognize my target. He's the older, meaner-looking guy who was with Andy the night Rose didn't come home. The guy I figured for a coach.

"What is wrong with you, you crazy bitch?" he hollers. Blood trickles from his nose. Pinching his nostrils together, he tilts his head up toward the ceiling.

"I'm not the one watching some girl sleep," I snap. Reluctantly, I sheathe my knife. "And you're not supposed to tilt your head back. It makes the blood run down your throat."

Andy appears from the kitchen with a couple of beers. "Holy shit, Ted, what happened?" His eyes flick to me and realization dawns on his face. His mouth twitches, like he's fighting back a smile. "I see you met my agent." Turning to Ted he says, "I told you not to wake her."

"Why is she even here?" Ted asks. He limps across the hardwood floor and collapses into the recliner.

I roll my eyes. How dramatic. I've never seen anyone develop a limp from being hit in the face before. "Why are you talking about me like I'm *not* here?"

"Relax. Both of you." Andy holds out a beer to each of us.

Ted takes one and holds it against the side of his nose. I can't help it. I start laughing.

"I should sue your ass for battery," he mutters.

Ignoring him, I wave off the beer and paw through my duffel bag looking for some clean clothes. "I can't believe I slept for so long. Is it all right if I take a shower?"

"Sure," Andy says. "Second floor at the end of the hall."

"She's *living* here?" Ted asks in disbelief. "How do your parents feel about that?"

"Don't worry about my parents," Andy says. "They don't tell me who my friends are, and neither do you."

I give Ted a dark look over my shoulder as I head upstairs. Andy's bathroom is almost as big as my bedroom. There's a separate claw-foot bathtub and Jacuzzi, with an L-shaped bench running between them. Behind the bench, a wooden door opens into a closet full of fluffy towels and baskets of soaps shaped like stars and moons. A strip of celestial-patterned wallpaper runs around the perimeter of the room. Someone has even painted a starscape onto the ceiling.

Stripping off my clothes, I step into the bathtub and turn on the water. As it pours down over my body, I try to relax, but I keep thinking about going home. Facing Jesse. What could he possibly say that would make things better? And then Gideon's offering to set up a memorial service. That's the worst of all. Doesn't he understand that part of my sister will continue to live as long as I don't fully accept that she's gone?

I try to block their voices from my head, embracing the pattering of the water jets against the marble tub. I crank the silver faucet farther to the left and steam floods the room. The scalding water turns the flesh of my arms bright pink. As my skin begins to burn, my mind clears.

I turn the water back to a bearable temperature. Hanging my head low, I watch the streams of water drizzle from tendrils of my hair. Then I step out of the bathtub, wrap myself in a towel, and stand in front of the sink. With one hand, I wipe the steam from a section of the large mirror. I use my fingers to start combing the snarls from my hair, the pain of each individual tug centering me, calming me.

Readying me.

You can handle whatever this day will bring.

By the time I'm done in the bathroom, Ted is gone.

"I hope Agent Asshole didn't leave on my account," I say.

Andy is sprawled out on the sofa, flipping through the TV channels. "Nah. He was in the neighborhood and just dropped by to do some prep work for a lunch meeting with a potential sponsor." He chuckles. "I can't believe you broke his face. That is going to be one awkward meeting now."

I sit on the opposite side of the sofa from Andy. "Why would he care if I was living here? Not that I am."

"Who knows? He probably thought you were Rose. I should have introduced you, but I try to limit the amount of information I share with him about my personal life."

"Why would he care if *she* was living here?"

Andy picks up a baseball cap from the floor and rests it backward on his head, both hands reaching up to curl the brim. "He found out she was a recorder and assumed that was the only reason she was with me. To get some shocking footage and sell it."

I wonder if Andy knows my sister *was* recording him, that she might have been doing exactly what his agent thinks. I twist my wet hair into a ponytail around my scarred palm, squeezing droplets of water from the end of it.

"Do you do that?" he asks. "Record people on the sly?"

"No. I'm more into stuff like—" I pause. I probably shouldn't tell him I break into companies and steal information. "Adventure sports."

"Yeah? Like what?"

I tell him about the shark diving that Jesse and I did in Florida, and about some of my other past ViSEs—including rock climbing and snowboarding in Colorado. Jesse and I trained for both of those recordings together. I remember the way he drilled me on the climbing safety procedures for almost an hour before he even let me slip into a harness. Then on the flight home he surprised me with a snow globe he bought from Rocky Mountain National Park. There's no way he could be so sweet and protective of me if he was in love with my sister the whole time. Something doesn't add up. Something major.

"That's awesome," Andy says. "You think you can hook me up with your boss? I would love to do a football ViSE."

"Are you serious? He would probably love that. But why would you want to record ViSEs? Aren't you going to make a lot of money in the NFL?"

"I just think it would be cool to share the experience with other people," he says. "When I was little, I loved it when they showed helmet cams on TV."

"I bet a football recording would go over huge with guys. You could make a ton of money."

"That makes me wish I had thought of it earlier," Andy murmurs.

Before I can ask him what he means, my phone buzzes with another text from Jesse and I notice what time it is. "It's after eleven. What time is your meeting?"

He glances at his own phone. "Crap. I'd better get going." He grabs his keys from the coffee table.

Touchdown appears from the doorway to the kitchen. He's got his leash in his mouth and a hopeful look in his eyes. Sitting back on his haunches, he whines.

"Shit," Andy says. "He needs to go out again."

"I'll take him out. It's the least I can do since he shared you with me yesterday." I smile at Touchdown. I hope Natalie is taking good care of Miso. "Go. We'll be fine."

"Cool." Andy flashes me a grin. "Make yourself at home. I'll be back in a couple hours."

"Sure." I smile tightly. Andy leans in and for a second I

think he's going to hug me, but at the last second he holds his fist out toward mine. I bump my knuckles against his.

"I still can't believe you punched Ted," he says. "Awesome."

Before I can respond, he's out the door, and I'm alone again.

Touchdown drops the leash and rests his chin on my leg. All right, so not exactly alone. I check my phone as I slip the chain around the dog's neck. I now have three texts and two voice messages from Jesse. I scroll through the texts as I stand up:

Call me. There are things you need to know.

There's something we can agree on. Too bad I can no longer believe anything Jesse says.

Please call. I'm worried about you.

Okay, fine. Don't call me if you don't want. But text me and let me know you're okay.

Touchdown wags his tail and bounds toward the front door, his long toenails skating across the wood. "I'm not okay," I tell him. He barks. "Jesse's just going to have to worry for now. I don't feel like texting him."

Touchdown places his paws up on the windowsill and whines.

"Fine. Let's go," I grumble, unable to keep from smiling at the dog. A blast of sun hits me as I open the door and we step out into a rare warmish day.

Touchdown starts pulling me rapidly down the block, but I don't feel comfortable going too far from Andy's house since I had to leave it unlocked. I dodge puddles of melting ice on the sidewalk as best I can. The dog finally pauses in front of a Spanish-style villa. An elaborately coiffed poodle peeks out from the front window. Much barking ensues. I wind Touchdown's leash tight around my hand and wait patiently as he circles a light post trying to decide where to pee.

My phone buzzes. And then again. I pull it out to silence the call and see that it's Gideon, not Jesse.

"Are you home?" he asks.

"Not yet," I say.

"Are you feeling any better?"

"Perhaps. Though I suspect going home will ruin that."

He pauses. "I forgot to tell you yesterday. I heard your diving footage is excellent."

I see the shark ramming the cage, feel my heart threatening to erupt through my wet suit. "You could say that."

Gideon chuckles. "That's going to be a big money ViSE for us. Hopefully we'll be up and running again soon."

"Speaking of big money," I start. "You know Andy Lynch? The football player?"

"Golden Boy turns Mr. Fumble?"

"That's him. It turns out he wants to make a football ViSE."

Gideon whistles. "Why? Is he worried about not getting a contract because of one rookie mistake? Pretty sure someone will pick him up in the draft."

"He said he just thinks it would be a cool experience to share. Like a helmet camera, only way more intense."

"How do you know Andy Lynch?"

"He and Rose were kind of dating, and he knew about her being a recorder. Yesterday I told him she was dead. I know he didn't have anything to do with it. I could see how upset he was."

"Okay. Give him my number and we can work out the details." Gideon pauses. "I'm glad you were able to share that with someone else."

Touchdown finishes his business and looks at me, tail wagging. My grip tightens on his leash. "Right." My voice wavers. "Are you back in town yet?"

"I'm getting ready to get on a plane. I'll be home in a few hours."

"Where are you? You've never stayed away this long before."

"California."

I cringe at the thought of him anywhere near where we used to live. "Why are you there?"

"Meeting with some people about the ViSE tech. Like I said, I'll be home this afternoon. I'd prefer if you go home too, so I know you're safe."

Maybe I *should* go home. I forgot when Andy said his parents are returning, but I've already made things weird for him with his agent. No need to cause problems with his family too.

"All right," I say. "If you promise you won't send Jesse up to keep an eye on me."

"I promise," Gideon says.

I say good-bye and slip my phone back in my pocket. I take Touchdown back to the house and release him from the chain around his neck. He lies down on the hallway floor as if the excitement of getting outside and visiting his poodle friend has been more than he can take. He lifts his head to watch me as I start getting my things together. I grab my phone and send Andy a text.

I had to leave. Call 555-2769 and ask for Gideon if you're serious about the ViSE. Thanks for everything.—W

When I arrive home, Baz is pacing in the hallway outside the penthouse. I can almost envision the multiple weapons strapped to his body. Better than Jesse, I guess.

"Do you want to come in?" I ask.

He shakes his head. "I've got this hallway and the roof of the building on security feeds in the office at Escape. I'm going to head back down there. Gid just wanted me to let him know when you got home." He pauses. "And to remind you that you can call me if you need anything."

"Thank you," I say.

Baz nods at me and then turns toward the elevator.

As the penthouse door closes behind me, it hits me how alone I am. I decide to call Natalie to check on Miso. I'll feel better once I can get him.

She picks up right away. "Your kitty misses you."

"I miss him too," I say. "Are you home? I could come down and get him."

"I'm actually working. Hang on a second."

There's some rustling and background chatter and then things go quiet again.

"Okay," she says. "Now I can talk. Are you doing all right?"

"As good as can be expected, I guess."

"Did Gideon figure out who . . . hurt Rose?" Natalie asks.

The image of my sister in that hotel bed flashes before me, burning itself into my retinas. I close my eyes for a second. "If he did, he's not sharing," I say. "Speaking of which, did you learn anything interesting about Phantasm while you were digging for Gideon?"

"Not really," she says. "Phantasm is owned by a larger Korean corporation called Usu. It seems like they own a lot of different companies—clothing, electronics, medical stuff."

Jesse and I figured that out when we were searching for the identity of the one-eyed man. "Did you hear anything about a man with one eye?"

Natalie pauses for a moment. "Say what?"

"I'm looking for a man who lost an eye, though I guess he might have a glass prosthetic now. I saw him in a picture at Phantasm. One of the Usu gatherings."

"Um, no. Nothing like that, but Usu employs boatloads of people, so maybe he works for one of their other companies." She pauses again. "Did Gideon used to work for them?"

"What? Why would you think that?"

"I saw one of the Phantasm executives reading that story about ViSEs when I was bringing him coffee. There was a photo on his desk—an employee ID badge from UsuMed. I think that's a drug company? Anyway, the name was different— a Korean name—I can't remember it exactly. But it was Gideon, I'm sure of it."

All I know about Gideon's work in L.A. is that he did some

kind of medical research consulting. He definitely could've worked for UsuMed. "Thanks. That could be helpful." A twinge of dread moves through me as I try to connect the dots.

"Okay, but you didn't hear it from me. And Winter, I'm really sorry about your sister . . ." Natalie trails off, clearly uncomfortable.

"Thanks," I say again. Sometimes I wish people would realize that their awkward condolences only amplify the pain of losing someone. It's like you're bleeding, and as soon as the wound begins to clot, someone comes along and starts picking at the scab. "And thanks again for the information. Call me when you get home and I'll get Miso. I appreciate you taking care of him." I hang up and toss my phone on the coffee table.

So Usu owns Phantasm and Gideon used to work for UsuMed. Coincidence? Probably not. Maybe Gideon stole something besides Rose and me three years ago. Maybe he took something from his job and now Usu has sent people from Phantasm to collect.

I sit cross-legged on the sofa and stare into the Kandinsky print. I feel like I have all the pieces needed to see the whole picture, and if I can just adjust my perspective, then everything will become clear.

I decide to call Detective Ehlers myself to see if there's been any news. I look up the number for the local police station. When the operator answers, I ask to speak to him.

"I'm sorry. Could you repeat that?" she asks.

"I need Detective Ehlers," I say. I start to spell his last name for her.

"We don't have anyone here by that name."

"But I talked to him just the other day," I start. "He works in—"

She cuts me off. "This happens a lot. You probably want the county police department, not the city."

"Oh. I guess it's possible," I say. "Thanks for your time."

I hang up the phone, a sick feeling in the pit of my stomach. I do an Internet search for the city and county police departments. Neither one of them has a detective named Ehlers listed on their web page. Next I do an Internet search for Detective Ehlers. There are about thirty results, all of which seem to point to pages based out of Vermont. I click through them until I can find a picture, just in case. Eventually I find a picture of him receiving a commendation from the department last year. It's not the same man.

I tell myself there's a reasonable explanation. Maybe I'm remembering the detective's name wrong.

Or maybe Gideon has been lying to me about everything.

No. That can't be true. Why would he do that? Gideon loved Rose. He would never have hurt her.

But then I think back to the overdose recording. The man who didn't speak was the same size as me . . . and Gideon.

I have to know for certain. I pull the ViSE of Rose's overdose from the music box and slip it into my headset. Flopping down on the sofa, I slip the headset on and adjust it. I press PLAY.

I'm in the masked figure's body. Across the room, Rose lies tied to the bed.

I fast-forward.

The smaller figure bends over me with the syringe.

It's just a shapeless black blob. It could be anyone. And then the smell of clove cigarette smoke tickles my throat. I remember smelling it the first time I played this ViSE and thinking it was because Gideon was smoking in the ViSE room.

My heart starts thrumming in my chest. I tell myself it's just a coincidence, that plenty of people smoke clove cigarettes. But then I rewind and watch the masked figure inject her with the drug again, and it seems so obvious. Gideon has done medical research; he knows how to give injections. His size, the way he tilts his head, even the angle his shoulders make with his neck—it's all Gideon. I don't know how I didn't see it before. *Because you couldn't. You didn't want to.*

The masked figure leans over me, gently reaching out to touch my face.

Trembling, I rip off the headset without even stopping the recording. A slight shock moves through me. I keep seeing the masked figure reaching out for Rose, touching her almost . . . affectionately. I can no longer deny it. Everything about the man with the hypodermic needle screams Gideon.

CHAPTER 37

Shuddering and nauseated, I race for the bathroom. I kneel on the cold tiles and try to make sense of things. Why would Gideon hurt Rose? *Well, she was sleeping with Jesse . . .* Maybe she turned in that recording for Gideon to sell. Could he have become jealous? Rose never told me exactly how or why they broke up. I was still kind of unstable when it happened and she probably didn't want to add to my stress.

I can't wrap my head around it. Gideon fell in love with my sister when she was working for Kyung. He knew she was a prostitute and didn't care. She used to tell me stories of their dates—how he brought her food and presents. He even brought gifts for me—books, usually. Stories to help me escape. She never told the other girls because she didn't want them to be jealous. While the rest of us were being used up and discarded, Rose was being cherished.

Gideon loved her so much that he left his whole life behind for her. He risked his freedom by getting us all fake documents. He risked his life by stealing us from the very hotel where we were working. Gideon's love for Rose never wavered, even though she slept with other men while he was planning our escape. Her sleeping with Jesse might have hurt him, but it couldn't have destroyed him. It couldn't have made her seem so worthless that she didn't deserve to live.

Unless perhaps he grew to resent her. He gave up every-thing to save us, and Rose's first action once we were free was to break up with him, almost as if she'd never loved him at all.

Locking away the flood of emotions, I force myself to con-sider the possibility. If Gideon overdosed Rose, that means the whole Escape burglary was as fake as the hotel room break-in. And just like with the hotel room, there's probably proof somewhere. Not at the club, where Adebayo or someone else might discover it. Somewhere Gideon knows no one will find it. Maybe somewhere here, in the penthouse.

I check the clock. It's only twelve thirty. Gideon won't be home for hours. Passing through the living room and dining room, I head to the study and flip on the lights. Half the room resembles a normal study, with a desk and chair, a file cabi-net, and several bookshelves. A long stainless-steel table and lab equipment take up the other side of it. A stack of cages sits empty in the corner, remnants from experiments Gideon used to do with mice.

I start with the desk drawers. The top one is full of office supplies. The bottom two are full of mail and papers. I rifle through them but nothing catches my eye. I move to the file cabinet, but all the drawers are locked.

No problem. I've picked locks before. I find a paper clip in the top desk drawer and unbend it. I slip the ends of the paper clip into the lock and start feeling around for the release mech-anism. Some people manage to pick locks just by flailing around and poking every which way. I learned how to do it properly on the Internet.

The locking mechanism disengages and the top drawer slides open. There's just more papers inside. Files in file fold-ers labeled A to J. Dropping to a squat, I pick the lock on the middle drawer. I pull out the folder marked K and see my fake surname, Kim, on some of the documents. What kind of pa-perwork would Gideon feel like he had to lock up? I peek down into it. It looks like mostly business and identification documents. I don't have time to go through everything here. I shove the folder under my arm and pop the bottom drawer open. I rifle through the S folder looking for anything with my real last name, Song. There's nothing there. It's all of Gideon's documents with his pretend surname, Seung. It occurs to me I don't even know his real last name. Turning away from the file cabinet, I keep looking. There's more to find—I can feel it.

Dropping the K folder on the desk, I go to the bookshelf against the back wall. I quickly yank out the books in sections, feeling for anything hidden. Nothing. A pair of Jackson Pollock prints hangs on the wall behind the desk. I peek behind each of them looking for a safe but don't find one.

I grab the folder and leave the study, pausing outside the door to Gideon's bedroom. I can't even remember the last time I set foot in his room. We're both very respectful of each other's personal space.

But not today.

I skirt around the king-size bed to the black lacquer dresser. A collection of pipes carved from gingko wood is displayed in a glass case on top of it. A Korean flag hangs proudly on the wall. I feel uneasy, like I shouldn't be here, like I'm violating an unspoken rule. Maybe I should just go through the paperwork I've already found. I force my eyes away from the flag's red and blue yin-yang and turn to leave. My gaze falls on the far corner of the dresser, on a lamp shaped like a gazebo.

The main hotel Rose and I worked out of in Koreatown looked out on a green gazebo with red trim, almost like the lamp. I think of the businessmen studying Rose and me with their quiet, careful eyes. Negotiating prices like we were animals.

I start to turn away from the hated gazebo but then stop. There's a faint outline of dust here, almost as if someone moved the lamp recently. If I were Gideon and wanted to hide something from me, I'd put it near this hated memento of my past.

I snatch the lamp from the dresser. The base is hollow and there's a piece of indigo cloth stuffed up inside of it. I yank out the fabric and something rectangular and metallic falls out—the neural editor. But that's not all. Six playback headsets and a thin metallic hard drive are also wedged in the base of the lamp.

My insides go dead. It's all the equipment that was supposedly stolen at Escape.

CHAPTER 38

I was right. There never was a break-in at Escape. Gideon is the one in the ViSE with Rose.

He overdosed her.

He killed her.

No. There has to be another explanation.

The room starts to fragment. I focus on the wall, on the yin-yang at the center of the flag, holding on to its familiar shape.

Some other explanation.

Something else.

Be strong.

The yin-yang's red and blue teardrops split apart. Furniture starts to melt into colors. Colors become black and white.

Gideon loved Rose.

Always.

I've never once doubted that.

Black and white begins to fade into nothingness.

I struggle to stay in control. *You can handle this.* "I can handle this," I say aloud. My brain wants to shut me down, but I fight it. I force the yin-yang back into formation. The dresser regains a bit of its shape.

Gideon saved Rose and me. He took us away from Kyung, away from Los Angeles. He brought us here so that we could start over.

The three of us.

It'll be just the three of us. That's what Rose always said.

And Gideon did his best to make it happen. He gave us jobs. He gave us a place to live. He's family. If Rose is dead, then he's the only family I have left.

My family killed my family.

Suddenly the penthouse feels like a prison. I leave Gideon's bedroom and pull the door closed behind me. Hurrying down the hall, I open the front door.

And then I realize I have nowhere to go.

Everyone I know besides Andy is loyal to Gideon. I have no friends of my own, no support network outside of the one he built for me. I should have realized this years ago and done something about it, but I never did because I had Rose. And because Gideon took care of us, or so I thought.

I shut the door quietly and retreat into my bedroom. I need to think.

I can't think.

Instead I lie facedown on my bed. Deep racking sobs claw their way out of me. It's like I'm vomiting out demons. How could Gideon take my sister away from me? He knew how much I needed her.

He needed her too.

But he lost her. And for a moment, it all makes sense. Maybe seeing her with Jesse made him snap. No wonder he didn't want me to go to the police. No wonder he didn't want me to look for her killers.

I turn over and stare at the ceiling. Another sob escapes my throat and I hug my arms around my chest. Reality starts to fragment again. The room disintegrates. Solids. Colors. Blacks and grays.

I debate calling Jesse. I am 100 percent certain he's not on the recording with Gideon. I know what it's like to vise from Jesse's point of view. I remember the slight visual distortion—you can't edit out something like that. The other man with Gideon had clear eyesight.

I imagine Jesse's voice. Soothing. Calm. The tears begin to dry on my skin. He cares about me, even if he lied, even if Rose is the one he fell in love with. He deserves to know what happened. If Gideon killed my sister out of jealousy, then Jesse could be next. I exhale slowly and the room regains its form. I dial Jesse's number.

"Winter." He sounds out of breath. "I'm so glad you called. Where are you?"

"Home." One word. Cracked whisper. This place doesn't feel like home anymore.

"Are you crying?" Jesse asks. "Are you hurt?"

I ignore his questions. "You might be in danger."

"What?"

"Gideon staged the break-in at Escape. I found the stuff that was supposedly stolen." The air around me buzzes heavy in my ears. I can barely hear my own voice. "He OD'd Rose. That's why he didn't want us investigating."

"Winter. Calm down." Suddenly it's Jesse who sounds anxious.

"Don't tell me to calm down." Without warning, I start crying again. I can't remember the last time I cried this much, but I suspect my sister was there to keep me from doing anything rash. "I'm going to the police," I say. "I'm turning him in."

"Okay," Jesse says. "But wait five minutes. I want to go with you."

I try to answer but can't. I am wailing now, a deep animal-like cry that seems to be originating from outside of my body.

"Stay there," he says. "I'll be right up."

When I open the door a few minutes later, I have managed to stop crying, but I still can't speak. Jesse stands awkwardly in the hallway until I motion him inside. He leans back against the wall, one hand thrust deep into his pocket, the other clutching a single printed sheet. I can tell he wants to touch me, hug me, make things better. But he can't. A cold space has sprung up between us, a barrier he's afraid to breach.

And with good reason. All I can see is him in the ViSE he tried to hide from me. Him and my sister.

And now she's dead.

"There's something you need to see," Jesse says.

"I have something you need to see too." I point at the neural editor and hard drive sitting on the counter. "I found this hidden in his bedroom. He killed her. It's the only thing that makes sense."

Jesse looks sick. "Winter," he starts. "Gideon didn't—"

I cut him off. "I played the ViSE again. The way the guy injected her. The way he touched her. I know it was him."

Jesse crosses the living room to the kitchen. He sits down at the table and immediately I wonder if he ever sat there with my sister. My dead sister. I can't sit. Can't stand. Can't exist in this apartment without overlaying her corpse.

I pace back and forth in front of the stove. Jesse hands me the paper he's holding—a news story printed off the Internet. There's a picture of a tall glass building. A red-and-green gazebo stands behind it. It looks like the hotel from Los Angeles.

"What is this?" I ask, skimming the first few lines of text. "An unidentified body found in the elevator of a hotel? So what?" But sluggish parts of me have flared to life. Not just a body, a girl. A dead girl.

In an elevator.

For a moment I feel the walls around me shrinking, closing in, trapping me. I smell blood. *Blood on my hands.* The paper slips from my grasp and flutters to the ground.

Jesse bends down to retrieve the article. He presses it back into my hands. "Look at the date. It's the day after you left Los Angeles—you and Gideon."

I glance down at the paper again. Sure enough, the date is from almost exactly three years ago. "And?"

"Winter. The girl who died in that elevator. It was Rose."

CHAPTER 39

"That's insane," I say. "Rose came to St. Louis with Gideon and me. I was so sick at first I had to be hospitalized. She slept next to me in bed. She took care of me. If it weren't for Rose, I would have . . ."

"You would have what?"

Suddenly I start to shake. I would have *died* without her by my side. "It doesn't matter, because Rose was there. And this girl was in L.A. Dead." *In an elevator.*

"Why were you in the hospital?"

"I was—" I stop. I remember the ambulance, restraints, IV drugs, the doctors saying that Gideon should leave me there for observation. Why *was* I so upset?

Jesse doesn't say anything for a few seconds. He just observes me carefully, as if he's trying to see the possibility settling in my brain. But it doesn't settle because it's *not* a possibility. It's an impossibility.

"But I talked to Rose the other night. Her stuff is still in her room," I say. "Up until last week she was dating Andy Lynch and making ViSEs for Gideon. I didn't hallucinate *all* of that. I didn't imagine the ViSE of her overdose. Everyone played it."

"I can explain," Jesse says.

"You don't have to, because you're *wrong.*" But for the first time, my voice lacks conviction.

And so does my heart.

Could I *possibly* have hallucinated Rose's presence in order to save myself? Like an imaginary friend? But that would mean I've been hallucinating her for *years*. And that's completely crazy. People like that can't function. They can't wake up and work out and get all As in their classes. They can't be trusted with dangerous work like recording ViSEs.

"Why don't you sit down?" Jesse suggests. "I can make you some tea."

"No." I back away from the table, shaking my head. "You're messing with my mind again. Dr. Abrams said I had post-traumatic stress disorder, which was normal. That's why I had bad dreams. That's why I saw things that weren't there." I start to crumple one corner of the printed page I am still clutching. "I'm better now, except I sleepwalk sometimes. I haven't been hallucinating my sister for *years*."

"Winter—"

I ignore him and keep going. "Why are you doing this to me? Did you and Gideon kill her and you're afraid I'll find out so you're trying to make everyone think I'm crazy?"

"I'm so sorry." Jesse's voice is laden with pity and it makes me want to lash out at him. Instinctively, I reach for a knife, but I don't have one on me and I feel exposed. Naked. I raise the article toward my face as if I can use it as a shield. The word *exsanguination* stands out amidst the blurring print.

Blood. Blood on my hands.

A fragment of a memory flits into my brain. An awful, terrible memory of blood spraying like a fountain. My sister is screaming. I am crying. And then Gideon's arms tighten around me.

I concentrate on the moment, but that's all I get. I don't even know if it's real.

"She bled to death?" I blurt out.

"Gideon never told me exactly what happened. Just that she died in Los Angeles. I found this online."

"Why would he tell you anything about her?"

Jesse looks down at the ground. "I told him how I felt about you. He wanted me to know the truth."

"The truth. You mean how I'm crazy."

"I mean . . ." He struggles for the right word. "I don't know what your therapist would call it."

Suddenly I remember the papers I found. Setting the article on the table, I turn and grab the file folder from the counter. A pair of Korean passports spill out from the middle. The first is mine. The photo looks about three years old. I vaguely remember Gideon taking pictures of Rose and me back in Los Angeles.

Holding my breath, I reach for the second thin, dark green book, my fingertips nervously tracing the gold Hangul on the cover. I flip it open and see the name Rose Kim. She has a round face and wider-set eyes. Her hair curls under slightly. Next to her, I am a mess of angles—pronounced cheekbones, a sharper chin. My hair is stick-straight.

She looks the way I remember her, but we look nothing alike. There is no way anyone could ever get us confused. But Andy did. And his agent did. And that makes no sense, unless I've been hallucinating them too.

Setting aside the passports, I flip through the papers without looking at Jesse. I skim the first page that has my name. It's the discharge summary from the emergency room, the day we arrived in St. Louis.

Patient: Kim, Winter
Diagnosis: Anxiety attack; acute psychotic episode secondary to
PTSD, as evidenced by
- *history of abuse*
- *repressing or suppressing memories of traumatic events and/or dissociation*
- *nightmares, flashbacks, and/or hallucinations*
- *explosive anger*

Visit summary: Patient admitted to ER by legal guardian because of unrelenting violent hallucinations. Guardian states patient's older sister died recently and patient has been struggling to cope. Elevated RR, HR, and BP. 4L of O2 given via non-rebreather en route by paramedics. Anxiolytics administered. Psychiatry consult ordered.

I skip past more medical jargon to the very bottom.

Recommended course of treatment: 72 hour observation.
Referred to Abrams, Cara, MD, for follow-up.
Chart signed by Bernard, Lance, MD

The pieces start to slide into place. I raise my eyes from the sheaf of papers. "I've been hallucinating Rose, so somehow Gideon faked that ViSE. To make me think someone killed her."

"Yes," Jesse says. "We shouldn't have tried to trick you, but Gideon thought if we could convince you Rose was dead, that your unconscious might accept it too. He apparently read a bunch of research or something."

"A bunch of research," I repeat woodenly. Like I'm an experiment. Like I'm a mouse in a cage. I swallow hard. "And you went along with this because you believed him? Or you were afraid he might fire you?"

Jesse stares down at his hands. "Both, I guess. I care about you, and Gideon's a smart guy. I hoped it would work."

"If you care about me so much, why didn't you just tell me the truth?" I ask incredulously.

"I wanted to tell you so many times, but Gideon said the hospital tried to orient you to reality when you were younger, and it didn't work. He said you got unstable. Violent."

I tremble visibly. I can almost hear Rose telling me she wouldn't let the hospital keep me. *Hospitals are for the dying, and we are only just beginning to live.* Only it wasn't real. None of it was real.

"It felt so lifelike." My voice wavers. "How did you do it?"

Jesse exhales deeply. "Baz grabbed you one night when you were being Rose. He and Gideon took you to Riverlights and shot you full of ketamine to mimic a near-death experience and some other drug to make you forget what happened, just in case."

"Being Rose?" I furrow my brow.

Jesse rubs at his scar. He glances toward the front door. "When are you expecting Gideon to get home?"

I ignore his question. "What do you mean, being Rose?"

"I'm not sure I'm the person you should be hearing this from," Jesse says weakly. "Gideon—"

"Is not here. Please, Jesse. You can't just come up here, tell me that my sister has been dead for years, and then not explain anything else."

He exhales deeply. "Okay. The ViSEs you and I have been playing are real." He pauses. "Gideon said you couldn't let her go. That you loved her so much you made her part of you. You let her . . . take over sometimes, in situations when you can't cope."

"Wait. You're saying that it's *more* than hallucinating? That I have . . . multiple personalities or something?" I shake my head violently. "No. That's not possible." But then I think about the blackouts. I think about the voice in my head that sometimes talks to me in Rose's words. "I see what you're saying, but the things she did—I would never have done those things. I *can't* do those things. You know that." Is Jesse really trying to convince me I danced with strangers at Zoo and made out with random switch-party guys? Is he trying to convince me I had sex with him and honestly don't remember?

"I mean, maybe this other part of you was there even before Rose died," Jesse says. "Maybe you created it to deal with your life in L.A."

I turn away. I need for Jesse to be wrong, for this all to be wrong. I flip through the papers, looking for something. Anything. I don't know what. There are a couple other visit summaries from hospital admissions that I don't even remember. The papers say basically the same things as the ER record: psychotic episodes, panic attacks, complex PTSD. Apparently several types of medication were tried, but nothing was effective against my hallucinations.

Below the medical records, I find Rose's fake birth certificate and some documents that show Gideon as our legal guardian. And then, at the bottom of the folder, a single picture of Rose and me mugging for the camera, wearing matching red dresses.

The entire memory floats back.

One of Kyung's men brought us to the hotel room. Gideon welcomed us inside; he was still Ki Hyun then. He bolted the door behind us and swept my sister—still Min Ji—into an embrace. I turned toward the blank TV screen to give them privacy and noticed the two boxes perched on the edge of the bed—long, flat boxes with brilliant red ribbons.

"Come here, silly Ha Neul." Ki Hyun pulled me into the hug, and for a moment all three of us were one, a tangle of arms and heat. "The preparations are almost completed."

"But where will we go?" I broke away from our awkward embrace.

"I picked a place for us." Ki Hyun's hand lingered on my sister's lower back. "Big enough to hide in, but small enough that no one would ever guess. I've already started buying things and putting them in storage."

"Things for our new life!" my sister added. "It'll be just the three of us."

Ki Hyun ruffled her hair playfully. "I just need to take some pictures of you both."

Min Ji immediately wrapped an arm around my shoulder

and posed—her smile bright, her free hand arranged in a peace sign.

Ki Hyun laughed. "As it's sort of a special occasion, I thought you might like to dress up first." He gestured toward the boxes.

Min Ji squealed. "Presents! Let's open them."

We tore open the boxes eagerly to find matching scarlet dresses, with gentle scoop necks and flowing skirts. They were two of the most gorgeous dresses I had ever seen. We got dressed in the bathroom, and my sister painted my eyes and lips with makeup. Then we posed for half a dozen photos, some proper for official papers, some silly just for fun.

The last photo we took was the two of us standing in front of the hotel window, both of us with our hands raised in peace signs.

This is the photo I am now holding.

We look so happy.

We look so hopeful.

You can see the fading cross-shaped scars on our palms—mine on my right, hers on her left.

A pair of sisters like matching gloves.

I'm left-handed. My sister was right-handed. It hits me that Rose's scar was on her right hand in the overdose recording. Which means Jesse is telling the truth.

Unless I'm remembering wrong.

"I need to play the ViSE one more time," I mutter.

My headset is on the coffee table, with the recording still loaded inside. I turn away from Jesse and cross the apartment in a few hurried steps, both anxious and terrified to know the truth. What's worse? That I'm clinically insane, or that the only two people in the world I trust killed my sister and are now conspiring to drive me crazy . . . and succeeding? Either way, Rose is gone.

"I need to be alone for a few minutes." I grab the headset

and disappear into my bedroom. Lying on my bed, I skip forward to the middle of the ViSE.

A rush of warmth pulses up my right arm. The kaleidoscope blurs into a rainbow and the smell of something sweet tickles my nose. A clove cigarette. The figure releases the tourniquet with a sharp snap and takes my hand. I can barely make out the cross-shaped scar carved into my palm.

My right palm.

I rip the headset off and fling it across the room. I can't breathe. I yank the comforter from my bed. Dropping to the floor, I wrap the blanket around me like armor.

Jesse peeks in through the open door. Tentatively he kneels down, maintaining a few feet of distance. "I'm sorry," he says, for what feels like the millionth time. "Gideon really thought he might be able to heal you."

I feel many things right now. Healed is not one of them. "Her ViSEs? I did all those things?"

Jesse fiddles with his hearing aid. "Yes."

My brain is spinning. Everything begins to make sense in the worst way. I'm missing pieces of time. I sometimes wake up feeling like I haven't slept. If I actually believed it possible that I might have killed my own sister, is it really a stretch to believe that I could have stayed out all night making sexy ViSEs? "I don't want to believe you," I say. "If I've truly been acting as Rose, that means Gideon and I—it means . . . who knows how many people . . ." Nausea wells in my stomach.

"No. Gideon never touched you. Not like I did." Jesse hangs his head. "I thought he was going to kill me, seriously. Once he saw how far your alter would go with your body, that's when he said we had to figure out a way to get rid of her."

How far your alter would go with your body. How can I have no clue about the things I've done or the people I've done them with? "If all this is true, how could you still want to be with me?" I think of all those strangers at the switch party, of the way I tried to convince Rose—myself—that I didn't need to be that girl.

Jesse scoots closer to me. "Winter," he starts. "None of that affects the way I feel about you. You're smart and kind and resilient. You're the strongest person I've ever known." His eyes fall to the initials tattooed on his wrist. "And I have known some strong people."

I want to feel his pain right now, but I can't. All I can feel is my own. My heart grows hard as my brain begins to fill in more blank spots. "When did it happen—you and me?"

Jesse looks down at the floor. "A few weeks ago. Not too long after we finished our snowboarding ViSE."

I think back over the past month. There was one morning Jesse had acted really odd. "The day you brought over breakfast."

He nods. "Gideon was out of town. You called me. I spent the night. I left to get food while you were asleep, and when I came back, it was like it had never happened. You turned me away and told me you had to study. I thought maybe you just needed time to process things, but Gideon came to see me in my apartment when he got home. He said we had to do something—that I had to help him if I wanted to keep my job. I agreed to keep his secret and watch out for you afterward, but I couldn't bring myself to be involved in the actual ViSE. So he used Baz."

Baz. The other recorder, the one who had felt almost emotionless. Of course.

"You planned this for weeks?" Suddenly every look he's given me, every innocent touch from the past month feels tainted.

"We talked about it. But then Gideon got some call from a paranoid viser and had the idea to make it look like retaliation for a recording. We just wanted you to get better."

"I can't—are you serious? You think this is *better*?" My left hand curls into a fist. "I think you should go now."

"Winter—"

"You helped him take my sister away from me in the most horrible way possible. Please, just leave."

"She wasn't real," Jesse says.

"She was real to *me*."

I'm still here, a voice whispers.

But I ignore it. She's not real anymore. Rose is dead and I am crazy. And Jesse is sitting on my bedroom floor with his scarred face, disfigured ear, and an armful of dead comrades. And he seems so normal in comparison, so whole.

Something shatters inside me and I am on him, tears falling, fists flying. It's like punching a granite cliff, but I don't care. A strike to the chest. An uppercut to the chin. Jesse's head snaps back. Pain explodes through my knuckles, but it doesn't feel real. Nothing feels real. It's like I'm watching myself from outside my body. *Stop,* a voice whispers. I should stop. I can't stop. I don't want to stop.

"Fight back," I scream. But he doesn't. So I hit him again, this time in the mouth. My bones feel like they're coming through my skin. Droplets of blood spray through the air, dancing across my eyelashes. I lash out once more.

"Enough." Jesse catches my fist and twists my arm behind my back. He pins my body to the floor. "I deserved a couple decent shots, but killing me won't make you feel better. I'm not the one who needs to fight back right now, Winter. This isn't you."

I wrestle beneath his weight, kicking upward with my feet. "You're wrong. This *is* me. Unstable. *Violent.* Those are the words you used, right? That's what I am." I struggle again, but Jesse outweighs me by almost a hundred pounds and he's not budging. "You can't pick and choose. The girl you care about doesn't exist."

"She does exist," Jesse says. "I was wrong. This is you, but it's not all that you are. You can fight the dark parts if you want to."

Tears leak from my eyes, each one feeling like a traitor, like maybe they're products of some secret piece of me controlled by someone else. "I don't know if I want to," I rasp.

Jesse sighs. "I know what that's like."

My body goes limp beneath his. I'm too tired to fight anymore. This is all too much.

After a couple of minutes, Jesse slides off me and sits with his back against the wall. Gradually I pull myself to a seated position and face him. His mouth is a mess of blood where I've split his lip.

I fight the urge to reach out and touch it, to take care of him. Jesse lied to me. I don't care what his reasons were. "You should go," I say.

"I'm not going to leave you like this."

"You're the *reason* I'm like this—you and Gideon." Each word hits Jesse like a separate stab wound. His shoulders hunch. His body folds in on itself.

"Try not to blame Gideon," he says quietly. "I'm the selfish one. Not him."

My eyes narrow. "What do you mean?"

"Gideon wanted to protect you. He kept hoping eventually your personalities would blend together, that if he loved you enough and gave you time, you would heal. I kept telling myself it was the same for me. I was playing along not to keep my job, but for your own good." He looks down at the carpet. "But the truth is, part of me just didn't want to share you. Not with club rats. Not with loser switch-party boys. Not with Andy Lynch."

The blood drains from my face. Oh no. Andy. I bite back a scream of frustration. How many other people did I sleep with when I was pretending to be my dead sister? "Like I said, you should go." Rising to my feet, I leave Jesse on the floor of my bedroom, still bleeding from his mouth.

I cross the hall into the bathroom. Punching the lock on the door, I lean back against it. My stomach twists with nausea as I consider everything I've just learned. I sink to the ground and bury my face in my hands. This cannot be happening. "Eonni," I whisper. I want my sister. I need her to come get me and take me to wherever she is.

"Winter." Jesse knocks on the door. "Are you all right in there?"

"I will be, once you leave," I lie.

I will never be all right again.

"Your phone is ringing. It's Andy. Do you want me to bring it to you?"

"Tell him I'll call him back once I figure out if I've slept with him or not." The words shoot out like spikes.

"Look. I know what we did to you might be unforgivable." Jesse sounds like he's crying. I've never seen him cry—not even when he talked about his dead army friends. "This isn't enough, it's not even a start, but I'm sorry. I am so goddamn sorry."

I look down at my bloody knuckles. "Me too," I whisper. I clear my throat. "Just leave, Jesse. Please. If you care about me at all."

There is a long beat of silence and then I hear the front door open and close. I strip out of my clothes and get into the shower. Hot water courses down over my body, igniting pain in the cuts on my fingers. Jesse's blood washes from my hands, staining the water beneath my feet a dull pink.

Minutes pass, or maybe hours, before it occurs to me that there's one major piece of information still missing from Jesse's little scenario of me being Rose being me: Who the hell was the guy who broke into the penthouse? Who got *stabbed* as part of this charade?

CHAPTER 40

When the hot water finally runs cold, I crawl from the shower to my bed, my eyes avoiding the bloodstains on the carpet. Jesse's blood mixed with some unknown stranger's.

Reaching out for my phone, I see that I have two texts. The first is from Andy:

I set up a meeting with your boss. Thanks for hooking us up.

Second text. From Gideon. Two words:

Call me.

Reluctantly, I dial his number. I should be angry. I should want to scream at him like I did Jesse. But once I do, I'll be completely alone in the world.

I'm scared.

"I'm on the way home," he says. "If you'll allow it, I can help you make sense of this. Or else you can just attack me like you did Jesse."

My hands are still throbbing from the punches I threw. "He told you?"

"Yes. He's worried about you. It's not like you to hurt someone who isn't fighting back."

"It's not like he didn't deserve it."

"You don't think you overreacted?" Gideon asks. "Jesse would never have touched you if he knew about your condition. I'm the one who lied to you for years. I made Jesse lie too. I'm the one you should blame, but I suppose I'm not as easy of a target."

"Maybe," I mumble. After six years of living in America and watching children disrespect their elders, that still feels odd to me. I've been inappropriate to Gideon several times since Rose disappeared, but there's no way I could bring myself to physically strike him outside of our sparring matches. Plus, Gideon risked everything to save me. Technically he risked everything to save my sister—I was just a collateral beneficiary. But he took care of me after Rose was gone. And he taught me to be strong.

It's hard to hate someone who has given me everything that I have.

"The cab is pulling up to the building right now. I'll be up in a minute," he says. "Perhaps you could put on some tea?" The call disconnects.

I head into the kitchen and dig through the cabinets for the teapot.

And then I stop. Gideon may have saved me, he may be the closest thing I have to a father, but he lied to me and kidnapped me and *drugged* me. I don't have to make him tea.

A few minutes later, the front door swings open. Wordlessly, Gideon slips out of his loafers. I take a seat on the sofa. He sits in a chair across from me.

"How was your flight?" I ask.

"Fine."

We stare at each other for a few seconds. I resist the urge to look away. I'm not used to making this much eye contact with him outside of our sparring matches. I feel as if I should let him speak first, but he seems more interested in listening.

"So it's true?" I start. "My sister died three years ago but I blocked it out and you concocted an elaborate scheme to make me accept her death?"

Gideon nods.

My lower lip trembles. "You said we were family." I think of that day with the red dresses, of how happy all of us were. "Family is all I have ever had in this world. You should have told me the truth."

He studies me with his dark eyes. "When we first arrived here, the doctors at the hospital told you Rose was dead. You refused to believe it. You threatened to hurt people. You threatened to hurt *yourself*. The nurses sedated you, and when you woke up, it was like you'd reset. You were back to believing Rose was alive, and you were calm. The psychiatrist who cared for you said there was no reason to force the truth on you at that moment. He prescribed you sedatives and referred you to an outpatient therapist." He pauses. "Dr. Abrams experimented with medications, but regardless of what she tried, you still saw your sister. She said she would work with you and help you deal with your past, but that when it came to your sister you were going to have to remember and accept the truth at your own pace. So I learned to embrace your reality."

"Rose has clothes, oppa. Furniture," I say sharply. "She had a phone. That's a bit more than playing along with some girl's imaginary sister, don't you think?"

He nods. "Some of those things I had bought before we moved. Some of them you bought for her yourself. You asked why we were never together, so I told you we broke up. After that, what started out as the guest bedroom slowly became Rose's room. The phone was just another way to keep an eye on you—who you were calling, where you were going. But you're right. I did a bit more than merely indulge your fantasies. It's just that whenever something felt off in your reality, it would upset you. I hated seeing you upset."

"Clearly you got over that," I say through clenched teeth.

"Do you remember why you quit vising?"

I shake my head. "I never vised, except a couple of times with you. I'm really sensitive to overlay. You know that."

"No, that's just something your mind has convinced your

body to believe. You used to go to sleep and then I would catch you out late or up early in the morning as Rose, using the beta tech to make ViSEs of just walking around the city. That's when I first realized you weren't just seeing her, that you were *being* her too. You were agoraphobic, but somehow as Rose you were able to go outside. And then as Winter you would play the recordings. I knew it wasn't normal, but it seemed therapeutic. I felt like you were helping yourself heal."

"So then why did I quit?"

"You started to figure things out. I suspect because of the scar on your hand. I tried to tell you the truth again but you didn't want to know who was really making the recordings." He pauses again. "I still have some of them somewhere, if you want to see. You went out a lot that first December to record the holiday decorations."

Another memory flashes back. Me lying on my bed, blankets pulled up to my chin, a ViSE headset secured to my head. Christmas lights, snowflakes, shiny decorations. Gideon is right. The department store windows were one of the first things that made me want to leave the penthouse.

"I remember," I say. "I can't remember her giving me the recordings, but I remember playing them."

"Believing Rose was alive seemed to strengthen you." Gideon's eyes get misty. "In a strange way, it helped me too. I would listen to you talk to her and I could almost hear her again. I couldn't bring myself to try to take your sister away from you when you were happy."

"Until now."

"Yes. I knew this other part of you had started doing things you wouldn't choose to do. And then I realized what a fool I'd been not to stop it earlier. I feared you would become unstable again if I told you the truth, or that you would hate me. I'm a coward, and I'm selfish. I had already lost your sister. I didn't want to lose you too."

"Are you really worried about losing me?" I ask quietly. "Or am I just the last piece of her you have left?"

Gideon rubs the bridge of his nose. "You cannot imagine what it's like to leave your whole life behind to start over somewhere else as a twenty-seven-year-old man with a teenager. And yes, having you close felt like hanging on to her—I won't deny that. But I've grown to love you, Winter. You are your own person—not a piece of her."

"And yet you used the fact I was dissociating to send me out to record your sexual ViSEs." I can't keep the bitterness from creeping in. "How could you do that to me? How could you treat me like a whore knowing everything my sister and I went through?"

"I never assigned you anything like that," he says. "You— your alter—did those things on her own. The behavior seemed like harmless acting out until after I saw what happened with Jesse. After that, I knew I had to do something before she put you at further risk."

"Sleeping with strangers is harmless acting out, but sleeping with a guy who cares about me is dangerous?"

"I never saw you be that . . . intimate with anyone else, or I assure you I would have taken action sooner," Gideon says. "I had Baz looking out for you, making sure things didn't get out of hand while you were recording at clubs."

"Why would you even let me leave the house if I was so far gone?"

He shrugs helplessly. "Was I supposed to imprison you? I tried to make you strong in every way that I could. You seemed to be functioning well. I thought maybe your actions at clubs were your way of taking back control from men after they hurt you."

It's the same explanation I gave Jesse a few days ago, but somehow it doesn't feel adequate now that I know *I* was the one doing it.

"Did you pay Jesse to watch me? Like you did Baz?"

"No. Jesse spends time with you because he cares deeply for you."

My cheeks go red as I think about exactly how deeply Jesse cares. "Jesse and me . . . How did you know about that anyway?" I ask sharply.

"The penthouse is wired with cameras," Gideon admits.

"Oppa!" I inhale a sharp breath. I glance furtively around the room, wondering where the hidden lenses are. "How could you?"

"Not the bathrooms or the bedrooms," he says quickly. "Just the common areas. For security purposes." He drops his chin. "I'm sorry. I know you feel adrift, like I severed your lifeline. But you're not the girl I brought here from Los Angeles. You're strong, Winter. You don't need Rose to survive anymore."

"So you decided to take her away from me. To kill her."

I'm still here.

Gideon lifts his head. "I was trying to orient you to reality in the least painful way possible."

"Well, you failed."

"Did I? You haven't hallucinated Rose in almost a week, have you?" His voice takes on a sharp edge.

"But I'm still *being* her. Who do you think saved me during the shark dive? Who stabbed the intruder in my bedroom?" I lift a hand to my throat. "Did you really hire someone to come attack me while you were gone?"

Silence. Gideon's eyes fall to the level of my bruised neck. He clears his throat. "That was not part of the plan. Initially, I thought perhaps the event was a hallucination and that your alter somehow procured a gun without your knowing. But I reviewed the security footage and clearly saw the intruder approach you in the hallway and force you inside the penthouse. I fear it might have been someone who works for Kyung."

"But why would Kyung—" I pause. There is only one

explanation that makes sense. "*You* worked for him, right? At UsuMed? That how you and Rose ended up . . ."

Gideon clears his throat. "Kyung was one of the UsuMed executives above me, yes."

"And it wasn't just us you stole, was it? There would be no reason for him to seek you out so long after we left if you hadn't taken something more valuable. Was it money? I always wondered where you got the money to buy the building and open Escape."

"It wasn't money," Gideon says. "I developed a number of drug prototypes for UsuMed, which I was paid handsomely for. In addition my father passed away shortly before I left Korea. He willed most of his estate to me."

"What then?" I ask.

Gideon dips his chin again. "I stole the neurochemical coding sequences for the editor. But it was *my* research that discovered them. UsuMed paid me to map the chemical sequences for different degrees of analgesia and relaxation in order to develop new types of painkillers. I saw the wealth of possibilities and kept going." He turns his lighter over in his hands and flicks the lid open and closed again.

"And then what?"

"I developed a procedure to map all of the afferent pathways—fear, excitement, heat, cold, all of the senses. The headsets and editor are mine, but Kyung thinks the ViSE technology should be his." Gideon sighs. "I've been in L.A., trying to reason with him. I offered to pay him for the information I took, but he wants the tech. I told him it had been stolen, but I'm uncertain if he believed me."

"So what's going to happen?"

"I don't know."

We sit in silence for a few moments. Gideon's lower lip trembles. He blinks hard and then looks away. Something about the emotion angers me. I'm the one who should be crying here, not him.

"I still don't understand how you could try to trick me into thinking my sister had been *murdered*! How could you pretend to grieve with me? You sat next to me and cried and it was all fake. Do you know how cruel that is?"

"She *was* murdered," Gideon snaps. "And it wasn't fake. It was three years' worth of pain that I let out all at once. Do you think it was easy for me to relive her death alongside you? Every moment of your agony was like a sword slicing into old wounds." He's practically yelling, something he never does.

"What if it didn't work, and I never figured things out, oppa? Were you going to pretend to investigate my sister's 'murder' forever?"

Gideon rests his head in his hands. "If this didn't work I was going to try to tell you everything again—to prove it to you with ViSE recordings, even if it made you unstable. Even if it meant you had to go back to the hospital."

My neck and shoulder muscles go taut. "I don't want to go back there."

"I know you don't. I've been doing a lot of reading. Plenty of people with dissociative disorders live normal lives. Maybe we can try going to therapy together. Or there are some support groups for people who have lost loved ones that we could join." He lifts his head. "I've also been looking into some residential programs for people with issues like yours. Nice places. More like college campuses than hospitals. Just so we can consider all the options."

My face falls. "You want to ship me off to some boarding school for crazy girls?"

"No, Winter. I want to be the man I should have been years ago, the family that you needed. I thought I was protecting you, but instead I failed you horribly. I failed both of us. I want to do better." Gideon's phone buzzes. He checks the display and swears under his breath. "Your friend Mr. Lynch is on the way here. Do you think he'd mind if I rescheduled our meeting?"

"That was fast," I say.

"Yes. He seems unusually enthusiastic about sharing his football experiences with the masses," Gideon says. "But it can wait a few days." He swipes at the screen of his phone.

"No, it's fine," I say. "Go ahead and meet with him. I could use a little time to . . . think about things."

Gideon nods. "He and his agent are coming here. I'll be in my study if you could show them in when they arrive?"

I flinch at the thought of seeing Andy, but I nod. "Wait." I reach out for Gideon's arm as he turns away. "How did she die?"

"One of Kyung's men caught me trying to sneak the two of you out of the hotel. Your sister attacked him, and he stabbed her. She died so that we could live." Gideon squeezes his eyes shut as if that will block out the memory. "I didn't want to leave her. I wanted to die by her side, you see? But she made me promise beforehand that I would never let anyone hurt you." He presses his fingertips to his temples. "It seems I've failed her in that as well."

When Gideon opens his eyes, they are wet with tears again.

I grab the ViSE equipment and the file of documents from the kitchen counter and take it all to my room. Rose's—my alter's—ViSEs are sitting on my dresser, taunting me. It's like I've been living half a life, sharing my body with a stranger.

My eyes skim past my collection of snow globes until they find my reflection in the dresser mirror. The girl who looks back at me is the girl I've always known myself to be. "Where are you?" I ask, narrowing my eyes, leaning close, trying to see some facsimile of my dead sister lingering beneath my skin. All I see is her silver necklace, hanging above my heart. "Why are you doing this to me?"

No answer.

I raise my right hand so I can see the reflection of my cross-shaped scar. Then I press my palm against the mirror. *Fingers to fingers, thumb to thumb.* The girl looking back at me is still identical, but in this position she feels like Rose.

A tear trickles down my cheek. "You made me into a freak. I want you to go away and stop hurting me."

I would never hurt you.

I freeze, unsure if I heard the words out loud or in my head. I watch my lips in the mirror as I reply: "What?"

All I ever tried to do was help.

"Help?" My insides seethe with rage. "You turned me back into a whore."

No, the voice says. *That isn't true.*

But the ViSEs all crash down on me at once—the dancing, the switch parties, Andy, Jesse. "Bullshit. I'm tired of people lying to me." Pulling my palm from the mirror, I rear back and slam my fist into it. The surface cracks and a handful of jagged shards fall like silvery tears to the top of my dresser. Curling my fingers around one of them, I study the scar carved into my palm. My eyes trail upward, the flesh of my wrist looking like so much blank canvas. Gently, I touch the broken fragment to my skin, but the edge is too smooth. I trade the piece of mirror for one of my throwing knives, its tip deadly sharp.

No.

I imagine a flower of blood opening on my wrist. It would be so easy.

You promised.

"Shut up," I say. "Get out of my head. Get out of my life."

We will make you stop, if we have to.

"Who the hell is *we*?" I ask.

No answer.

I press the blade against my skin. "Tell me."

You promised!

"I didn't promise you anything," I say. "You're not her. Quit pretending."

But you promised her. Don't let her death be for nothing.

Other-me shouldn't be talking. Other-me shouldn't even

exist. But she does. And whoever—whatever—she is, she's right. Hurting myself would dishonor my sister. I pull the knife away from my wrist and tuck it into the pocket of my hoodie. "So what now? How am I supposed to live like this?"

No answer.

"How am I supposed to live without Rose?"

You have me.

"But you're not Rose."

I can be the Rose that you need.

I'm not convinced of that, but I won't let my sister's death be for nothing. I need to know exactly how she died. I need to know who killed her so I can make him pay.

But first I need help.

I dig through the top drawer of my desk until I find a business card with Dr. Abrams's name. With shaking fingers, I dial her number.

Her receptionist picks up right away. "Greater Midwest Mental Health. This is Shelly. Can I help you?"

"Hi, Shelly. My name is Winter Kim. I'm a patient of Dr. Abrams. I need to come in for an appointment."

"One second while I access your file. Looks like you haven't been here in a few weeks."

"Yes. It's definitely been too long."

"When would you like to be seen?"

"The sooner the better."

The receptionist pauses. "Is this an emergency, Winter?"

"No," I say. "No emergency. But is Dr. Abrams available? I wanted to ask her a quick question."

"I believe she just got out of a session. Let me check."

A couple of minutes later, Dr. Abrams picks up the phone. "Winter. So good to hear from you. How are you doing?"

"Did you know?" I blurt out. "Did you know I had a separate person living inside of me?"

"What do you mean?" she asks slowly.

"I mean some girl who thinks she's my dead sister. Apparently she takes over my body when she feels like it."

"She's not a separate person, Winter," Dr. Abrams says. "What you're feeling is another part of you."

"Are there more *parts* of me I don't know about? How could you not tell me any of this?"

"Winter, I had my suspicions, but I never saw direct evidence of Rose or any alter persona in our sessions. Mr. Seung told me about some of the things you were doing that troubled him, but it wasn't enough to say for certain that you have dissociative identify disorder." She pauses. "The truth is, your collection of symptoms is quite rare and I wasn't sure what all we were dealing with. And I didn't tell you my suspicions because forcing reality on people often has negative consequences. We were working toward some realizations together when you started skipping your sessions. I've been hoping you would call me back."

"Did you know what Gideon had planned?"

"We talked briefly a few weeks ago because he felt your behavior was escalating. I gave him some information about residential treatment facilities in case the two of you wanted to go that route. He told me he wanted to explore one last option first. I assumed he was going to try hypnosis, or perhaps returning to the scene of the crime."

Not exactly. "Can I come talk to you?"

She pauses. "I can see you at six if you want to come in at the end of the day."

"All right," I say.

"Winter," she says. "Are you alone right now? If this is an emergency, I can have my receptionist call 911 for you. The hospital can stabilize your condition until I'm finished seeing clients."

"I'm fine," I murmur. "See you later." I hang up the phone and for a few minutes I truly feel, well, not fine exactly, but stable. If anyone can help me make sense of this, Dr. Abrams can.

Now to start filling in the gaps in my memory. Grabbing the music box, I separate the ViSEs into three piles—ones I've played, ones Jesse played, and ones with Andy. I'm starting with the third pile. I'm going to have to figure out how to explain this whole mess to him. But before I do, I want to know exactly how close we've gotten.

I slide the first recording into my headset and close my eyes, but I can't focus. It's too bright. I keep thinking about what's on the other side of the wall—Rose's room that was never Rose's room at all.

I gather the ViSEs together with my headset and duck out into the hallway. I knock gently on the door of the study. "I'm going down to Escape," I say. "I need to go back through some of these recordings, but I can't concentrate here."

Gideon opens the door a crack. His eyes are red, like maybe he's been doing more crying than preparing for his meeting. "Are you sure that's a good idea? Perhaps you could review them with your therapist."

"I called and made an appointment," I say. "For six. I can take the train there."

He shakes his head. "Sebastian can drive you."

"Fine." I don't really want a ride from Baz, but I don't feel like arguing.

Baz is waiting just inside the door to Escape when I arrive.

"Just get me from the security office when you're ready to leave for your appointment," he says.

I arch an eyebrow. "That's all?"

"Was there something else?"

I'm less mad at him, because he's just a guy who works for Gideon, not someone who claimed to care about me. But still. "I know what you did," I say. "I know everything now."

"That's good," he says, like I told him I just aced a calculus exam.

"Wow. You don't even feel bad, do you?"

"I don't feel much of anything, Winter." His eyes flick around the club. "I did what my boss asked me to do. I can assure you I've done worse."

I shake my head. "How do you live like that?"

He shrugs. "It used to be hard, but I adapted. The world is full of terrible people and I'm one of them. I've made my peace with it."

Shaking my head, I turn away from him and duck into the nearest ViSE room. Reclining back in the chair, I try to prepare myself for the things I might learn. "It's better to know the truth," I say. I just yelled at Jesse and Gideon for lying to me. I can't lie to myself anymore.

There are five ViSEs with Andy—two at the casino, two at dance clubs, and the one at his party. Other-me is flirty with him at the casino and kisses him once while we're dancing together, but none of that really means anything. I finish the first four recordings with a sense of relief. That just leaves one more. I slip the ViSE of the backyard party into the headset. I fast-forward past the hot tub and the time spent in Andy's bedroom. I start at the point where I storm out and see Baz out on the street, praying that I don't go back to the house.

Andy rushes up to me, pale faced, all apologies, begging me not to leave. "I need you," he says. Slowly, he cajoles me back inside. He shuts the front door and leads me back to his room. "I'm sorry about tonight."

"It's all right," I say. "I'm not mad." I flop down on the bed while Andy paces back and forth. I see tears forming in his eyes. "What is it?" I ask.

"I screwed up," he says, sitting next to me. "I did this terrible thing and I feel like it's going to haunt me forever."

I reach up to run my fingers through his hair. A ribbon of warmth twists through my body.

The tiny surge of desire I feel is terrifying. It's almost enough for me to stop the ViSE. But I have to know.

"Shhh. Whatever it is, it's all right. We all do bad things."

"I've been gambling a lot," he says abruptly.

"I'm aware," I say. *"That's how we met, remember?"*

"Higher stakes," he mutters.

I look up at him. "How high?"

"I got in a half a million. I offered to pay them double after I get my signing bonus, but they didn't want that." His eyes get watery again. *"They wanted something else."*

"What do you mean?"

"I threw the national championship," he says. *"The game was fixed."*

"What? How could you—"

"They threatened my family. It was the only choice I had." He's crying freely now. *"If anyone finds out, my whole career is over."*

I wrap my arms around his neck. "Shh. No one is going to find out."

He buries his face in my hair. My wig. Which slips slightly forward, obscuring my view. I feel his hand on the back of my neck. His fingers graze metal.

"Is that a headset?" Andy's voice goes cold. *"Are you recording this?"*

"I can explain," I say.

But then a shock races through me and the ViSE goes dark.

CHAPTER 41

My eyes flick open. My heart threatens to explode out of my chest. This ViSE is a time bomb. If it got out, it would destroy Andy's life. He would never be able to play for the NFL. He must have paid someone to attack me outside the penthouse. And now thanks to me, he knows Gideon's identity and where he lives. He's probably upstairs right this second, demanding that Gideon turn over a recording he doesn't even know exists.

I yank off my headset and flail for the door to the ViSE room. I have to get to Gideon before it's too late.

My phone rings. I lunge for it but my stomach sinks when I see it's Jesse calling. "I can't talk right now," I say breathlessly. There's no time to explain. I slide the phone back in my pocket and hurry across the gaming floor and into Baz's office.

Baz's eyes turn flinty. "What are you—"

"Gideon's in trouble. The meeting with Andy is a setup."

"What do you mean?"

"Ro—I recorded him confessing something that could ruin his life."

"Shit." Baz reaches for his phone.

"I'm heading upstairs." I turn and rush toward Escape's exit. Behind me, Baz is yelling for me to stop, to wait for him. I don't even slow down.

I race across the lobby toward the stairwell as Baz heads for the elevator. For one brief moment I consider going with him. It would be faster. Easier. But I still can't bring myself to do it.

I hit the stairs running. Blood roars in my ears as I take the steps two at a time. My muscles tremble. Sweat beads on my upper lip.

As I race up the stairs, my mind slots this new information into place. Andy developed real feelings for Other-me and confessed to fixing the game while he was secretly being recorded. Then my alter ran away and started avoiding him, so when Andy met me he struck up a friendship to see if he could find out what happened to the incriminating ViSE. He or someone working for him tried to threaten me, and when that didn't work, he got me to lead him right to Gideon.

I fly out of the stairwell on the top floor and see that the door to the penthouse is cracked open. I peer around the doorframe. The air is thick with the metallic smell of blood.

Two men stand in the living room. They have their backs to me, but I recognize them—Andy and Ted, his agent. Gideon lies in the center of his fluffy white rug, arms and legs splayed out at awkward angles. His face wears fresh bruises, but his lips and eyelids are pressed together in what looks like sleep.

Around him, the living room is a kaleidoscope of glass and blood. Bits of white sofa fibers hang in the air. The coffee table is completely shattered. Baz is crumpled in the doorway to the kitchen, facedown, not moving.

Andy bends down toward Gideon's body. For the first time, I see the blood pooling beneath it.

"Don't touch him." I crouch low and slide my throwing knife out of the pocket of my hoodie. The black blade trembles with a life of its own.

Andy spins around at the sound of my voice. "Winter. Thank God you're okay. I was about to call 911."

"I'm sure you were." My voice wavers. "Get away from him."

The curtains twist wildly in the breeze. Air whistles through a gap in the sliding glass door. A tear sneaks down my cheek as I push past Andy. Some part of me knows it isn't safe to be here, that there's no reason for them not to shoot me too.

But I can't abandon Gideon.

With my knife still clutched in my hand, I bend down and feel for a pulse at his throat. His skin is cool and motionless.

"Please," I mutter. "Oppa, I need you." My fingers search desperately for any sign of life. Was that a beat? I press harder. I can't tell for sure.

"We saw the guy who did it," Ted says. "Asian guy. I think he went onto the deck. Maybe climbed into the next apartment."

"There is no next apartment. Gideon owns this whole floor."

"The roof then," Andy says.

I hold my ear above Gideon's lips, listening for any hint of breathing. "Cut the bullshit, you two. I found the ViSE. I know what you came here for."

Andy pales slightly. "What ViSE?"

"The one where you confess that you fixed the national championship."

"Don't say anything," Ted says. "We don't know shit about any ViSE."

His words trigger a memory. *I don't know shit about that little whore.* Then I remember the way Ted was limping at Andy's house. I must have stabbed him in the leg.

"You're the one who almost strangled me, aren't you?" I ask. "And then you came here and attacked my boss." I slip my phone out of my pocket to call 911.

"You almost *strangled* her?" Andy gives his agent a look of disgust. "That's your idea of handling things?"

"I wouldn't have had to be involved at all if you had taken

care of it at the time. I was trying to protect both of us, and for that I got stabbed." Scowl lines form in Ted's forehead. "But I didn't attack your boss. Like I said, it was the Asian guy. A big dude with an eye patch."

My finger freezes, a tenth of a millimeter above the 1 key. "What did you say?"

"The guy who shot him had an eye patch, like a pirate or something."

Before I can speak, before my mind can even begin to process what it means that the one-eyed man from my dreams who showed up in a photograph at the Phantasm offices was apparently here in this room, the front door of the penthouse swings violently inward.

I flinch. My phone slips from my sweaty grasp.

Jesse rushes toward Gideon and me. "What the hell is going on?"

I wave him off, trying not to focus on his split lip, on the bruises that I inflicted upon him. "Check on Baz. I think he got shot." Reluctantly setting my knife on the carpet, I place one hand on Gideon's forehead and the other on his chin and tilt his head back to open his airway. Just because I can't find a pulse doesn't mean he's dead. I will give him CPR until the medics forcibly remove me.

It's too dangerous, Other-me whispers.

She's right. The one-eyed man will bring death. But I'm not leaving Gideon. "You two," I snap at Andy and Ted. "Call 911. Get out of here. Stay away from the one-eyed man."

They head for the door, Andy with his phone out. I hear him say there's been a shooting.

Baz groans from behind me. I glance over my shoulder and see Jesse fashioning a bandage from part of his shirt. I pinch Gideon's nose shut and blow a soft breath of air into his mouth. Lacing my fingers together, I place the heel of my left palm in the center of his chest. "You can't be dead. I can't lose you both." I press down firmly on Gideon's breastbone.

And he coughs.

"Oppa!" I brush his hair back from his forehead. "Hang on. An ambulance is coming."

And then, from behind me:

A soft mechanical whooshing.

"Ha Neul, is that you?" a man's voice asks. "You look so grown up."

A whisper of a shadow of a memory settles at the edges of my consciousness. A man who worked for Kyung. A man who used to forcibly retrieve the girls if the clients didn't finish on time. A calm but violent man. I close my eyes for a moment and reach out for the fractured piece of my past.

"Sung Jin," I say. Slowly, I rise to my feet and turn around. Sung Jin stands before me, a patch over his right eye, a gun pointed at my chest. His black hair is flecked with gray, but otherwise he looks exactly like the man from my dreams. I fight off a tidal wave of memories. Sung Jin blowing smoke in my face. Sung Jin calling us whores. Sung Jin beating a man who refused to pay. But the Sung Jin I knew in L.A. had two eyes . . .

"That's right. My employer sent me to retrieve what is his. Be a good girl and get it for me."

The ViSE equipment is stashed inside my bedroom. I take a moment to consider my options. Gideon seems to have lost consciousness again. Jesse has disappeared from view, but I have no idea if Sung Jin saw him when the elevator first opened. My knife is within reach, but there's little chance I can grab it, throw it, and hit Sung Jin before he shoots me.

"Don't make me hurt you," he says. "No one else needs to die."

"What you're looking for is not here." I just need to stall him until the police arrive. I pray that Jesse doesn't do anything rash before then. "It was stolen."

"If that's the case, then you're useless to me." He starts to pull the trigger.

"No, wait," I say, my hands in the air. "You're right. I'm sorry, It was stolen, but we got it back."

"Where is it?" Sung Jin asks.

I lick my lips and try to think of an answer. I want to get him away from everyone so no one else gets hurt. My mind is empty. Finally I blurt out, "We hid it. It's in a safe deposit box."

A lone siren blares in the distance.

Sung Jin swears. He's on me before I can even go for my knife. The barrel of his gun presses into my ribs. "Come on."

"Let her go." Jesse steps out from the kitchen, his own gun drawn.

Again, my first instinct is to look away from his bruised and bloodied face. But I force myself to meet his gaze. How many things can I convey with a single look? *I'm sorry. Don't die for me. Save yourself. Find someone less broken.*

Sung Jin chuckles. "Oh, Ha Neul." His voice is hot in my ear. "What is it about you and your sister that inspires men to such rash stupidity?"

"Go to hell," I say.

Jesse takes a step forward, his weapon still out and ready. "Let her go," he repeats.

Outside, the siren draws nearer. "Jesse, don't—" I start.

"There's no time for this," Sung Jin snaps. He pulls the trigger twice. Jesse flies backward into the wall of the dining room, his neck snapping forward, his body crumpling to the ground.

"No," I shriek, flailing toward his fallen form. As furious as I am at Jesse for lying to me, as destroyed as I am at the realization that we've slept together and I don't even remember it, some part of me cares deeply for him. Some part of me has made him my family. I can't lose him too.

But I might.

With the gun still pressed into my side, Sung Jin drags me toward Gideon's private elevator. Rage turns to terror. "Not the elevator. I can't," I try to say, but the words don't come. My breath catches in my throat as he hauls me inside. The doors close behind us and my chest goes tight. I am weak. Limp. I am a thunderstorm of sobbing and tears. I collapse onto the floor with Sung Jin staring down at me.

The elevator begins its descent; the red numbers count down: 14 . . . 13 . . .

And then I am back in L.A.

I am in an elevator. I can see myself reflected in the dull steel walls. Not just me. Rose and Gideon too. Only they are still Min Ji and Ki Hyun. Ki Hyun managed to sneak us out of the hotel room, but we still have to make it out of the building and all the way to the airport. And then to somewhere safe.

It seems reckless. It seems almost hopeless, but I sense joy in the way my sister squeezes my hand.

I cling to the red numbers: 10 . . . 9 . . . The elevator chimes merrily as we descend. It doesn't stop until we hit the second floor. I see Ki Hyun tense up. My sister steps protectively in front of me. The doors open. Sung Jin is waiting. My eyes drop immediately to the knife clutched in his hand.

"No!" my sister screams. She steps forward to punch the door-close button. Sung Jin thrusts himself into the elevator. My sister lunges for him, pushing him against the wall. Silver flashes in her hand. It's the tiny vegetable knife I found in her pillowcase. The blade sinks into Sung Jin's eye just as his much larger knife tears through my sister's body. Blood spurts out from the center of her, a fountain of sideways rain. "Go," she yells. "Save her." Sung Jin is screaming in pain, flailing for the knife still stuck in his eye. My sister is slapping and clawing at him, lashing out even as her life pours from her wound.

"No!" I reach out for her. Blood. Blood on my hands. And then the elevator opens again and Ki Hyun is gripping me around my midsection, pulling me away. "No!" I scream again.

"I love you," he tells my sister's fallen form. And then he is running. He is carrying me to safety.

6 . . . 5 . . . Now the numbers are white, the walls mirrored, and Gideon is not here to save me. Rose is gone, but once again her killer stands before me.

It all makes sense now. This is why I am afraid of elevators. I watched my sister die in one. My alter whispers inside my head. *Remember. Don't let her death be for nothing.*

I will not let things be for nothing.

This man is part of the reason I've been living half a life.

I sweep my leg suddenly, hooking my toes around the back of Sung Jin's ankle and landing him on the floor beside me. He raises the gun but I slap his arm to the side. The gun goes off. The barrel burns my hand but the bullet misses. Behind me, a wall of mirror shatters to fragments. Leaping to my feet, I grab the gun with my other hand and try to wrench it away. But Sung Jin is too strong. Grunting, I slam his elbow against the wall of the elevator. The gun falls to the floor. We've reached the lobby now. Then the basement. The doors open onto the parking garage.

Sung Jin hisses like a snake as his foot connects with my stomach. I stumble. The elevator doors slide shut but the compartment doesn't move. He kicks me again. The pain makes my body fold in on itself.

I struggle to stay on my feet, dancing back from his cobra-like strikes. I can't beat him at martial arts. He's a master and I've been training for only a couple of years. I duck low under his sweeping elbow but his other fist connects with my jaw. I scream in frustration as my body slams hard against the control panel. I taste blood. The elevator begins to climb back toward the penthouse. Once again, I remember the curved knife. I see the blade slice into my sister's body, the spouts of red that follow.

Rose is dead.

Gideon is probably dead.

Jesse is probably dead.

But I am not.

If I am going to die today, I'm going to die fighting.

I throw myself at Sung Jin. We end up on the ground. Fists fly. My hands find flesh. They find floor. I am all screaming and tears. I barely feel the blows landing against my face and ribs. I have no idea if I am dying. I keep lashing out. At one point my head ricochets off the back wall of the elevator and I swear I feel my brain bounce against my skull. But then somehow my fingers find the gun and all I feel is the death I'm about to unleash.

You don't have to kill him.

A second voice: *Yes, you do.*

I *want* to kill him.

I don't even have to think about it. Ever since Jesse taught me how to handle a gun, part of me has been dying to shoot one. Flame explodes from the barrel. Once. Twice. Three times. The recoil of the gun shocks me all the way to my shoulders. Sung Jin slams into the wall. He gasps, reaching out for me as he falls to the ground. The gun smokes in my trembling hands. As the elevator continues skyward, Sung Jin's eyes turn to glass. Still shaking, I bend to feel for a pulse at his neck. Nothing.

The doors open with a sharp chime. We're back at Gideon's penthouse. I step over Sung Jin's body and head immediately to check on Gideon, wondering what's taking the paramedics so long to get up here.

Gideon's face is gray, but he's alive. "Ha Neul," he breathes. "Forgive me."

I fall to my knees and take his hand in mine. "Hold on," I plead. "Don't die."

Blood trickles from the corner of his mouth. "I left everything to you. The building, Escape, the tech—it's yours now." He wheezes. Droplets of blood land around his pale lips. "There's an envelope with your name on it in the safe downstairs." He whispers the combination to me.

"I don't need that," I say. "Because you're going to be fine. You have to be fine."

A tear leaks from his left eye. "I'm so sorry for bringing this upon you."

"I forgive you." I press his hand to my chest. "I love you. You are my family."

He smiles faintly. "So beautiful," he murmurs. "Inside and out." Then his eyes fall shut.

"Oppa, no." My heart wrenches open.

But his body goes still.

My world dies. I have lost everything important to me today.

"Winter."

No. Not everything.

From the doorway to the dining room, Jesse reaches out toward me, his face contorting with pain. "You've got to get out of here."

Blood covers his arm, bathing his tattoos in a curtain of red. More blood flows from the wound in his side each time he exhales.

I cross the ocean of carnage to kneel beside him, brushing away a sweaty point of dark hair that's glued itself to his forehead. A lump forms in my throat as I run my fingers across the bruises left by my fists. I should apologize. I *need* to apologize, but there's no time.

Quickly, I survey his new injuries, mindful of the sirens growing louder. He's been shot twice, once in the side and once in the shoulder. He's bleeding a lot, but his face still has color and his pulse is strong. The bullets must have missed his major vessels.

"I don't want to leave you," I say.

"You have to," he chokes out. "I don't want you to get sent away."

He's right. Four people have been shot, and I'm the one holding the gun. There is no way I will escape an investigation if I am found here. "The medics will be here soon. You're going to be all right."

"I know." Jesse clutches his side. "Wipe the gun on your shirt and put it in my hand."

"What? Why?"

"Because then you were never here."

"But I shot him three times," I protest. "They might try to say that isn't self-defense. And the forensics will look like—"

"Screw the forensics," Jesse says. "Baz will back me up. We can handle it."

"Do it and then get the hell out of here, Winter," Baz yells from the kitchen. "And take the ViSE tech with you."

I wipe the gun off and place it in Jesse's right hand. "Promise me you won't die."

"I'll be fine," he says. And then, "Play the end of that ViSE. It's important."

Before I can tell him that it doesn't matter, that I believe him now, a phone rings, sharp and shrill. The sound is coming from the elevator. Sung Jin's phone. Probably someone checking to see if he's completed what he came here for.

Returning to the elevator, I kneel down and fish a cell phone from Sung Jin's breast pocket. I hit the button to answer the call as I hurry back to the living room, but I don't say anything.

Neither does the caller.

I can hear him breathing.

I hold my breath.

When he speaks, it's in Korean. "Did you get what I need?" he asks, with a trace of irritation. I know that voice. It's Kyung.

I still can't speak. The silence stretches out. Outside, the sirens crescendo. Through the broken sliding glass door, I see an ambulance and a pair of cop cars approaching from down the block.

"Ki Hyun?" It's a question.

"No." I swallow back a sob. I refuse to give him the satisfaction.

"Song Ha Neul," Kyung says. "Well, this is an interesting development."

"Ha Neul is dead. I go by another name now," I say sharply, finding my voice at last. "If you're calling for Sung Jin, he's also dead."

"Then he won't be bringing me what is rightfully mine. Which means you'll have to—"

I cut him off. "My time taking orders from you is long past."

Kyung chuckles. My bones turn to ice. "Keep this phone," he says. "You are mine again."

Before I can tell him that I belong to no one, the call disconnects. More sirens sing in the distance.

I grab the ViSE tech and a throwing knife from my room. I return to the living room and pause just long enough to retrieve my other knife from the floor and to give Jesse one last look.

"Winter. Go!" he yells.

I go.

CHAPTER 42

I am halfway down the stairs before I realize I don't know where I'm going. *Play the end of that ViSE.* I left my headset and recordings at Escape. I can hide out there for a few minutes, try to clear my head in the quiet safety of a ViSE room.

I tuck my bloody hands into the center pocket of my hoodie as I cross the lobby of the building, suddenly grateful that I'm wearing all black. I let my hair hang forward to cover most of my face. Adebayo looks up from behind the bar as I enter. "What is happening?" he asks. "I heard sirens."

"Not sure," I lie. I trust him, but I don't know what story Jesse and Baz are going to tell the cops. It's better if I don't give him any conflicting information. "I left some things in a ViSE room. I'm just going to go get them."

"Of course." He adjusts his glasses. "Are you certain you're all right? You look . . . disheveled."

"I'm fine," I say. "I've been sparring." I force down the tears. Now is not the time to fall apart.

When I slip back into the ViSE room and shut the door, it's like locking out everything I can't deal with—the people, the lies . . . the love. I try not to think of Rose dead, Gideon dead, Jesse and Baz bleeding. My headset still sits on the chair in the center of the room. In Florida, I thought Jesse wanted me to see the end of the recording because it proved I was the one who recorded it. But maybe there's something else . . .

Reluctantly, I recline back into the chair and slip the ViSE of Other-me with Jesse into my headset. Closing my eyes, I skip forward past the parts I've already played and the parts I'm not ready to play. The very end is Jesse and Other-me snuggled together under a blanket on the sofa. I back the recording up about thirty seconds and press PLAY.

I lie encircled in Jesse's arms, my head pressed to his chest. His heart beats, quickly at first and then slower. His eyes are closed. A smile plays at his lips. I am warm, inside and out.

"Your heart is beating erratically," I inform him.

"That's your fault," he says.

"Why is that?"

He brushes my hair back from my face. "Because you totally own it right now."

"You're such a girl," I tease.

"Yeah, well. Some of the girls I know happen to be pretty badass."

A tiny pinch of pain radiates outward as my heart flutters in my chest. "So you're not scared anymore?"

He shakes his head. "I'm more scared now than ever, but it doesn't change how I feel. I love you, Winter."

Heat surges through me at his use of my name, at the word love.

I brush my lips against his. "It's going to take some time for me to learn how to love someone."

"That's okay," Jesse says. "I'm not going anywhere."

"You're not allowed to die," I whisper. My phone chimes with an incoming text. I stop the ViSE and sit up in the dark, but when I access my messages, there's nothing new. Then I realize it wasn't my phone that chimed. It was Sung Jin's.

My heart climbs into my throat. I should ignore that phone. I should throw it away. I should smash it to pieces and set it on fire.

But I don't.

With shaking fingers, I check the messages. There's a text that says, "I will see you soon." It has a link to an airline page, highlighting the flight schedules from St. Louis to Los Angeles.

Leaving tomorrow.

If Kyung thinks just because his thug killed Rose and Gideon that I'm scared enough to travel to L.A. and do his bidding, he's dreaming. I don't care if Gideon stole the neural mapping codes or the editor or the entire ViSE technology. I owe Kyung *nothing.*

Nothing but revenge.

I'll take the money Gideon left me and disappear to a place where Kyung won't find me. Then someday when he least expects it, I'll come for him. I will make him pay, the man who sold me like I was an animal, the man who sanctioned the killing of my family.

Almost as if Kyung can read my thoughts, a second message arrives.

It's a photo of a Korean boy who looks about sixteen. There's something eerily familiar about him. *Meet your brother, Jun. He works for me. We are both eager to see you again.*

I nearly drop the phone. Brother? I stare at the photo. No, it can't be . . .

Only it could. My mother might have given Rose and me away, but kept a boy child. Even today, many Korean families can afford only one child and it's imperative to continue a bloodline. I zoom in on the boy in the picture, looking for Rose or me inside his high cheekbones and wide-set eyes. I can't be certain. It could be a trick.

Or he could be my brother.

I dial the phone and wait for Kyung to answer. "What do you want from me?" I ask.

"Bring me the technology and I'll let your brother live," Kyung says.

"The way you let my sister live?"

"She brought about her own demise," Kyung says. "I was quite sad about that. Min Ji was one of my favorites."

"You disgust me," I say. "And maybe you haven't heard, but the tech was stolen."

"Then you have three days to find it," Kyung says. "Or else I send your brother to you, in pieces." The phone goes dead.

I text back.

How do I know he's my brother?

The return messages come rapid-fire. Each message contains a picture. My mother tightly clutching the hand of a dark-haired toddler. My mother looking older with a school-aged boy. I'm about to denounce them all as forgeries when the last message chimes: a picture of my mother clutching a woven basket. A baby slumbers inside of it.

I remember that basket. And then I remember the long train ride—how I was hungry, thirsty. Each time I would reach for the basket, my mother slapped my hand away. Not because she didn't want me to have food, but because she didn't want me to wake the baby. Could I really have blocked out the fact that I have a little brother? Why wouldn't Rose have mentioned him?

Or maybe she did, and I just don't remember.

I call Natalie.

"Hey," she says. "I'll be home in like ten minutes if you want to come by for Miso."

"Actually, can you watch him for a few more days?" I ask. "Something came up and I have to go out of town."

"Sure. He's a doll. Is everything okay?"

"It will be. I just have some stuff to take care of."

"Not a problem. He'll be waiting for you."

I remove my headset and stuff everything into my pockets. Glancing both ways to make sure the hallway is clear, I cross from the ViSE room to the back office. I spin the combination to the safe and open it. I find the envelope with my name on it that Gideon was talking about and slip it into the center pocket of my hoodie. Bundles of cash are stacked neatly next to a folder of financial paperwork. Feeling a little like a thief, I help myself to some of the money before I shut the safe.

I slip out of the office and turn toward the exit. I'll die before I turn Gideon's technology over to Kyung, but if I have a brother somewhere, I have to find him. I have to save him. And I have to kill the man who took away the rest of my family.

I leave Escape and pull the hood of my sweatshirt up as I pass through the lobby of the building. Two detectives—real ones, I presume—are questioning a couple of men at the bar.

I step out into the bright but cold evening and head for the nearest MetroLink station. I'm about three blocks away when an ambulance roars past me.

Jesse and Baz should be to the hospital by now. I know no one will give me information about Jesse's status over the phone, but if he has a room number that means he's probably alive. I look up the number to the hospital and wait impatiently for the call to connect.

"Thanks for calling St. Louis Medical," the operator says in a bored voice. "How may I direct your call?"

"Hi, I was wondering if you could give me a patient's room number. Jesse Ramirez?" I dodge a patch of ice on the side-walk and nod at a man who's methodically unwrapping silver and green garland from a light post. The walk signal turns red as I approach the corner.

"One moment." The operator puts me on hold and I get to listen to some elevator music while I wait for her.

The light turns green, but I'm still waiting. I duck into a recessed alcove in front of a pizza place, my phone trembling in my fingers.

"Mr. Ramirez is currently in ER-3," she says finally.

My body goes weak with relief and I have to lean against the glass window of the restaurant to keep from sinking to the ground. "Thanks. Can I ask about one other patient? Baz, er, Sebastian Faber. They were in the same . . . accident."

"Faber. F-A-B-E-R? Yes, here it is. Mr. Faber is in ER-4."

"Thank you." I like that they are next to each other.

I leave the shelter of the alcove and return to the sidewalk. I barely see the people who push past me. I barely feel their bulky coats brushing up against my arms. It's like I'm playing the ViSE of the overdose again: I'm back in that rushing tunnel of light, but instead of death, it's freedom awaiting me at the end. Rebirth. Like I'm once again shedding my skin and becoming someone new.

When the MetroLink station rises up in front of me, I pause for a moment at the stairway to the platforms. East leads to Dr. Abrams's office. West, to the airport. I know which way I should go, but unfortunately it's not the way I need to go. I hurry down the stairs toward the westward platform. There's no time to waste.

My brother needs me.

My vengeance is waiting.

Acknowledgments

As always, endless thanks and love to my family and friends for putting up with my mood swings and neurotic middle-of-the-night e-mails during the drafting and revision of this book. You help more than you know.

More thanks:

To my agent, Jennifer Laughran of the Andrea Brown Literary Agency, for supporting me in writing whatever books I want to write. Also for being level-headed, laid-back, informative, and basically everything I am not.

To my editor, Melissa Frain, whose feedback encouraged me and pushed me to keep making the book better and better. Your enthusiasm for Winter's story was evident throughout the process, and that kept me energized and motivated during some tough revisions.

To my publisher, Kathleen Doherty, for making this book possible. To Amy Stapp, for taking such good care of my manuscript (and for teaching me how to use Word!). To everyone else at Tor Teen, for the editorial, design, publicity, sales, and marketing support and for a cover that is everything I dreamed of and then some.

To everyone I met while I was living and working in South Korea. Thank you for sharing your stories with me and for being part of an experience that changed my life forever. To the authors, librarians, booksellers, bloggers, and readers in

St. Louis who were supporting me way back when I actually wrote this book. To my rock star blurbers, Lindsay Cummings and Victoria Scott. Gratitude times a million.

To all of my beta readers and experts. The following people were kind enough to provide feedback on elements of story, psychology, biology, technology, medicine, adventure sports, and Korean culture: Marcy Beller Paul; Jessica Fonseca; Cathy Castelli; Antony John; Heather Anastasiu; Philip Siegel; Tara Kelly; Kristi Helvig, PhD; Christina Ahn Hickey, MD; Peter Kriepke; Paul Suhr; Eli Madison; Elizabeth Min; Minjae Christine Kim; Yun-A Kwak; Jen Albaugh; María Pilar Albarrán Ruiz; Debby Kasbergen; Stacee Evans; and Sarah Reis. Any mistakes are mine, not theirs.

To all of my amazing industry friends and colleagues: the girls at Manuscript Critique Services; the YA Valentines; the Apocalypsies; my street teamers; and all the bloggers, booksellers, librarians, and teachers who interact with me in person and on social media. I couldn't do it without you.

And finally, to the readers. I couldn't do it without you either. I will never forget that.

Author's Note

Winter's history is fiction, but according to the United Nations, over two million people across the globe are victims of human trafficking at any one time. This is not a problem that happens predominantly in foreign countries—cases have been reported in all fifty states. Anyone can be trafficked regardless of gender, age, race, class, education, or citizenship.

In addition to sexual exploitation, victims of trafficking are forced to work as domestic servants, manual laborers, soldiers, street beggars, and more. They are coerced and controlled by fear, and many are afraid to seek help from local authorities. Some do not even realize that what is happening to them is a crime.

For information on how you can help or get help, visit:

The National Human Trafficking Resource Center
www.traffickingresourcecenter.org/report-trafficking

The Salvation Army International
www.salvationarmy.org/ihq/antitrafficking

Unicef
www.unicefusa.org/mission/protect/trafficking

U.S. Department of State
www.state.gov/j/tip/id/help/index.htm